# Comes The Hunter

# Comes The Hunter

A novel by James Tannehill

ISBN:978-0-6151-3919-7

While the planning and the actual writing are solitary efforts, and sometimes fraught with periods of staring at a blank page, with no words forthcoming, the end result, the finished, product, requires some help for the struggling writer.

He, the author, or she, as the case may be, needs editing, guidance, criticism, and perhaps most of all, encouragement. I got all this from a good friend.

Thanks for it all, Bob.

And a special thanks to my wife, Barbara, who suffered quietly through the creative process, or whatever it was. As well, my children, Kathy, Susan, Keith, and Carol, always had a word, encouraging or otherwise, though I think they secretely wondered if I would ever finish the novel. Thanks to them.

And then there is J. A special nod to him.

Jack Morgan appears to be nothing more than one more wealthy man living on a private island in Florida.

In his former life he'd been much more: a shooter, a sniper, hunter, the best solo hunter and killer the Marines had known.

Now, mostly as a favor to his old boss, he has agreed to search for, and hopefully find, the daughter of a U.S. Senator who has gone missing while working for the Peace Corps in Haiti. He knows the country.

What he doesn't know is just where the hunt will lead and who is the real prey.

The trail leads to Mexico, Europe, and eventually to the heart of both power and corruption: Washington, DC.

The story is more than a tale of a shooter, his agony, violence, struggles with conscience, the demons of guilt.

It is also a love story.

# ONE

Things weren't all that bad. Not yet anyway.

The dirt floor was hard and I kept shifting around trying to find some position that might be at least bearable, but there didn't seem to be any such thing. Nor was there any hope of relief from the heat that lay on me like a wool blanket.

So far, aside from a little pushing and shoving by the guards, and a few well placed kicks, I hadn't been treated too badly. The rough stuff was yet to come, but I wasn't too concerned about that—I'd been there and done that in worse places. With that thought in mind, I suddenly remembered a technique told to me by an old hand at captivity, Captain Bryan Savage. The simple trick of it is, he said, was to first relax the body to a state of jelly. Relax the body and let the mind go blank. Then when you get to that state, let your mind picture you floating gently, like a Lily pad, in a clear, cool mountain stream. Let your mind take you there— make it real. Of course, he had added, with his odd little smile, it is a bit more difficult when one is being beaten and tortured continuously. He was British, an instructor on loan from SAS (Special Air Services) to the CIA facility in Virginia, and in his own unassuming way he understated a lot of the truly difficult things he was trying to teach us.

At the time he'd shared this bit of wisdom with us—long before I was obliged to use it—I thought he might be a bit round the bend, as they say. I was young and naive in those days. But his lessons proved to be some of the most valuable training I received.

There are people that for whatever reason remain a vivid memory, a clear picture in our minds forever. For me it was a teacher in the eighth grade that I fell madly in love with. Never forget her face. And there was the Drill Instructor at Parris Island: a mean face with the high cheekbones of an American Indian, big, menacing, right in your face, a chest full of ribbons. He was a nightmare. And in a far less menacing place was the British officer with the fancy mustache that twisted up across his face, and the funny little smile. On one rare occasion I saw him in uniform (the only time I would normally see him was in training and that was in fatigues, without decorations), and he had a chest full of ribbons. He seemed not the type to mention that kind of thing.

When you are totally alone, open to the varied whims of the mind, life passes by in a strange parade of things, places, and sights.

The hot, stale air smelled of dirty earth, a strange sweetness that must have come from rotted fruit—though as far as I knew there was none

8

nearby—human sweat, and overpowering it all the indescribable scent of fear. It was mostly quiet around me except for the occasional moan of despair or pain, a cough, or the sound of a metal door opening and closing which probably meant some poor soul was being taken out for interrogation. I had the feeling that the door was never opening to freedom. Ironic I thought, how this was one of the few times I'd been in a country, this or any other, for an honest, legitimate purpose and look what happened. Maybe that was my mistake this time.

***

A gray and damp morning at Heathrow as I looked out from the terminal at the huge BA 747 that would take me "across the pond," as the Brits say, to the land of the Magic Kingdom at Orlando. As always, when I saw the monstrous chunk of aluminum close up, I wondered how the damn thing even got up in the air, let alone stayed aloft. That kind of thing had always baffled me.

The huge crowd waiting to board, I noticed, was mostly families with kids barely able to control their excitement at the thought of seeing Mickey Mouse and the gang. What with the currency advantage of better than half again for the dollar to the English Pound, America, and especially Orlando, was a popular destination. This flight appeared to be booked to capacity. How sad, I thought, a bit smugly, being in first class I would miss all that family togetherness.

I had learned early on that rank—be it military or in the civilian pecking order—or being rich, had its privileges. Being rich had more. This is not to say that I was anywhere near the wealth of the many multimillionaires of today. Being wealthy had assumed new dimensions that we'd never dreamed of just a few short years ago. Let's say that I could live comfortably in a better than average lifestyle.

Two weeks ago I had thought it might be a good time—after the remodeling work on the house was completed—to visit one of my favorite cities, and as well, hop over to the Channel Islands and check on my finances. My work, if it could be called that, paid well and was all off the books—meaning the IRS could never find it in a million years—and what with a bonus here and there, coupled with careful investing, my stockpile should last a lifetime. That is if my advisor was strictly tending to business. And I was pleased to find that she was.

So with that good news in mind I wasn't overly concerned at the outrageous prices in the London shops. Still, since I had come from modest means to say the least, I had the occasional twinge of guilt at spending the US equivalent of $180.00 for a shirt. But it was only a fleeting thing. Living well is truly the best revenge.

I could appreciate the saying, but the word *revenge,* along with memories and bad dreams of the past, I kept locked away in a dark corner. Sometimes I tried to keep them away with booze. Sometimes it worked.

The flight was nothing out of the ordinary: the crew was constantly serving something; a passenger snored too loudly, keeping many from sleeping; my seat mate talked too much; I drank and ate far too much. When I woke up from whatever sleep I had, the taste in my mouth was foul, the woman next to me was asleep, and I called the attractive attendant for a fresh cup of coffee. From watching the entire crew board the aircraft, then seeing who tended to us, it seemed to me that the prettiest were assigned to first class. On the one hand I thought this was the worst form of discrimination and prejudice to put the best looking to serve the big spenders. On the other hand, her name was Pamela, trim figure, short blond hair and the most charming accent. She was delightful. On balance I suppose the airline knows best.

I sipped and thought back to my visit.

My borrowed flat in Chelsea, courtesy of an old friend with MI6, was spacious, comfortable, and in a nice location, very near one of my favorite restaurants. From the flat, it was a short ride on the tube to a special pub near Covent Garden called the Prince of Wales, where the attraction, in addition to the friendly crowd, was the lamb and vegetable pie. Unfortunately, the place brought back some bad memories with the good. That happened a lot in some old, favorite places. But for the most part it had been a pleasant visit to London.

The trip over to the Channel Islands, beautiful, but brooding I always thought at seeing them, was a refreshing change of scene. A different world existed in those islands.

I dozed for a time. Then, quickly it seemed, we began our descent over the flat, lake-covered land of north central Florida.

At Orlando the world jumped ahead a lifetime from London: the crowds of excited tourists coming and going bedecked in souvenir hats and shirts; glittering shops; busyness of Americans going somewhere in a hurry-- underdressed and overdressed, various shades of sunburned skin; the tram ride into the terminal with the perfect Disney voice giving instructions. This was a country on the move.

Showing my valid US passport in the name of Jack Morgan, which always brought a twinge of anxiety no matter how much I worked at being calm (I had done a lot of traveling in the old days, under a few different names), I cleared customs with only a casual glance from the inspector, snatched my bags from the carousel, then went down to get a rental car for the drive home.

Sometimes when I came back from a trip tired, or just didn't feel like being bothered with a car and driving, I had used car service. But today was a beautiful day and I felt good. This was a day for a convertible. My trip home was a matter of thirty minutes of easy driving east on the BeeLine—a new toll road that cut a straight swath through the open country from Orlando to the coast—then south on Interstate 95 for about the same amount of time, east again to the Indian River and across the water to my house. After a mostly sunless time—weak and cool at its best—in London, it was great to ride home with the top down in full, cancer-giving, glorious Florida sun.

Home was a large, but unimposing house on an island in the Indian River, about mid way between Melbourne and Vero Beach. Since the Dodgers, first from Brooklyn where they were the glorious "Bums," and then from Los Angeles (a different type of fan), had wintered in Vero Beach for years, most people had at least heard of that city. With no baseball team, and a low key, small town image, very few people knew of Melbourne. Funny thing is, an awful lot of people liked the city for those very reasons.

About a year and a half ago I started to remodel the house, make it more old Florida with wood siding, new, bigger windows, metal roof, and a porch all around. In a burst of enthusiasm I painted the whole thing light green in color, added a second floor, and brought in lots of rattan furniture with brightly colored cushions. I hadn't done any "jobs" for a while so doing the work on the house myself was good therapy. Claire said I'd gotten fat, lazy and was becoming an irritable person. She also said it would help me forget the past and move on with my life.

Claire thinks she is getting wise in her old age, or wiser, and I can't tell her otherwise.

I owned the other two houses on the island and I selectively rented them to people I felt were self reliant (that is, from appearance, and a few discreet questions about employment, should be able to pay the rent), and people who would generally leave me alone (not the nosy type of personality). So far I hadn't been wrong in my landlord decisions.

A few years after Marv first put me to work, and after a few jobs I found myself with a pocket full of money (ill-gained many might say, and in the light of today I might have to agree), I bought the island for a future hideaway. It was close enough to things but still an island. I didn't know it at the time but I had acted just before the developers got their greedy hands on the place. This section, it turned out, had been singled out for

11

mass development by a large California conglomerate. I'm not against progress—which here in Florida means a whole gang of people moving into too little land—but some places are better off left alone in more or less their natural state, which is how I tried to keep the island.

So to be totally honest, it wasn't any great ecological fervor that prompted me to buy the island. I'm no tree-hugger. Though only a quarter mile from shore, the island provided a discreet extra measure of security. I could never be sure of course, but it was reasonable to suspect that there could be people out there holding a grudge, hoping to find me and looking to settle an old score. There were those who never forgot.

The relatively few in my line of work weren't active socially and didn't make a lot of friends. And while I wasn't paranoid to the extent that I put in sensors around the property, electrified fence and the like, the house did have the very best security system.

Reminds me of a writer, English I think, who said "the past is a foreign country; they do things differently there." I did things much differently in my past.

The rental would be picked up at the dock—for an extra charge. I transferred my things and sped off across the water in the inflatable that I used for supply runs and mainland visits. This was one of the few runs I could make without my shadow, a chocolate Labrador I had named "Harry" after my London friend, he of the flat in Chelsea.

That time in England was different for me, different and difficult in many ways.

Anyway, Harry it was. As soon as I hit the dock he came bounding down the grassy stretch in front of the house, jumping, tail wagging, looking to lick me and smother me with affection. He was that kind of dog. As far as temperament and general demeanor, he was like a child, but a pain in the the ass when we went out fishing. He was a water lover. Whenever I made a cast he jumped in and took off after the lure. I mean what the hell, he was a retriever. I had to stop taking him along if I wanted to do any serious fishing.

I got Harry one day when I was driving along US1 and saw a sign: "AKC Labrador pups with papers." One look at that cute little furry, brown ball, with the big eyes, and I was hooked. Besides that, he looked like the pick of the litter to me.

When I brought him home Claire wasn't all that happy, not at first anyway, and for the longest time she never used his name and put out his food with an indifferent attitude. And the times that he wet on the kitchen floor were tense indeed. In time though, she like me, was won over by the big, friendly creature with brown eyes. In fact, after a while, she even

12

stopped complaining when he came into the house and shook himself off in a shower of water all over the floor. Now, she gets after me about brushing him, trimming nails, exercise, proper food, the whole bit.

Harry pretty much ruled.

The house was quiet, which meant Claire was probably lying down. She was doing that more and more lately. And I knew that despite getting her the best medical care I could find, she was losing ground in her fight with the cancer.

I unpacked and lay down for a nap. Harry was right behind me. He circled around several times before picking a place to flop next to the bed. I wondered about that. The whole floor looked the same to me.

Though the so-called experts strongly recommend that one not lie down after a cross Atlantic trip, I always chose to ignore that bit of advice. What I did find though was that the west bound trip was easier than the eastbound. That business of arriving in London six hours earlier in the day was too much for my aging body to handle.

Claire, my all-around house person, critic, spiritual guide, and mother, always said that I acted and spoke like a Brit when I came back from my occasional visits. As far as I knew she'd never had much to do with the English, but somehow it never sounded like a compliment. For the last ten or twelve years she ran the house, along with Harry the last two. She was a great cook. When I first sampled her cooking at one of those diplomatic things at the home of a French official in Haiti, I decided then and there to steal her from the unappreciative frog. And I did just that. All this, of course, happened in that period of my life when I was into something new in service to the government; it didn't work out and I went back to what I knew best.

Not until much later did I learn her story. The daughter of a missionary couple whose small church was burned to the ground on some trumped up political charge, with the parents in the church, she made her way into the city of Port-au-Prince and started out on her own. She was a child and she survived. By the time I came to know her she had worked her way up into the well-to-do circle of mulatto families, and from there into the international diplomatic group.

But I came to learn that she was far more than just a good cook. She was a warm, caring human being with a heart as big as her ample body. She was my rock in this world. Of course, we did raise some eyebrows the few times she insisted I go shopping with her.

When she went in for a routine physical exam, that I insisted she have, she was soon diagnosed as having a rare form of cancer. She was never anything but positive about her condition. There were many trip to specialists all over Florida and many experimental programs tried. At this point, the best report was that she was in some dormant state, not remission, and that was fine with me.

After a restless nap which did little for my jet lag, I got up and put on shorts and a decent tee shirt and went down to the kitchen where I knew coffee would be waiting. Harry tagged along behind me.

Claire called from the laundry room. "Have a good trip, Mister Jack?"

"Not bad," I said. "What are you doing?" Nothing would ever change her habit of calling me "Mister Jack."

"Putting in a wash. You want that new shirt washed before you wear it don't you?"

She'd been in my room and taken the new shirt. The woman was impossible! "Yes. Thanks, Claire. I don't think I'll be needing it right away."

"Can't complain. Sure is a pretty shirt."

"It should be. Expensive as hell."

I heard a chuckle before she said, "Only kind you buy."

Wandering in to stand next to her in the laundry room with my coffee, I asked her if she was okay. She looked thinner to me.

"I'm fine, Mister Jack." A pause while she opened the top and readjusted the load which was lopsided—the machine thumping. "A man called while you were away, couple of times, wanted to know when you'd be back, said he had to talk to you."

"And...?"

"I told him today and he said he would be here tomorrow."

"Here in Florida!"

"He was in a big hurry to talk to you."

"He say anything else?"

"He hung up right away. Must be a busy man."

"Odd," I said mostly to myself. "He didn't give you a name?"

She turned to look at me. "No. He talked like he was an old friend. Said he'd be here tomorrow without fail. Does he mean trouble, Mister Jack? You aren't back in that government business again are you?"

'Government business' to her meant travel; she had no idea of my real work and if she did know I doubt that she would even be under the same roof with me. "What business?"

"You know, all that travel. You're getting too old for that stuff." She smiled.

"Too old! You're the one who's getting too old."

"Not that old," she said, pushing me away. "Now get out of here and let me finish the wash. Oh, that woman called."

14

"What woman?'

Big grin. "Now how many women be calling you here, Mister Jack?"

"Not enough."

"That woman with all the money. The one who wants you to help with some charity thing."

"And what did you tell her?"

"I said you'd be gone for a month."

With all my travel absences—far fewer now than in previous years since I had "retired"—it was still difficult not to become some part of the local community. I did go to mass on a fairly regular basis (not regular enough according to Claire) and one does have to reply when spoken to, which means slowly becoming involved with the speaker over a period of time. The woman who had called, Marjorie Bogart, was one of those speakers who gradually came to know me to a tiny degree, though to hear her tell it we were the closest of friends. Anyway, she telephoned me periodically to help her out with some social cause; these were usually of the "Save the Tit Mouse" variety, of which I could care less. Claire had done well to fend her off for at least a month.

A month was more than I could usually hope for. I said, "Claire, you are a devil—a good one! Good work. What's for dinner?'

"After the food you've been eating over there," she said, separating clothes for ironing—the woman seemed to be always in motion—"I figured you would need a good home-cooked meal."

"And what do you put in that category?" She gave me a funny look at the word but didn't comment." By the way, English cooking has come a long way. It's quite good now."

She grinned. "There you go with that English talk again. 'Quite good,.' she mimicked. "I had some fresh sea bass delivered from those new people in Sebastian. Figure I'll fix it in a light herb sauce."

"Light!"

With a glance at my waist she said, "trousers getting tight. I can tell in the wash."

"How can you tell in the wash! Claire, you're impossible."

"Maybe. But somebody has to look out for you."

I couldn't think of a reply to that one. No matter what she said the meal would be superb.

"Now get out of here." she said. "You should take Harry for a walk. That poor dog has been in the house all this time."

I knew very well that Harry had been out for a run every day. I said, "Yes mam," giving her a salute. "Harry and I are out of here."

15

"Dinner be ready in an hour. And put something on besides those ragged shorts."

When Harry and I got back from a walk and a quick dip in the lagoon, I did just that: I changed into a freshly pressed pair of short and a short sleeved shirt—also fresh from the iron.

Perhaps from her years of working with the better off Haitian, then with the diplomatic group, who tended to dress for dinner, Claire insisted I show up for dinner in some respectable form. God knows she wasn't any kind of a snob—breakfast and lunch were very informal—but she did have set ideas on some things. And on balance it was a good practice.

I was sitting out on the deck in back of the house, watching a trio of dolphins make their leisurely way up the lagoon, leaping in and out of the water (dolphins here are dark brown rather than the lighter color in tropical waters), with a cigar and the last of a bottle of a California white wine when the phone rang. I picked up and heard a familiar voice: "Jack?"

"Sure is, Marv. How are you?"

A grunt. "Same as ever. Listen, I'll be there around eleven tomorrow—in time for lunch. "Marv was never one to waste words. He told me what time and that he wanted to be fed. With his mention of lunch I knew he was angling for his favorite of lobster salad. I'd have to mention it to Claire.

I started to ask where he was coming in and if he wanted to be picked up. But he was already off the line.

*** 

In the morning, knowing Claire would lay on something big and special for Marv, I ate a light breakfast, then went for a run and a long swim, with Harry of course. We went over in the inflatable at 11:15 and Marv was waiting with a briefcase in one hand.

Marv was Marv Millman--no one used his last name; in fact I worked for the man for almost a year before I even knew what it was. When we were in operations he was my controller. Seeing him again triggered lots of memories from my active days, some good and some not so good. Marv was a solid professional who became Director of Operations at one point, then later was one of the few career people to be appointed Director Central Intelligence Agency.

In appearance, Marv never looked finished, or at best, one who had dressed in a hurry with little regard to matching jacket, trousers, and tie with each other. His tweed jacket was too heavy for Florida and his tie had every other color but one that matched--anything. A cigar stuck out of the

16

top pocket, the two side ones bagged though they appeared empty. In general, he looked as if he should introduce his jacket to his trousers.

He greeted both Harry and Claire warmly and they both made a fuss over him.

The day being a pleasant one, still early in March and without the oppressive humidity that would be along soon, we ate out on the deck. We made small talk since there wasn't time for much else, what with Marv eating everything in sight. At a rapid pace he went through a cold soup, fresh-baked rolls with a pate of some kind, a huge lobster salad with avocado and hard-boiled eggs mixed in, topping it all off with a bowl of fresh fruit slices. We had both settled back with a cigar before he got down to business.

"I need you to do something for me, Jack," he started slowly, twisting the cigar, watching the smoke rise.

Here it comes. "I'm listening, Marv."

A pause while he studied my expression, then, "I know what you're thinking—and it's nothing like that. This is a simple job in Haiti."

Haiti! Why in Haiti? "Jobs for you are never simple, Marv," I said.

"Believe me, this is different and it's simple."

"Different doesn't do anything for me. They were all promised to be different. And damn few were. Simple I like. And before you say another word, you of all people know I'm out of the business."

Marv waved an arm. "It's nothing like that, Jack. I know you don't do that anymore." He looked away out over the water as he went on to explain about a senator's daughter, in the Peace Corps, who had disappeared. Could I go look for her?

Seemed simple enough, I thought, on the surface anyway, trying to keep an open mind. I had to wonder why he wanted me. Sure, I'd worked for Marv a lot of year—what seemed like a lifetime, and in a way it was. And yes, I had been in Haiti for a time working with their army. This hardly qualified me as the expert to be sent back in on a search. Even beyond the time in Haiti, which was a relatively short period in my overall career, I only worked within a defined area of operations—a very specific area. I was good at my job. Maybe too good. Some of the memories are always there waiting to come alive when I least expect them, nor want them.

This isn't what I did and Haiti had been nothing special. I finally said, "I don't think this is for me, Marv. Believe me I feel sorry for the senator and I can imagine how he feels about his daughter. But it's not my kind of job and I'm not into the missing persons thing. The Peace Corps! I don't think so."

He puffed on the cigar, looked at me then away, then back at me. "Jack, bear with me on this one."

"I'm trying to do that, Marv. But I just don't see it. This is not my kind of thing. I'm not a cop. I'm not even an intelligence officer. And I sure as hell am not Missing Persons. You know what I did."

"Yes, I know all too well what you did, Jack and I still have nightmares about some of it. Hopefully, we'll never go there again. Right now, I need someone out of the agency, out of the loop as they say today, someone I can depend on to handle this kind of situation in a mature manner. These kids today are so busy being politically correct they trip over themselves. And God forbid they have to assume the responsibility of a tough call, let alone see it through to the end. No, I need you, Jack. If this should get rough I know you can deal with it." A long pause. "And besides, it pays well—very well. Let's face it. You know Haiti! You lived there. This should be a walk in the park for you."

"What do you mean by 'get rough'?"

Marv shrugged. "You know how these things can go. The point is, you know how to handle yourself."

I thought about what he'd said so far. I could have an expense paid trip to find a missing girl in a familiar country. Not only expense paid. Well paid personally. How bad could it be? In recent years I hadn't done all that much traveling and the London trip renewed my interest in seeing other places and other people. And even in revisiting.

Marv and I shared the common bond of being a Marine. That kinship was what first got us together--that and his initiative to find and recruit me—and it was what moved us beyond being merely employer and employee. His passion was fishing. He had a cabin in the Maryland mountains on a lake—a quiet kind of place where he went as often as he could get away—where he indulged in his passion, and as well I'm sure, spent moments of contemplation, satisfaction, and probably regret. Since my work was in the dark part of our world I sometimes met him there in private to review and critique an operation.

He was a good fisherman, with his own lures, different rods and all the gear, and he usually reeled in the fish one after another while I sat there watching my slack line. Very often he slipped into fishing metaphors, so I figured at this point he probably felt the hook was set in my mouth and all he had to do was reel me in, slowly, taking in the line bit by bit. I had no idea at the time just how badly he wanted to land this particular catch.

And he was correct.

I said, "She into drugs?"

Marv looked at me sharply. "Why do you ask that? She's a kid—maybe all of twenty four."

"All the more reason to ask. Well, was she? Is she?"

"Not that I know. And that's the truth. But this isn't about finding some strung out kid, Jack."

Though honesty in its true form was rare in our business, knowing Marv as I did, I had to respect his use of the word with me. Looking back, I think I felt some faint warning signals at the time. Was it something in his face when he said it wasn't about one kid on drugs? I can't be sure. In any case, if the signs were there I ignored them. I asked Marv how he fit into this since it seemed way out of his area.

"Simple really. I owe the senator. He's the one who organized the move to get me the directors job." Marv looked away then, a kind of wistful look on his face. "I'm not sure why. I hardly knew the man."

His words and that look told me that Marv had been greedy for the job and that the senator owned him in a sense. It wasn't something to be happy about. I said, "So what's the big deal? You're retired now—out of it all. You never played politics, Marv."

"Sometimes that game had to be played, Jack," he said thoughtfully. "And a debt has to be repaid, in one form or another."

"I guess so," I admitted, not happy with a side of Marv I'd never seen. My thoughts went back to the time Marv had saved my ass from a firing squad in Guatemala, and other times. He alone had backed me in many a hairy operation, some successful, and some that had gone sour, backed me when the brass and the suits on the hill wanted my head on a platter. Yes, I could make a point that I owed Marv. I could, but I wasn't going to give in yet. I pressed him on the woman.

"Give me the rest of it, Marv."

"What rest!"

"The rest of it about the woman. Seems to me there has to be more than finding the wandering daughter of some senator you owe, more than finding some kid out to save the world in places she has no business being in the first place. Either that or this is a job for some young hotshot just up from the farm on his first assignment."

I waited out a long silence.

He seemed to sag in the chair. "That's all there is. Now will you do it?"

"I'm not convinced, Marv. From what you've told me so far my feeling is that this is a job for someone else. I'm wondering why you even asked me."

Holding eye contact he said, "A favor, Jack. I'm asking you to do me a favor."

Was this only a favor or was there more? The senator would have access, if he pushed the issue, to some very secret files in the agency, files that should never be seen. Could there be something in those files that gave the senator even more leverage on Marv? Was I overreacting?

"A normal favor I'd do for you anytime. You know that. But you haven't convinced me that this is worth my time or yours." Looking at him I could picture the wheels spinning: how to reset the hook; his catch was slipping away.

"It's a favor, yes, but this is a big payoff for you, Jack. The senator will deposit a half million when you agree and another half if you find her. Now, does that sweeten the pot?"

With a smile I said, "It is a nice pot. But I really don't need the money." Then I added, "Is the senator's daughter only worth one million! This guy is cheap."

"I can get more—much more and very easily."

I wanted to do this. I stalled, wanting to get as much out of him as I could, knowing that he would hold something back—he always did. I wanted back in the action, any action, even minor league missing persons (maybe that was bush league), no matter, it still made me a player. And I think Marv knew.

We were quiet for a time, enjoying our smoke and the after feeling of a nice lunch on a beautiful day. Finally he turned to me and spoke softly. "There is one other thing, Jack."

Here it comes. "And what is that other thing?"

"Do you remember Hannah? Hannah Bergman?"

"Hannah is dead."

"No. She's very much alive."

A shock wave rolled over me. But there was more.

"The girl is her daughter."

Stunned didn't begin to cover my feeling at that moment. I had worked with Hannah, slept with her, and I was in love with her—I had loved her and then she was dead. An anger rose up in me. "What the hell are you saying, Marv!"

"I'm saying that she didn't die in that plane crash. She was never on that plane. She is very much alive, Jack. You were told of her death for the good of the operation. None of it matters now. The father is Senator Blackwood. Now you know why I'm asking you to do this."

I stared out at the gentle water. Senator Blackwood: Chairman of the Foreign Relations Committee, self-serving and typical of the breed. If this were just for him I'd laugh in Marv's face. Finally I said, "Is this the truth?"

20

"Yes," he said. "I spoke with Hannah last week. She didn't want you or anyone else to know about the woman being her daughter. You and I go back a long way, Jack, and I've always been square with you...well almost." He smiled at himself. "I know how you felt about Hannah and I knew you would want to find her daughter."

How I felt about her? I wasn't sure myself. Someone had written that the fire of yesterday was but the cold, gray ashes of today. And Hannah was yesterday, not a cold ash maybe, more like an ember still warm to the touch. But she was not today.

"So, what's the story, Marv?"

"Then you'll do it?"

"I'll go. I'll find her."

"That's great, Jack," he said with a smile, obviously relieved. "I brought along everything I have on the woman,hoping you would accept. And remember, this man has money and this is a bonus job. I'll get you a nice payoff here."

"Money is not the issue. I don't really care about it one way or the other."

"Easy for you to say. You're a young man with a lot of years yet, might as well live them in style."

"Oh I will, Marv."

"I'll let him know right away and get the deposit in your account. Where is it? Caymans?"

"Channel Islands. I'll give you the account number. You did include a photo?"

"Everything we could find,including a passport photo, not too old." Silence for a moment then he added, "I think you need to do this, Jack. For a lot of reasons."

Had he heard of my so-called drinking problem? Probably. But that and a lot of shrink sessions were in the past. I'd given up a lot of today to get rid of my past.

He stood and said, "Got a plane to catch. Keep in touch."

We didn't have much to say on the ride back across the lagoon, both deep in our own thoughts of what was and what might be now. At the dock I said, "I'll be talking to you. Your cell phone still the same number?"

"Yeah. But I want to set up something new for us. Let me know if you need anything. Anything. You let me know and you got it."

When I got back to the house, one look told me that Claire wasn't too happy about my visitor. Harry didn't care and showed it by running around with tail wagging, jumping, and pesting me in his usual way; he loved attention and made his feelings known. Claire, on the other hand, while not saying much nor giving her feelings away in any physical way, gave you a clue to her inner feelings by the expression on her face. I moved to stand beside her. After a moment she said, mostly to herself, "Hardly get unpacked." Then she turned to me. "I better get your things together. You be going north or south, Mister Jack?"

"South, Claire. This should be an easy one."

## TWO

At a glance, the woman sitting by the window, with an empty seat between us, immersed in her book and off in another world, made me think of Hannah. Not that she looked like her. Hannah loved books and spent every spare moment reading.

This was just two days after Marv's visit. On such short notice—once I'd made up my mind I wanted to be on my way as soon as possible--there was no way I could get a first class seat. On a short flight like this one it wasn't a big deal. But I had made the effort, and I somewhat reluctantly accepted the idea that I'd gotten into self-gratification in my old age. Instant gratification. Something that annoyed me about the younger generation. I could make the point that I'd paid my dues, and that at my age I was entitled. It seemed a weak rebuttal.

The flight out of Miami to Port-au-Prince was almost fully booked, not with tourists for that was a thing of the past (who wanted to visit a poor, barren country without decent facilities or drinking water?) but with Haitians bringing back clothing, food, and other items to help ease the rough life in that country. The poorest of the poor in Miami probably lived better than the average Haitian.

The woman who had brought Hannah to mind reached out for the bottle of water she'd dropped in the seat between us. She hadn't turned from the book and her searching fingers weren't finding the bottle. I picked it up and guided it into her hand. That caused her to look at her hand first, a bit awed at the wonder of it appearing, then up at me. "Good idea that," I said. " A lot of water is recommended--flying dehydrates."

She looked at me for a long moment, as if deciding how to respond, maybe wondering whether I was an intruder, courteous fellow passenger, or magician. "Thank you," she said finally. "That's what I read somewhere." And with those brief words she went right back to her book.

For whatever reason, haste or inattention to details, or simply an oversight, I didn't have a book to read, so I had my nose in the mail-order book from the pouch on the back of the seat in front of me. Nothing interested me in the catalogue so I moved on to the airline publication—even less interesting. The only thing left in the pouch was a paper bag for you-know-what. I went back to the mail-order book. I was trying to find something of interest in that when she gave me another few words. "Your first trip to Haiti?"

"No," I said, glad to get away from the boring reading. "I've been there before. Are you going on vacation?"

"No. I live in Haiti."

Her answer surprised me because in these times not many Americans, or whites for that matter from anywhere, lived in Haiti. There had been a time, way back, when the country was calm politically and affordable—like Costa Rica is at the moment—that many Americans and Europeans came to live in Haiti. That was history.

Over the years—a lot of years, going back to before World War II—the US had spent a lot of time and money, aid in various forms, in a continuing program of assistance to Haiti. Looking at the overall program in progress at any given time, as it was being administered, it seemed to be working in each sector. But the general condition of the country, surprisingly, at least to those who were involved, remained unchanged. Perhaps the hard work at the grass roots level wasn't enough to offset the greater incompetence, or indifference (probably both), and the graft and corruption at the top. That problem remained an enigma.

At any rate, to that impossible dream, a small number of Americans--engineers, teachers, agricultural experts, and the like--worked in Haiti on government projects. In addition, there was the diplomatic and military personnel--not a large group. As well, there was the religious, and others with a humanitarian purpose. All told it didn't add up to a lot of people. So I was curious as the where she fit into that picture. I would bet that she wasn't diplomatic or military. That left...?

Since the older (I should say more mature), but none the less attractive flight attendant, had lined me up with two tiny bottles of Smirnov--the only vodka option and a poor choice in my opinion--I was set with drinks. The woman in the window seat had turned back to her book and I sipped and wondered what might lie ahead for me. Without the connection to Hannah, however fragile the link, on balance I wondered if I would have taken this on. Was I that eager to get back in the game? And if the answer was yes, then the question was why? But I knew the answer to that one.

Christine, I was thinking, bringing her picture to mind, was a pretty girl (had to be with a mother like that) with long, light brown hair, who had finished her tour in Haiti and was overdue to come home. She was close to her parents and bright, having graduated from Georgetown, one of the better schools, with high grades. That said a lot. Nothing in her file indicated she was anything but the average young woman who wanted to change the world. In different ways, I considered, and stretching a point,

24

we were working on the same project: Christine in improving society and me in exterminating the vermin that moved in to destroy it.

A voice cut into my thoughts. "I think I was being very private, again, and you were being social. Bad habit of mine: being too private."

"Nothing wrong with being private."

"There is when you've spent much of your life alone and someone wants to talk."

"Oh. Sounds like you're being very hard on yourself. Has your life been that lonely?"

She didn't answer right away. "Much of it." She held up her book which was a history of Haiti. "All the time I lived there and I didn't know a thing about the history. Well, I did know a little."

"A little is about what I know. And I lived there."

"You lived in Haiti?"

"For a time. A very short time. Jack Morgan," I said, putting out my hand.

She took it with a firm grip. "Anne-Marie. Anne Marie Calder."

With a deep tan and strong, thin face, good bone structure, no-nonsense, outdoor person, one who would age well, I would call her a handsome woman. Whether she might be flattered or insulted I had no way of knowing. But I could easily picture her forging across the plains in a covered wagon, braving the elements, standing up to Indian attacks, tending to the wounded, and offering comfort to the other settlers. I saw all this in a most complimentary way.

And I doubt that she was bothered by a few gray strands among the long brown hair that hung in a low ponytail.

After a beat or two looking at her, I said, "Do you work for the government?"

"Oh no," she answered with the start of a smile.

The "Oh no" put her in the humanitarian or religious groups. I said, "Living here, I suppose you speak French?"

"I can get by in French--my mother was French. But I'm much better in Creole." She turned reflective for a moment and added, "The others I worked with, the women, came to call me Amy." I didn't see any connection so I waited for her to explain. "I was always questioning, you see, not one to follow blindly so it was 'Am' for Anne-Marie and 'why?' Amy! We were a very close group. I haven't been called that in years."

Wondering who the others might be, weighing her words, I concluded that she seemed a very serious person. Was it school? Fellow employees? Then, to my surprise, she accepted my offer. "Maybe I'll have what you're having."

25

"I don't think so," I told her, shaking my head.

"What then?"

"Something a bit lighter." I signaled the attendant and asked for a Gin and tonic. When it came I mixed a weak drink for her, leaving half the Gin in the little bottle. She sipped, looked at me, then sipped some more and smiled. Glancing at her book, I said, "So, now you know all about Haitian history?"

"Not all certainly. More than I knew before reading this. Do you know much about Haiti?"

"Far less than you I'm sure. I do know that their past is a violent one. I can't imagine anyone treating the blacks here worse than their own kind treated them."

"Odd isn't it?" she said.

"Not so odd. Look at Africa: the slaughter goes on and on and it's all black on black."

"Do you speak any Creole?"

"Barely enough to get by. There's an old Haitian proverb I liked. I don't remember the thing in Creole but it went something like: It is shoes that know if the socks have holes."

She smiled. "I like that one." Then she asked, "Are you on vacation?" When I told her I was on a kind of vacation, she said, "How long will you be in Haiti?"

"That depends. I'm not really sure."

"That sounds a bit mysterious to me," she said with a broad smile.

"No mystery at all. I just don't know how much time I'll need to wrap things up here. Mine is a dull life, Amy." It was the first time I had used her name and I liked the sound of it.

After a long moment she said, "Somehow I doubt that."

The rest of the flight passed quickly as we made small talk about the country and the world in general. Listening to her talk I realized how well read she was and that she was far ahead of me in intellect. But none of it came out in a pretentious way. She was very down to earth and a no nonsense woman, one I would like to see again. Hinting at that, it turned out that she had no phone and only a vague rural address. That wasn't uncommon but it would make any contact difficult. I was left with the feeling that any possibility of seeing her again was slim indeed.

Turned out I was wrong.

After a period of calm, level flight, I felt the plane shudder through a patch of warm air turbulence, veer sharply, then steady in a curving glide downward. At that angle I could make out bare stretches of brown hills deeply rutted by erosion, the very same hills that had once produced a

26

profitable crop of mahogany. It was the flagrant abuse of the product, coupled with the lack of conservation and replanting that had turned those magnificent trees to dust, and their economy with it. I read that their mahogany, for the few shops still making mahogany products, was imported from Guatemala and extremely expensive.

We steadied then on a due west course for the landing strip--the new runway. Long after most other countries in the Caribbean had caught up with the jet age and improved facilities accordingly, Haiti finally put in longer runways and built a new terminal building. If it came at all, progress was at the pace of a snail on this end of the island shared with the Dominican Republic. The local telephone system had changed little since it was first installed by the US Marines in the early thirties. Across the border was a different world.

We hit the strip with a thump, bounced, then raced along the irregular tarmac before slowing down with the roar of a reverse thrust of the engines.

From what I could see nothing had changed in the years since I had been here, nor had I expected to see any. Thatch-roofed *cailles* were visible on one side of the runway. Everyone and everything looked dry and dust-coated, colorless, like a photograph of the old west. Off to the east, toward the border, stood a range of hills with a large lake at the base of the mountains.

In a flash of memory complete with sights and smells, I could see myself back at the lake for an evening crocodile hunt in the warmish, muddy water. In those days the crocs were so plentiful as to be a nuisance. I had heard they were gone now--along with the sugar, coffee, fertile hillsides of fruit and mahogany, and of course tourists. I felt a sadness at the thought of what was, what might have been, and the reality of today.

Moving to the cabin door, I was suddenly hit with a wave of heat, mixed in were the familiar scents of spice, burnt wood, sugar cane, and rotting vegetation. With that, and the flood of memories, there was immediately the feeling of the indescribable presence of the dense population struggling to survive on arid land, poor and starving, still hoping for the seemingly impossible: a wise and benevolent leader who would take care of them. In the mood and thinking of today, no doubt that would be considered a racist thought.

Inside the muggy terminal of yellow stucco and glass, sparsely furnished with wilting plants and shabby furniture, I caught a brief glimpse of Amy then lost sight of her as I moved through the inspection lines. The luggage search, while performed by bored, indifferent men and women, seemed thorough enough and I wondered if they would pull people out for having too much food, or too many appliances. The whole picture was rather pathetic.

Once outside the terminal in the blazing heat, which wasn't conducive to lengthy bargaining, I spoke with several drivers before settling on what I thought was a reasonable fare with a man named Lafond. Actually the problem wasn't the fare. The problem was that he couldn't understand why I wanted to go to the hotel I gave him because it was neither well known nor fashionable. The man made perfect sense but I was determined. Finally, after even more talk, he reluctantly agreed to take me to my destination. When he led me across the street to his vintage Ford Fairlane I wondered if I'd made the right choice. Maybe I had lost my touch at this sort of thing. I was almost totally convinced of this when I found out he had no air conditioning.

Anyway, with the windows open and the hot air at least moving across my face, I settled onto the lumpy, plastic-covered seats and gave myself a vote of confidence. This was all well and good as long as we were moving, but almost immediately the traffic slowed to a crawl. We inched along the narrow, twisting, bustling road that led down into Port-au-Prince and I looked out the window, seeing, but in the back of my mind wondering just how I would go about finding Christine. Loaded donkeys plodded along the roadside, steadfast, determined, oblivious to the noisy machines in competition, almost as if flaunting their continued existence in the face of such awesome mechanical progress.

People were everywhere but seemingly going nowhere, standing in clusters along the road, looking, talking, unsmiling for the most part. There were the vendors: a ragged line of lace goods, mahogany bowls and figures, animal hide rugs, paintings, and much more. Lean, hard women trudged down the steep road with baskets of produce balanced on their heads; the weight of the basket was cushioned by the *troquette,* a roll of brightly-colored cloth twisted into a small circle and placed under the load. Only within the last ten or fifteen years, I'd read, had the women of Haiti been allowed to travel about the country without a special pass. Prior to that they were considered chattel.

Gradually the mass of cars, mostly tiny and foreign, with unfamiliar names, began to move and shortly we were in the large, grassy square in front of the palace. From there a narrow, cobblestone road, walled on either side to hide what had once been grand plantation homes, brought us to my residence of choice: Hotel Sans Souci. The French name meant, literally, "without concern" and from what I remembered was a perfect choice, not only for the hotel but for the general population, in a positive way, considering how they managed to deal with the harsh life of the poor.

I looked the old place over as we drove into the circular driveway in front of the hotel. In the best of times--assuming that period was when I was here before--the hotel seemed almost proud to show what I considered a seedy appearance. What could it look like now? I had expected the worst with the passing years and I was not disappointed.

Sitting on the western edge of an irregularly shaped triangle of land, the three-storied structure of brick, wood, tall pillars, balconies, tile floors, and tall arched doorways in the French mode, had been built near the turn of the century (a standing joke among the regulars was which century?) as a grand home for a French plantation owner whose name I never heard. Now, looking at the peeling paint, sagging portico roof, and overgrown vegetation surrounding the place I found it difficult to picture it in those days of glory. The French had indeed fallen a long, long way.

Few tourists found their way to the Sans Souci, nor should they. As is often true of places such as this, with a faded ambiance of its own, it was the guests, mostly residents, some of spurious means, that gave it a reputation and made it unique. Those who lived there were lower level embassy personnel on a tight living allowance, French and American for the most part, pensioners without a lot of pension, small shop owners (always on a strict budget), and a few writers working in search of that elusive first successful novel--a truly eclectic group. This was where Graham Greene should have stayed when he wrote his novel about Haiti. But I don't think he did.

As if the clientele weren't enough of a draw, with the food surprisingly good, another attraction was the bartender: a tall, thin, affable fellow named Luke who, according to those who would know such trivia, made the best Rum Punch in Haiti, and possibly in the entire Caribbean. So, on balance, the Sans Souci was a popular place for many to visit, an oddity to see, an almost tourist attraction for those looking to observe the other way of life. A discriminating, select group (or maybe cheap few), chose to actually stay there. In short, Hotel Sans Souci, while clinging precariously to the rock edge of survival in a monetary way, and to respectability often, oblivious to time, and unique in a manner of getting by on its own terms, was to some people *the* place to stay.

I knew none of this when I first took up residence. It was a place I could afford.

Looking among the foreign cars parked around the driveway for the old owner's Mercedes, and not seeing it--it may well have died by now--I went up the steps, across the tiled porch, and into a small room used as a reception area. If the old French plantation owners had such a thing this might have been called a parlor room. A woman suddenly moved in behind the desk from the dining area, which was a rather small, pleasant room in the front corner of the main floor. She was a stunningly attractive mulatto who, after a brief moment of eye contact, told me her name was Claudette. Aside from the woman, as I looked around, as usual nothing seemed to have changed, or improved. But then with the addition of such a beautiful woman, nothing else really had to change did it? From the owners point of view anyway.

A few moments later, in my second floor front room, I unpacked, showered, then lay down in my shorts hoping for a brief nap. Even with a soothing, gentle warm breeze drifting through the room and a long, tiring trip, it seemed like a long time before I fell asleep. Before I did, I wondered about Christine, once again. Would I find her? What was her story? And perhaps more importantly, where would I even start the search?

## THREE

The man who rose from his desk to greet me was wearing a
seersucker suit and bow tie. The suit was perfectly normal attire for this
climate. I had owned one myself. The tie was a statement of some sort.
He said, "Good Morning, Mr. Morgan. I'm Roger Wilson. What can I do
for you this morning?" Then he sat and waved me to the only other chair
in the room.

I smiled and said, "Jack Morgan." He was about my age, I guessed, with
a full head of gray hair, almost white, with a body at that dangerous age of
turning to fat around the middle. Idly, my thoughts drifting momentarily, I
wondered if his tie was a clip-on. Bow ties were rare these days. Since it
had that rumpled, kind of off-center look, I thought it was probably a real
tie.

Starting from absolute zero, with no plan and not the faintest idea of how
to start my search, or even where, it had come to me during the period of
sleep--as those directions sometimes do come (not often enough)--that a
good place to start might be the American Embassy. Not a brilliant
thought but it did seem logical. I didn't expect a whole lot of help or much
in the way of hard facts. From personal experience I found the embassy
group could be somewhat cliquey and very often out of the real picture of
what was happening, especially in a small country. That is not to say that
there were not some good people working for State. But in a general way,
they seemed to think they had their finger on the pulse while in reality the
blood pressure number was off the scale. But then, what else was there?

Earlier, a Marine guard in tan shirt and blue trousers with the blood
stripe, as we used to call it, had shown me, after a moment to check some
ID, to the office of the Cultural Attaché (read spook).

As he shuffled some paperwork out of the way, I couldn't help but
compare the past to the present--an upsetting thing to do because it made
me think of all the years gone by, and feel old. So typical of that time, and
so full of character, the old embassy was a big, wooden structure with a
wide porch and columns, huge rooms with tall shutters, creaking floors,
and a winding staircase that led to the upper floor. What stories that place
could tell if it had a voice.

The American Embassy of today, an ugly combination of cement boxes
and glass, all sharp angles, so clean, efficient and impersonal, was no
doubt a secure fortress by design. It too was a product of the times--an era
of violence and terrorists. Was this progress? I wasn't sure about that.
Certainly it represented the passage of time, but I'm not sure that
represented progress.

31

I had to stop thinking of the past.

I waited. His desk had all the props for a scene of the busy cultural man. No doubt there were many who wondered--I certainly would have if I hadn't been associated with the embassy situation--what a Cultural Attaché did in a country of constant political turmoil, and a starving, mostly illiterate population. That is not to say that the starving artist in his poverty does not create art, and does not bring forth a culture. Even with an annual average earning of $400.00, music and the arts do exist, and even thrive.

Still, the position of Cultural Attaché in a country like Haiti would hardly warrant a person devoting their full time efforts.

I said, "I'm not sure what you can do for me, Mr. Wilson. I'm hoping you can fill me in on the Peace Corps: where they operate, who's in charge, and who I might talk to about their people."

After he studied me for a moment he asked, "Are you a reporter?"

"No."

"Writer?"

He seemed to be looking for some point of reference, to put me in some category, so he could deal with me comfortably. I didn't want to disappoint him, and I wanted him to open up and tell me something, so I told him yes. What harm could it do? As long as he didn't get into technical stuff or details. I told him I was a freelance writer.

He said, "I see," slowly as if it now made sense. Now he had me in some sort of box. "Well, I'm sure you know that the PC is nonpolitical and has nothing to do with the embassy. In fact, they make a point of staying far away from us. With that in mind, how can I help you?"

"With that in mind of course, I'm sure you know something about them. Maybe a sub-heading under culture in Haiti."

He frowned at first then ended up with a smile. "In a way I suppose they are, or at least they will have an effect on the general culture--in time. My main concern, as you probably know, is with trade and the arts, that sort of thing. Not a whole lot I can tell you about them. A group lived up north, not far from the Citadel. Do you know Haiti at all?"

*To be sure: trade and the arts; and running agents on the side.* He didn't seem to be the type. But then they aren't supposed to be are they? I suspected this was one of those he-knows-that-I-know-that-he knows type of situations. "Yes I know Haiti. I lived here for a time."

"Good. Then you know the country. You were with the government? With State?" I didn't want to lead him anywhere so I told him I was a tourist at that time. That brought a raised eyebrow but no comment. A pause then he said, "If you're interested in just general information about the PC I'd suggest you contact their headquarters directly."

"You mean in DC?" He nodded. "A bit out of the way." I saw an ashtray and lit up a cigarette, though his frown told me it was strictly for show. Too bad. "I may end up doing just that. But I would like to see them in action, get a feel for their mission here. You know what I mean?" Another nod. He knew I was bullshitting him but I pressed on anyway. "I'm not looking for anything secret here. I'm trying to write a Sunday Special (whatever that might be) on the good work these people are doing--a human interest piece."

"There's really not much here, Mr. Morgan."

"And why is that? All I need from you is a name."

"I can't give you one."

"You can't give me a name!"

"I could, but it wouldn't matter now."

"What does that mean?"

He let out a soft sigh and turned away, as if bored with visiting idiots like me, having to deal with tourists, writers, whatever, all those without any idea of the complexity of his work, no grasp of the enormous internal problems he had to deal with in his demanding job. I could read it all in his face. I'd seen it before. "Mr. Morgan," he finally said with an effort, "the Peace Corps was ordered out of the country three months ago."

Three months ago. Christine should have been home three months ago. I ground out my smoke and wondered why he hadn't dropped that one on me in the beginning. Maybe he enjoyed my company. More likely he was hoping to get something out of me. "Why was that? Why were they kicked out? Why would anyone throw out a bunch of do-gooders who could only help this place?"

With a shrug he said, "A decision by the president."

"Theirs or ours?"

"The president of Haiti of course!"

"Of course? Why of course? And who is it now? But the serious question is why."

"He was informed that they were engaged in anti-government activities."

"The Peace Corps!" I was tempted to ask if they were because he would know. But of course he'd never tell me. It was pointless to go down that road. I said, "I can certainly understand them getting kicked out, what with teaching the Haitians to irrigate the land, rotate crops, reforest the hills, personal hygiene, that sort of thing. That is definitely subversive stuff. I'd be worried if I were the president."

33

He stared at me for a moment, not absolutely sure if it was sarcasm, then said, "We didn't agree of course, fought it all the way, the Ambassador in constant sessions with the president. But what could we do? It is their country after all."

*Since when?* I really wanted to answer that question, to say that we could have some balls, kick some ass here, stand up to this clown. After all, the man wouldn't even be in the palace now if it weren't for the US military and a policy that wasn't a policy at all. We could have gone on down that path of discussion. But what was the point? It all had nothing to do with Christine. I said, "It's been a pleasure, Mr. Wilson. Thanks for your time." I didn't mean a word of it.

Politically correct in my book is the ultimate oxymoron.

\*\*\*

From 28 years of experience with the Agency in countries all over the world, and dealing with all kinds of people in all kinds of conditions, Roger Wilson had developed an inner alarm that went off when he felt things weren't quite right. The alarm had gone off after Jack Morgan left his office. He had the strong feeling that the man was neither a tourist nor a writer. The question was then, who is he really and what is he doing in Haiti? Then as he pondered that question he wondered if he was over reacting, after all very little was happening here these days and he could be making something out of nothing--chasing meaningless shadows out of boredom. Still, he trusted the old instincts and decided to run a check on his visitor. You never know what might turn up.

\*\*\*

A hot, gritty, stifling wind hung in the car. I sat near the open window smoking a cigarette that tasted foul. Earlier, after leaving the embassy and going back to the hotel for breakfast--an ordinary meal served in the breezy front room made more enjoyable by Claudette swaying around--I'd changed to comfortable shorts and sandals and decided to go for a walk. I needed a bit of space, a time to think and question and I did that best when walking.

I headed off down the narrow, cobbled street, walking along the stone wall. More people in the streets than I remembered, more with nothing to do but search for food and a place to live--the hopeless in a land where hope was no more than a fleeting shadow, or a puff of teasing smoke in the wind that could be seen but never grasped.

I walked and thought. The Peace Corps, and Christine, was no longer in the country. So why am I here? Did Marv know that from the beginning? If so, why did he steer me to Haiti? In knowing me, did he think I would take hold of this and follow to wherever? Follow each small lead and do what had to be done? Did he include killing?

He knew I would do this largely because of Hannah. What else did he think I would do? He knew I would scour the earth because of her, and because I owed him, and because he owed the senator. Starting with me all debts were going to be paid in full. I was the key to it all. Was there more to it?

As is often the case in this unpredictable life of ours, fate, chance, karma, God, call it what you will depending on your persuasion, someone was moved into my space. A taxi came to a screeching halt at the curb beside me; horn blowing and the driver shouting in Creole. Reacting on instinct, I dropped into a crouch and grabbed at my waist for a weapon I didn't have, then seeing there was no danger and embarrassed at my ridiculous position, straightened and relaxed. No one on the street paid any attention to me.

"Hey!" LaFond yelled. "You want a taxi? I show you everything. I drive all over Haiti. Special rate for you."

Special rate! A guy surprising me that way could get killed.

After some talk I took his special rate for the day, figuring I could at least see where the PC had worked, ask a few questions, see if anyone knew her or of her, and maybe get a feel for where Christine had spent a part of her life. Doing so would at least clear my conscience and I could leave tomorrow. This would be a nice, easy way out. But it was not meant to be.

I crawled into the back seat, settled down and lit a cigarette. The car was like an oven, though it cooled just a bit with the breeze of moving. We headed north past the airport, paved road turning quickly to dirt, nice homes giving way to simple dwellings in small towns, and these finally replaced by shabby villages of wattle-and-daub cottages out in the countryside. Children, covered almost white from the dust, played by the road. Looking down from a narrow wooden bridge as we crossed a nearly dry gulley, I saw women washing clothes in the trickle of water that in the rainy season would be a small river. A strange land I thought, staring out, a place where voodoo and the Catholic Church shared a space in the hearts and minds of the people, each getting a certain reverence in a special way for perhaps the same end result; a place where the village voodoo priest, or *houngan,* was sometimes more powerful than the priest, or at any rate more feared. In retrospect it was easy to understand how "Papa Doc"

Duvalier had bullied his way to power using that fear and superstition of voodoo to sway these mostly uneducated people. The bowler hat that he wore, and the big glasses that gave his eyes an owl-like appearance, were merely props to enhance his mystical image. With that going for him and a building fear enforced by his gang of thugs, the dreaded TTM's (*Tonton Macoutes*), he created a cruel dictatorship, a power that gradually drained the resources of the country and virtually enslaved the population. In time he was succeeded by his son, "Baby Doc," who proved to be a branch of the same tree. All the while the US continued to pour money and resources into the crumbling nation. Perhaps the bitter sweet irony of it all was that the son, persuaded to abdicate, finally, and flown out by a US aircraft, was last heard to be living in France, destitute, reduced to doing common garden work to survive. The stolen millions were gone, squandered on a lavish lifestyle he'd brought with him from Haiti and thought was his due. The stupid, greedy bastard didn't have the brains to manage his money.

Who said life wasn't fair?

At his request I was calling him Al now, more Americanized I suppose, though I wasn't sure why he would want to do so. For a city cab driver he seemed to have an excellent knowledge of the countryside, claimed to have a rough idea of where the PC worked, and promised we would be in that area shortly. Over the next two hours we stopped in three small towns, villages actually, with the same results, or lack of them: hesitant, guarded conversations in Creole that Al translated; yes they knew of the PC people who did good work and were liked; no, no one knew anything else about them, why or just when they left the country. Somehow I wasn't surprised at how little we learned, for I had an unexplainable feeling of a deeper mystery in this. One person did recall a young woman with long hair among the group. This narrowed it down to almost any American female and really amounted to nothing. We were drinking warm cokes and smoking during this interview. At the end I said,"I guess that wraps it up, Al. We might as well start back."

In all honesty I wasn't unhappy with our non-accomplishment. The more I thought about it the more I was convinced that it was a mistake to come here in the first place. Marv and her father, the senator, certainly had to know that Christine wasn't in Haiti since they had unlimited access to information and intelligence reports. That aside--which I didn't know at the start--while it had been a pleasant thought to see my old "home" again, struck me that it was a closed chapter, finished and put away, and not a trip I would even consider if I had nothing to do.

Whether Al was concerned with our failure to turn up anything, or anxious to give me my money's worth, in a quiet moment he said, "You like to see Citadel? We are very close. Very interesting place to visit. I can take you all the way to the top if you want."

"No thanks, Al. Been there and done that--the donkey ride up that mountain crippled me for days."

"Okay boss," Al said with a grin. "We make it back to city before dark. No sweat."

I told him to thank the villagers and I went back to the car to smoke and think. I remembered going up to see that fort.

The *Citadelle La Ferriere,* as it was formally known in French, was the brainchild of Henri Christophe, a name as familiar to Haitians as George Washington to Americans--though not for the same reasons. Around 1805, after the assassination of Dessalines, instead of turning the presidency over to the next in line, who was Christophe, the educated mulattos in the government turned away from the barely literate black man. In retaliation he seized the northern part of the country and set out to prove he could create a masterwork in tribute to himself--quite an ego. His empire was ruled from a grand palace called *Sans Souci* near the town of Milot.

Over the following 16 years, roughly, the people under near slavery conditions built the massive stone fortress. Thousands died. The stones, cannon, cannon balls (weighing 25-50 pounds), mahogany, iron, and furnishings, were carried up the mountain by hand; a matter of a two hour climb on foot, carrying nothing; an incredible feat when you consider the loads they must have carried. The fortress was 3,000 feet above sea level-- straight up!

Christophe quite literally fell from power during the construction of the strategically worthless fortress. Weakened and partially paralyzed from a stroke, he nevertheless dressed in his white uniform to review his troops from astride his horse. In front of his men at *Sans Souci* he slipped from his saddle and fell to the ground.

It is said, and believed by many at the time, that he shot himself with a silver bullet, after which his queen dragged his body up the tortuous 5-mile track to bury him in the fortress. In any case, his tomb is today in the awesome structure that covers some 80,000 square meters and is considered to be the 8th Wonder of the World. It stands in mute testimony to the French and English engineers of Christophe.

I sat with Al in the front and we started back along the dirt road to the city. The earlier bright sky showed the first traces of an impending storm, the clouds gathering quickly in a swirling black mass, wind picking up without a break in the humidity.

Offering the pack, I said, "Smoke, Al?"

"Yes," he said enthusiastically. "Thank you. They are very expensive here."

He took one and I shook out the pack. "I'm sure they are. Take a couple. For the road." After a moment I asked him if he had a family.

"Oh yes. I have four children in school. You have a wife? Children?"

"No. Never got around to it, Al"

He was a big man and he had a big laugh. "There were women?" I smiled at the thought and nodded. "Not good. Not good for a man without woman and a family." We smoked for a few moments, Al inhaling deeply, both of us glancing up at the sky, then he said, "This girl you are looking for. Your woman? She is pretty and has long hair?"

"My woman? No. Not in that sense. She is the daughter of someone who knows a friend of mine. He asked me to look for her."

"Must be very good friend."

"Not so much a good friend. More like someone I owe a favor. I like to pay my debts."

That brought a glance. "A good habit. It is not so common in Haiti." He watched the road for a moment, and the sky. "What will you do now? The woman is not here. Maybe she has gone to another country."

"Maybe. I've nothing to go on here, no leads, not even a hint as to where she might have gone. I might as well go home tomorrow."

"That is too bad. I would like to be your driver. You are, I think, a good and honest person. If you change your mind and decide to stay, get in touch with me. Any driver can tell you how to find me. Is it that you don't like Haiti?"

"Not at all. But this isn't a vacation. I lived here for a time and I like Haiti." That brought a glance at me but no comment. "But I have a life in Florida."

"Florida is very hot?"

"Yes. It is very hot in the summer. But it is very nice in the winter when the snow if falling up north."

"Snow? Do you know New York?"

"New York City? Sure."

"I would like to go there and makes lots of money," he said with a grin.

"You could make lots of money in New York City. The thing is, it costs a lot to live there. And I don't know if you would be happy there, Al. It's all relative."

"Relative, yes," he said as if to himself, thoughtfully.

"Must be tough here with a wife and family, to raise them and all. You must do a lot of driving."

"Oh yes, I do that. As much as I can. But we have no tourists now and it is difficult. My wife works at CMC."

He said the name as if I would know it. "What's CMC?"

"A big factory where they make American sports equipment. Long hours and low pay." Then he pointed out to the right where I could make out two large, yellow buildings. "That is the place of Caribe Manufacturing."

"Is it owned by the government?"

"Not the government. Someone close to the government--Colonel Sauvain. You know of him?"

"Never heard of him."

Nodding, he said, "It is better not to know of that man."

On that ominous note, one that would have piqued my curiosity if I planned to hang around that is, I went back to watching the now menacing sky.

The rain started.

In an instant, the water splashed against the windshield, and all around us, in a torrential stream. I rolled up my window as far as it would go but there was a gap at the top and I was taking on water badly. Al fared no better as his window went about half way up. I saw him straining to see the road from behind feeble wipers not up to the task. The car's better days, if indeed it ever had any, were a long time ago.

Al seemed a bit tense at the deluge. It wasn't as if we could go to shelter and wait it out. Aside from the factory a long way off, there wasn't a building or a hut in sight. We seemed to sway and veer a lot, whether from the wind or from Al making an attempt to dodge the many potholes. If it was the latter he wasn't doing so well because the car thumped and banged constantly.

Suddenly we hit what must have been the "Mother" of a hole in the road. We came out of it leaning to one side, shaking and rattling, then losing speed until finally going off the road to a dead stop. Looking at each other, Al said, "Sorry. I think we hit a hole. It is not good." He smiled before adding, "But we get it fixed."

I nodded, but I didn't have a good feeling about this and I definitely didn't share his confidence in getting whatever fixed. We weren't a cell phone call away from roadside assistance, even if I had a cell phone. I remembered that at one time there was a car rental office and even AAA in the city. I had my doubts that they existed today. Out here in the country we were at best hours, if not days from any qualified help, and I had the feeling that we needed qualified help. What I did feel, vividly, was the flight to Miami leaving tomorrow without a Jack Morgan on the passenger manifest. I lied and said, "No problem, Al. We'll wait out the storm and then get help."

He believed me. "Right," he said. "No problem." Then he leaned back and lit a cigarette.

After about twenty minutes of waiting, with the rain pounding, silence, much smoking and no conversation, both lost in our own thoughts, the storm gradually weakened, then passed, the sky returned to blue as if it all had never happened.

Al got out to check the car and came back to tell me that the "wheel is gone."

"The wheel is gone. You mean the tire? The tire blew?"

He shook his head. "The wheel must be fixed. The garage tell me, maybe a week ago, that I need shocks and a few other things."

A few other things. Shock absorbers and a few other things. What it needed was a new car! Shit.

Unperturbed, which I suppose is a good way to be when one lived in Haiti--maybe the only way to exist--Al smiled and said, "A village is not too far away. I will go and get help. No problem."

I immediately regretted using that expression. "Right," I said. "I'll be here. You still think we can be back in the city tonight?" A touch of sarcasm there, which he missed or ignored. He took off down the road.

The evening sky on the horizon was splashed with shades of purple and pink, the bugs out in full force, when Al finally came back. He was riding in a beat-up truck with two other men. They all got out and proceeded to check out the car in great detail. The sad-looking car was slanted over with the front end in a pool of water. After much shaking of heads and much animated conversation full of "I don't knows" (that I knew in Creole), Al told me the obvious. "We will have to spend the night in the village. I have many friends there. No problem. I will take you back to the city in the morning. No extra charge." He showed a big grin.

With the air heavy and still, probably made more so by the rain, it was a pleasure to ride in the open back of the truck, feeling the wind against my face, and feeling good. The ride was a short one to the village where we turned down a muddy road and stopped in front of a small, but neat, three-bedroom house painted green and white. Al, warmly greeted by a man and woman with a bunch of kids, introduced me and we went inside. The main room was large with sturdy, wooden furniture that looked functional if not comfortable. Later I found out that many of the houses in the village were nowhere near as grand as this one, often without water which

40

was bought at the single well in the village and carried home in metal cans, and just as often without an indoor toilet.

After a meal that would be a dieters delight, some vegetables and a piece of meat, none of which I recognized, we went out to sit on a small porch and smoked something Al told me was a local blend. Whatever it was, it seared my lungs, watered my eyes, and made me the main topic of conversation.

This was only the beginning.

Shortly, someone lighted a huge fire in the street. Then after a few moments a bottle of *Clairin*, their fiery home-brew, was passed around with much talk, laughing, and looking at me. Without hesitation, for I was anxious to use this rare opportunity to improve racial relations in the hemisphere, I drank. The clear liquid wasn't as bad as I had anticipated--it was much worse! This was like having a butane lighter, lighted of course, shot down my throat. Surprisingly, the second drink was better, and the third one quite enjoyable. Before long, what with passing the bottle around, and me carrying on a conversation using Creole words I thought were long forgotten--and using some I never knew--we were all great buddies.

Ah, the mind is a marvelous thing when freed from the darkness with a few nips from the bottle.

Al said, "Do you hear the drums?"

I told him negative, then made a point of listening, wondering if he was the one with too much *Clairin*. After a moment I did hear the boom-boom seemingly floating in the night--an eerie sound.

I looked at Al: his eyes were wide, the light from the fire dancing on his face, turning him into what I perceived to be fierce warrior, perhaps a chief sitting at a tribal gathering to talk of war, or peace. He spoke and startled me out of my thoughts. "We will go to the ceremonies. You want to come with us?"

I was surprised at the invite because traditionally, from what I remembered anyway, no white men were allowed into these secret gatherings--not to the real ones. For the tourists, back when they had them, shows were put on complete with drums, chickens, blood, the whole bit, but it was completely phony. Had times changed or was I included in the group with Al as my guide? Either way, the idea of attending was an intriguing one. What the hell. I didn't have to get up in the morning. I probably wouldn't be able to get up in the morning.

And so off we went, a long line of us, some carrying torches, some chanting in a deep, soft murmur, many silent, a long procession across barren land and then into scrubs and small trees. Eventually we came to a larger village some twenty minutes away. It all reminded me of a black and white John Carradine film of long ago, of zombies and dreadful music. For me, thankfully, it was a sobering walk.

The rhythmic thumping of the drums grew louder, as did the babble of voices from people joining us from out of the darkness. This was an event that drew all who could possibly make it, including the crippled and the lame. By now the crowd was massive. We came to what Al told me was called the *"Houmfort."* He explained that the cult center featured what was called a *"peristyle,"* a shed partly walled or banked by benches on three sides. The roof was thatch or corrugated tin and supported by a large wooden post down which the *"Loa"* (spirits) descend during the ceremonies. A sanctuary opens onto one end of the *"peristyle."* Saints and virgins, as well as the *"Loa"* are invoked at the beginning of the service. From Al's description of it all I could see a faint resemblance to Catholic liturgy--far out, but faint.

Entering the shed we sat near the front, off to one side, and the chanting began.

I looked around and took it all in, fascinated by the spectacle. Behind the altar hung two huge roughly drawn posters, one of *"Damballah,"* the Snake God, and the other of *"La Sirene,"* female of the sea, a mermaid with a fish in one hand and a conch shell in the other. Al told me that in other times I would have seen a poster also of *"Baron Samedi,"* one of the best known *"Loa"* who was made famous by "Papa Doc," the former president, who wore dark, somber clothes and owlish glasses similar to the baron, except for a top hat or bowler. Legend has it that a virgin must be deflowered before death or risk rape by the baron who lives in cemeteries and traffics with the souls of the dead.

Heady stuff.

Heady stuff made even more so by the crush of humanity around us, the oppressive heat, pounding drums, a strong human odor mixed with damp earth, pungent *Clairin,* and the sweet smell of whatever was being smoked by the crowd. The beat of the drums had reached near deafening proportions. I lighted up the last of my cigarettes and drew heavily. This was all getting to me and I tried to keep a grip, a level head for whatever reason--probably habit. Later, I could question that thinking; if I'd been a bit more relaxed when things started to happen, I might have reacted differently.

We were close enough to the altar to see necklaces, stones, earthenware jars, and several bottles of what I assumed, from my own upbringing, to be wine. A lean goat with spindly, quivering legs was tied near the altar for sacrifice.

A hush settled over the crowd as the *Houngan* entered from the sanctuary and proceeded to call upon the first *Loa*. Moving around the altar, stalking, shaking the *Asson,* sacred rattle, he called in chants for *Legba,* guardian of the crossroads, to open the gates leading the way to communication with the other world. Looking around I saw many whose eyes rolled around in swaying heads, unseeing, bodies possessed, already in another world. The chanting and wailing increased, both in numbers and volume.

What with all the noise, absorbed as I was in the ceremony, I wasn't aware of a different kind of commotion starting in the back of the shed until Al grabbed my arm. Annoyed at his interrupting my concentration, I turned and asked what was going on. He didn't answer, but indicated with a head movement rearward. I turned and followed his look. In among the people who now were screaming and pushing to get out of the way, were a group of khaki-clad soldiers, or police, moving through the crowd knocking people around and hustling some of them outside. For whatever reason they seemed intent on breaking up the ceremony. Some of them swung a short club at anyone within range. Al was pulling on my arm and telling me that we had to get of there, pronto! Too late, for I spotted two of them blocking the doorway nearest to us. No matter, we started pushing and shoving our way in that general direction.

"What the hell is going on!" I screamed.

Al kept moving and I was glued to his back. To this point it was only a question of pushing bodies out of our way and to keep moving. Suddenly, Al took a hit from one of the swinging clubs and he stumbled and fell. The soldier was standing over Al as I moved in, grabbed his arm and twisted until he dropped the club. I found his face in front of my hand so I gave him a push. Al moaned and tried to stand up but someone fell on top of him. After I helped him up we started moving again, slowly, between bodies pushing and shoving, I fell down twice, but we were able to keep going in the right general direction. Seemingly out of nowhere a soldier, officer I saw, stepped in front of me with pistol drawn, puts the damn thing in my face and screamed, "Come with me!"

No way. I wasn't about to do that nor was I about to let him shoot me, which he looked perfectly capable of doing, and even willing to do. He was close, so close I could smell his bad breath, see the violence in his eyes, and see big, white teeth. I repeated the move of grabbing and twisting, but he was big and strong and his arm barely moved. Still holding his arm with my left hand, I threw a punch with my right, with all I had, aimed at his stomach which is usually a vulnerable soft spot. Not much happened, to him anyway, he sort of shuddered but didn't go down and didn't move away from me. My whole arm hurt like hell. Incensed at my resistance, he was screaming at me now in Creole, probably cursing, as we jostled for control of that pistol, with his arm, my hand attached, swingy wildly. I wasn't gaining any ground on this guy. In a desperation move I shifted so that I had both hands on his arm holding the pistol. What I was trying to do was slide my hand down inside the trigger guard so that I could control when and where the damn thing went off. Nice thought. To his surprise and mine it did go off. I knew it was my point when I felt him go limp, sag down away from me, eyes roll up, and go on down to the floor. I stood there staring at him as a patch of blood appeared on his shirt. As for myself, I was soaked in perspiration, chest heaving like I'd gone ten tough rounds at Madison Square Gardens, and felt like my guts would heave at any moment. Aside from that I was great.

Not quite what I had in mind for a night out in Haiti.

Next thing I know Al and I are outside and he's pulling me by the arm. "You must get out of here," he said. "They will arrest you."

Probably, I thought. "What ever happened to self defense?" I offered lamely. "What about unjustified use of excessive force?" I was clearly out of it--except to myself.

Ignoring my stupid comment, he pointed off into the trees. "Go now! Go to the village and take the truck."

"What fucking truck?"

"You must go. We will be fine. Go quickly."

"What truck? What about a key! Where is the damn truck?"

"No key needed," he told me with great patience, under the circumstances. "Go now. Take the truck and go back to the city."

A sane section of my brain that surprisingly still functioned told me that he was giving good advice. Besides, I didn't have a whole lot of options. I wasn't operating here in the "Home of the free and the brave." Brave maybe but definitely not free. What bothered me was leaving him. My profession not withstanding, where I worked alone, leaving someone involved with me in the operation behind was never an option. Those who went in with us came out with us. But I wasn't "operating" here in the strict sense of the term. This was his country, his problem, and his call to make.

I ran. And I kept on running until the night turned quiet. The only sound was my heavy breathing and the thumping in my chest which could surely be heard for miles around. Fearing a heart attack, I dropped down to catch my breath and looked around. There was nothing but black in all directions and I hadn't the faintest idea of how far I'd gone or where I was. Sitting down in the dirt, I tried to collect my wits and think in some logical fashion. From where we had started, eaten, and left the truck, it had been about a twenty minute walk to the ceremony. It seemed to me that I'd been running a lot longer than twenty minutes. But in what direction? There was no sign of any village. Had I run the wrong way? Away from the village? Maybe it had been in a circle? Both were strong possibilities. The fact was that I was in the middle of nowhere with no idea which way to go. Overhead, a moon passed through an opening in the dark clouds, then disappeared again. Which direction was the moon? Without some gadgets--a compass would be nice--I hadn't a clue.

After a few moments I stood and stumbled up a rocky rise to where I might have the advantage of height. Along with my still pounding heart, my arm had gone numb. With all that I still would have like a smoke.

Off to my left I saw dim lights. Was that were I wanted to go or was it the place I'd just left? A different village? Providing the lights didn't indicate the place I just ran away from, it could be some kind of help, maybe even where the truck was to take me out of here. I started off heading for the lights, thinking as I moved, reviewing my situation. Not good. For starters, if that guy died I could be facing a murder charge. In some other country--I could think of several, but not in this part of the world--I might be able to go for justifiable homicide in some form or other. I doubted if that term was even known in the Haitian legal vocabulary. Round up the usual suspects. Hell. I was the only one on the list. If there was one other white person at the ceremonies I didn't see him, or her. My thought train seemed to be taking me nowhere and it didn't take a brain surgeon to realize that I had to get out of the country and fast. Let the embassy worry about any charges, in absentia of course.

When I did reach the edge of a village I entered carefully, from training and habit, moving down a dirt road, looking for any sign of activity. But then, this wasn't an enemy village and I relaxed a bit at the sound of a dog barking, realizing that life meant help here. The dog was quickly joined by several others in a howling chorus. All the noise was bound to awaken someone. Suddenly aware of the smell of wood smoke, wet vegetation and raw sewage, I went deeper into the village.

Being in a strange place at night wasn't new to me, What was new was being in without backup, without some organization behind me knowing where I was and how to get me out. A creepy feeling. No matter how fucked up a situation might become, and it often did, at least there was a plan to fall back on. And behind that, if necessary, a new plan would be devised. There was no one here but jack Morgan.

From the road, which seemed to be the main street, other streets, sometimes only a path or track, branched off to show the bare outline of

45

houses and an occasional soft light. If I was having any luck at all, and if I was in the right village, down one of these dirt roads I hoped to see the truck. After all, there weren't a whole lot of vehicles of any kind here and the truck would stand out. More streets off to either side. Sure enough, there under a tree I thought I could see the glint of moonlight on steel. Moving closer I saw that it was the definite outline of a truck. Was it the one I was looking for? No light in the house and no sound. I got to the truck and reached for the door handle.

Suddenly I was choking and gulping for air, something tight around my throat. "Who are you?" A voice asked harshly. "What do you want here?"

"Wait," I croaked. "Al sent me. Lefond."

The pressure eased but was still in place. "Where is Lefond?" I told the voice in all honesty that I didn't know, that I left him back at the shed. The arm around my neck slacked off. "Tell me what happened." I did, leaving out the shooting, which I thought wasn't a good thing to bring up now. "He is right. Take the truck. I have more gasoline." With that he moved off, then came back with a can and stood by the truck. I heard liquid sloshing into the tank.

Good idea. Wouldn't be much of a getaway on an empty tank.

As quickly as he had appeared he was gone. Opening the door, which made one helluva racket, I climbed in and hit the lever where a key would be. Nothing happened. Three times before the engine started with a racket that might well be heard in Port-au-Prince. But then who would care? There were no soldiers here. I backed out and roared off, hopefully in the direction of the city.

A smoke would have been nice.

As if driving on a narrow, unfamiliar dirt road wasn't bad enough, a broad swath of black clouds moved in and blocked the only light one could hope for out here in the country. But things weren't all that bad: one headlight was working at half power. And of course the upside, if one were an incurable optimist, was the lack of traffic. Other than wanting to get back to the safety of the city as soon as possible--a delusion actually, since there was no place to hide if they, meaning the authorities, wanted to find me--there was no need for haste. The confusion back at the shed would take time to unravel, and even if it were decided that I was the wanted one, it wouldn't be right away.

All very logical. Still, I drove as fast as I could without running off the road.

I zipped right along, struggling all the while with a serious case of nicotine withdrawal, and trying to see the road in more than the tiny

46

patches of headlight allowed. Coming to the crest of a steep hill I missed the curve off to the left, at the bottom, and went straight. Serious trouble. For a few seconds I was airborne. I kept pumping at the brakes but of course nothing is happening in mid-air to slow me down. Then I slammed down hard onto solid ground, still pumping the brakes out of reflex action. I kept going, careening down the slope, slamming into rocks and trees, the horrible sound of twisting, stressed to the limit metal glancing off immovable objects, we finally meet, head on, something big that didn't give.

The last thing I remember is being thrown into the windshield.

# FOUR

Opening my eyes and coming back into the land of the living, the first thing I realized was that I was lying naked under a sheet on something that might be a bed, except there was no mattress. Maybe it was just a hard bed. In any case, I was alive and I didn't think it was a time to complain. I ached all over and was soaking wet, the sheet limp and soggy around my waist.    Stifling hot in the room.  Above me was a fan with long, thin, wooden blades, motionless on a white ceiling where the paint was peeling off in ragged strips.  Turning my head, painfully, I saw a small, wooden table in one corner of the room; on it was a yellow, china pitcher that was painted with flowers.  The descriptive word that came to mind was austere, or more accurately, poor.  Of course I did have a private room.

Where the hell was I?

A man came into the room and studied me for a moment.  "So you're back with us?" he said with a smile.  From those few words I figured he was American, from New England somewhere I'd guess. "How do you feel?"

An obvious question to which I'm sure he had an answer just from looking at me. "I'm not sure yet," I said in all honesty.  I was looking at him and trying to get my bearings.  He had long hair worn in a ponytail, sunburned face, beard, a thin man whose face showed a lot of mileage, the kind that was difficult to match with an age.  He could have ten years on me either way.  His  white jacket over a dark brown tee-shirt had missed the last laundry call, showing a mixed bag of stains. "Not bad, all things considered," I finally told him.  The sound of my voice had a hollow, almost alien tone.  I asked the usual questions as to where I was and who he was.

"Never mind that now.  You need to rest."

Didn't they always say that?  I leaned back down from him on my slab. Was it alcohol I'd smelled on him?  Medicinal?  I began to wonder if I'd dropped down some hole into the hands of some wacko, a mad hermit living in the boonies.  "Mind telling me where I am?  And who are you?"

"My name is Fielder. Marshal Fielder.  Most people around here call me Doc."

"With good reason I hope."

"Depends on who you ask."

Not really a confidence builder, I thought.  But I was hardly in a position to go look for a second opinion.  From what little I'd seen of this place so far, what you saw was what you got and you were damn lucky to get it.

Perhaps sensing my doubts he offered, "Don't worry. I did graduate from medical school."

In what percentile? He could have been at the bottom of his class. No stethoscope around his neck. Since when was a doctor without one? I felt a bad headache coming on but I persisted. "Where are we anyway?"

Putting his hands in the pockets of the grubby jacket, he looked around the room then back at me. "You are in...well, there is no official name for this place. It's a clinic, and a school, a sort of home for a lot of these people. The Haitians call it simply, 'Sister's Clinic.' Does that help?"

Not really. But I nodded as if it all made sense. "And...ah...where is this clinic? Are we in the city?"

"Oh no. Nowhere near Port-au-Prince. The closest town of any size is Gonaives."

That did help because I remembered that Gonaives was on the coast, northwest of the city, and not all that far from where I was last night. At least I assumed it was last night. After a moment of the two us staring at each other like two strangers, which we were, I asked, "How did I get here? The last I remember was driving along in the dark heading for the city. Now this!"

"Not surprising under the circumstances," he answered in a doctor's tone. You're a lucky man...?"

"Jack. Jack Morgan."

"Yes. You're a lucky man, Jack. You had an accident and ran off the road. You were in the truck, unconscious, when Andre found you--he's one of the men who help out around here. Anyway, he was on his way to work this morning and saw the truck off on the side of the road, said the truck was a total wreck and wondered how you were still alive. He brought you in here."

"Guess I owe him one. This morning, huh? What time is it now?"

He went over and looked out in the hallway then came back. "Almost five thirty."

"I've been here all day?"

He nodded. "Sleeping."

The sound of kitchen activity, a faint rattle of pots and pans, and an aroma of food, which I possibly imagined, made me realize that I hadn't eaten in a full day and was starving--even in pain the body does need energy. At that point, as if to perhaps gain my confidence, Fielder, in a serious tone, assured me that he was a doctor, and though his appearance gave me cause for doubt, I figured I'd let well enough alone. After all, there did seem to be some sort of medical presence about him. I said, "Anything broken? Any serious condition I should know about?"

49

He fidgeted for a moment, as someone might who needed either a smoke or a drink. "Nothing really serious. You're banged up of course, cuts and bruises, the usual, and you may have a fracture in the leg, bump on your head but it's only an external injury, I think. I can't confirm either without an x-ray. I did immobilize the leg just in case." He smiled and added, "You won't be running the hundred for a while."

"The hundred? You a sprinter, Doc?"

"Used to be...a long time ago...in college."

"Where was that?"

"Boston."

That could mean anything since the city of Boston was one big campus with a dozen colleges or more. I nodded as if did mean something. "Thanks for the care. Guess I owe you, huh?"

"I'll send you a bill. You just take it easy for now. Sister will be back soon and you'll get something to eat."

"Sure. Thanks again. By the way, any smokes around here? I'm dying for a cigarette."

"Not something to ask your doctor," he said, smiling. "You may well die from them. I don't have any but I'll see if I can find some for you. Andre may have some."

Watching him leave the room, I wondered about "Sister," hoping she came back from wherever with an appetite as big as mine. From memory I pictured a stern face in habit, peaceful, serene and spiritual on the outside and with the attitude of a Drill Instructor. Some things you never forget. They all had beautiful skin. And why not! No drinking. No smoking. No sun. No lots of things.

An aroma of food in the air! And this time I was sure it wasn't my imagination or wishful thinking. Right now I wouldn't turn up my nose at broiled leather sandal, if properly seasoned.

In an attempt to maybe get closer to that aroma, I tried to stand up, with the sheet wrapped around my waist I could at least see what was cooking. No go. The leg wouldn't take my weight and I flopped back down on my slab.

Moments later, though it seemed an eternity, the sound of a vehicle, sans muffler and probably other parts as well, broke the quiet early evening, with the noise stopping in front of the building. Sister? Food? I could make out a female voice speaking in Creole, the rustling of paper bags, a trunk closing, then more talk. The voice came closer.

She stood in the doorway with a bag under each arm. "Feeling better?"

Amy! I pulled the sheet up to my neck.

"You must be starving. Let me put this stuff in the kitchen. You're lucky because today is shopping day and we have chicken tonight."

Wonderful. Chicken is a big deal? What do they have on other nights? Still, it sounded better than broiled sandal. I thought it best not to mention cigarettes.

I heard her talking in the kitchen, then she was back holding a pair of khaki shorts, a cotton shirt, and my sandals. The clothing looked used but recently laundered. Holding them up in the air she said, "Look what I found for you!"

Still in mild shock at her being "Sister," I couldn't say anything for a moment. Amy! What were the odds on running into her again? A thousand to one? I finally said, "Thanks. I'm not sure I can get up to put them on."

"I'll help you. We eat in the kitchen next door to this, but if you can't manage I'll bring your meal in here."

"No. No. If that's where we eat I'll make it." I stared at her for a moment. "So...you're the Sister I've heard about."

"That's me," she said with a big smile. "I assume you were expecting Mother Superior, grim face, habit and all?" She sat down on the end of my slab. "It is true, at least about my being a Sister. I was in an order here and yes I was a Sister. I left the order about two years ago because I felt I could do just as well, if not better, in helping these people, without the restrictions of an order. Times have changed. The thing is, these people know me in that role and I don't think that will ever change with them. And that's okay; with or without that title and the organization behind me, I'm the same person. Now I expect you, Jack Morgan, to see me as just another woman."

"That's asking one helluva lot. I have the feeling you're anything but just another woman. But if that's what you want, so be it. I'm still in shock. You never mentioned being a Sister on the plane."

"I saw no reason to mention it. What difference does it make?"

"None, I suppose." I didn't really agree with that because people like her were in a different world from mine, until now anyway, and to me it made a big difference. I still wondered why she left a profession that was a way of life in itself. That was a big move.

As if reading my thoughts she said, "You're wondering why I left?"

"As a matter of fact I am. That's quite a change in lifestyle. You mentioned doing as well without the higher-ups, the bureaucracy, the politics of it all. I think it had to be more than that. But it's none of my business."

51

She looked away in thought, then back at me. "That question is always there in people's faces when they find out I've left the order. I've answered that question a hundred times and it's never the same answer. It was a combination of things: changing times of course, a gradual lessening of support from our Mother House in Miami, a change in me and a growing if you will, liberation of women, a realization that I could do all that I'm doing with my life without the restrictions and problems of a religious vocation. There came a time in my life when it seemed the natural thing to do. Does that shock you?"

"No." This was heading down the road to a discussion I didn't want to get into because it made me feel uncomfortable and ill-informed.

She got up and said, "I'll go see if I can help in the kitchen. When you're ready, give a holler and I'll come back and help you in to dinner."

"Thanks. I was wondering how you support this place?"

Stopping in the doorway, she said slowly, "That's the trick. We somehow manage to do it with patience, prayer, and the help of many loving, generous, hard-working folks. We manage to get by, and believe me, I often wonder how we do as much as we do."

So do I. I managed to get dressed without too much trouble since it was only a matter of shorts and a shirt. As promised, she came back when I called, and with one arm over her shoulder we moved slowly out of the room and down the hall. I learned later that this was the short leg of the l-shaped building that was the clinic. Passing what she said was her room we moved into a large, open area that was the kitchen. The simple room, high-ceiling, white walls, a number of long, wooden tables set up in a line cafeteria style, wood floor, and bare walls except for a crucifix was just what I expected. Near a big old iron stove was a woman, thin as a rail, in plain cotton dress, staring at me in what I would call an unfriendly attitude. Her look made me feel guilty, as if I were surely here taking food from the poor and starving. Which I was. But not by choice. And I was certainly not poor nor needy by any definition of the terms. At the moment I was totally under their control.

After Amy got me seated in an uncomfortable straight-backed chair, with a hemp seat, I looked around at my dinner companions. She made introductions, first waving an arm at the lean woman. "That's Marie, our cook. If she likes you, you're set. She'll take very good care of you where it counts."

"I don't think she does," I said softly, meant only for Amy.

"Does what?"

"Like me."

She spoke loud enough for everyone to hear. "Don't pay any attention to that look on her face; she takes a while to warm up to strangers." Then she added with a big smile, "I can see that she likes you already." That food aroma was getting to me, but I tried to pay attention. She pointed then to an older man dressed in rumpled sport shirt and faded khaki pants. I'd seen faces like his in other countries: wise and worldly with age, having experienced the cruelty and injustice, yet filled with compassion; hardened and yet soft to the needs of others. It all showed on his face. "There," she announced, "is Father William B. Smith, known as Father William."

"Call me Bill," he said. "And never mind Amy with her speeches. Would you care for a bit of scotch? Jack is it?"

"Jack it is." Scotch! Now here was a man after my own heart. Did he smoke? Empty stomach or not, I was ready for a drink. "I'd love one, Father...Bill." When he leaned over to pour me a generous portion, in a water glass, I noticed and was a bit surprised that it was one of the better brands. He was a bit overweight, balding with wisps of white hair swirled around his head, ruddy, friendly, round face with wire-rimmed glasses, and an unmistakable, at least to me, look of mischief in his eyes. I formed the immediate impression that here was a man I could trust and depend on, and learn to like if given time.

"You're American? Sorry we have no ice."

"No problem. I've spent enough time in London to get used to not having ice." I thought I detected either an English or Irish accent, however slight. "Do you know London?"

"Ah, yes I do. But I much prefer Dublin."

"Would it be an old place near Trinity College?"

He glanced around the table before winking at me. "I know such a place. Perhaps more than one."

"I can't say that I know Dublin well. But I have enjoyed the city on several occasions."

"To have been there is to know Dublin well. And what is it you do for a living, Jack? If you don't mind my asking."

"I'm retired." It was an honest answer as far as it went, and I didn't want to go any further on that subject. He gave me a curious look but didn't comment. Doc came into the room and the conversation shifted easily into a community mode about their problems of the day. I looked and them and listened to their talk. This was a close group who shared a common goal and common beliefs. I felt uncomfortable to say the least among these people whose very existence was for giving, to saving lives, whereas mine had been the opposite.

53

The simple meal was satisfying and filling and I asked for, and got a second helping. The others drank bottled water or tea while Bill and I drank scotch. I was suddenly very tired and didn't catch most of their talk, nor wanting to, waiting for the right moment to make my exit. It came quickly enough when someone brought up the incident near Milot where a white man, believed to be American, had been involved in a shooting and was being sought by the police. I caught Amy, then the others at different times, staring at me. How could they not know? How many Americans were wandering around the country these days? Not many. I told them it was bedtime for me, thanked the cook, bid them all good night and managed to get out of the chair.

"Do you need help, Jack?" Amy asked.

"No. Thank you. I'll be fine."

"One day when you're fit you must get over to the school for a visit," Bill said.

"I'll try to do that."

I shuffled slowly down the hall, stopping several times to let the muscles calm down, aches ease a bit, and wondering why I'd turned down the thoughtful offer of help. In the room I saw that some kind soul--I had no idea who since I didn't notice anyone leave the kitchen--had straightened out the sheets and left a glass of water and some aspirin near the bed. After gulping them down I fell on the bed and in moments went into a restless sleep. The dreams came back.

*My arms were lashed tightly behind me; I was on a rough, wooden chair; a leather thong around my neck was tied to my hands, pulling my head back into an awkward, painful position. An olive-skinned man in camo fatigues with long black hair and beard; he was of the jungle, unwashed, a strong smell of earth about him; he slapped me again and again. I had no voice to answer his relentless questions. Someone threw a sweet, sticky liquid on my face. I knew, but I couldn't tell him what he wanted to know. I saw another man in the crosshairs of my sight...his head disappeared; the crowd screaming as they ran from the square. The dark man raised a pistol and held it to my head. NO!*

It was over--this time. I raised up from my slab shaking and soaking wet.

Amy was there. "Are you okay? I heard you yelling." She sat at the foot of the bed.

A long moment before I said, "Yes." These dreams, nightmares really, were an occasional happening, not often, and it had been a while since the last one. But I knew the truth: I might never be completely free of them. This wasn't the time to go into my past with Amy, and perhaps the right

54

time would never come, perhaps that was the reason I still had them. Pushing it all back into a dark corner, I said, "I'm fine. Sorry I woke you."

"Do you want to tell me about it?"

"No. It's nothing."

"Do you want something for the pain? Something to help you sleep?"

"No. Nothing. I'm sorry for the disturbance. Please go back to bed."

A long time later I finally went into a dreamless sleep.

***

For the next couple of days I did nothing but limp around the compound, sit in the sun, and generally be an additional burden to Amy. She came looking for me and checking on me periodically throughout each day. Then there was the unknown someone who changed the sheets and tidied up my room. I saw the men, women, and many children who came here for treatment, the truly needy, and I felt more than ever that I was an outsider, a fraud, here under false pretenses, an intruder with no business being in this community.

One day Amy, perhaps sensing my growing boredom, offered me her book collection. In my early days, when the youthful brain was like a sponge and I should have been reading, I wasn't interested. But in recent years, what with the time and a new interest in all things, I found the pleasure and treasure  of the printed word. I was only too happy to delve into her library, and at the same time get an idea of  how she lived. Most of what was carefully lined up in her bookcase--a sturdy wooden thing of many shelves that took up most of one wall--was paper backs with brown pages, religious in theme, lots of highlighted text, pencil notes in the margins--heavy stuff. What else did I expect? My patient search did finally pay off when I found, nestled among the mass of study material, a Graham Greene novel. Aside from the fact that he was an excellent writer, I wondered how his novel came to be in this group. Of  course he was a catholic, of sorts, and maybe that accounted for it. But then so was I.

When I wasn't soaking up the sun, walking to exercise the leg, or spending time with Greene's troubled visa clerk in Africa, I found my way into the clinic to watch. I'm sure I was mostly in the way but no one yelled at me. A long line of waiting patients--I learned later that the line formed in the early morning, way before the clinic opened, and lasted most of the day--stretched out of the treatment room, down the hall, and out into the blazing sun. There were men of course, but for the most part the waiting were dust-covered women holding babies who were covered with sores, swollen hungry bellies, all with the dazed, bewildered look of

55

the forgotten.  One old man I saw, crippled and barely able to walk, partially blind, stood silently in line for the hour or so that I watched. I have no idea what medicine Amy gave them, if any, maybe a kind word and a show of concern was enough.  She told me the same people showed up every day and that the line for a meal was even longer. While finding that hard to imagine, I again wondered how she managed to maintain the clinic.

As she ministered to these people, she mentioned that she knew of someone coming out from the city, and suggested having some of my clothes brought out. I declined the offer. While I did find her company pleasant, I wasn't comfortable in the general setting of such people. As well, my leg would improve daily and I wanted to get back to my own world, back to the obligation of my search, though at this point I saw it all but ended.  The large amount of money involved troubled me, pushing me on to offset the inner guilt.  These were all new feelings to me and I wasn't sure how to handle them.

# FIVE

A fifteen minute drive up into the mountains from the city, far enough away to distance itself from the urban poverty, and as a bonus much of the stifling heat, is an area known at Petionville. The section was for the better off, the very well off, and the connected, and included a wide range of homes, some perched along the hillsides in the California manner of secluded grandeur.

One such home, for more reasons than unusual design, was far different from the others.

Constructed as they all were of cement blocks, now a faded yellow in color, the house, or more accurately the compound, was completely enclosed by a high stone wall and was entirely hidden from public view. Though ugly and secretive from the outside, the house itself was lavishly furnished and tastefully decorated; a long section of sliding glass doors led off the living room onto a large slate patio and a gorgeous view of the valley beyond. A sophisticated lighting and security system maintained an around the clock watch on the property. To enter, for whatever reason, one had to first satisfy a guard at the massive steel gate at the front.

The owner of the property was a tall, trim man in his early forties, a man of considerable charm and intelligence named Sauvain, Colonel Lucien Sauvain, Chief of the palace guard. He was the son of a wealthy mulatto mother and a black politician father.

Sauvain had smoothly stepped into each vacuum when superiors were fired or disappeared, working his way up the chain of command until he headed the president's personal army. Among his men he was known for his excessive neatness. Since he couldn't tolerate an untidy appearance, or the slightest stain of perspiration on his uniform, he sometimes changed several times a day. He was a crack shot on the pistol range. His romantic affairs were almost legendary. To most people, with the possible exception of the president--or maybe him most of all--Sauvain was a man to be feared.

Showered now, in freshly pressed sport shirt and slacks, he paced the patio in thought, concerned about a possible threat to his latest enterprise. The first glass of Johnny Walker Black in his hand, almost empty, wasn't enough to soothe his anxiety--the first never was, it merely nibbled at the rough edge of the day. He emptied the glass and poured a generous refill. In times of stress, or even near stress, he leaned to excess in his drinking, becoming abusive with his now absent mistress who was in Miami on a shopping spree. Of French parentage, his current love was a beautiful woman, now nearing middle age but still of fine figure, with long, thick dark hair that still shined, a narrow waist, and full breasts. He was usually furious at her extravagance when she came back from shopping and he saw the bills. But she easily turned his anger into passion and release when she modeled, then removed her new things, and then knelt naked in front of him to do whatever he wanted.

What troubled him was the incident in the north: a disturbance that might bring attention to that area, too close to his new base of operations. With his Mexican connection set, if he chose to move some product that way, and the supply from Columbia open and flowing, he was anticipating the huge market and profit in the US. The demand was there and he would be the supply. With all the billions spent, he thought with a smile, the Americans were only putting fingers in the dike. It was his feeling that nothing short of all out blockade and war, which they refused to do, would stop the flow. On top of that was the prospect of moving special goods from Russia--arms and nuclear components. Fringe elements in the US, facing increasing calls for legislation against gun ownership, were searching for a source of weapons from across the border. His potential for profit, as he saw it, was unlimited.

Sauvain knew only too well that the man behind the harassment such as the incident last night, the one keeping the pot boiling and happy with the general unrest and discontent, was the former president. There was a man, he mused, who having once tasted that sweet nectar of power would never settle for the ordinary, would never be content with the common place, and would never accept being one of the people. The man had an ego the size of an elephant. And he had been a priest! How did he go so far astray?

As if that wasn't bad enough, the man actually believed that he was the only one who could rule this country, and that he was the only one who could solve the problems of this hopeless, black republic.

Fortunately, Sauvain considered with some satisfaction--though he had no idea why, since the former president seemed to be in some heraldic realm that he thought gave him extraordinary vision and knowledge--he still had some influence with the former president. It probably came back to power and the preservation of that power. And he, Sauvain, controlled the palace guard, and for all practical purposes the army. Without him the president was in a paper building. One of these days he would try to talk him out of his current campaign of disruption. But that was a separate problem.

The Peace Corps woman was a mistake that shouldn't have happened if they had listened to him and shot her on the spot. But orders were orders and they wanted her alive. Sauvain might be a big man on the local scene, but in the larger picture he was just a face in the crowd.

What was of immediate concern was the American and the shooting. Was he CIA or DEA? Might they possibly know of Sauvain's activities and be in the process of closing in on him? Improbable yes, but still a possibility. Since he had far ranging power to investigate almost any incident, no suspicion would arise from his personal involvement. But was that wise? The last thing he wanted was for any attention being brought to that area. The raid itself was bad enough. But another American! Coincidence? He took a large swallow and let the liquor take hold. Maybe his imagination was running too far afield. Still, there were too many unanswered questions. He was too close now to the really big money and the thought of such wealth was intoxicating in itself.

Where the hell was that woman when he needed her! Of course he knew where she was and what she was doing. He insisted on knowing her every move. But his need for her was now. Still pacing, he drew slowly on the smooth Cohiba cigar, staring at the cloud of smoke that hung in the humid air. An idea, a plan of sorts was forming in his mind. Before any thought of interrogation, of which he had plenty of ideas, he first had to find the American. First reports said that the American might be injured. There was no record of treatment at the city medical center. But the incident was two hours from the city. Where else could he receive decent treatment? He hadn't returned to his hotel. Being in the country only a matter of days, how could he know anyone to offer help? Where would he go? A white man in these days of few tourists would stand out wherever he went. The American Embassy might be informed, and might have some information; but his relationship with that man Wilson wasn't one that led to cooperation.

The American must be found. He would send men out to all the villages in the vicinity of Milot.

# SIX

The next day I felt stronger and a bit more adventurous, so much so that I hobbled some forty yards from the clinic to the school run by Father Smith. The scruffy area in front of the building, some grass but mostly dirt, was filled with noisy children at play. They were uniformly dressed in white top and dark blue skirt or trousers. The only play equipment I saw was a set of battered wooden see-saws, a contraption to climb on, also of wood, a swing made up of a tire at the end of a rope hanging from a tree, and a sagging net on rusty poles that might be for volley ball. There was no ball. Nevertheless, the children seemed to be having a grand time. The wonder of children, I thought idly, is not only their total lack of guile, but also their capacity to adapt and to survive.

The school building itself didn't look much better than the playground in that mildew stained the faded, peeling white paint, and the place had a general run-down look. Inside, I wandered around until I located Father Smith in a plain, unadorned room, with a mahogany crucifix on the wall behind a cluttered desk. Along one wall was a tan row of filing cabinets. A single chair was next to the desk. Looking up he seemed glad to see me. "Jack! Top of the morning. The leg must be improving to get you over here." He waved an arm at the chair. "Sit. How do you like our school? Sorry I don't have coffee to offer."

"No problem."

He smiled. "You must be here early for coffee; the pot goes fast."

I looked around and offered what I hoped was a neutral comment. "Nice place you have here."

"Oh, I know it's not much of a school by some standards. We do our best under...how shall I say it? Adverse conditions? We could use so many things here." He looked away for a moment. "But I won't bore you with my troubles. Lord knows, there's plenty here without my adding to the list." He offered a cigarette from a crumpled back. As much as I wanted one, I declined, knowing how expensive they were and how difficult to get out here. When he lit up I noticed his fingers bore the stains of a heavy smoker. In place of a beard, which I would have expected, his ruddy face showed a fine white stubble of growth. He reminded me of a famous English actor whose name I couldn't think of at the moment.

After a time of sniffing the aroma and enjoying the cigarette vicariously, I asked, "How did you get here...Bill? I mean how did it happen to be Haiti?"

When he pushed the glasses up on his nose the name of the actor came to me: Trevor Howard. He said, "By way of Africa, lad. Can you imagine that! Not much of a story. I'm a White Father. Do you know anything about them?" I told him I didn't. "No matter. I trained at our center up in Canada, few other places as well, served all over the place, then I was off to Africa for five years. After that Haiti."

He seemed a modest man and I suspected there was much more to his story. "So you, your order, work with the blacks?"

"Mostly. A bit of irony there," he grinned. "White Fathers!"

"I would say so. Are the two countries much the same?"

"Oh no. Haiti is much different."

"How? Both black and both in constant turmoil."

"Different in every way, lad," he said, putting out the butt. "In Africa we had little by way of equipment and supplies to work with, more than here, but what we did have there was a lot of young men looking for ordination. Unfortunately, while the bishop was supportive in our efforts, he wasn't too quick on bringing Africans into the priesthood. We had far less government interference. In the beginning it was very difficult to get anything done."

"But you wore them down-- the hierarchy."

"Yes, finally we did. You Catholic, Jack?" I nodded that I was and let it go at that. "Yes, that's just what we did over time. Lord knows we had fewer priests every year and they didn't want the local lads at first. We could have lost it all in Africa. Lucky for us the man saw the light." He paused for a moment. "I sometimes wonder if they'd have been better off left alone."

I saw the sadness in his eyes, a portion of his young dreams unfulfilled, a life spent in search of something better for others, he thought then. Here, their own leaders were defeating him. "You can't do that in Haiti? Wear them down?"

"Not without a bigger fight than I can manage. Maybe I'm getting old." He lit another cigarette and again extended the pack. "Sure you don't want one?" This time I gave in and joined him. Marlboro. Surgeon General be damned. "Sad to say, I've pretty much given up on trying to convert. Now I'm content to help ease their burden in this life, teach the children...do what I can in whatever way is open to me."

"Sounds like enough to me."

"I often wonder," he said thoughtfully. "So much for us to do. So much for the church to do." He came out of his thoughts and smiled broadly. "One day, when we have more time, I shall tell you about my African wife."

61

"Your what?"

He stood and came around the desk, taking my arm. "The children will be coming back in now. I have a moment to show you around."

Up close I noticed the full length white vestment he wore: clean though threadbare, a twisted braid of black cord was a cincture. As we walked down the hall he told me he only wore the cloth, as he put it, during business hours and that it helped with teaching them a bit of the faith. "A little respect for a man of the cloth never hurt; what with their voodoo priests and the like."

"I totally agree." Here was a man who would never survive in a stateside parish. Which was probably best for both him and the church. He was a rogue--a lovable rogue. I asked if the slight accent I heard was English.

"Heavens no, lad. I've not come that far from home. What you hear had better be Irish!"

"Sorry. I'm not good at that. Your Irish-accented Creole must be something to hear."

He laughed out loud. "You should have heard me with African dialects! Yes, the family came over from Ireland, settled in Boston...potato heads we were...but that too is for another time."

I wondered if I would ever have the time to hear his story, or stories.

We had finished touring the classrooms and were heading outside when the relative quiet, what with the children back in school, was broken by the arrival in a swirl of dust of a jeep full of soldiers and a dark Mercedes sedan. I asked what was going on.

"I'm not sure, Jack. It looks like trouble of some sort." We walked in their direction and watched as a man in neatly pressed uniform, medals, and pistol belt, stepped out of the car. The soldiers had formed a ragged line in front of the clinic. "That's Colonel Sauvain's car."

"Who's he?"

"Someone you're better off not knowing. But that's not him--one of his flunkies, I'd guess. A clone of that terrible man."

"Gee. Medals and all huh?"

"Battles fought only on paper, Jack. Or maybe with the whores in Port-au-Prince." He turned to me and winked. "Lots of fighting there."

"One of those."

"Yes. One of those. A bullet coming his way would dirty his pants, I'd think. You stay here. I'll go see what they want here."

He moved off and I, ignoring his advice, moved closer to the action. Amy came out of the clinic and stood on the porch, hands on her hips; no nonsense, this woman. She wore a white apron over her pants and shirt and looked tired, a strand of hair over her face, a curious but drawn

62

expression at the crowd. She spoke to the officer. "What do you want here? Is one of your men sick? If he is he'll have to get in line."

She is either stupid or brave, I thought. From what I knew of her it had to be the latter.

The officer didn't rise to her hostility, to his credit, smiling, in heavily accented English, he said, "Good Morning, Sister. I have come only to talk." Amy said nothing to that, waiting, showing her impatience at being interrupted in her work. "I am here on a mission for Colonel Sauvain." This brought a buzzing in the crowd, the name being well known, and not in a positive way.

If Amy had concerns she didn't show them. "And what mission is that, captain?"

"The colonel would like to talk with a certain American."

"There aren't many here these days are there, captain?" She glanced around and caught my eye, holding it for only a few seconds. "Why come here? What makes you think the American is here at the clinic?"

"We were informed that he is here, Sister."

Though I do have a good tan and am dark for a *blanc,* might even pass for a Latino to an untrained eye, there would be no mistaking me for a black. Aside from that, the rest of the crowd, regardless of shade, all appeared to belong here--they had the look and clothing about them--while I stood out like the proverbial sore thumb. There was little room for deception. What got my attention was that bit about an informant. I could be reasonably sure it wasn't anyone from the village. I was very sure it wasn't Lefond. Who did that leave? Someone at the clinic. But who and why? At any rate, it wasn't worth worrying about at this point.

The captain turned away from Amy and searched the crowd, taking only a moment to settle on me. "You must be the American," he said rather proudly. An obvious conclusion, I thought, a no-brainer for sure. I didn't say anything but looked at Amy for her reaction. "I think this is the man we want," he announced as he turned back to face Amy.

"Maybe," she said." You said you wanted to talk. So talk."

He shrugged and looked around. "We cannot talk here, Sister. He must come with me."

"We can talk right here, captain."

"No. He must come with me."

The people gathered around seemed to sense a confrontation and the buzz of talk grew louder. Realizing that this was more than the routine of bringing someone in for questioning, and feeling the growing hostility, the soldiers tensed and straightened, bringing their rifles up from the ground to a sort of sloppy port-arms, almost like a real army. I felt the tension. I

63

knew these people, this community, would be loyal to Amy and the clinic and the last thing I wanted was to be the cause of a problem for them. Hell. I was willing to talk. After all, that business at the ceremony was self-defense, in my opinion, forgetting of course that I was in a land where justice had never visited.

As I started to move toward the porch, Amy spoke quickly. "No, Jack! Don't go with them. Let me handle this from here."

Before I could say anything, Bill grabbed my arm. I hadn't noticed him moving right along with me. "She's right, Jack. I've heard lots of stories about the prison from these people over the years. You go along with them to that place and you may never come out."

I could see that he was concerned, for me, and I didn't doubt for a moment that what he said was true. In fact, I'd heard similar stories in other places. Even so, it didn't seem right to have these people--these new found friends who were dedicated to helping the Haitians, and who deserved more help than they were getting--become involved in my minor problems. There was nothing heroic about it, but rather a simple question of taking responsibility for my actions. I tried to reassure Bill that I'd be okay, and that his was a matter that had to be straightened out between me and the law. "No big deal," I told him. He didn't seem convinced but he didn't say anything.

Then Amy came down from the porch to give Bill some help, urging me to listen to him and reconsider going along with the soldiers. She started to give some examples of her own bad experiences but I interrupted her before she got too far along. "This is not a big thing, Amy. I'll go along with them and answer all their questions and explain myself. They'll see that this was an unfortunate accident that could have happened to anyone when you've got a riot going and soldiers, or police, or whatever they are, are waving guns around." I guess it wasn't my day to convince because she just stood there looking at me with the same doubtful expression that Bill showed me.

Giving her my best and biggest smile, I said, "Keep the chicken warm." She didn't comment, just gave me a pathetic bit of a smile, the kind you show to someone you think isn't quite all there. Since my stuff was all back at the hotel, and I had very few possessions to collect her at the clinic, I was ready then and went along with the captain.

\*\*\*

"What were you doing there, Mr. Morgan?"

I had been brought up from a dark cell somewhere below ground to a room with light. I knew only that hours had passed since I'd come here from the clinic. At least it seemed like hours. Stalling for time I said, "Doing where?" I wanted to adjust to the light and get my bearings, get some kind of handle on my situation. I was seated on a wooden chair, dim light overhead, heard a questioning man, and saw a sullen soldier by the door. It was all so familiar. I'd been there and done that in other places. As the great Yogi Berra had once said: *deja vu* all over again.

It had never been pleasant.

I took stock: aside from an aching leg, hurting ribs (someone had kicked me along the way), an empty, growling stomach, and a God-awful taste in my mouth, I was okay. That was the important point I always tried to focus on. Then I tried an old trick that usually bought me some time, not much in most cases, but a measure of breathing room. I took an offensive position. "What the hell is going on!"

I got a few minutes, no more. The questioning man, an officer I could see now, just stared at me. When he spoke it was nice English with the barest trace of an accent, French maybe. "You are hardly in a position to question anything, Mr. Morgan." At least he was being polite. "You are here on a serious charge and you would be wise to cooperate with me. I am, by the way, Colonel Sauvain."

Staying on the offensive I said, "Good for you. Now would you mind telling me what this is about? I've explained everything to the captain who brought me in here, in great detail. Why the questions?"

He lit a cigarette, all too carefully I thought, as if maybe knowing the smoke would drive my starved habit into orbit. "I'm sure you told it all very well, Mr. Morgan. Now I would like you to tell me."

In this commercial world of ours there is a market and a price for everything. I tested the market. "Can I have one of those?" Without a word he gave me a cigarette and a light. With that, I had the strong feeling that I was dealing with a trained interrogator: be pleasant and friendly as long as there was hope of getting what you wanted the easy way. So I told my story once again, leaving out any mention of Lefond by name, just saying some driver. "How the hell would I know his name!"

A pause as he smoked and moved around the room. "Are you aware that an officer, one of my men (he was stretching the point here, since his men, in the strict sense, were around the palace), was shot last night? Shot by you!"

Following his every move, I smoked and watched. "Shot by accident, colonel. I was an innocent victim. The man attacked me with a gun. I don't know about in your country, colonel, but in mine, in civilization, there is a condition known as excessive force." As soon as the words were out of my mouth I knew I'd gone too far with the civilization thing. I quickly said, "I think it is my right to see someone from the embassy."

Sauvain glared, thinking he'd learned nothing and been insulted in the process. This man Morgan was no doubt an experienced operative, certainly no tourist, but as to what or who he really was...? "Your are right! Mr. Morgan. You are not in your country now. You have no rights but the ones I choose to give you!"

He was pissed and I couldn't really blame him. "In any case you owe me a phone call."

"I owe you nothing!"

A staring duel in which neither one of us blinked--no winner. I was bluffing with a weak hand and I think he knew it. What the hell. You can't win it if you're not in it. Then he literally screamed in my face. "Take him back to the cell! I will deal with him later."

I was okay. I kept telling myself that this wasn't a question of *if* I'd get out. This was a question of *when.* Unlike the middle of the night round-ups in this part of the world, and other parts with a much colder climate, I had Amy and the gang going for me. They knew where to look for me. Those other poor souls might be gone forever. I had someone who would ask the right questions in the right places and that was a definite plus in my favor. I had no doubt that Amy and Bill would leave no stone unturned to find the rock I was under.

My cell had a large wooden door (was everything here made of wood?), a small square hole set high in the scarred timber, through which I could look out, if I so desired, to a dim light in the passageway. It was dark inside but this didn't really bother me. I always chose to work at night when I had the choice. Daylight, when I was exposed to the world, was my natural enemy. Today I might ask if it was guilt. In those days I acted in a noble cause. I was not ashamed of my past, even though times had changed and I saw my role now in a different perspective. What we did in the passion of our youthful, and often naive idealism, was in the past and nothing could change the past. And yet, it seemed to me, that is exactly what we try to do today in our obsession with making amends for past injustices, or the cruelty of times gone by. Are the times so good for us today that we turn to this monumental guilt trip about the past? How much does it really mean to those in the present to receive payment for what we now consider to be debts of another era? The forefathers who lived with the pain and injustice of their time could hardly benefit from our belated efforts of today. Was this for them? Or was it to ease a guilty

66

conscience of those who had the everything of today? I wasn't sure. But my thoughts roamed in the darkness.

It would be easy at this stage of my life to recognize and embrace the excuse of having done things of the young. And perhaps that is valid. We change a little with the passage of time, hopefully for the better. But have we really changed? Are we not the same person forever? I could see my life now as a long train of events, linked, traveling in the same direction, yet each car separate and locked. At the end of the journey the locks would be opened and the contents examined. What was found then, and how it was viewed in the present would be far different from what first went in--another time. Time capsules were a frightening thought. But what the hell. I wouldn't be around for the opening.

After all these years Hannah was still a clear memory--in a separate car to be sure.

She was born in Sweden, a small town somewhere in the mountains I found out later, and was attached to their embassy in London when we met. I simply assumed she worked in some clerical capacity. Of course, she never said anything to indicate otherwise. We met in a pub.

I had returned to London, banged up, exhausted and disgusted, from a rare mission in East Germany--rare not because missions were scarce, there were plenty for a person with my specialty, but rare for me since I normally operated in the Caribbean and Central America. There was simply no one else available. From the beginning I'd had bad feelings about the assignment. Perhaps it was because it was a new area for me, or maybe a premonition. As it turned out my feelings were well founded because the thing went sour and lots of innocent people were either killed or imprisoned, on both sides.

The important part is that because of that shitty mission I ended up in London on R&R and met Hannah. But I'm ahead of my story.

After the usual debriefing, which meant answering a lot of dumb questions for a designated bright person who would make it all logical, profound, and maybe important in the larger scheme, someone who actually didn't give a damn about my personal problems in the process, it was decided that I should stay in London for a time. The thinking seemed to be that I was a nut case who needed time to find my place in the world, if there was such a place. They seemed to need guys like me but hated to deal with the fallout. He said things like: the political ramifications were enormous; public reaction and the newspapers would bring down governments; speculations would be wild about what happened and why, what might happen to the future of Europe. I personally didn't give a shit. I had a job and I did it.

His mere suggestion of a remote and guarded safe house out in the country was unacceptable to me. What was the point? No one knew my identity. I had to be about six layers down in any intelligence file, if mentioned at all.

In the end I was given a tiny flat in Knightsbridge and what amounted to free rein for an undetermined period of time. The flat had a nice collection of novels so I read a lot and slept a lot. Despite some opinions in the organization that I was nothing more than an illiterate thug, a stereotype assassin, I loved to read. I went out at night to eat. So it was several days before I ventured out in the daytime to visit the famous Harrods store which was but a few blocks away. Once discovered, the food courts alone in that fascinating place--just part of one floor--consumed hours of my day. After a time, when I felt rested, and bored, I went on to explore Soho, Covent Gardens, did lots of walking, and in time found my way to a pub called "Prince of Wales."

Hannah had a cold the day we met.

She had taken a day off, slept late in the morning, taken her medicine, and by early afternoon felt well enough to go look for a new dress, and maybe earrings to match, at the stalls in Covent Garden. She told me all this later. An embassy affair was coming up and she had nothing decent to wear. She commented on how expensive everything was in London.

She found the pub by accident--it wasn't all that far from where she was shopping--and staggered inside with an armful of boxes and bags, with her face flushed, and a red, runny nose. She sat down in a booth behind me to unload and rest, then went up to the bar to order lunch. I actually didn't notice her until she was coming back to her table with a glass in her hand. More accurately, I noticed her when her foot caught in the flooring and the glass of something pink spilled on her and on the floor.

It was far from love at first sight. But it was the start of something good.

My mind was off in another place with Hannah, the blue of her eyes, blond hair in a pigtail hanging halfway down her back, precise, perfect English. I heard a voice then but it wasn't hers. It came again from behind the wall. "Boss. It's me, Al."

Could this be a trick? No. There was no way they would know to use the word "boss."

"I didn't tell them. I tell them nothing."

"Tell them what, Al?"

"About you. They want to know about you."

"I know. Don't worry about it. You okay?"

"I am fine, boss. They try. But they get nothing out of me."

His words caught me for a moment. Why would someone I hardly know show this kind of loyalty? I'd seen far less from my own kind. I had to help him. "Al, tell them anything they want to know about me. Look out for yourself. They can't touch me here, but you...? Cooperate and make it easy on yourself. Do you understand me?"

Nothing for a moment, then, "I can't do that, boss."

"Why!"

"These men are not my people. They are the enemy of my people."

"That's great, Al, very noble. But think of yourself."

"They will get nothing from me."

A patriot. Shit! They could be the worst kind--or the best. "Just hang in there, Al. We'll get out of this, both of us. Trust me."

"I trust you, boss."

I knew someone would look for me and when it happened I could only hope the duty officer wasn't Roger Price. In a head-to-head with Sauvain I didn't give him much of a chance. But I'd been wrong before. Some of these agency types, the good ones, hid a pair of balls behind a keen mind, and did it well.

***

"Someone to see you, Mr. Price," said Alice Jennings from the office doorway. "A woman and a priest."

Price had a status report due today and didn't have one word on paper. Looking up from the blank paper in front of him, annoyed, he said, "What is it, Alice! Is this a cultural matter?"

"No." She held eye contact. "Not exactly a cultural matter." In a twenty-two year career with State she had seen them all come and go: the good and the not so good; bright and stupid; drunks; the self-serving and the righteous; and mostly the useless who'd made big contributions to the current administration, the ones on a paid vacation. Many of them, she'd found, were impressed with themselves for no good reason other than that they had money. Few had impressed her and certainly none of them had intimidated her. She also knew that the best State had to offer, the trained career men and women, were in a position one level below the ambassador, from which the embassy actually was run. She hated politicians. As well as her own job, she had a working knowledge of every area of the embassy. She made it a practice never to put up with bullshit from anyone. And here, she thought, unless her instinct was was way off, which only happened rarely, was a matter for Roger Price, Cultural Attaché/CIA.

"They why..." he started.

"I think you should see them."

With that look and that tone, thought Price, it was best to go along with her. "Very well. Send them in, please." He stood in greeting, and when he saw their faces his mind automatically went through his files to place them. The priest had to be Father Smith from the school out in the country. There weren't a whole lot of white religious still around. And for good reason, he thought. Smith had an interesting file: reportedly married--a shocker to start with by church doctrine--or at least lived with a black woman in Africa. He was considered to be, but not definitely established, active with revolutionary groups who wee unnamed. He was nearly defrocked more than once both in Africa and at home in the US, and in fact there was some question about his being in good standing at the moment. Price seemed to remember that the Vatican had never responded to official inquiries on Father Smith. Did he know Aristede? In some ways they seemed to be birds of a feather.

The woman was the "Sister" from the clinic, a popular figure among the people out in the boondocks--some looked on her as a saint. She was every bit as interesting as the priest. She had been in Guatemala during the trouble there and narrowly missed being murdered with the other sisters. No known political affiliations. There was some question about her credentials in the church as well. Rome was never queried on her. A mention in the file about an attempt to recruit both her and the priest as agents. Unsuccessful. Dumb idea (personal comment). Striking woman (another personal comment).

This was all part of the trade, his gift of memory and details.

"Thank you, Alice. I'll take care of it from here." He shook hands, offered them chairs, and when they were seated asked what he could do for them.

"I'm Anne Marie Calder. And this is Father Smith."

Price smiled. "A pleasure to see you both. I've heard of you of course...your good work with the people. Now how can I help you?"

Shifting the narrative between them, they told of Jack Morgan and his being taken into custody. Amy stressed the injustice of it all and Father Smith, less patient, demanded action on the part of the embassy. "What are you going to do about this?"

Since Price hadn't been the Duty Officer for the past twelve hours he knew nothing about this, and even if he did, he wasn't about to make any kind of commitment without more information and a conversation with Langley. This was within his province and he was annoyed that he wasn't informed. Who was on duty? Prescott? Probably. Some of these people, he thought, not with the Agency, took these things too lightly, as if this was just another posting along their way to retirement. Prescott was one of the worst! He was writing a goddamned book about Haiti and didn't know the first thing about the country--didn't even speak the language. Where does State find these jokers!

Price watched Father Smith light a cigarette, saw him out of focus, his mind working. Colonel Sauvain being involved was a question, a complication he didn't understand at all. What did it mean? The ceremonies hardly came under the heading of Internal Security; but Sauvain did have free rein in any matter he chose. Where was the connection? Was it coincidence? Price had never accepted the idea of coincidence. No. There was a connection. Of course, this was coming from the priest and a sister and had yet to be confirmed. Still, he had to wonder about the incident. These two weren't the type to tell tales out of the blue. His instinct told him to accept their version as the truth, at least for now. And he still had that damned report to finish. No reply on his inquiry on Morgan. Might that change things? Possible. Anything was possible. Too damned many questions as usual. At this point he could only stall for time. This was becoming a shitty day, early.

"Well," he said finally, "this isn't exactly in my area of responsibility. You do know that?"

Amy and Father Smith looked at each other then back at Price. They knew he was agency. Everyone in the country with half a brain knew he was agency, at least anyone who took a moment to think about it. Amy said, "We know that, Mr. Price."

"And even if it were, what is it you expect me to do? I can hardly interfere in their legal process. This is their country."

"Since when?" Father Smith said just loud enough to be heard.

"Legal process!" Amy snapped. "You know as well as I do that there is no such thing. Legal process? Haitian men and women have gone into that jail and were never heard from or seen again. This is an American we're talking about here."

"Amy," Father Smith said, putting a hand on her arm, "easy now." One unfiltered cigarette was lighted from the last, he drew heavily and blew out the smoke, sighed, then said, "Mr. Price, as the big men in Washington would say, or in Dublin, God help them, let's go right to the bottom line. What we have here, very simply, is one of our boys being held, unlawfully I might add, totally without representation, no just cause, and all the rest of the legal stuff, and we want him out. Pure and simple. Now that strikes me as an easy task for someone like you." He smiled broadly. "Seems to me that's what your job is about, among other things." He watched an ash

71

drop on the floor. "I think you can have a friendly chat with the colonel and straighten this out. Might be a good idea to do it right away. From what I know, that jail is no place for any person, let alone an innocent American, to linger for long. The fact that he's in there at all is a disgrace. Is that a clear statement of the facts, Mr. Price?"

"Colonel Sauvain is hardly a friend."

"Is that so? I would have thought what with your wives, or women, playing tennis and all..."

Amy cut him off with a sharp look.

Another ash fell to the floor.

Price was silent. As with all of these people, he was thinking, those that were untrained and therefore unqualified to deal with such matters, the priest's view was a gross oversimplification of the problem. What is it with them! Doesn't the church have enough to keep them busy? If they weren't protesting some minority cause, or helping illegal immigrants get freebies they weren't entitled to, abortion, capital punishment, you name it, they were out running for political office. Even president! Look at Haiti. They were all off in the clouds somewhere, out of touch with reality. The nagging question here was whether this was a deliberate provocation in the president's behalf, though he couldn't imagine why, after all we did install this damn government with our own troops. Or was it a simple misunderstanding? Either way it was another problem in a country, and a government, already full of them.

"I understand your concern," he said finally. "And while I'm not in a position to interfere in local matters, I will see what I can do about Jack Morgan. I'll give the colonel a call. Maybe we can get this straightened out in no time at all. How's that?"

Father Smith spoke through a cloud of smoke. "Good. You see what you can do. You know, the people out in the country, out where we work, simple folks, they're upset about this. Did you know that? They wonder why an American, innocent at that, can be treated like a common criminal. That's not good for that new democracy we gave them and not good for our image. Isn't that so?"

Amy had to smile because she'd seen before how Father would drift into a folksy manner when he wanted to catch someone off guard and drive home a point. Matlock on old TV was a favorite of his. She was again surprised at how easily it came to him, as if he'd done it all before. And he probably had.

Price squirmed a bit, running a finger around his collar. "Rest assured I'll get to the bottom of this." With that he got up from the desk to signal the end of their meeting. "And thanks for coming in with this."

"You'll be in touch?" Amy asked.

"Just as soon as I have any news."

*** 

In this place no news is *not* good news. Sitting on the floor with my back to the wall, I idly watched a family of roaches in motion, wondering where they might be gong. I seemed of little interest to them but I did swat them away when they got too close. It was evidently a social period because in a moment a rat was suddenly in my space (maybe that was why the roaches moved on). His eyes were little glowing dots in the darkness. A big guy, in a sniffing mood, first around the seatless toilet, which was a nice touch, then he showed an interest in me. I am not your dinner! Not even an appetizer! I backed into an opposite corner, flicking a leg in his direction. As much as the leg hurt I wasn't about to have my demise happen this way, not if I could help it. When he inched close enough I made sure I connected with a leg kick--hurt me more than him, or her. Giving me one last look, as if offended at my attitude, he scampered off into another black corner and disappeared, maybe off to visit Al. He'd know how to deal with the big guy--maybe strangle the damn thing.

It seemed like a good time to take stock. I was okay. I wasn't cold; one point for me. But I was dirty, starving, worried, in some pain, and my future looked bleak; that made it five to one in their favor. But this was only the first quarter. I did have friends out there; bringing it to about a tie. Not bad with three quarters to go. Stupid thoughts to pass the time. I again wondered where this could go and how it might end. I didn't see a bright picture. I could easily die here, rat or no. A smoke would be marvelous! I took long, deep breaths like they told me in Smoke Enders. I failed that course twice. What I got for my efforts was a lung full of stale air, hot dirty air, along with the heightened sense of earth, fear, and death. What the hell. At this point it was a tie game.

Lafond called out of the dark. "You okay Mister Jack?"

At least he'd stopped calling me boss. "Never better, Al." This was true when I compared myself to him: what chance did a Haitian have? And with no friends of influence outside. "How are you doing?" I'd heard him being taken out of the cell more than once. "You okay?"

"I am good. It will take more then these fellows to break me."

What are they after with him? Where is the connection? "What do they want to know, Al?"

"I don't know. I tell them nothing. They ask about warehouse."

"What warehouse?"

If he did answer I never heard his reply. My turn again; big, sweating man with a bald head and tiny eyes. Different soldier sitting at the desk writing. The big one used a section of rubber hose every so often on my back and shoulders. Foreplay? The same dumb questions. They didn't seem to care about the answers--going through the motions. What kept me going was the delicious thought of payback for this one--maybe with a rifle butt, or a solid hunk of two-by-four thudding on his shiny head. It might never happen, but it was a pleasant picture and I had always believed in payment for a days work, in full.

Back in my cell. How would it all end?

I was okay. This was one where the final period would determine the outcome.

## SEVEN

Abruptly awakened from what seemed to be only moments of sleep, I was hauled to my feet and led out of the cell. This was a good thing actually because wherever I'd been was a frantic and disjointed place-- anything but restful. Twice I was sure come creature, maybe the big rat with the beady eyes, was crawling over my hurting body, tiny feet running up and down looking for a place to settle in and grab a bite to eat. It could have been my imagination. In any case the feeling was reality at the time. God only knows what creepy crawlies had explored my body in the darkness.

Out in the passageway that led along between the cells I was aware of a dim light, the sounds of bodies stirring, coming to life, so I assumed it was some hour in the morning. Whatever I smelled in the musty air sure wasn't morning coffee. I thought of Claire bringing that delicious first cup almost as my feet hit the floor. One of life's daily simple pleasures taken for granted.

What I did smell was unwashed humanity.

A different direction this time, up some wooden stairs and into a similar room of pale green walls, a table and two chairs. The same disinterested, but sleepy guard by the door. The cast was different as well--Price stared at me from across the room. If he was trying to hide a shocked expression, he failed because his face told me that I looked like hell and that he was pissed at my condition. Good for him. Beside him stood the colonel: calm, smug, and neat, either unconcerned or indifferent to the condition of the miserable creature led into the room. Had we been in his home I think he would have called an exterminator. Without waiting for an invitation I dropped into the chair, sort of folded actually, curled up and waited for the talking to begin.

While I felt that Price hadn't shown me much so far, I did feel better having him in the room. After all, I didn't really know the man; the few moments together in the embassy were hardly enough to condemn the man. After that cell, the friendly vermin, or maybe discriminating vermin, and the rubber hose treatment, anything that happened from here on in was a positive. With the sudden realization that I might get out of this alive, very probably, everything changed in an instant. I would see the morning sun, feel the cool water rushing by as I swam, enjoy the balmy tropical air. And I could enjoy the thought of inserting Colonel Sauvain as the first name on my repayment list, well, maybe second after that bald head with the hose. I'm not vengeful. I do believe in justice.

75

Price was staring at me a long while before he said anything. Gee. Maybe it was the purple bruises and bits of blood on my face, or the dirty clothes and horrible condition of this fellow citizen. Maybe he knew about the subtle, unseen effects of the rubber hose. I was looking into his eyes when he lost it-- literally lost it. He screamed into the room at no one in particular. "I protest, colonel! This is an American citizen! Is this the way you bring someone in for questioning? You can be damn well sure the president will hear about this. I want him out of here. Now!"

The Price stock jumped ten points!

Visibly unimpressed, the colonel said, "I was not here to supervise the questioning." With a shrug he added, "these things happen."

"And that makes it acceptable? This is the last straw,colonel. Our ambassador is going to have a long session with your president, your boss."

I watched and listened to the rhetoric. In politics--and this was definitely politics, no matter the setting--the so-called truth was an illusion, a sleight of hand to please and delight the crowd. But then maybe I'm a cynic. I asked Price for a cigarette even though my mouth was so dry I could hardly swallow. He moved over to me and shook out a pack of Marlboro, put a silver Zippo to it (I thought they went out with the OSS), then moved back. It might well be bad for my health, but I took a big hit and let it out slowly--wonderful. No one said anything for a moment, a long moment, the air thick enough to molded like clay. I said, "I must have missed the meals and the linen change, huh colonel?"

Price looked pained. The colonel missed or more likely ignored my brand of humor. Price said, "I take it that everything is in order?" Without waiting for an answer he went on. "I'm taking this man out of here. If there is need for anything further, questions, whatever, Mr. Morgan will be available at his hotel. Right, Mr. Morgan?"

"Yeah. I'll be around."

The colonel, looking off into the middle distance in thought, came to the conclusion that this man knew nothing about his operation, nothing more could be gained here, and it was time to move on. In an effort to mend a strained relationship with Price he said, "You can be sure, Mr. Price, that I will look into Mr. Morgan's treatment here and those responsible will pay the price. You are free to go. As far as you both are concerned this matter is closed."

Very nice, I thought. Neat, simple and clean. Too simple. Why were Al and I put through the wringer for such a simple matter? It didn't make sense. What was he looking for? The man was hiding something. What was the story on this guy? While I made up my mind to find out, at some

76

point, the matter of finding Christine came first; that was my paying job at the moment and my reason for being here in the first place. The colonel was definitely an addition to my growing list.

Price said flatly, "Let's get out of here."

I managed to get on my feet, then sat down again, too tired to make the effort in one shot. Besides, I had unfinished business with the colonel. Looking at him, I finished the smoke and dropped the butt on the floor. "So," I said. "That's it? This is all over and done with? Case closed?" He nodded. "There is one other matter."

"And what is that, Mr. Morgan?"

"I want a man named Lafond released."

"Lafond?"

"Yes. The man in the cell next to mine. I want him released."

"Mr. Morgan..."

I cut Price right off. "If I go, he goes with me. Simple as that. The colonel just told us this thing is closed. Why hold Lafond? He was with me. Get him in here. We walk out of this place together--or not at all."

"I don't know..." Price started.

"Lafond is Haitian, Mr. Morgan," the colonel said sharply. "We will deal with him as we see fit. He had nothing to do with you."

*"Au contraire,* colonel. He has everything to do with me. We leave together."

The colonel, with an expression that told me he didn't suffer fools gladly, said, "Mr. Price. Take this man out of here before I change my mind."

"You don't have that option, colonel." Then turning to Price I said, "What is this bullshit! Haitian or not, Lafond is an innocent man. Either he goes with me or I stay. And that gives the embassy a big problem doesn't it?"

Price moved over to the colonel and spoke softly. "Let's go outside for a moment."

While they went out for their conference I took another cigarette from the colonel's pack left on the table. With Price here I figured I had the upper hand: he either had some embassy clout, or better still, if he was good at his job, had something to use on the colonel in the form of leverage, we all have some skeletons in our closet. I was forcing him to use whatever he had in reserve. An old Marine custom was that we never left our buddies behind, even frozen bodies from the Chosin Reservoir; some were left there of course because there was no transport; they were buried in the frozen ground, but we tried. Lafond had paid his dues as far as I was concerned and he was one of us. Let Price work it out.

77

After what seemed like ten minutes but was probably only two or three, the two-man jury came back in with their verdict. Needless to say, I didn't rise.

Price said, "Lafond is being released. Our agreement calls for you to leave Haiti within 48 hours. We can go now."

While I thought it a stiff sentence for an innocent man, the time frame was quite liberal; I'd faced many shorter ones in other places. In any case, I wasn't about to press the issue. Throwing me out of the country was probably a face-saving thing for the colonel. That's how these things usually worked.

Maybe Price was afraid of losing what he thought was a good deal. "You ready?"

"Oh yes. I'm ready."

"Well, let's go."

"Let's wait for Lafond."

Price stiffened but didn't say anything. Neither did the colonel for a moment. He kept staring at me with those black eyes, like a cobra searching for an opening, biding his time, knowing he'd win out in the end with patience and cunning. Looking at him I was sure of two things: I hadn't seen the last of him, and that he was a deadly adversary I'd have to be on the lookout for, constantly. But on the plus side, I'm good at what I do and I would take him when I was ready.

\*\*\*

The village of our misadventure, Al's and mine, never had an official name according to Price. He proved to be quite talkative, and informative, on our ride from the jail to my hotel. Al had been released with me, we shook hands, promised to keep in touch, and he went on his way.

Those living in the area knew it as Miel. Price didn't explain any further and he left me wondering. I thought about it but I couldn't find any sensible reason for the name, though some interesting possibilities came to mind. In French the word meant honey? He gave me a quick rundown on the political and economic problems of the country, his work in negotiating our release, the visit of Amy and Father Smith and that they had called his office repeatedly for information. He seemed a decent guy trying to to a job under difficult conditions. Join the club.

No fanfare at the hotel for the freed victim: a few stares (could they know or were they merely curious of anyone?), a few friendly words from Claudette.

In the room I lay on the bed thinking, wondering how things had gone bad so quickly, annoyed at my lack of results in the search for Christine, all the while trying to find some comfortable position for my body. Again, there didn't seem to be one. In a matter of moments I was soaked from the humidity. I got up and had a cigarette, roamed around the room, then decided to call Amy. While she was certainly an attractive woman this wasn't sexual. I wasn't sure what it was. The thought of being with her brought some stability, some sanity to this mess, a strong branch held out to a man sinking in quicksand of non-accomplishment and wrong moves. After about five minutes of being almost connected, to someone, followed by noisy disconnects, and lots of just plain dead wire, which was a normal occurrence, I finally reached her and set up a date for dinner at my hotel. It worked out because she happened to be in town on errands and would spend the night with friends in the city--a sometime thing for her, and lucky for me since my days here were limited.

Later, I had just fallen asleep when Claudette brought me a sandwich, iced tea, and a bag of ice to put on the hurting parts. Watching her as she adjusted the ice, fluffed the pillow, and checked that the shutters were full open, moving around the room, I wondered idly if she would be receptive to my questionable charm and amorous advances, that is if I felt like using them, which I didn't. Maybe another time. But then there wouldn't be another time would there?

The rest of the afternoon was spent in fits of sleep, some good and some bad. I came out of it as darkness was closing in around me. The bag of ice was gone.

After a shower and shave, and in presentable shorts and shirt, I felt surprisingly good and went down for a drink before dinner. I was warmly greeted at the patio bar next to the pool by a smiling Luke--the dispenser of delicious and very generous drinks. Settling in with a Rum Punch I asked him what was new.

With a shrug he said, "Nothing is new in Port-au-Prince." Then, laughing he added, "Except my drinks!"

"How right you are, Luke."

Warm and humid night, as usual, the slight breeze carried the scent of wood smoke and a sweetness from the flowers surrounding the lawn beyond the stone patio. A few seats down from me a pair of older men were engaged in serious talk, speaking in French, with that look of diplomatic people who were responsible for the world. Candles were lighted, flickering in the glass globes on all the tables, though only two were occupied. A young couple of maybe honeymoon age were at one, holding hands, with eyes for only each other, talking softly. The other customers were an older couple with that comfortable look of a shared lifetime. I had to wonder how they found this place. A Haitian couple came out of the hotel, arm in arm, soft talk and knowing smiles at each other as they went to their table. Watching them, I envied their special moments. I took it all in, smoked, waiting, feeling a bit sad, pushing the past few days into a remote, and very closed section of my mind. I could do that.

Then a strange man, literally, as well as someone I'd never seen before, was standing next to me and introducing himself. When he paused for a breath, I turned to look at him. "Who are you?" I saw a thin, dapper man in a cream-colored suit, purple shirt, a many-colored ascot, Panama hat, carrying a walking stick with a gold head. He told me his name was Marcel, saying his name as if it would, or should, mean something to me. With a tilt of his head and a shrug, Luke walked away. I stared at Marcel in his rose-tinted glasses.

Outwardly insulted at my question and swaying at the thought, he waved a thin cigar in the air. "I am Marcel," he repeated. Still no connection. When I didn't say anything for a moment, and he was out of patience with me, he said, "You have read my column?"

"Sorry. I must have missed it."

"No matter. You are new to our country and of course wouldn't know how famous I am."

"Really."

"Yes. Everyone knows Marcel. Everyone reads Marcel. My column *is* what's happening in Port-au-Prince. Oh, I know what you're thinking. But it is far more than gossip."

"I'm sure."

"And you...you are Jack Morgan?...are a happening here."

"I somehow doubt that, Marcel."

"Oh don't be modest. May I call you Jack?"

"No."

He handled rejection well, in fact ignored it. "The shooting in...what was that little village? ...Miel? Going to our jail! Exciting stuff for my readers. Surely you have a story for me, Jack. That is not the sort of thing I normally use but things are slow now. You do understand? My readers demand the latest and the juiciest news."

"Not really, Marcel. I don't have a story for you and I'm not news. And don't call me Jack."

We both turned, as, thank God, Amy was suddenly with us. Marcel bowed deeply, touched his hat, and gave her a long, careful look from top

80

to bottom. "Your friend?" he said. "Good bone structure. Attractive in a plain sort of way. But that outfit?"

Amy said a pleasant hello. I said, "Goodnight Marcel."

This one could not be insulted, at least by me. And he was persistent. "If you change your mind," he said, handing me a business card, "you can reach me at that number--anytime." With that he turned and strolled off toward the hotel.

"Friend of yours?" Amy said, taking the chair next to me.

In a simple white blouse, flowered skirt, hair pulled back and tied off with a piece of yellow cloth, Amy was that attractive plain that millions of women paid good money for and failed to achieve. I told her I'd never seen the man before. "Ever heard of Marcel?...in the newspaper?"

"That was him! I don't have the time to read his column, but everyone in the city knows the name. What did he want?"

"A story. Nothing important. Would you like a drink?" Luke had returned.

"I have the feeling we've had this same conversation before," she said smiling. "I think I'll have what you're having."

"Wise choice," I told her with a straight face. I gave Luke the order and he moved off, smiling all the while.

We took our drinks to the table, a far one at the end of the patio, under a huge tree that cut us off from the night. The pale light from the candle softened the strong lines of her face. Raising my glass to her I said, "To you. Thanks for your help."

"Thanks for having me to dinner. This is a rare treat for me."

"Don't order chicken. Will it be a treat even if the meal isn't so good?"

"Doesn't matter. I know it will be great. Just to be away and eat different cooking is enough for me."

"I hope you're hungry."

"Famished."

"Great. So am I. Let's order everything!"

"I could never eat everything. How are you feeling?"

"A few aches and pains, but no complaints. Let's say I've been worse."

She seemed to be studying my face for a moment, perhaps wondering just what I meant by that, and maybe wondering is she should ask. She didn't, just stared and sipped her drink. Then she said, "You never did tell me why you came down here. If it was supposed to be a vacation it didn't turn out too well did it? I heard that you have to leave Haiti. Is that true?"

She may be out in the country, but she knew what was going on. "Yes. That's what I was told."

"Too bad," she said thoughtfully. "Since you just got here. If you don't mind my asking, why did you come here? I'm still not clear on that part. If I'm prying just tell me to keep quiet."

"You're not prying. It's not a big deal. A friend of mine--a good friend or I'd never have agreed--asked me to come down here and look for someone."

"Look for someone? I don't understand."

I held up a cigarette and asked if she'd mind my smoking. She didn't so I lighted up. "Well, it seems this guy's daughter was here with the Peace Corps--and just disappeared!"

"How could she simply disappear? There must be more to it than that."

I told her about what Al and I had been doing, about the ceremonies and all. After a moment she said, "That's odd."

"Odd that she disappeared?"

"Yes that certainly. Plus the fact that you didn't learn anything about her. Those people with the Peace Corps were very community oriented, lived and worked in the villages, made friends and had ties with the people. Seems like someone would know of her. But then you really didn't have much time to look and ask questions, did you?"

"That's true."

"Another thing. They had to get around out there and they needed a vehicle. I seem to remember a beat-up yellow Land Rover they used. Did you ask about that?"

"First I've heard of it. Good point." She started me thinking. If I really wanted to find Christine I realized I'd have to comb the villages again, and keep looking until I found out where they lived. From there something had to turn up. Someone had to have seen that vehicle. The girl just didn't disappear into thin air! Of course there was one major flaw in that thinking. I had maybe one day to do it. For more than one reason I made up my mind to give it another shot.

"I think I'd like another drink, please."

I'd been talking so much I didn't notice our glasses were empty. I ordered two more and we got into the menu. It wasn't an extensive list and after a brief discussion we both settled on the local lobster. They were small but we had a good time cracking and slopping our way through the things. They were good. When we were pretty much finished making a mess of ourselves and the table, I asked her to tell me about herself.

"There isn't much to tell," she said, obviously not comfortable talking about herself. "And it's not very interesting."

"Hopefully, we don't think we're interesting, and we shouldn't. But others might. Try me."

"I think you might be interesting."

"Far from it. Now get back to you. Where were you born?"

"A small town in Connecticut; only child, good parents--seems to be an unusual thing today--parochial school upbringing; I decided to become a nun when I was quite young."

"Any special reason?" While she thought about that I ordered coffee for her and a desert wine for myself. "Now, where were we? You were becoming a nun. Why did you do that?"

"It was an accident." Smiling she added, "Literally. My mother and I were coming back from shopping one day--I had just gotten my license and was driving--and we were hit by a car that ran a stop sign. It was terrible. Anyway, she was in the hospital in critical condition for two days. I didn't know if she would survive. While I was waiting to hear about her I decided that if she lived--which had to be God's work--I would dedicate my life to God and helping others." She looked down for a moment than back at me. "Does that sound foolish?"

"Of course not! It's not something I can relate to, but I can see where you were coming from at the time. And after that?"

"School and training. After some other places I finally got transferred down here."

"Any regrets?"

She let that linger for a moment. "No regrets. I'm needed here and I love these people. What I'm doing is important in their lives--and in mine. You said you couldn't relate to what I did. What do you mean?"

"Not that I couldn't relate to what you did. Well, that too. But I'm not sure about the why. I often hear people say, 'How could God let that happen?' God doesn't *let* anything happen--people do. People do good and they do bad (I was getting a buzz on here and talking from someplace I didn't know existed). People make war. People kill. If we wanted to spend more money on research than on arms, we could find cures for everything. People make those decisions."

"Where does God come into this?"

"If people listen to God's teaching they will do good things. But someone has to be listening and believe the good way is the way to go. If no one is listening..."

"Go on."

"I've said more than enough already. What about your life?"

"You haven't said too much and I'm interested in how you feel."

"Forget it. What about your life."

"My life is satisfying. Now, get back to you."

"No way. I'm duller than tan wallpaper. Let's not spoil a nice evening."
She didn't pout but she was close to it, and I knew she wasn't about to let
me off the hook without a little more. So I gave a little, said I had a
typical upbringing (which was far from true, actually anything but), some
time in the Marines. That's about it."

She sat back and looked at me in a curious way. "You left out a lot."

That was certainly true. "So did you."

"Yes, I did. But with you I have the feeling that it goes much deeper."
She sat forward and finished her coffee. "But it's getting late. We can save
the rest for another time. I'd better get going. Thanks for a nice dinner and
a lovely evening."

"I don't see how there can be another time."

"If it's meant to be you will find a way."

"I guess so. The pleasure was all mine, Amy. You are a beautiful and
remarkable woman."

"Well thank you. Such compliments!" Giving a big smile, she said,
"And you are a beautiful and remarkable man."

"Should I have Marcel put that in his column?"

"Maybe you'd better not."

I signed the check, added my room number and a decent tip, then we
walked through the hotel and out to the porch. A taxi driver was waiting
beside his car. Standing by the open door, I kissed her, lightly on the lips,
at which she gasped, gave the driver some money and watched the car
drive off. She was so different from Hannah in a way I couldn't define,
and yet I knew I wanted more of her, more time with her, more talk, more
everything about her. Unfortunately we moved in different worlds and I
could see no way they would ever come together.

It was a long time before I got to sleep.

# EIGHT

By the time I got the body parts moving--something that seemed to take more effort than I remembered needing in the past--showered, shaved, got dressed and had breakfast, then finally located Al, it was near ten o'clock. I had hoped to get an earlier start on this last day for searching. Claudette kept me up to my eyes in coffee.

Al showed up in a borrowed car and we drove out into the country. I had explained what I had in mind, that we had a lot to do, much ground to cover and Al had recruited lots of men and women from his village to help us. None of them would take the money I offered. Transportation was a problem because there simply weren't a lot of working vehicles to be had. Our group started out in two cars, of questionable longevity, and two trucks with even less. We had worked out a plan whereby we would drop people off along the way in the villages we passed, let them scour for information, then we would pick them up on our sweep back at the end of the day. I stressed the new information from Amy about the Rover. Our hope was to flood the area and find something! While I didn't hold much hope for success, I felt I had to give it a try. As it turned out I was wrong.

A long, hot and dusty drive brought Al and me to the farthest village from our starting point. If the place had a name I never knew it; but the people were friendly and helpful, giving us water and something to eat, spending a lot of time in animated conversation with Al. And though all the talk seemed like a positive sign to me, at the end I found it was just a matter of isolated people sharing common thoughts and problems--a social visit. Mid afternoon by the time we left and I was tired and disgusted.

Al, sensing my mood said, "Don't worry, boss. My people will find her." Chain-smoking (my cigarettes of course, which I didn't mind), he drove like a wild man all the way back.

In thought as we rode, I had to envy his optimism both about our search and his life in general. "I hope the others did better than we did--a big zero."

"Trust us, boss."

"It isn't a question of trust, Al. Do you think I'd let you smoke all my cigarettes if I didn't trust you?"

He glanced at me to see if this had been a serious question. "That my only vice, boss."

"I doubt that."

Puffing away, he laughed. "We will find that woman, boss."

"I wish you'd stop calling me boss."

"Okay boss. But you are in charge of this. That makes you boss."

"A technical point, Al."

"That may be."

"By the way. When will your car be fixed?"

"Hard to say. Maybe this week. Maybe next week."

"That definite huh?"

After a moment. "What did you do back in your country, boss? You a rich business man or something?"

"Or something, Al. Not a rich man but I'm okay."

"All Americans have money."

"It might seem that way to you, and by comparison I guess you would say we all have money, certainly more than most Haitians. But we have our poor, lots of poor."

"Those Peace Corps people didn't have much money. Why you looking so hard for that woman?"

"A long story, Al. Like I said, it's a favor."

A long silence then. The mention of money made me realize that I never checked to see if my down payment was in the bank; that used to be the first thing I did. Things were different now; I was different now. And somehow the money didn't seem to be all that important. That puzzled me.

Dark by the time we got back to the village and gathered our troops together for debriefing. In this part I could only stand by and let Al do the talking, frustrating as it was. I heard a lot of chatter and the general mood, it seemed to me, was good, although as I'd learned earlier in the day at our village, it could be nothing more than friendly talk and gossip. Maybe they were glad the day was over. Maybe they were just happy to have seen new people in other villages. I had no way of knowing. I tried to stay positive.

Later, around a fire with food and *Clairin* to loosen tongues and spirits, our debrief, if it could be called that, got started with Al as the coordinator. Looking around the group, it seemed to me that I was the only one anxious to get down to details. I studied Al as he spoke with different groups, trying to read something in his face or in the talk. Beneath it all I was pretty discouraged and down. Suppose we did learn something about Christine? What was the point? I still had to leave tomorrow.

Even so, every time he turned to me with a nod or a smile, I took it as a positive sign. Wishful thinking? Maybe he was looking for a cigarette. In that case he was out of luck because we ran out some time ago on the drive back. He wasn't trained for this and I wondered if he wasn't off into stories and folklore. Who knows? He talked on, laughing and drinking,

86

then later smoked a pipe of something, having a grand time. Finally the talk eased off into a few murmurs, then quiet, and, Thank God, it ended.

He took my arm and we walked off a distance. "Boss," he said, "we have good news and bad news." With no preference in mind I didn't say anything. "The good news is that we learned about your woman. She was here. We spoke with no one from the village where she lived, that is further north. We know where she was last seen."

"That's the good news?"

Al shrugged and continued. "Her car was seen at the factory."

"Sauvain's!"

"Yes. Her car was there for two nights." He offered me the pipe but I was in no mood.

"So what about the factory? What could that have to do with anything?"

"Is it not odd that the car was there in the night? Two nights!"

That didn't make sense. If she had visited the factory, and I couldn't imagine why she would, she would certainly go back to her home at night. "What do they make at the factory?"

Al gave his familiar shrug. "They make sporting goods and things like that."

"I don't see a connection. You sure we can trust these people? Maybe too much imagination? You know?"

"Could be. These are country people and very..." he laughed..."superstitious. But one thing for sure: these people speak the truth and there is something strange about that place. They have bad feelings about factory."

And this was the good news? "Al, that makes no sense at all. What the hell does sporting goods have to do with anything?"

"Maybe they do other things."

"Like what!"

He looked at me for a moment. "Not many will talk. Some think it is the white powder."

"Drugs!"

"Sauvain is very powerful. No one want to get involved."

"Drugs here? First I ever head of it. How could Sauvain be into drugs and no one know about it?"

"People may know but afraid."

I couldn't dispute that. It sent me off on another track. If it was drugs, and Christine somehow found out about it, which was not a farfetched thought, then there were a lot of possibles. None of them good. And if she knew, then who else might know? Marv? Price? Amy? It might account for the questioning, by Sauvain himself. It still seemed like a wild scenario.  While drugs was getting into an area I wanted no part of, if it involved Christine I had no choice but to go on.  If this was true, the vague and rambling tales from the villagers wouldn't carry a lot of weight in court.  If I wanted to pursue that line, which wasn't what I was about here, I would have to get facts, and proof.  That part was all very interesting but not where I wanted to go at this point.  Maybe something I could hang on Sauvain at another time.  "Is this the first time you heard about this, Al?"

"No.  I have heard before."

So there might be something here.  "Do you think there's anything to it?"

"Not for me to think about, boss."

"Stop calling me boss."  We both laughed.  The bottom line, I realized, was to have a look inside that factory.  And it  had to be tonight!

*** 

I was bone-tired and now smoking the pipe.  Al pulled our truck off the paved highway onto the dirt shoulder and we sat looking at the factory about 100 yards away.  We had to be almost invisible on a dark night on a road without lights.  From what I could see, which wasn't much--how I longed for night vision glasses, or even plain binoculars--the building looked like any other factory except for the newness, and what I thought was excessive security.  A high chain link fence surrounded the building and the loading bays in the rear.  At the front gate was a small guard shack.  The whole place was bright as day from powerful lights mounted on the fence.  Seeing no power lines going in, I assumed there was a generator inside--useless information since we were hardly prepared to hit the power first as in a full scale assault.  The place was a fortress and I was beginning to see this as a hopeless venture.

Al kept looking from the factory to me but didn't say anything.  I hated to disappoint him if he was looking for some brilliant plan from me.  I kept watching a pair of headlights piercing the black night as a tractor-trailer eventually came abreast of us, went by, then slowed and pulled up to the gate.  I noticed the load on the flat trailer was a sea-going container rather than a box with doors at the rear.  But  that didn't tell me much one way or the other about the cargo except that it probably came from out of the country.  The guard took a few minutes to check paper work before opening the gate, then the truck went around to the rear docks, which was were the only lights and signs of activity showed.  If I were to gain entrance to the building it had to be from that point.

After about five minutes of quiet another truck came by and went through the same procedure. This was all very interesting, but aside from knowing where to get inside, and the fact that good security was in place, I was getting nowhere.

"Lots of night deliveries," said Al.

I nodded while not really hearing him because the flicker of a plan popped into my mind--a weak plan was better than none at all. "We need another truck."

From Al's expression I might have spoken in Polish. "Another truck?"

"Yes. Pull out onto the road and stop in the middle. Put the hood up as if you've got some kind of engine problem." He was staring at me. "Do it! Now! Get out there!"

Al followed orders and stopped on the road. Before he got out to do his hood thing I explained my plan. He asked, "What do I do after?"

"You get off the road and wait for me."

After a pause. "If you don't come back?"

"Then you go home and forget all about tonight."

Shaking his head, he looked away then back at me. "That part not good."

"Get out there!" I told him, when I saw the lights of another truck. "Get out and do it. Give me an hour. If I'm not back by then get the hell out of here."

Bathed in the light as the truck neared, I flattened out on the seat. I should hear the sound of air brakes very soon...or? First the frantic blast of the air horn, the swoosh of air, then the shudder of the big rig going into a forced stop. I could feel the tremor from the road. Well at least the damn thing stopped. I slid out the door and ducked around behind the truck, scurrying in under the trailer looking for the spare tire rack. I was in luck: not only did he have one but it was empty! Crawling up into the metal rack and pulling myself as close as possible to the trailer bed, I felt my straining muscles seize up and I knew I couldn't hold that position for very long. I could hear Al and the driver talking and I knew it would be a few minutes before we'd move. I eased my back down onto the metal frame-- better, but far from comfortable.

After what seemed like an eternity our truck moved away and the trailer was moving to the gate. Though I would be fully exposed in the lights if the guard even glanced underneath the trailer, he hadn't before, so I used the moments to relax the muscles. Presently the sound of gears being engaged and we were off to the loading area. It was a short ride but I ached all over when the trailer stopped and I flopped down onto the concrete ramp. I lay still--I couldn't really do anything else but lay still while I caught my breath--and waited for things to settle down. I could feel something, probably dirty oil that had dripped from the trucks, seeping into the back of my shirt.

If the place was full of workers what could I hope to find? That is if I did get inside and did get a chance to look around. I didn't give a damn about the drugs if there were any. That wasn't my problem. Christine was my problem. Did I actually expect to find them holding her inside? The more I thought about it the more I thought this was a dumb move.

I finally got inside, picking my moves and sneaking around the place. There were some workers, loading and unloading mostly, and I was able to cover the large factory almost from end to end. Nothing. From what I could see they made sporting goods. I was making my way back out, not even thinking about the guard at the gate, when two men, one with a gun, grabbed me from behind. The one was shouting in Creole; but I didn't need to know the language to understand what he wanted. They started marching me towards an office in the back of the warehouse.

We never got there.

I heard a thump and a groan behind me, some scuffling, then I turned around to see Al holding the gun on the one left standing. "I thought you might need some help, boss," he said, grinning.

"Don't call me boss. And how the hell did you get in here!"

"Walked right in the gate, boss. The guard is a cousin. You know the back of your shirt all dirty?"

"I should have known."

No one seemed to notice us, or maybe they did and didn't want to get involved, which was more likely, so I figured we might as well take the guy into his office and find out what he knew about the business. We sat him down in a chair and Al started with the questions. The man was sullen, quiet, and uncooperative. Al tried again with no results. I took a moment to go to the door and see if anyone was coming our way. When I came back things had changed. Al was holding him up in the air with a handful of shirt in one hand, slapped him twice with the other, then shook him like a bag of rags. Now Al is a big guy and he quickly adjusted the man's attitude from non-cooperative to blabber mouth. We found out there was a separate section sealed off from the factory by a false wall.

"Never mind that, Al. What does he know about the girl?"

The two of them talked for a few moments and in a break I asked, "So, what's the story, Al?"

Al dropped the man back into the chair with one last back-handed slap. "He doesn't know much, boss. He say the woman was here and then she was gone. They drove her Rover away."

"Where did they take her?"

"He doesn't know. He has heard them talk of a ranch in Mexico. The big boss lives there. Somewhere near a place called Durango. That mean anything to you?"

"Yes," I told him thoughtfully. "It means she's a long way from here and I've got a long way to go to find her." Durango. Years ago, I read somewhere, it had been a place for movies and movie stars-- money. It could mean expensive homes and big spreads which meant a lot of land to search. Not much to go on. "Well, I guess it is a start, Al. Thanks for your help."

"No problem, boss," he answered with a grin.

# NINE

From personal experience, I have found that one can leave a country in short order with a police escort, almost as quickly, I would imagine, as with a diplomatic passport. After all, the undesirable and the politician have a common bond. Two of Haiti's finest--or more likely whomever was assigned to the job--showed up very early to pound on my door. They did that, and kept at it, because I was tired and groggy, needing a few moments to wake up and get my wits about me, and then finally open the door. With a minimum of words, and many gestures, they made it very clear that I was to pack and be ready to go to the airport at once. After I got moving and started to think about it, I thought it odd that while it was barely dawn, the only flight out of here was at mid-morning. Haiti wanted nothing more to do with Jack Morgan. Their loss.

What would they have done if they had found the room empty? Which it damn near was.

By the time we had gotten back to the city it was well into the early morning hours. Al wanted me to stay and help make life miserable for Sauvain and the whole bunch, which was an interesting and flattering thought, if out of the question, even if I wasn't in trouble with the authorities. I had to convince him that it was best for me to get back to the city and get thrown out as ordered. And I did have a life.

Thus, I'd gotten very little sleep. What we'd gotten from the factory foreman told me that my next move was to Mexico, via Miami of course since there was no direct connection from here. Had there been one I doubted I'd be allowed to get on the flight. There still seemed to be no reason for taking Christine that made any sense. If she had found out about the drugs, which was entirely possible, and even probable, why take her as a hostage? Why not simply shoot her on the spot? Not a nice thought. But from a practical viewpoint it made more sense than taking her along. She was taken and kept alive. Why? Because she was worth more alive than dead. Simple. But to whom and why? They were the tough ones. Then as well, maybe this was just one of those screw-ups that happen. And maybe, just a thought, maybe I was being used in something much bigger. But again: why and by whom? Did Marv know more than he was telling me? A strong possibility because that had always been his way. And even if that were true, I still basically trusted him and his motives.

This was all going through my mind as we rode to the airport. One of "the finest" sat in front and one in the back with me, neither saying a word to me or each other. I took a bit of pleasure in wondering how they would handle the taxi fare because I wasn't about to pay. Send the bill to Sauvain, I thought, with a smile that puzzled my guard.

As for Christine, I *could* simply report back to Marv that I'd found the girl and that she was in Mexico. End of story. I did my job. And in one sense that would be enough to get me full payment for services rendered? Maybe. But was that all I wanted ? Was that enough to make me feel comfortable with this?

These things were running through my mind as the plane raced down the runway and lifted off from the parched land. Looking out, I couldn't help but think that these people, who hadn't gotten a break in a hundred years, deserved better. And unfortunately, the prospects for any change, now or in the immediate future, looked dim indeed. And while it wasn't my problem at the moment, nor likely to be in the near future, having seen it up close was a disturbing thing. It made the work that Amy and the others were doing all that much more important, even if it did seem to me to be a drop in a very large bucket. They were doing the job.

And on another level and in a different way, Christine deserved better. Here was a problem that I could do something about and I was wavering, not sure if I wanted to see it to the end. I wondered why. I had never left a job unfinished. As long as I could get in, do the job, and had a decent chance of getting out alive, there was never a thought of anything less than completing the assignment.

Climbing nicely for a time, we hit a spot of turbulence passing through to the cooler upper air, then settled down as we neared the cruising altitude. The flight, one of those bag-of-peanuts-can-of-soda type, was full and there was no first class--not that I had the option anyway. Next to me in the middle and aisle seats were a mother and daughter, the mother giving me only fleeting glances for a while before we bridged the racial gap and started talking. Turned out she was Haitian-born, left to live in Brooklyn, then returned, divorced and with child, to be near her parents. She had a job at the radio station in Port-au-Prince. With the ice broken, I finally ended up drawing pictures for the daughter on her writing pad. She loved them and thought they were wonderful. Her mother and I exchanged knowing looks--they were awful. I always had trouble drawing a straight line. Turned out they were visiting relatives in New York and on the return trip home would be carrying lots of things to help make their life a little better in Haiti.

After that I got to thinking about another daughter--Hannah's. Who was thinking about her? I'm sure Hannah was, but she was in no position to do anything but worry. Her father? Well, he had put up the money to find her and I guess that had to count for something. And in a manner of speaking I had found her. I didn't need the money and I was getting too damn old to be doing this. I was trying to rationalize my way out of this and knowing at the same time that it didn't set right. Maybe it was because of my own orphan upbringing, a terrible feeling of being alone. Christine had a mother and father in her life--a wealthy mother and father. But wealth didn't mean they cared about her or spent a lot of their time with her. Children young and old, everyone, needed someone to care about them and love them. And maybe her parents *were* loving, caring, and worried parents.

With all that in mind, and stalling on a final decision, but close, I took a room near the airport rather than going home. Time was important to Christine. I had no idea what she was going through, how long she might be alive, or even if she *was* still alive. Maybe she was going through the worst days of her life, suffering indignity and abuse, maybe torture. But I was tired and still sore all over and I didn't want to go--I couldn't go there. After dinner and a bit of reading I was asleep before ten o'clock.

Lately I'd found that eating a big breakfast wasn't the pleasure it used to be, but this morning, however, what with an early turn-in and a late rising I was hungry and ready. Or so I thought. At first I dug into a plate of pancakes, eggs and bacon with gusto. But in a moment my appetite slowly faded away as a tiny thought of Christine crept in, then continued to grow. Suddenly the eggs seemed to be staring at me like two accusing eyes and I shoved the plate aside. I'd picked up a map of Mexico in a travel agency near the hotel and I looked at it for a few moments: big country with lots of open spaces. The colorful, accordion map, which included some related facts and a bit of history, told me that the city of Durango was the capitol of the State of Durango, a large state located just east of the Sierra Madre Mountains which ran down along the West Coast, almost the length of Mexico. From what I could determine, the state included some barren, rough country, much of it uninhabited. While the roads didn't look like much, there appeared to be a decent highway leading from the coast city of Mazatlan, up through the mountains and then down into Durango. A map symbol indicated an airport in Mazatlan and one in Durango as well. And while I didn't know if anyone cared about strangers one way or the other, on balance it didn't seem like a good idea to announce my arrival in Durango by flying in to a small field.

While I could no doubt buy decent equipment in Mexico--I'm sure they made good boots--I preferred to get them here where I knew and trusted the brand name. Walking in was not new to me, but this trip would be without the usual goodies like camo clothes, weapon, GPS, night vision equipment, radio, and backup to name a few. Like the rest of our citizens

94

today--and disturbed at the thought that I might be joining them--I'd gotten spoiled not having the high tech goodies of our times. But the difference, it seemed to me, was that I *could* live without them.

Was I getting old?

Wasn't that long ago, or so I preferred to believe, when we went in with nothing more than a gun, a knife, and a compass. Well, we did have a bit more than that, but not much more.

Yes. I was getting old. Still, all things considered, and not spoiling myself, I would at least like a good rifle--my rifle. If it came to that Marv could always arrange delivery. And thinking of that made me think that it was time to contact him and see if we had any useful asset I could use in Mexico.

Later in the day, back at my hotel after a bit of shopping, I put in a call to Marv to bring him up to speed on my activities thus far. He said that he didn't have anyone he wanted to use in the city--the organization there was too much of sieve. But, oddly enough, he did have an old, reliable asset in Durango. Within 12 hours he would send off a package to me to the embassy with full information and what he called "equipment."

I repacked, then called Mexicana Airlines and booked a flight under another name, one that I had a credit card for and photo ID. One of the simplest ways to track someone unaware, or inexperienced, a no brainer in fact, was to simply check airline passenger manifests which were available to intelligence agencies, police, and someone with connections. I couldn't know if anyone was that interested in my travels just yet--it was a possibility if word got out of Haiti. And I did know that using a different name on the flight would hardly delay a professional for very long. Still, I wasn't going to make it that easy to track my movements.

I went to check out. Behind the counter was a pleasant Indian woman--Eastern Indian I guess you would call her today, dark skin, black hair, a red dot on the forehead--who took care of the paper work, all the while talking about the recent hurricane that had brushed the area. Since I hadn't heard about it I could only listen without commenting. They must have hurricanes in India. Or did they? She seemed so fascinated by the whole thing, more so because they got away with no damage. Finally, she stopped talking and phoned for the shuttle van.

On the drive to the airport I mulled things over in my mind. Prior to Haiti only Marv and the senator knew about me. Since then more had gotten into the picture, probably more than I was aware of, and it seemed logical that the boys in Mexico would soon learn of my activities; they would know I was looking for the girl and be prepared for me. Who knows? Maybe they knew already. The bottom line was that I should start looking over my shoulder and watching my back.

There was plenty of time to spare after I checked in for the flight so I went off in search of a bar near the departure gate. By now, I was sure, somewhere in the world if not here, the sun was over the yardarm, as they say, which meant it was now a civilized hour to have a drink. If I interpreted that old saying correctly it meant noon, which seemed pretty liberal to me. After I had scanned the room and saw no one of a suspicious nature--though I did see several I wouldn't want to socialize with--I settled in with "USA Today" and a double tequila on the rocks with lime. I ordered a double because I'd forgotten I wasn't in a place where one got strictly a measured shot, such as in the British Isles. It was annoying to order a drink and see a puny quarter inch of liquid in the glass.

The Miami terminal building is a non-smoking facility. This means that if one wanted to smoke it meant going back through the departure area, a long walk, again past the scanning procedure, which meant emptying my pockets, and then out to the street. A discouraging process that I was too tired to make.

The newspaper, of the generic type I thought, and with the traveler in mind, gave good coverage on happenings around the country and the world, but of course little on the local scene. Fine with me. Starting from the back section, "Life," covering entertainment, health, books, computer things, and the like, I had moved on to the "Sports Section" when I was aware of the slight touch of a body moving in on the stool next to me. I heard a "Sorry," answered it with a "No problem," and went back to my reading. The home run hitting competition, I read, was in full swing (no pun intended) and both men were on a pace to better the record. An article about the Miami Dolphins gave the usual drivel that they were considered to be a Super Bowl contender. Probably a bit of wishful thinking on the part of their new coach. With Dan Marino out of there at quarterback they'd be lucky to make the play-offs.

"Your football is very big here," came from a voice at my elbow.

I said, "Yes it is. College football is even more so here in Florida." I kept reading and didn't look up.

"You live here?"

"Florida? No." At this point I did look up and turn to see who wanted to talk to me. Next to me was this attractive woman with light blue eyes and what appeared to be genuine blond hair in a long braid down her back. She was a woman who would bring a second look and I gave her a long first one in anticipation of more. Very professional looking in a dark pants suit, one trim leg crossed, an arm resting on a flat briefcase on the bar, I

96

thought she was one stunning woman. She was smiling and I kept looking at her--nice teeth and nice smile, friendly and real.

She said, "I've become a fan of the Dolphins while I've been here on business."

Still staring I asked, "And what business is that?"

"A travel agency. I'm a part owner," she added in what I considered a modest way.

"You're traveling on business now?"

"Oh no. That part is finished." She took a sip of her drink then glanced off before coming back to me. "Now I'm on holiday," she said brightly. "I'm taking time off to wander, to see Mexico and maybe some of Central America."

We started talking. She asked where I was staying, knew the hotel and recommended it for a nice visit. She was in a hotel just down the street. Turned out that she was born in South Africa of Dutch and Irish parents, then after an education went into the business which was based in Europe.

One of the delights of travel I'd found, on the rare occasion that I indulged in talk, was meeting people from all over the world. It occurred to me that if we all got together on this basis, no matter what we spoke or how we looked, the world would definitely be a more peaceful, friendly place. We were, after all, travelers on the same journey.

"Are your parents still there? In South Africa?"

"No. They were killed in the troubles there."

I nodded but didn't comment. Her speech carried the faint trace of an English education and I found it very enjoyable. In the time of silence then, I glanced away and re-scanned the room. Very few Mexicans; either they weren't drinkers, which I doubted, or they were smarter than I and wouldn't pay these prices for tequila. Across from me sat an over-sized, fake blond with lots of hair, in too tight clothes, telling everyone within hearing of her many enjoyable trips to Mexico. Evidently she stayed in her hotel and was unaware of the crime problem. Beside her was a tanned surfer-type in sagging tank top and long, stringy, bleached hair, who pretended to be listening to the boring tales. He kept looking over at the woman next to me. Next to the surfer, his woman, was his female clone but with the gaunt look of either a drinker or a user. Going on around the bar was a man talking on his cell phone. Brain surgeon? A middle-aged couple who seemed to be in a constant argument. Two men in suits, alone, engrossed in their own thoughts: what could they use to make the big sale? Would they be among the next to be let go on downsizing? The Brits-- bless their simplicity and directness, and so far, their disinterest in being politically correct--called it "redundant." Either way it meant being fired.

97

How the hell do you make that sound better? Who made up these expressions and who benefited from this strange correctness that obsessed us? Was the little guy "vertically challenged?"

We were a country going downhill fast, I thought, losing our heritage, our identity, and our power. We were in a decline ever since the Big War. We had a win in that one. Then, arguably, a tie in Korea. A loss in Vietnam where the whole thing fell apart. That oil thing in the Gulf? A fantastic display of our technology and no doubt a great tool for arms sales. So what if 200 soldiers got sick, permanently, from some mysterious source of what had to be chemicals. We left with the pipelines open and the same tyrant in power. A spurious win to say the least. Bosnia? Where was it and who cared? We bombed the place to rubble, let the Russians in, and again left with the same guy in power. What could you call that? Wasn't NATO set up to defend against that ice pile where the Mafia ran the country? Seems like downhill to me.

But then what do I know?

"What are you thinking about?" she asked.

I shrugged. "Nothing important. You might call it the bitter and no doubt cynical thoughts of an old man. It's the drink," I added, only partly kidding.

"You don't look old to me."

"Well I'm not young."

"For that matter neither am I," she said.

"Anything under 50 is still young."

That brought a smile. " In that case I'm still young. Is your trip to Mexico a vacation or business."

"Mostly business," I told her. "I'm thinking about having another drink. Would you like one? Or would you feel more secure buying your own?"

"Secure?"

"Secure," I repeated. "Whatever it is with the modern woman."

With an embarrassed smile she said, "I don't know this term."

"You look like one. But I don't know what you are. I do know you're under 50 and going to Mexico." With that I waved an arm at the woman tending bar. "Now or never."

Ignoring my offer for the moment she asked, "Do you think that woman behind the bar is a modern woman?"

"No."

"Why not!"

"Tending bar is not a woman thing; women have been doing that for centuries." She just stared at me shaking her head in disbelief. "You want that drink or not?" I asked.

"Okay. I accept. A Margarita, please." She glanced at my glass. "I don't know what you're having but it looks strong. You sure you want another one?"

"It is strong and I do want another one. I'm a social drinker and I'm being social with you." Her question did give me pause. Though it was mostly in the past now, I well remembered the times I'd had a second, and a third, and sometimes beyond. I told myself that drinking would chase away the demons, the dreams, and make me feel better if I kept at it long enough. Of course it never did. And why now? Maybe it was because this is now, the present, a time I'm not at all sure of. My drinking had never reached the addiction stage, thank goodness, but it came close.

I came out of my thoughts to her staring at me, again. Putting out my hand, I said, "Jack Morgan. And you are...?"

She watched the woman bring our drinks. "Thank you. I'm Kimberly Durden."

"Nice name." Looking up at the departure screen I saw it was time for boarding. I took a few gulps and said, "We'd better be off to our gate." After she stood up and looked at me, I added, "And if I should ever see you again...I will call you Kim. Would that be all right?"

"Quite," she said smiling. She turned back and tossed off her drink. "Jack, I do believe you are an unusual man."

"I've been called worse. And you are an unusual woman."

"Enjoy your trip," she said. And with that she was gone.

Arriving in Mexico after an uneventful flight, I bought a ticket for the taxi ride into town, then went outside and into a typically heavy shower to have a smoke. The rainy season is June to September. As usual in the tropical part of the world, which this definitely was, the downpour did nothing to relieve the humidity and heat. Nor did it weaken the chemical fumes and smell that hung in the air. The city of some 20 million or so, I'd read, about 25 minutes from the airport, was one of the oldest cities in the hemisphere. I had passed through the city before, though I didn't really know it, only because it was an agency hub. What a lot of people might not know is that the city has an excellent subway system.

The traffic was much like anyplace else, maybe more of it. Watching it I thought of the worst possible combination for "road rage"--this heat and the Latin temperament.

I'd chosen my hotel, Galeria Plaza, part of the Westin Hotel deluxe chain in the Zona Rosa because it was busy, in the middle of the action in this city, the place to get information, and loaded with tourists for me to hide among. No one should notice me here. If Christine had gotten mixed up

99

in a drug operation--and at this point that seemed the most likely possibility--the ring might well be part of a vast network with *mucho* workers, players, dealers, and money movers. Conceivably, anyone of these people I passed on the way into the lobby might be a part of this thing. While that was an interesting thought, I had no idea how that might help me. It seemed ridiculous to even hope that I'd learn the names of these people or the exact location of the ranch by roaming around Mexico City and asking questions. I could only hope the contact Marv gave me was up to speed on this place.

Crammed into the elevator with a group of mostly older and overweight tourists in garish clothes, I questioned this venture in my mind and had worked myself into a foul mood. What the hell were all these people doing here? Had they never read the State Department advisory warning about travel in Mexico? Many Americans, it seemed, had the idea they could go anywhere, anytime, be welcomed and be perfectly safe. Well, we were a young and naive country.

We got to my floor and I squeezed out, found my room, then  spent frustrating minutes trying to get the damn card to work in the lock.

Might have been better if it hadn't worked.

As soon as I opened the door and stepped inside, a pair of huge hands grabbed me by the shirt and threw me across the room. Thinking that he had to be a big man and maybe not too fast, I got my arms under me and tried to turn and get up. Wrong. I caught a kick in the ribs and felt the pain shoot through my body. I doubled up trying to protect myself. Yanking me over onto my back, he bent over me, so close I could smell his foul breath. "Stay out of this, gringo. Go home before you really get hurt." With that he kicked me twice; one caught me in the ribs and the other I deflected off my arms. But they both hurt.  "It will be worse next time," he growled. "Be on the next plane."

Two countries; physical abuse in both.  This was not a good start.

I heard the door close, then quiet, as I lay there unable to move without causing more pain. After what seemed like a long time, and realizing I couldn't stay on the floor forever, I managed to crawl to the bed, get myself up, then flopped down and reached for the phone. To the accented voice that answered I yelled, "No! No goddamned Espanol!  English! Send ice up here. Lots of ice. Bags of ice. Now! Pronto!"  I hoped the ice would keep back the muscle spasms that would surely follow. Some of my aches and bruises hadn't healed yet from Haiti. At that moment I wondered if I'd ever walk upright again.

After about five minutes a man came in with a bucket of ice--one bucket. He took one look at me and started for the door. "Bring more ice!"  He came back with two buckets. I sent him for more. He never came back. I pulled off my shirt and covered my chest and arms with ice cubes, then pulled the spread up over me to keep the slippery things in place. Now I not only hurt like hell but I was also freezing.

In my situation in an ideal world I would have drifted off to a restful sleep, then awakened pain free to go off and fight the bad guys. The reality was that while I may have had some moments when I drifted off-- and it sure wasn't restful--the pain and cold never left me. And as far as the bad guys, I didn't even know who they were and I really didn't care. Well, I did care, and I sure as hell would tighten up my whole profile here. This was a different ball game now. First I wanted sleep. I was hungry. I wanted a drink. Then came the bad guys--this one in particular: he wasn't Spanish; something about it wasn't right. Then I slept.

When I woke up later I wrapped myself in the bedspread, scattering what was left of the ice cubes all over the carpet, made my way slowly to the liquor cabinet, then opened two little bottles of tequila. I poured both of them into a glass. Ice wasn't a problem--it was all over the place. I emptied the glass and repeated the process. Sitting on the bed I fired up a smoke. Sure, both are hazardous to your health, but oh so good at that moment.

A knocking at the door. I figured the guy with the big hands and feet would hardly come again, knocking. "Who is it?"

"Its me. Kim."

Without thinking about how I looked I went over and opened the door.

She stood there, staring at me, around the room, back at me, the carpet, then finally held on me. With a broad smile she said, "Am I interrupting something? Perhaps something very personal? Something odd?"

"This isn't the way it looks, Kim."

"It never is, Jack. Maybe I should come back another time. Maybe not at all."

"Oh come in and close the damn door! Some guy was in here waiting for me." She looked gorgeous in white shorts and a light blue top, hair hanging down loose, face pink from the sun. She gave me a skeptical look but finally came in. "Want a drink?"

"I think so," she answered slowly." You look like you've had one already and need another one."

"Just let me put some clothes on."

When I came out of the bathroom she asked, "What happened to you? What do you mean by someone was waiting for you?"

"It's not a long story: a guy was in here waiting for me and when I came in he did a job on me." I walked over to the cabinet. "What would you like?"

"Tequila?"

"I drank it all. Next choice?"

"Vodka and tonic?"

"I can do that."

She watched me fix her drink. When I handed it to her she said, "Why would anyone do that? Do a job on you as you put it?" After a moment she smiled. "That is different."

"What's different?"

"That ice-and-carpet thing. I don't know that I've ever seen that before."

"Very funny, Kim! What are you doing here?"

"You first. Why would someone be here waiting for you?"

"I haven't a clue."

She sipped her drink and nodded. "Odd don't you think?"

"Quite," I said mocking her way. "Might I ask, again, what you are doing here?"

"Being social, Jack. Besides, I believe I owe you a drink."

"You don't 'owe me,' but it is a nice thought." We held eye contact for a long moment. God, she was delicious to look at. "Okay. Why don't we have dinner and talk about all this?"

"All?"

"All if you do the same."

"Bargain. You sure you're up to this?"

"Telling all or going to dinner?"

"Both."

"We have to work on longer sentences, Kim. Makes for better dialog."

After a frown she smiled. "I suppose I could work on that. You Americans are a bit..."

"Odd?" I suggested.

"That might do."

"Now, how about dinner?"

"Do you know a place?" she asked.

"No. I thought we might just look around and find some place suitable."

After a moment she said, "No. That won't do. We are both tired from our trip and you are in no condition to be walking around. I did read of a place, just a few blocks away, that is highly recommended for food and a wonderful Margarita."

Of course she would know a place--it is her business. She is not only different, I thought, but bright, charming and capable, and lovely.

102

Considering myself a lucky man, I said, a bit smugly, "Meet you in the lobby in...an hour?"

***

A hushed darkness of evening was settling in as we left the hotel; the lights on the street and in the stores gave the city a sort of generic, big city feel as so many others, but the heat and the language, clothes, sidewalk vendors, and the music drifting in the night from somewhere turned it into Mexico. She had changed into a simple cotton dress (it looked simple to me but was probably a very expensive frock), hair pulled up in a casual, sort of sloppy neat way that suggested salon design. Nothing about her seemed totally casual and yet she had no airs, nothing phony, or at least I didn't see it. At this point, in our very early relationship, while I did feel that she was someone wonderful and refreshing in my life, there was, unfortunately, an underlying feeling of doubt, of suspicion if you will, that she was too good to be true. Time with her, I hoped, and looked forward to, would tell.

By Mexican standards, she was telling me as we walked, we were eating very early--dinner at ten in the evening was more the norm. I was half listening and at the same time glancing behind to see if we were being followed, which wasn't easy in my condition. Coming back to her conversation, I asked how she knew so much about the country and she told me that she had visited before on business, both here and in Central and South America briefly.

"Are you sure you are up to this walking?" she asked more than once.

I was plodding along slowly, sort of bent over with my arms across my chest. "I'm good, Kim."

Frowning, she said, "Maybe this was not a good idea."

"No problem. I always walk this way in Mexico."

Letting that one go, she grabbed my arm and turned us to the right down a narrow side street, through glass doors and into a foyer where a beautiful woman in native dress greeted us as if we were old friends; she held a leather-covered menu in one hand across her lovely chest. We were shown to one of the several small rooms off the larger main room, all in candle light with just a few tables widely spaced. We settled in to a small table and ordered drinks.

"This looks like a real find, Kim."

Pleased obviously, she said, "And the food is supposed to be every bit as good as the ambiance."

I was trying to enjoy every moment of this evening but the doubt lingered. Let's face it, I never had the charm or the looks to attract anyone like her. This was a matter of fact and not modesty. In every respect she seemed a woman who knew where she was going, why, and how to get where she was going. Too bad I didn't.

"Mind if I order wine?" said Kim softly. "I know an excellent red."

Again, my kind of woman--red wine. "Is it expensive?"

"Terribly," she admitted.

"Then by all means...be my guest."

"Thank you," she said with a thin, kind of awkward smile In a younger woman I would have taken her look for embarrassment. But she was surely too old for that and had certainly heard many complimentary words before mine, and very often I suspect. If not, the male world had gone blind. I personally felt that people weren't being completely honest when they said that money was no object. Money is always an object, maybe not always the most important, but it is always in the running. In this case, however, having dinner with this beautiful woman, money was truly of no importance.

She spoke to the waiter for a few moments and ordered the wine in what sounded to me like perfect Spanish. I asked her about her languages.

"Aside from my own? I do pretty well in Spanish and French. I could probably get by in German."

I nodded without comment, feeling like a dunce: I barely knew a few words in any of them.

After looking at me for a long moment, she said, "I have this odd feeling about you. Can you tell me what you're really doing here and why someone would be waiting in your room to do bodily harm? That is if you want to tell me."

I was feeling better suddenly, the tequila numbing my body, easing the aches and pains, chasing cares away temporarily, yet knowing it would all come back tomorrow. Of course, tomorrow might never come, while today is here. Even so, while just looking at her was slowly eroding my defensive wall, with pieces falling away by the minute, I still wasn't quite ready to tell all. "Like I said, Kim, I'm here on vacation and I haven't a clue about that guy in my room."

She shrugged and didn't comment.

In short order our meals came and there was no more talk for a while. At almost the same time our wine was brought to the table and uncorked. I sniffed it, seeking the "nose" (whatever that might be, I was never quite sure) rolled the ruby red liquid around the glass, sipped, letting it adjust to my mouth, breathing in the body--and to my audience of two apparently searching for the very essence of the wine. Then, with an all-knowing, educated smile pronounced it fit to be consumed. Our waiter took it all in with no expression whatsoever. Perhaps he even thought I was a wine expert. Kim on the other hand, suspicious and doubting my whole routine, and with a delightful smile, rolled her eyes at me.

Later, I was smoking; she was back on our earlier subject. "You have to admit it's unusual for a tourist to get beaten up in a hotel room. It's unheard of!"

"*Au contraire,* Kim," I said, using up most of my French. "From what I read, crime is a major problem in Mexico City."

She smiled and rolled her eyes. "You speak French!" After we both laughed she said, "Now let me try and guess at what you are really doing in Mexico City."

"I already told you that."

"Perhaps. Let's see. You stole a huge sum of money from retirees in Florida and are on the run from the FBI. You're into some kind of drug deal gone bad, owe lots of money and they're out to kill you. You're wanted in the states for spousal abuse--she was gorgeous but a bitch and you darned near killed her. How's that?"

"Terrible, Kim. And such language. Is that the best you can do?"

With a shrug she said, "Okay. We'll let that go. You already know why I'm here." She again told me about her travel agency, European Grand Travel, and that she was here to explore, basically.

What she said made sense to a point, as any good story should--the fact that I was even thinking that way showed my doubts. Maybe I'd become overly suspicious and doubting in my old age. Of course, if she was in any part of our trade, which was the way I was leaning, and she was good at it, there would be at least a bit of truth in her story. That was basic in our training. So where did that leave me? It left me in the company of a gorgeous woman that I didn't know enough about. How bad was that? I decided that it was something I could definitely live with.

For whatever reason--and there were many, the wine simply one among them--I decided to confide in her. I told her about Christine, leaving out some of the details, making it out to be a simple search for a missing woman.

"And you're doing this for a friend?" She paused before going on. "The man in the room doesn't make sense. I don't see any connection to Durango? I'm wondering if this could be a mistake, a case of mistaken identity? I must check with the manager on who had the room before

105

you." She was into it now and kept going. "Maybe this woman, Christine, fell in love with a man in Haiti and just took off with him to live in Mexico? The young people do that now. And in that case how could you take her back? Do you want to take her back? Does your friend want her to be taken back?"

"Whoa. I don't have any answers, Kim. From what little I know of the woman I'm not inclined to believe she went off with a lover. It doesn't fit. As far as taking her back to the states...? My job is to find her."

"You're making a big assumption about this woman, considering you know very little about her."

"True. I'd like to start out believing in her."

"Is that important...that you believe in a woman?"

Was this about her or Christine? I said, "Yes it is, to a degree. It's important that I believe in what I'm doing and in those I'm involved with, no matter how it looks to others. More importantly by far, when it comes down to it, and it usually does, is to trust in me alone." While Kim was still a bit of a question mark, what I'd told her so far wasn't revealing any big secrets, no matter whose side she was on. I had to believe that she was somewhere on my side, or near it, though in a general way that covered a lot of people, a lot of alphabet groups in the drug, law enforcement arena. Then again, I could be way off base here. She could be just what she claimed to be.

She seemed to be reading my thoughts. "Even if people aren't exactly what you think they are, Jack, or even what they claim to be, it doesn't mean they're not on your side."

"True again, Kim." *Are you what you claim to be?* "You want anything else? After dinner drink? Maybe a walk?"

"Definitely not. I'm full, and bushed, and you're in no shape for anything but bed. This has been a wonderful evening, Jack. Wonderful dinner. Can I split it with you?"

"No way." When I got the bill I saw that she was right: the wine was very expensive, almost as much as the expensive dinner. Like I said, money was no object when spending time with a woman like Kim.

The walk to her hotel was a short one, the air sultry and with the faint sweetness of flowers, despite the smog--a pleasant stroll. In the lobby, we stood looking at each other for a long moment with no words being said, wondering about each other, and in my case, about a tomorrow. Then she suddenly reached up a kissed me, quickly, more a touch on the lips. "Good night, Jack," she said softly. "And thanks for that lovely dinner."

"Will I see you again?"

"That seems very likely."

The walk to my hotel was different, lonely, and not as pleasant.

Needless to say I went into my room with a bit more caution this time. I flicked on the light and jumped to one side of the doorway. Had anyone been watching they would have definitely thought I was mentally challenged. But there were no surprises. Now I felt tired. I got undressed, went into the bathroom and set the stopper in the tub, then sat on the john and smoked, watching the water level rise, wondering where things would go from here. I had a lot to do tomorrow and the truth was that I didn't know where to start. Kim was out of the picture while I looked for whatever it was I hoped to learn. All I could do was find out all I could about Durango and then go look for Christine. Seemed simple enough.

When the water was high enough and hot enough I eased my aching body in for a long soak--let the bath do its soothing, magical work.

Then the phone rang.

Damn! Slopping water all over the floor, I grabbed a towel and dashed into the other room for the phone. Who would be calling me here? Kim? The phone slipped out of my hand and bounced on the carpet. I got it in my hand and yelled, "Hello!"

"You don't have to shout, Jack. It's me, Marv. Just wanted to let you know your package will be at the embassy first thing in the morning. Anything new?"

"I'm shouting because you got me out of a nice hot bath, which I was enjoying very much." The phone slipped out of my hands and bounced on the carpet. Picking it up I said, "What could be new? I just got here."

Marv made a snorting sound. " Since when do you take baths?"

"Whenever my body gets beat up." I told him about my visitor.

"Hmm," he murmured. "Could be nothing."

"Getting worked over is nothing?"

"You know what I mean. About what you're doing there. Anyway, be careful."

"I always try, Marv. Anything new on your end?"

"Nothing new here. I'm calling because I just heard from the senator. He wants us to work closely with his office and pass along, right away, anything you find. As you know, I like to cooperate with the boys on the hill. So, what do I tell him?"

That sounded odd to me. As long as I'd know the man--and that was a lot of years--I had never know Marv to freely share information with anyone unless he was under a lot of pressure. He was very much like me: he worked alone wherever possible and he trusted no one--right up to and including the White House. What I thought he was really telling me was that he wasn't all that sure about security in the senator's office and that I should pass on as little as possible, while still keeping them satisfied with my progress. He might even have company as we spoke.

"Tell them I'm working on a slim lead that Christine may be here in Mexico.

"That's it? Want to put a little more meat on the bone?"

"No. Don't give him any more than that right now. Tell him I'm on it but it's going to take time and that he shouldn't be looking for daily reports. You and I know what I'm doing. Let's keep it that way."

"I read you, Jack. If you need anything, anything at all, get in touch with me at my office. By the way, a cell phone is in your package, the very latest."

By *office* he meant his cell phone that went through a secure satellite connection. "Nothing at the moment. Oh. There is one thing. Run a check on a Kimberly Durden. Might not be easy. She comes from South Africa and works out of an office in Europe. Get in touch if you come up with anything."

"Will do. Is she friend or foe?"

"Friend I think."

"You think?"

"It's still early in our relationship, Marv."

"Like that huh? Okay. Want me to send a speak Spanish book?"

He was trying to get an idea of how long I'd be in Mexico. "I hope that won't be necessary. I can always get an interpreter. But thanks anyway. Gotta go." I didn't *have* to go anywhere except back to my soaking; I'd said as much as I wanted to say and this conversation was over as far as I was concerned. He hung up without another word and I went back to my bath--the water now tepid but still enjoyable. Marv's comments made me wonder about the senator: maybe I should be checking him out instead of Kim. How far could that go? Investigating a senator! If he did have any skeletons they'd be way too hidden to uncover without a very deep dig. Still, the senator was a subject to ponder.

\*\*\*

Bright sun streaming in the window and a new day in the land of the Aztecs. I lay there listening to the smooth hum of the air conditioning, the room pleasantly cool and crisp. When I did finally get up and roll out of bed, the body still ached and I felt old. It *looked* old when I was facing the mirror to shave. Still, I considered, it wasn't a bad face (the company of a younger, gorgeous woman will bring such thoughts). There was nothing wrong with maturity. The deep tan hid some wrinkles, as well as old scars

108

and bruises. Managing to get the job done without any cuts, I found a pair of shorts and polo shirt that survived the flight in fairly good shape, slipped into sandals and went down for breakfast. With the morning chores finished, all in all, I felt pretty good, and hungry.

In the crowded room which was dominated by a long buffet table in the center, I slowly scanned the faces, searching for anyone who looked even the least bit interested in me, and especially for anyone resembling my sparing partner from yesterday. I saw no one in either category.

While looking over a thin copy of "USA Today," I picked at a plateful of almost everything offered at the buffet table, then after I'd done a good job on the plate, and still seeing no one to arouse my interest, or suspicions, I went out to the desk and checked for messages--there were none. While I was at the desk I got a detailed map of the city, located the US Embassy, which was within walking distance, and set off.

From the information I'd gotten, along with the map, our embassy was on Paseo de la Reforma, Colonia Cuauhtemoc (this was one of the hundred of districts in the city), a wide main drag that ran east to west, coming in from the east through a park, past the zoo, and into the Zona Rosa in the heart of the city. From there it swung on up to the northeast where smaller countries had their diplomatic buildings. The US Embassy, I read, was open 9-2 and 3-5. Pretty decent working hours. But I knew that those were hours open to the public--the actual working hours, for some of the staff anyway, were much longer.

I went into the imposing white building and spoke to the Marine guard. He was almost robotic, polite, impersonal, and looked to be about 16--a sure sign (another one) that I was getting old. In some cases these were kids thrown in way over their heads. Years later, in the wisdom of older age, they might very well wish to have that portion of their life redone. It is a flagrant cliché but so true: Youth is wasted on the young.

I showed him real ID, told him that I had diplomatic mail, which brought a quick second look, and was directed inside and down a hallway to the Officer of the Day. A heavy man with curly hair and a thin beard, named Harold Gross, introduced himself then went off to get my mail. When he came back with a package for me he looked as if he'd like to ask questions. He didn't. I took it, signed my name and was out of there.

While I didn't even peek at the package from Marv until I got back to my hotel, and into the privacy of my room, the weight of it alone kept me curious. Interesting to say the least. What he'd sent, among other things, was a nice little .9 mm Glock Automatic (if the State Department only knew!) a cell phone out of Star Trek, and a packet of information on the narcotics situation.

Unbeknownst to me, as I looked at the stuff from Marv, our president had signed into law the Kingpin Act which established a sanctions program targeting the big drug traffickers on a world wide basis. It even named names. I didn't see Santana on the list.

Another document was on International Narcotics Strategy (Strategy was misspelled). It was a summary of the problem in general, some statistics on harvest and what was impounded, and what would be done in the future under our ambitious plan. Reading through some 14 pages, I got the general impression that it was a question of "maybe tomorrow" with the Mexican officials. One section caught my eye: "The continuing revelations of corruption even within vetted units poses a serious challenge to Mexican law enforcement institutions, to bilateral counter-narcotics cooperation." In plain English that tells me that we're on our own in this one.

Another interesting item from the same document. "In September 1999, a Mexico City judge found sufficient evidence to issue arrest warrants for eight federal agents (Mexican) on kidnapping charges, abuse of power, and violations of the organized crime law. Four had been vetted under U. S. standards and three had been trained by the U. S. but had never been assigned to a vetted unit."

In the statistics chart I noticed that total arrests in Mexico, from 1991 to 1999, had gone from 8,762 to 10,464.

That was all State Department stuff. On his own, Marv went on to point out that this Santana, while not on the Kingpin List for whatever reason, was one ruthless character who controlled the relatively new Pacific Route of drugs from Columbia into the US. Santana had not only shot to death employees who stole or crossed him, he had killed the entire family. Here was a man who would put a bullet in your head if he didn't like your face.

And it seemed likely that this guy had Christine!

I read on and began to sweat, even in the cool room. I lit a cigarette and read through it all a second time. On the ranch itself there was very little of any use except an aerial shot from a low-flying plane. All it showed was a big house, lots of open space around it, and what looked like a race track. What it didn't show, I thought, was an electronic defense perimeter that had to be in place.

How could I possibly get into the place to even find out if she was there?

And if I did find out then what? Getting her out would take an army. But that was not my problem.

I smoked and kept looking at the material until I was so full of questions and problems, that I couldn't take any more, for now. I changed into a bathing suit and went down to the pool, but even there, doing laps and

110

pushing my body as hard as I could, my head was still going on the same subject.

Later, after a brief nap, and remembering that with all that Marv hadn't sent maps, I decided to talk a walk and find some tourist agencies--maybe I'd pick up something on the terrain and local situation..

In the first one I came to, a few blocks away, a young, darkly attractive woman was friendly, gracious and attentive to my questions about Durango, but was of little help, explaining in perfect English that the interior was no longer the *in* place for tourists--everyone these days went to the beaches. Still, after pleasant talk and broad smiles, I left the office with not only a good map of the country, but with a smattering of Mexican culture as well.

Another agency stop and then a book store added to my general knowledge, but I had the feeling I had as much as I was going to get without actually going there and nosing around.

In the late afternoon, now after siesta time, the bustling city was again in full swing, the heat and humidity still oppressive. The sidewalks crowded with shoppers and gazing tourists, traffic at daredevil pace, the noise at record level. As far as I could tell no one was following me. Sitting down at a sidewalk cafe, I had a cool lemon drink of some kind, lit up a cigarette, and settled back to watch the world go by. Some of the people passing by, I thought, could probably have told me where to buy crack, heroin, or whatever the boys in Durango were offering at the moment. But I could hardly grab one of them and ask for directions to the main supply center--not like I was looking for Office Depot. A few "ladies" passed in bright, tight-fitting attire, working the street early, giving out invitations with a look, a toothy smile, and a wiggle.

It being a bit too early for cocktails, I went back to my hotel and down to the pool again. This time I accepted the offer of a massage from a shapely woman I'd seen around the pool. She certainly didn't need any massage. Her body needed nothing. In the moments before I went off to sleep on the table, I decided to rent a car and be off on the road to Durango first thing in the morning. Though flying up to Mazatlan and making a short drive over the mountains would make for a shorter trip, I would stand out at any small airport like the proverbial sore thumb. Oh yes.

When I woke up she was gone, as were most of the party crowd around the pool. The sinking sun cast long shadows across the water and my watch told I'd slept for a little over an hour. Not that I had anything pressing to do.

At the front desk later, to check on a car rental, I first had to listen to a short, mandatory lecture on the perils of traveling alone in Mexico. Once that was taken care of I arranged to have a Land Rover waiting for me in front of the hotel at dawn. I specified a full tank of gas, two additional 5 gallon cans of gas, sleeping bag and two cans of water. I would have included food but he was giving me strange looks. He assured me--I think he was annoyed at my suggestion of a backward land-- that there were plenty of gas stations, many places to get water, and that I wasn't going to be traversing the Gobi. Nevertheless, he carefully wrote everything down, still glancing up at me, maybe to see if my madness was visible to the naked eye. Finally finished with the paper work and credit card process, he gave me a broad smile and said, "All is good, Senor. It will be waiting for you in the morning."

"Thank you"-- I looked at his name tag--"Manuel."

Seeing that I had no friends to eat with, and didn't feel like talking with strangers, I had dinner sent up to the room. Besides, I wanted to turn in early. I was lying there watching Spanish TV, with the sound off (it actually made more sense to me that way because from the picture I could be pretty sure of the dialogue), when Marv called.

"Semper Fi," he said.

"Same to you. What's up?"

"Your friend checks out." This was good to hear and I told him so. He added, "She is what she claims to be. Is she a looker?"

"None of your business, Marv. I'll be off first thing in the morning for Durango."

"You got my mail?"

"Yeah. Nice package. Want to tell me more about Santana?"

"Not on this line. Be careful and keep in touch."

"Will do. I'll check with you later on that contact."

With that we both hung up.

I had barely turned back to the television when I got another call.

Kim said, "Hello! Did you have a nice day?" After I told her about my day, briefly, her comment was: "Too bad you fell asleep during that massage. Was she very pretty?"

"I think so."

"What time are you leaving in the morning?" she asked.

Without thinking about it I quickly said, "Early. I hope to be on the road by eight."

"Good. I'll see you then. Good night."

I yelled "What!" into a dead line. Calling her back right away I was informed that Miss Durden requested no calls to her room. Damn! For a few moments I was furious. I even thought about getting dressed and going over to her hotel. The truth was though, after I thought about it, was that I felt good.

***

My wake-up call from the front desk was followed in a few minutes, as I'd requested, by a pot of coffee at the door. My body doesn't start well without that infusion of caffeine, first thing. In Korea, or anywhere in the field, even when it was brewed in a canteen cup and had that awful tinny taste, it still got the weary body started. I'd slept well, felt rested, and after a shower I was ready to get going. Of course while the coffee does give a jolt and a start, the old body won't go far without fuel. So I went downstairs for breakfast.

The view from the main floor dining room wasn't much. From what little I could see of the outdoors, this was another great day with the sun coming up in splashes of pink and orange. Much like Florida, there weren't a whole lot of bad days here, except for the occasional hurricane.

Turning reflective, I wondered why I was up so early. A few hours one way or the other wouldn't make a whole lot of difference. It wouldn't matter to Christine, because if she was there in Durango, and being held against her will--a most likely assumption in view of what we learned in Haiti--I was in no position to charge in at first light and rescue her. Or at last light. Maybe she didn't even want to be rescued. I couldn't believe that. But the sad truth was that I wasn't all that sure about where she fit into this. And I sure as hell had no idea of what I was going to do when I got to Durango.

In any case, the bottom line about my early start, was that it always seemed the proper thing to do. One starts early on an adventure into the unknown. Columbus sailed at sunrise for his little jaunt around the seas, discovering, or so they would have us believe, almost every country west of the Atlantic Ocean.

I think he did.

My hearty breakfast finished, body and mind fully awake by now, and functioning, my thoughts turned from Christine to Kim. Another unknown. There were pros and cons to her coming with me, and I had to admit, the pros had it by a good margin. For one thing, she was hardly a hothouse flower that needed my special tending and care--something I was never good at doing. She was in full bloom and seemed quite hardy to me. Time could prove me wrong, but I had the overall feeling that she would be good company, and as well, take care of herself. As far as my "mission," when the time came for me to go off and do my own thing, I

113

didn't see any problem. She could go off and do her exploring to her hearts content. And last but certainly not least, she was beautiful.

Since the vehicle was waiting as ordered, and I was feeling good after a long restful night and a full breakfast, and with Kim in mind, the day was full of promise.

Unfortunately Kim wasn't in sight when I went outside.

My vehicle was a green Land Rover. I opened the door and looked inside--four wheel drive of course, but also leather seats, sun roof, what looked like a map system screen on the dash, lots of gadgets I would never use. It seemed to have all the bells and whistles of a high end model. Stalling and looking for Kim, I opened up the back and checked over the items I'd ordered and made sure everything was properly stowed. The morning already hot and humid, I saw a lot of people pass by, but no Kim.

Finally, with no further reason to delay and assuming she wasn't going to show up, I got in and started it up, opening the windows to clear out the hot air, then closing them and putting the air conditioning on full blast.

I had barely pulled out and gotten into the traffic when a taxi cut me off, pulled over right in front of me. I jammed on the brakes and started to swear at the idiot. Then the door opened and Kim jumped out of the taxi. She was carrying a bulky, black bag. The taxi took off in a hurry.

Grinning all the while, she threw her bag in the back and jumped in the front seat next to me. Then, with an expression like a child awaiting a reprimand, she said, "Sorry, Jack. Never got my wake up call. Really had to rush."

What does one say to the apology of a gorgeous woman for being late? If he is wise he will say nothing. He will smile and be glad she made it at all. Her thick hair, damp and curly, was loose and hung down around her face and over her chest--a golden frame to the portrait. She had on a tan shirt with lots of pockets, cargo shorts, and hiking boots. I could see a lot of slim, tanned legs.

After staring at her for a long moment, I simply smiled and said nothing about her tardiness. Horns from the traffic behind me started to blare.

"I humbly offer my apology," she said. "Now you'd better get moving before we have to deal with some Mexican road rage."

Then we drove quite a way without either of us saying a word.

Though a tail would be more difficult to pick up on the busy, crowded city streets, now that we'd reached the outskirts of the city, having gone past both the shacks and elegant homes to open country, I was sure no one was following. I relaxed a bit and glanced at Kim. She had pushed the seat back and sat with her legs up against the dashboard, looking out the window.

114

"Feel like going for a drive?" I asked.

"Lovely day for one," she said with a glance at me.

"Big bag you have, lady."

She smiled. "I need lots of things.

We were quiet then for a time, rolling along in our cool cocoon, kept comfortable at max settings. Outside I knew it was hot from just looking at the parched land and seeing the waves of heat dance on the highway. Soon we were well out in the country. Knowing the Rover was a gas-guzzler, and wanting to save our own supply in the cans, I started looking for a service station before we got to the point where all we would see were cactus, scrub, Iguana and rattlers.

"You looking for a gas station?" Kim asked.

"Yeah. We're not too far out of the city yet so I'm hoping we can find one before too long. I'd like to save what gas is in the cans for an emergency."

"Sounds like a good idea. You never know what might come up in country like this."

Shortly we came down from a small mountain and into a valley that was relatively flat. Off to our right I spotted a run-down building that could be a store, and in front were what looked like two gas pumps. I hoped they were still in the gasoline business; the pumps with an "ESSO" logo went out about twenty years ago, maybe thirty. Kim said, "If you'll get us a couple of cold drinks, cold anything, I'll handle the pumps."

"Deal," I told her, opening the door and climbing out into the furnace. Turned out it was a country store overfilled with stuff, junk actually, but I did find a battered thermos chest with cold drinks. Reaching down through what was mostly water rather than ice, I pulled out two of the coldest bottles of some kind of light green liquid--the Spanish label probably meant something important as far as calories and sodium but it was Greek to me. I popped off the two tops, draining mine in two gulps, then grabbed another bottle, popped it, and went outside. It had an awful taste but it was cold.

Kim had company: two young, muscular men in bright shirts and jeans stood in front of her, close I thought, and not friendly close. Off to one side was an immaculate, old car, worthy of Classic Status in the states, one of those over-sized things with lot of chrome and shiny metal. A flag of some kind was tied to the antenna. My first glance told me these were unwanted guests coming on to Kim and I sensed it was a violence thing as much as sexual. There was a tension in the scene that sent off my alarms. They looked at me and seemed to disregard me as a threat, then turned back to her. Setting the bottles down next to the pump, I moved in close. "Problem, Kim?"

"Nothing I can't handle." Cool and calm, she gave me a half wink which I interpreted as, "I'm confident. Get ready." Whatever was happening here was something she'd either dealt with before or had been trained to handle. Another little item that added to the mystery of this woman. She seemed totally in control. The two men were talking and laughing like a couple of good old Mexican boys having fun, maybe bragging about what they could do with this beautiful woman. Kim had plans of her own and when one of them put his hand on her shoulder things turned serious in a hurry. She brought her right knee up, quick and solid, right between his legs. He doubled up, howling in pain. Before the other one could react I'd stepped in close with my leg between his, delivered a straight stiff arm into his neck, and yanked his leg out from under him. He went down like a felled tree. Kim pushed her guy backwards onto the dirt. Mine still had a bit of life in him and I put a foot on his neck to hold him in place. "Don't even think about getting up!" There didn't seem to be a language problem because he stayed put.

While this close-in stuff had never been my thing--I worked from a distance, sometimes a long distance--I had been trained a long time ago and the moves came on instinct. In any case, it was time to move on. I grabbed our bottled drinks and we climbed in the Rover and spun out of there onto the highway. For a time we drank without a word. The drink was still cold. "Nice moves back there," I told her after a few moments.

"You weren't so bad yourself."

We shared a grin. "I hope that's the last of them."

"Me too," Kim agreed.

But it wasn't.

The road was straight and flat for a time, a black ribbon cutting through the bare, brown land, off to our right a range of mountains that we would eventually have to cross, and my thoughts drifted to another time...

Marvin Millman had been Captain Millman, USMCR, my company commander. I was Corporal Sean Gardner, USMC, and we were a part of George Company, Third Battalion, Seventh Marine Regiment. He seemed poorly cast for that role in a physical sense. Unlike the stereotype, poster Marine, he was short, overweight, balding, and whatever he wore was always in a rumpled state; an unlit stub of a cigar was a permanent part of his mouth. But beyond that unimpressive appearance was a keen, perceptive mind that was able to encompass all in a glance, adjust tactics as needed, and perhaps more importantly, at least to us in the company, placed the needs and safety of his men as his first priority.

I learned later that he had been a High School Math teacher in real life, somewhere in New Jersey.

One day he walked up to me and told me he was moving me into the unpopular, unwanted and ever lonely job of company sniper--inside three months we'd lost four men who'd had the job.

There was a bounty on snipers.

He never told me why I was picked. Perhaps there was no *why*. Maybe I was the first face he saw that day. Or maybe I had the best shooting numbers in the company.

At any rate, I took up our company sniper weapon, a Winchester Springfield 30.06 with an 8 power scope, and began to learn my assigned trade. The first time out I zeroed in the rifle at 500 yards, a comfortable distance for me, and I worked at that range for a while. Gradually I worked on up to 1,000 yards and, in a few cases, got off shots at sometimes a bit further.

It was slow going at first, and since I chose to work alone (our snipers usually worked with a partner who could act as a spotter, and as a relief on the rifle, giving constant coverage on the zone), my kill numbers were low. I made all the beginners mistakes like rushing my shots, underestimating the skill of my opponent, staying too long in one spot, and setting up poorly planned hides with no escape route. It was a learning process that I somehow survived.

The captain showed a lot of patience with me and in time I was coming back to our area with much better results. Battalion would send out patrols to verify my shots and keep the area clean. The area might be clean but I was anything but. I'd come back smelly, dirty, hungry and tired. No one wanted to get near me for days.

I survived and became proficient at my job. Unlike some shooters I heard of, some becoming well known, legends in the Corps, I never kept score, never joined the contest, never made a game of the killing. To be successful at hunting, whatever the prey, the hunter needed not only the accurate shot, but great patience as well, waiting for that proper instant to make the kill. Some nights when I was in position, perhaps being in the same spot for days, waiting and watching, the captain would make his way to me and we'd talk softly for a few moments in the steamy darkness. He was never personal, only positive and reassuring. Once he told me that we all have a time to die and that mine wasn't here yet--exactly what a sniper wants to hear.

Marv was later in the Operations Division of the CIA and found himself in need of a person like me. Actually, within the contract employees, of which there were many, there were plenty to choose from already, but we

117

had a relationship he was comfortable with and could depend on and he went looking for me. At the time, I was slowly going broke trying to make a go of an air freight company in Miami. I loved the independence of the industry, the free spirit they had, and it didn't take a whole lot of cash to get started: all you really needed was a plane that flew, a customer, and a few employees to load and unload. A bit more complicated than that yes, but that was the basics. And there were the temptations to fly dope and illegal cargo--offers that boggled the mind with the money to be made. Somehow, as money poor as I was, I resisted all that and at times I wondered why.

Marv came along as a consolation prize, offering me good money to eliminate our enemies. One could debate the morality of both undertakings: transporting drugs and the killing. At the time it was a clear cut decision for helping democracy and the American way. In later years, the reflective ones when we have the wisdom of age, it was not so clear cut.

At any rate, with my acceptance of that employment, and the other life it involved, the official record of Corporal Sean Gardner would show that he was killed in action.

So long ago...

Coming back to the present I saw a few wiry, bent trees along the side of the road, the dry earth, scrub growth and the cactus, all hanging in there against the odds of nature, in the absence of life-giving water. This was not the area of tourist cameras.

Kim sat staring straight ahead.

In a moment I noticed movement on what had been the empty road behind us: a big, shiny car that looked familiar was gaining on us. "I think we have company, Kim."

She twisted around in the seat for a look. "Oh no."

"Oh yes." She kept looking back and I watched in the rear view mirror. "Well. Let's see now. While they have the speed in that chrome monster, we have four-wheel drive and traction they can only dream of. Let's try off-road."

At a point where the glistening metal beast was about three lengths behind, I switched into four-wheel drive, yanked the wheel over, and took off into the dirt, the LR digging in for purchase and spurting ahead. The chrome thing flew right on by like it was in a timed speed run, then in a cloud of burning rubber screeched to a halt, spun around and in no time at all was churning up dust behind us. I really thought the tactic would gain us more time than it did. All I could do now was hit the worst pieces of land, or maybe a steep ravine, and hope they followed the leader into a

118

place where we'd come out and they would stay. It was a simple game that required simple minds. On I drove over small mounds, holes, whatever I saw that looked ugly, scraping off whatever was trying to grow in the damned area. They were still on our tail.  As good fortune has it sometimes, I came down into a narrow valley with a stream ambling along in the middle. Driving right through the water I went up the bank on the other side, then down and across the water again, ending up the way we had come. The chunk of chrome went in, and even up the other side, but flipped over in the water on the second leg as he tried to come down the bank at speed. Simple minds.

Once we got back on the highway and alone, I went back into regular drive, lighted up and puffed away with a certain pride in my efforts. "Can I have one of those?" asked Kim. I gave her one and after a few drags she said, "Interesting tour your company runs here, Jack. Do you get many customers?"

"We take pride in our trip, mam," I told her in my best tour guide pose. "We aim to show the breathtaking,  beautiful face of Mexico in all its gory.  Make that glory."

"Breathless might be a better word. You think we can do this in one day, Jack?"

"We probably could if I pushed. But it would mean driving all night and us getting in there bushed. I figure we can pull up into the mountains a bit and catch some rest.. That way we can get into Durango fairly fresh."

She looked at me out of the corner of her eyes. "Fairly fresh? I don't know about that."

"It's all in the eyes of the beholder, Kim."

"I was never good at beholding."

# TEN

Earlier that same day a White House meeting was held in what was still known as a *basement* room, though it resembled such a place only in that it was underground--this was truly a finished basement. From the huge, oval, oak table and thick carpeting, to the vast array of electronic gear that monitored the activity of the entire world, the room, installed in the 70's and upgraded almost annually, was an awesome place to sit and talk. The meeting room itself was divided from the electronic area by a clear panel of custom made sound-resistant and bullet-resistant material.

In attendance for this general meeting, with the sub-topic for discussion of "Mexico/Drugs," were high level representatives from the military, Department of State, intelligence agencies, Attorney General's Office, and narcotics. The only female among this power group (powder group she called it in the press for its sometime shoot-from-the-hip approach to problem solving) was Captain Serena Wilson of the Coast Guard. A small woman with short, gray hair and glasses, she looked more the academic than military, but was known as a tough negotiator when it came to her annual budget battle on the hill. And now, what with the stepped up role of the USCG in the drug battle, she was even more of a presence in the political arena and more of a headache to the committee scalp hunters.

The morning session had been devoted to routine old business, some new thoughts, cost figures and projections for various programs that were pets of the president, and a smattering of situation reports from trouble areas.

With the lunch dishes cleared away, the talk had resumed in a different direction, with the thrust on new ideas or thoughts about the ever growing drug war.

Harry Weniger, Intelligence Advisor to the president, a man with a quick and intelligent mind, never at a loss for words, and never uninformed, with a calm manner on the outside (and hiding an ulcer from the press), chaired the meeting. In public appearances he always wore a poorly tied bow tie and buttoned down shirt; the attire seemed to make an already prominent adams apple stand out even more. A no smoking rule was generally observed at his meetings and he winced as a cigar was lit. "Do you have to do that, Marv?" he asked softly.

All heads turned to the offender. "Yes, I do, Harry," Marv told him, holding the cigar up and rolling it around in his fingers. "These things calm my nerves and clear my head. God knows it can only help with your bunch running the show. So far, in this drug business, we're still at zero results. Have been for a long time." Marv knew he annoyed Harry and most of the others but he really didn't care one way or the other. Now retired from the agency on a hefty pension, he was attending what he considered to be another stupid meeting as a consultant and adviser to the Director Central Intelligence Agency. His being there, as both he and the DCIA knew, was strictly for show. Due to the very nature of the matters the agency dealt with every day, their agenda, secret and sensitive, was often on a course known by only a few.

So screw them, thought Marv. State had a block on any real action toward Mexico. So what could really be accomplished here? He'd tuned out most of the dull morning session and was doing pretty much the same now. Doodling on a lined, yellow pad in front of him, writing the name "Alan" several times, circles, drawing arrows pointing to the name, his thoughts drifted off. Alan had been a good kid and good student before he jumped from the 14th floor of a New York City hotel. Drugs had destroyed their only child. He had been away a lot and he lived with the guilt of not being there for Alan. Could he have prevented the terrible tragedy? Many of his friends, parents themselves, had told him not to go there, not to go down the road of guilt because there was no end. We all did the best we could at the time, they said. No matter the upbringing, every family had such horror stories.

Oh yes he had memories. And he had a plan now to cut off the head of the snake in Mexico

Richard Cernera, from the AGs office, a forceful young man, often openly at odds with the AG herself for whom he worked, and was usually under the threat of the ax, was talking when Marv came back from his hollow place. "What we need is a plan to apprehend that guy in Mexico and bring him in. I'll prosecute him myself! I don't get it! We know who is shipping the stuff in here. Now I've got a plan..."

Remington Ball from State interrupted, shaking his head like he was correcting the misguided thinking of a young student; at one point he had been a professor at Harvard and he made sure everyone knew about it. "You just can't go off half-cocked like that, Dick. You know how delicate relations are with them. We've got things moving in the right direction now and 1 don't want to see that fall apart. Does your plan include participation and cooperation on the part of their government? Without that we can't even consider any kind of covert move."

Marv couldn't believe what he was hearing: Get the cooperation of a crooked government, who confiscates the drugs then sells them back to the dealer, to go after the dealer. Unbelievable.

"Covert, shmovert, Rem!" Cernera said sharply. "I keep hearing this diplomatic bullshit that ties our hands at every move. They're crooked. Don't you get it, Rem? From the top to the bottom they're bent. You're in a game with a crooked dealer and phony cards. This guy Santana passes out weekly bonus checks like a CEO. And some of them go to the government. How the hell are you going to get their cooperation!"

Remington kept shaking his head. "You can't do anything like that in Mexico, Dick. And besides, you're oversimplifying a very complex problem that starts in Columbia: unstable government, a military that is without direction or allegiance, rebel militia factions from the left and the right taking drug money-that country is near collapse. Mexico isn't the root of the problem. We need a massive rescue here or Columbia goes down the tube."

"Columbia is another problem, Rem. We're talking Mexico here, our neighbor. You have a better idea on that problem? On taking this guy out of the picture? If I'm not mistaken we just had one of our DEA agents tortured and murdered down there? Doesn't that tell you anything!"

"Gentlemen. Please," Harry said, raising his arms over the table. "We've been over all this before. There's no sense in going over it again. Our programs are in place and working. Let's move on."

Wade Thompson from DEA smiled inwardly; the agency had just gotten a huge appropriation to step up their operation in South America, a plan many critics, mostly in the military, feared would mean the heavy involvement of US troops in another quagmire. Vietnam was long gone but not forgotten. At the moment, Thompson was definitely ahead in the turf battle. He said, "Our new operation should cut down some of the flow, Dick."

Dick looked at him for a long moment but said nothing.

Marv took a deep pull on the Cayman Supreme--from Cuban seeds he was told and every bit as good as the ones from Cuba--and saw the frustration on Dick's face. No wonder: we were defeating ourselves in this so-called war with internal fighting for money, the lack of a unified plan, and the lack of balls to make the moves that had to be made. Now, he had read, the Coast Guard was into heavy lobbying for more money in light of the increased demands on their resources. Everyone, it seemed, had demands for more except the taxpayer.

No. This would not do, thought Marv. Someone has to make the moves to stop this shit from coming in over the border. They had to be made without the problem of diplomacy and with the use of secret programs and secret funds. He was convinced that someone was himself--and Jack Morgan. He was depending on Jack to do the job that had to be done.

122

This could be one last, grand operation for the old Marine, Sean Gardner, and for Marv. If things went as planned Santana would be out of the game. Of course there was still the problem of demand--perhaps the greater problem. But that was another program to be worked out and applied.

And while we're at it, he thought, smiling, we just may smoke out some others as well.

Yes he was using Jack, using him for a good cause, and yes, he wasn't told the whole story because there was no need for him to know, not yet. Marv told himself this and wanted to believe it was true. Still, he hated the use of that agency terminology with an old comrade like Jack. Marv knew damn well who had Christine, knew she'd been in the wrong place when a drug flight came into Haiti. And he had a good idea of where she'd been taken. It was the *why* he wasn't quite sure of and therein was the real question to be answered. There were more players in this game.

Sean Gardner. He was the best of them all. Oh sure, there may well be some young hotshot out there now who could match Sean, maybe even better him a bit. But could he be counted on for the really long one? Could anyone else handle the pressure? Make the call that had to be made and do it? These young ones were too sensitive for the real work.

Marv looked over at Thompson and saw him smiling. "You always have a new plan, Wade. And you always get more money. What is it we're spending now every year? Thirty billion? More? And you know, I don't see a helluva lot to show for all that spending. Maybe you should ask the army for border troops. Send in..."

The smile was gone when Thompson interrupted. "That's not fair, Marv. And you know it. We're planting new crops, training the local forces, strengthening the government...lots of things coming out of this."

"Not from where I sit, Wade."

A general murmur from the group, then General Watson spoke above the noise. "Never mind sending troops down there to get picked off one by one, in the damned jungle where they don't want us anyway. How about we just blockade them! Shut them down! Or are we talking about too big a chunk of their economy?" The room has quieted down some when the lean, soft-spoken. gray-haired general spoke. "What kind of a war are we in here, Wade? Seems to me it's a war in name only. How about we seal up our own border if the stuff is pouring in from Mexico? We've got the manpower. Or would that be stepping on someone else's patch? Upset our diplomatic applecart. Of course an innocent farmer might get shot now and then, but people do get killed in a war."

Dick Cernera spoke into the silence that followed. "Let's go in and get Santana."

"Don't start that again," from State. "We have no right to go into a country, our neighbor at that, and take that kind of action."

"Perhaps if you gave us some of that new money," Serena Wilson offered, "we can widen our surveillance, do more intercepting at sea, stop the stuff coming in by water."

The buzz of talk got louder and Harry stepped in. "Gentlemen. Please. This isn't getting us anywhere."

"It never does," Marv said just loud enough to be heard.

Harry glared at him. "I'll kick this around again with the president and see if we can come up with something. In the meantime nothing changes without approval from the White House. Are we all clear on that?" Some of those around the table nodded, but no one gave a verbal approval. Then the rustle of papers as notes and plans, the useless but necessary paperwork was packed up and put back into briefcases. "We'll get back together in say...three or four days," Harry announced.

*Three or four days.* Marv stayed in his chair and a smile slowly crossed his face, a look that said he knew more than Harry, and that the old need to know was still in business.

Through highly secret talks with the Director, the president knew of the plan. And it was still on.

This was the classic political football game, thought Marv: if the game was won the owner would take full credit for assembling the team and calling the right plays; if it was lost he would deny having any part in acquiring players, and of course had no part in calling any of the plays. It wasn't a complete no-lose situation, but there was a built in face-saver. And either way, the careers of some of those in command could be put on hold.

This would get done. He had been in touch with Fort Bragg. General Sadowski had assured him that the "black forces"--uniforms and equipment untraceable, Spanish speaking--would be ready to move out at a moments notice. Jack Morgan could kill from a thousand yards out if need be. Marv Millman could kill from several thousand miles.

A dangerous game.

## ELEVEN

With a glance out at the orange ball of sun hanging in the sky to our left, I estimated it must be around three in the afternoon--my watch, a bit more accurate and reliable, told me it was four-thirty. We would have lots of daylight since there was only flat country and flat water in front of the sunset.

Ours wasn't an uneasy silence, but rather a contemplative one, at least on my part. We'd been driving for a while now, light traffic, little talk between us, only the hum of the big tires and the wind as we moved along by the base of the mountains.

Kim had a large, black bag in back and I wondered what it contained. And I still had the feeling, way down, that there was more to her than I knew. She had come back clean. But if there was more, and she was working for someone, some where, wouldn't she have a perfect background in place? A history that would stand up to verification? Then I looked over at her and wondered how that could be.

Was my imagination running wild?

If she was in this as a covert operator, like myself, she would have backup somewhere. How close were they? A cell phone call away. I smiled at the idea of us both walking off alone to contact our people.

I looked at her as she casually pulled her hair back from her face with both hands, then tied it at the crown in one deft move. The high pony tail hung below her shoulders. The skin at the back of her neck was lighter in color, soft and smooth, and I thought the exposed neck made her look younger somehow, vulnerable, inviting. But it wasn't wise to go there. The one thing I couldn't do was let feelings in that direction get started. It was unprofessional and it could be dangerous to my health. That's what the book said anyway. But then so was smoking.

I said, "I think we need a break, Kim."

She looked at me and nodded. "You're right. Been a long drive. I'm thirsty."

"We'll find a shady spot and pull off."

"I might even take a nap if you can find us a cool place." Then she added with a grin, "I missed my siesta."

We pulled off into a shady grove of trees at the base of the mountains, parked, drank plenty of water, then sat in a grassy place for a smoke. After a long silence she asked, "Are you really working alone on this, Jack?"

Thinking that our thoughts had been running on a parallel course, I smiled. "I could ask you the same question."

125

"Yes. But I asked first."

"Ladies go first."

"Not this time. I yield to the gentleman." After first flicking her hair up out of the way, Kim was lying with one hand under her head, looking up into the trees as she talked.

"We're assuming a lot here, Kim: that we are a lady and a gentleman."

"Why not! I can vouch for me."

"Okay." What harm could it do? I was 99% sure that at least she wasn't working for Santana. And I liked her. In a manner of speaking, yes, I am working alone," I told her.

She drew deeply and exhaled. "In a manner of speaking! You sound like some politician, Jack. You're either alone or you're not." She grinned, not looking at me.

"I'm alone. But I can get help if I need it. That satisfy you?"

"I think it does," she said slowly. "I'm in this alone as well. And help is available if I need it. The thing is, before we get any help, which might take some time, our lives depend on each other. Right?" She went on without waiting for an answer. "And I was trying to figure out if I could depend on you in a tight spot."

"And?"

She turned to look at me then, held eye contact for a long moment. "I think I can."

"Ah. But can I depend on you?"

"That's for you to decide. If you don't know by now you never will."

There was truth in what she said and I did know. "Good. Now that we settled that we can move on." She turned to give me that look of hers out of the corner of her eyes, but didn't comment.

We didn't move anywhere for a time. She finally broke the silence. "You have any kind of a plan here, Jack? I mean just how you're going to get the girl out of there?"

"Not a clue at this point," I told her truthfully. "We'll just have to see what the situation is there and make some kind of plan when we get the lay of the land."

"Lay of the land," Kim repeated. "I like that. Sounds formidable. Do you know anything about this Santana? All I really know is that he is one bad *hombre*."

"What do you have on him?"

"Not a lot. I'll have whatever we have on the guy sent to me in Durango when we get settled. Might be a help to know something about him."

"I agree. I'll do the same." Not totally honest here, but I didn't want all my cards up.

126

"I'm going to stretch my legs," Kim said, getting up. She went over to the Land Rover for a moment, then walked off out of sight. I figured she was contacting her people on the cell phone, which was a good idea, so good that I decided to do the same.

Marv came on right away in his gruff voice. "Where the hell are you!" When I told him we were heading for Durango, he said, "Who is *we*?"

"I'm traveling with a friend."

"A friend! You mean a Mexican?"

"No, Marv. I'm with a beautiful woman."

A rather long silence. "Oh. You mean the one you had me check out?"

"The very same."

"Can you trust her? We've got a lot at stake here, Jack."

I let that one hang for a moment. "I think I can trust her. After all, she's not going in with me. She's traveling to Durango, touring. She's a travel agent, Marv. Remember?"

"Yeah. I remember."

"So what's the problem? What's bothering you?"

Silence for a moment. "Maybe because she came back too clean."

"Too clean! What the hell more do you want? You've been in this business too long, Marv. Trust me on this. My gut feeling is good on her."

"Gut feeling? You sure it isn't lower?"

"That's beneath you, Marv. So you think Santana has Christine?"

"From what I have and what I sent you, it seems likely that he does? You have any other ideas?"

"Not at the moment," I told him in all honesty.

"Watch your step with this one, Jack. This guy is bad news."

"So it would appear, Marv. Who is that contact in Durango?"

"Go to the Casablanca, big, old fashioned colonial hotel, you can't miss it. Ask for a guy named Karl Gruner. He's a part owner."

"You're kidding. Sounds like a movie plot."

"I'm not kidding. He came over after the war, had some intelligence background and we made use of him. He's been out of the action for a long time now, but from what I know he's solid. Anything else?"

"Not at the moment. I'll be in touch."

"Good. Watch your ass, Jack."

"Very little there, Marv. And it's difficult to even see my ass without throwing my back out. But I do have a nice one to look at."

A grunt. "Some things never change. Bye Jack. Let me know when you get into Durango."

When Kim came back we had more water and a smoke. The sun was dipping fast now, turning the western horizon to a pink hue, with slashes of orange, red and yellow. The coming night was like a descending curtain on the stage of the mountains.

I didn't hear the shot, sensed it, felt the wind as it passed, close, then heard the bang on metal as it hit the Land Rover. "Get down, Kim!" She was already moving to the back of the vehicle, grabbed something out of her bag, then ran in a crouch to a stand of trees about 5 yards away. I was busy rummaging in my bag for the Glock, but another close shot made me forget that idea. I followed Kim and knelt down beside in what little cover we had available.

"We have company," she said calmly, looking up into the hills. "They're on the high ground." I saw what looked like a dark, Glock automatic in her hand. Full of surprises, this woman.

"See anything?"

"Not yet," she answered calmly," turning to look at me. "We only have this between us"--she glanced down at the automatic--"so I have to ask you to decoy."

"No problem." Without another word I took off at full speed for a group of rocks to our left. These shots I heard. I didn't see the puffs of dirt around me, and nothing hit. I dropped down behind the biggest rock, gasping for breath. I heard three quick shots from where I'd left Kim. Then a long quiet. While these things seemed a long time, I knew it was only a matter of minutes for an ambush and a killing--if it worked. If it didn't work, it could be forever. After what seemed like enough time for something to happen, anything, I stuck my head up and looked around, mostly uphill. I didn't see or hear anything. Taking a chance, I ran back to our original position behind the trees. No shots and Kim wasn't there. Could they have grabbed her? Not enough time. More likely, if she was as good as she seemed to be, she would have circled off to our right and gone up after the shooter, or shooters.

The moments of nothing stretched out. Where the hell was she? I leaned against the tree, watched a lizard of some kind scamper up to my feet, red tongue darting in and out before it left, finding me uninteresting, smoked, and waited. What else could I do? Being a shooter myself I felt useless and out of it. With my trusty "friend" I could be in this game. I wasn't happy at all with a woman, beautiful as she was, doing my work.

Where the hell was she?

Then I heard two shots that, from the sound, had to be Kim's Glock. There is a difference to the trained ear.

128

Three cigarettes later Kim came scrambling down the hill, dust-covered, strands of hair in her face, weapon hanging at her side. "What happened?" I asked.

"I got one, young, dark guy, no weapon left behind, and no casings. The other one got away. I think there were only two of them." She plopped down beside me and I gave her a smoke.

"Any point in my looking over his site?"

"I don't think so. He didn't set up well and wasn't there long. I think it was a quick shoot and run, more to scare off than kill."

"It wasn't one of the guys from the gas station?"

"No." With a smile, she added, "Whoever he was he had expensive boots."

"That helps." She didn't say anything and we were quiet then for a time. Where did a travel agent get this kind of savvy? She had the training and the knowledge to react to the threat, was familiar with the terminology, and showed the poise of a professional. As if this wasn't enough to wonder about, there was also the question of *who* and *why*. As well, I began to realize that this might be something bigger and more involved than I'd thought at first. I'd have to be a lot more alert, sharper, smarter than I'd been thus far. I'd been taking this far too lightly. That attitude had to change.

Kim had ejected the clip, slide back, which meant the weapon was clear, and was wiping it down with a handkerchief. It *was* a Glock. Whoever trained this woman had done one helluva job. As if reading my mind, Kim said, "I did well?"

We were holding eye contact and I said, "Yes. You certainly did rather well. In fact you were fantastic." I was still asking myself: *Who are you?*

"Then you would have me as...your buddy? Is that what you say?"

"That's what we say. And my answer would be yes. In the blink of an eye."

She showed a big smile. "In the blink of an eye. That *is* fast. I'm flattered. I don't think I've ever been a buddy before."

"Welcome to a select, very small group," I told her. We smoked and then I asked if she was hungry. "The hotel fixed some kind of lunch for me."

She made a face at that, like a kid seeing tuna salad that wanted peanut butter and jelly. "Probably dull. Let's move on and get some real Mexican food to eat."

"Move on where?"

"Stop at the first house we see."

"Just walk into some strangers house and ask for supper? Is that what you did here before?"

"I've never been here before."

"Wonderful. Incredible."

With a shrug she said, "Just stop, Jack, at the first house that isn't falling down, the first place that looks like they can feed us. I'll do the rest. Trust me."

"Trust has nothing to do with hunger."

"In this case it does."

And she was right.

I don't know what she said to the people in a modest, stucco house, fenced, with goats in the back yard--while I sat in the Land Rover--but in a few moments she signaled for me to join her.

***

As late as it was, the sky still had a dim glow from the setting sun, now out of sight to the west, bringing dawn to some other part of the world. We were back on the road with a full stomach and pleasant memories of a generous family of six in a small house, but with a large measure of friendship and hospitality.

Kim sat with her feet up on the dashboard, boots off. Patting her stomach, she said, "That Chili was good."

"It sure was. Nice people. I won't ask what you told them."

Kim looked at me and smiled. "I told them we were lost and hadn't eaten in two days."

"You didn't!"

She kept looking at me with that big smile without a comment. I let it go and changed the subject. "I'm looking for a spot to pull off for the night. You can sleep in here if you want; lots of bugs and things around."

Shortly I found what seemed like a good place, pulled off and parked. I got out a sleeping bag, found a flat spot without rocks and settled in for the night. The air had cooled quickly and the lightweight, summer bag was just right. Looking over at Kim, I saw that she was still sitting in the same position with her feet up, staring into space. Maybe she had a lot on her mind and unlike me couldn't lock it up for the night. I lay there smoking a last cigarette, then crushed it out and turned over--I'd be asleep in moments, or so I thought. I was in that period when the conscious faded away, an instant from going into the deep unknown, when I was jolted back to reality. The zipper went down and Kim crawled into the bag. It didn't take more than a second or two to realize that she was naked.

She lay with her back to me and I put one arm around her waist; I could feel her trembling. She spoke softly. "I'm not only that confident, cool

130

and collected woman you see on the outside, Jack. Inside there is a fragile woman who needs love and understanding." I waited out her long pause. "I can do my job. But I've never gotten used to taking a life as I did today. Sometimes I wonder if there is something missing inside me. And I wonder too how long I can go on doing my job. You know what I mean?"

Welcome to the club, I thought. "Yes. I know, Kim."

"I wanted to prove something to myself..."

"You don't have to prove anything to me. Or to anyone."

"You seemed strong and directed, confident in yourself, and I wanted you to see me as a capable woman who could handle anything. I think I liked you from the first moment we spoke. Do you think I'm attractive, Jack?"

"Yes."

"More than that?"

"Much more. But I don't think you need me to tell you that you're beautiful."

"You're wrong there, Jack." She backed up into me, nestling along my body, then laughed, her mood lighter. "As well as strong, directed, and confident, you know the right words to say, Jack."

"Sometimes."

A long silence, then, "Hold me, Jack. Just hold me."

I held her, feeling the soft curves of her body, the whole presence of her a part of me, wanting her, then she was soon asleep. She had aroused not only the physical but had opened all the memories I'd locked away, awakened the demons, the fear, the loneliness.

Sleep finally came. And then the dream: *I climbed aboard the bus with my small case in the early, bitter cold night; not quite enough money for the ticket but the driver waved me on. I was six years old and I had run away. Curling up on the seat, I pulled my coat around me and tried to sleep. The ride from the boarding home to our house was a long eight hours. I saw the snow flakes sticking to the window. I slept a little. Then the driver called me to say this was my stop. My case was small but heavy and I struggled off the bus into the dim light of the terminal. The walk to our house took a long time, dragging my case in the snow. No one was on the streets at that hour. Finally I came to our house and stood on the sidewalk. Looking at the old, wooden house I was filled with the joyous memories of family, food, lights, presents, the smell of a turkey cooking, the warmth of people I knew and loved. I let go of the bag and went up to the door. It was open. I ran in filled with the excitement of a boy coming home. The house was empty.*

Kim was in my face shaking me, kissing me through the hair hanging on her face. "Jack! Wake up! You were screaming. Are you okay?"

I wasn't okay for a moment, shaking and chilled with the memory, the dream so vivid. I pushed her hair back then took her face in my hands and kissed her on the lips, gently. I kissed her eyes, her nose, and her neck. Holding her in my arms I felt as if there were nothing else in the world but the two of us. And for a time there wasn't.

# TWELVE

Late afternoon in Paris.

"Madam," Paul said, trying to be patient with a good customer, "You are booked for a cruise tour. What that means is land and sea. Yes, this is something relatively new."

Paul Girard, co-owner of the travel agency, had reluctantly taken over the call when no one else in the office could satisfy the woman. He continued, "You will fly to Venice where you will see the famous Piazza San Marco, and other highlights on a walking tour. The next day you will ride in our motorcoach--which is quite comfortable I might add--to Florence where your tour features the imposing Duomo, the Piazza Signoria, and the Santa Croce Church, where Michelangelo and Galileo are buried. Then it is on to Civitavecchia, the port for Rome, where you will board the ship."

He listened for a moment, then, "No. Rome is not on the Tyrrhenian Sea. It is some twenty miles inland, Madam. However, you will be able to visit the beautiful city from there. No. Your ship is not an ocean liner, Madam. A Clipper ship that can go in shallow water to the smaller ports. Yes, it has sails. Not like the pirate ships, Madam. Your cabin is quite comfortable with all the amenities. Yes. There will be younger men aboard." Finally, with the customer satisfied, at least for the moment, he told her goodbye and hung up the phone.

He sighed and sat back in his chair. This is one of the many problems, he mused, of running a dual operation. Most of his tiring day had been spent on the phone with "regular" business.

Unfortunately, in one way, Grand Europe Travel had caught on. From an austere, small room over a book store, operated by the two people who "owned" the business, it had grown to a rather grand suite of rooms over a bank, with six employees. The business was now turning a nice profit.

What very few people knew was that the business was a front operation for Interpol.

Paul's wife called then, wanting to know what time he'd be home--her parents were coming for dinner, a special occasion, for her. He gave her an approximate time and quickly got her off the phone. He needed time to think.

Their well placed informant in Washington, DC--a woman highly paid by the bureau--was the top advisor to the senior senator from Delaware. On a European vacation some years ago, the woman had gotten herself into a compromising position, literally, that was set up and recorded by persons who sent it on to Interpol--for a fee. From then on she was most cooperative with the bureau.

Her background check on the American, Jack Morgan, had turned up nothing out of the ordinary, and since Kim's request had indicated a strong feeling that the man was something more than met the eye, she was checking further. It could be nothing, thought Paul, these were complex matters and he wasn't expecting any quick results. Nevertheless, for Kim's sake, he wanted to stay in the office and wait for the final results.

He lit a Silk Cut--he preferred English cigarettes--and stared out the window to the busy street below. The phone was quiet, thank God. And just suppose the American was something other than what he claimed...an intelligence operative for example? Suppose this American had operated in Europe? Was he then obligated to follow that course? Maybe implicate him in other Interpol cases? He thought not. Enough is enough. Such an imagination.

They were now in pursuit of the man known as Luis Santana. He had used other names in his visits to Europe, names known to them, and in fact had barely escaped the last attempt to nab him in Spain. The man, now a prosperous drug dealer with important connections in Mexico, had been nothing more than a common terrorist in Europe.

Paul's partner (and fellow agent) in this business venture, told a different story as a part of her cover. But the truth was that Santana was behind the bombing that killed her vacationing parents in Brussels. No wonder she had become obsessed with him. The question in Paul's mind, one of the many, was whether she would settle for simply finding the man and keeping a watch on him. There was little question about his real identity, and since Mexico had ignored all requests to even consider extradition, Interpol now wanted to track his movements, hoping to catch him if he visited Europe.

While she was no longer sanctioned for such operations, early on she had been trained as a sharpshooter, and there was nothing stopping her from taking out Santana. Nothing that is except present Interpol policy which now forbid such actions. Now, he thought sadly, Interpol had become an investigative and intelligence gathering organization, less dependent on humans and their product--and, of course, their failings-- sophisticated and technical, so totally civilized in a world turning less so. He had always felt that it was the human element in the organization that gave it breath and feeling, gave it a life and character of its own. The world is changing around you Paul, he mused. You must keep up or you will be lost.

He chain-smoked and waited for another call.

***

Late morning in Mexico.

Coming down out of the mountains and turning onto Highway 45 that led to Durango, the land changed from barren and rocky to a fertile valley of cattle and crops. A place of great contrast, I thought: extensive forests, picturesque deserts, lush plains, and of course the special land by the sea. It was easy to see how such diversity here, coupled with a great climate, and a cheap labor pool, had drawn the film industry.

I don't know what I was expecting in this city that was half way between El Paso and Mexico City. But it certainly wasn't the wide and paved streets laid out in a perfect grid, nor the spacious parks that dotted the area.

"I'm impressed," Kim said. "Nice little town. Do we have a place to stay?"

Aside from a "good morning," these were the only words out of her since we got up and on our way. It wasn't a tense quiet between us--on my part anyway, and from her looks and a soft smile for me I don't think on her part either--more reflective, wondering about our relationship, and about what Durango held for us. Then as well, I wondered why she had come to Durango in the first place. It might well be a nice little town with an interesting past as a movie center, but as a big time tourist attraction for Europeans? I didn't think so. Cabo San Lucas over on the Baja Peninsula maybe. But Durango? So, while on the one hand I had the strong feeling that she was other than what she presented, and felt that I should find out about her, on the other hand I wondered if it really mattered. She wasn't on their side so she had to be on mine, somewhere on mine.

I said, "I don't know about a place to stay. But I do have a contact here and he does own a piece of a hotel. That's a start."

"A good start, Jack. What's the name of this place?"

"Casablanca."

She gave me a full thirty second look. "You're kidding?"

"Why would I be kidding? That's the name of the place."

"And your friend is named Rick?"

"I take it you've seen the movie?"

Big smile. "One of my favorites."

"Too bad. My contact is named Karl."

With a shrug she said, "maybe they'll have a nice white piano."

Having spotted our destination I let that one go and pulled in to park. It was, at first look, the Sans Souci (now in Spanish motif) transported from

135

Port-au-Prince to Mexico. For no good reason, I took that as a good omen. There was something to be said for ambiance. Wasn't there?

I was filling out the card for adjoining rooms when Kim said, "the locks are probably old anyway." When I looked at her, she added, "between the rooms."

"Probably." I left a message for Karl.

Kim stood beside me at the counter. "I don't know about you. But before I do anything else I'm going to soak in a long, hot bath and wash my hair."

"Sounds good. Maybe I'll join you." She gave me a roll of the eyes without comment, then went off to her room. I stood there finishing a cigarette, hoping I'd hear from Karl soon, because there wasn't much point in going anywhere until I spoke with him. Whatever he could tell me about Santana and the ranch was a plus, a start anyway. With Kim out of the way for a while soaking, I figured I'd take a ride out and look at the place, maybe get a feel for what I was up against. When I thought about it I found it odd that I wasn't getting more pressure on this. Maybe Marv was keeping the senator off my back, and if he was successful in doing that, fine--good for Marv. It would take some doing. The small men who had made it to any small form of power thought they were suddenly big, magically changed to some other higher form of human. The only urgency I felt was my own doing. The way I saw it the sooner we found Christine the better: she wasn't spending her time at some fancy resort with gourmet meals, spa treatments, and fascinating company. I found it a lot easier not to go there, not to think about what she might be going through. If I went there I'd lose the clear head I needed to make this work.

There would be a time for that, for a moment of revenge. A time for justice, Morgan's Way.

When I was on my way back into the hotel with an armful of stuff from the Land Rover, I found him waiting for me.

"Hello," he said, putting out a hand. "I'm Karl Gruner."

I looked him over as I shook the hand. "Jack Morgan." A short, sturdy man with a round, pink face and shaved head, alert, questioning eyes, he wore faded, wrinkled khakis and bush shirt. Two cigars poked out of the shirt pocket.

With a broad smile he said, "I can't even remember the last time I got a phone call from Washington. Though I haven't the faintest idea of why. Must be important. You must be important. So, what is it I'm to help you with, Mr. Morgan? What could possibly interest them here in Durango?"

"I need some information."

"What kind of information?" he asked with a curious look.

136

"I need to know about a man named Santana."

He held eye contact for a long moment, then gave a nod of understanding. "I see. Perhaps we had better go to my office." He led me down a hallway and into a small room that could be opened onto a tile patio. The room looked comfortable, more like a den than an office, with a small, carved wooden desk, leather high-backed chair, bookcase along one wall. He opened the doors to the patio, stepped out and waved a hand to a canvas chair. Around the patio was an adobe wall, solid on one side, lattice on the other two sides so that a gentle, warm breeze moved across the space.

I sat and pulled out a cigarette. "You don't mind?"

"Not at all. Would you join me in a Monte Cristo?" he said, pulling a cigar up out of the shirt pocket. "Cuban."

"Maybe later." I lit up and pulled deeply, drawing in the smoke then letting it drift out. I felt a bit tired suddenly, and at the same time feeling fearful for Christine, wanting to get this over with as quickly as possible. Karl had been watching me, I saw, his eyes studying me as he went through the routine of carefully snipping off the end of the cigar, then firing it up. There was a ritual to it all that I liked, though I didn't smoke many cigars myself. "So, tell me about Santana."

He puffed and shrugged, a thin smile forming. "Where does one start with a man like that?"

"At the beginning. No. Let me make it easier for you, Karl." I told him all about Chistine and what I had so far and where I hoped to go from here.

The only word he said for a long time was, "well." Then after another pause, "if this man has the girl, I fear for her, Jack. Santana is a brutal, ruthless man who rules this part of the country, a man who kills for the pleasure of seeing people die. So, you are here to find out if the girl is here?"

"Yes. For a start anyway."

"For a start," he repeated, nodding. He blew a cloud of smoke in the air. "Even that will not be easy. The man has a ranch that is a fortress. You could never get near the place. He is known here and he is powerful. Let me ask you, aside from the woman--she is quite beautiful by the way--does anyone else know you are here?"

"Oh. You saw Kim?"

"Kim? That is her name?"

"Kimberly actually."

He puffed, then smiled broadly. "I haven't reached the age--and I hope I never do reach such an age--where I stop looking at a woman like that one. She is not one to be missed. Is she a part of your team?"

"Team? No. I only met her in Miami on my way here."

He nodded thoughtfully. "And what do you know about her?"

"Not much when you come right down to it. But I trust her."

"And what was her purpose in visiting Mexico?"

"She runs a travel agency."

"Ah.. That would be a satisfactory reason for her travel--a perfect one. I suppose you have checked her out at home. In Washington."

"Yes. She came back clean. I can understand you being suspicious. I am too. But what's the worst she could be? An intelligence rival?"

"Possibly. But I must agree with you. Whoever she is, she most certainly is not with the drug people. She might well have her own objective here, which is fine as long as it does not interfere with your work."

"Whatever. I trust her. Why do ask about her?"

"For the same reason I would ask about anyone coming here--except you. On the surface things may look peaceful and calm here in Durango. And in a way that is true. But we all live under the power of that man Santana. He has the police on his side. He has everyone on his side, probably right up to the president." He puffed on the cigar and shrugged. "Perhaps not that high up. But very close. Aside from me, you will find little help here."

"Of course. I understand. How far is this ranch?"

"A little over two kilometers out of the city. I have never seen it. From what I have heard you would not get within--he paused to make the calculation--a thousand yards of the house."

"That part of it is for another time. At the moment my concern is to find out if he has the girl. Any ideas on how to do that?"

Karl reached out to the ash tray on the table between us, carefully flicked off the half inch of ash that had formed, then slowly turned to me. "There might be a way." I waited out the silence for his thoughts to form words. "It means asking a lot of questions. That in itself is dangerous. But that is the only way we will learn these things. If I'm not mistaken, one of my girls here has a sister, cousin, some kind of relative, who cooks at the ranch."

After all these years he still spoke with the hint of an accent. "Will she help?" I asked.

"I don't know. But we can try. *We're* certainly not going to get close enough to find out anything."

138

"I think you're right about that."

"In addition, I have lots of friends in this town. I'll ask around, discreetly of course."

"Of course. You'd better be damned discreet. We're not putting these people in any danger are we? By talking to them?"

"It is a chance we must take."

"And what about yourself?"

"Me? Who cares about the idle questions of an old man?"

Wondering who might care, and hoping he knew what he was doing, I put out my smoke and got up to leave.

He waived an arm in the air and said, "Sit for a moment. I know you are anxious about this. But there is really nothing you can do at this point, Jack. Before you do anything, let me ask around. You will learn nothing by standing at the fence of the ranch and looking. No?"

"I guess you're right, Karl."

"Besides," he said with a smile, "we do an excellent lunch here which you must try. Then a bit of siesta. After that, we will get together with your friend Kim and talk again. How does that sound?"

"Sounds good."

"I am curious to meet your friend. Now I must be going. Would you like lunch here or in the hotel?"

"Here would be fine (without Kim it didn't matter). And thanks, Karl. I'll see you later."

It *was* later when I woke up, disorientated--with good reason I suppose in view of the last few days--looking around the room and searching for some base for all of this.

Lunch had been a large salad with strips of marinated beef in it that were grilled, black on the outside and pink in the center, and freshly baked rolls. I passed on soup or vegetables but added a Margarita. All told, a memorable event. And since I did find myself feeling a bit guilty about doing nothing as far as Christine--even though I rationalized that there was really nothing I *could* do at the moment--I had a second Margarita. A siesta had seemed like not only the logical conclusion, but the inevitable one.

Lying there, I had the unshakable feeling that something was wrong. I got up quickly then, splashed some water on my face and knocked on the connecting door to Kim's room. No answer. It was now 3.30 in the afternoon. Was she up and gone already? To where?

In the lobby I asked about both Kim and Karl. No one had seen Karl but Kim was out front in the parking area. I spoke to her standing beside the

Land Rover. "Hi Kim. What have you been up to?" A light and casual opening that hid my concerns and bad feelings.

"Well. Hello, Jack. You finally wake up? I knocked and knocked at your door. You must have been in some deep sleep."

"Yeah." I let that go and went on to tell her about my talk with Karl, about him being my contact here, and his plans to ask around about the ranch and Christine.

"I was out there," she said. "To the ranch. Not much to see from the road."

"You were out there already!" She didn't say anything. "Why would you go there?"

"Because I'm interested, Jack. And because I'm a part of this now."

"I don't see that, Kim. The last I heard you were a touring travel agent."

She shrugged me off. "It's a woman thing, Jack. Come on. Jump in. I'll take you out for a look see. I know you have to see the place."

We drove out there and she was right about nothing to see from the road. In fact the two goons who came out of a small guard house beside the road weren't about to let us linger to see anything. Beyond them, way off in the distance I could barely make out a white building. Going out there was frustrating and a total waste of time.

We didn't talk on the drive back to the hotel.

I went on in ahead of her and asked at the desk about Karl. No one had seen him. "Was that unusual?" I asked. "Is he always around?" The clerk told me that Karl--who owned the place, the clerk was careful to say--was always here to see that things went smoothly. Did I have a complaint? No.

My information told me that he was a co-owner. The government a silent partner?

I brought Kim up to speed. She said, "I wouldn't get upset just yet, Jack. You saw him a few hours ago. If he's out nosing around it takes time."

"You're probably right."

"You're getting spooky in your old age, Jack," Kim said with a smile. "Let's go for a swim before drinks and dinner. You need to unwind."

We went up to our rooms and changed, then met at the pool. She took longer than I but I'm not sure why since she had less body to cover. And she did it so well. Kim not only looked great in a two piece bathing thing that only the very young can wear comfortably--or more likely the only ones who should wear such things--but as well she swam like a fish, beating me easily on laps. God I felt old, gasping for breath and admiring her as we clung to the side of the pool. She said, "You're still worried about Karl?"

"Yes there is that. I'm also worrying about getting old."

140

"You've got a ways to go, Jack. Thanks for letting me win."

"What makes you think I *let* you?"

We got out of the water and dried off, ordered drinks, I had a smoke. In a few moments she said, "If Christine is in there, how do you plan to get her out? There's an army surrounding the place and you would need an army to get in the house." Even though Paul Girard, in his last phone call, had told her that nothing irregular had turned up on the check on Jack Morgan, she still felt she was right about him: he had to work for some government agency. And what if he did? She didn't see how it made any difference one way or the other. If he didn't take Santana out she would. That was the simple fact.

"I know. Did you notice any hills around the property?"

"I think there are some in the back. But they're far away from the house--too far for a shot if that's what you had in mind." She watched to see his reaction.

"Something to keep in mind and pass on the the unlucky ones who have that job."

*Well, that seems to rule out the military or him being a shooter.* "Whoever is going to do it will need equipment," she offered.

"I'm sure they can get anything they need."

"They? Aren't you going to stick around for the finale?"

She was probing and I didn't want to give her anything about my part in this. Of course that was partly because I didn't know at that point. "If you remember," I said with a smile to keep it light, "my job was to find Christine. Nothing more. I've done that and I'm not here to do a Rambo."

"Rambo?" she said, frowning.

"Never mind. If they send a team in here to take that ranch so be it. Has nothing to do with me."

"But you can be a big help to them in such a plan."

"Maybe you're right about that, Kim. Maybe I'll keep an eye on the place until a decision is made along those lines. Good point."

"Thank you. And I have a sneaking suspicion that, whether you admit it or not, you want to be here for the end. Am I right?"

"You could be."

She looked at me for a moment. Then she put an arm around my shoulder, moved in close and gave me a slow kiss. "It's going to work out, Jack. Karl's got contacts. He has to come up with something. When we find out more we can help set this thing up."

Smiling, I said, "*We* can set this thing up? Since when is a travel agent into planning operations?"

141

"My major was in travel. My secondary was operations. Now I think we should eat."

After dinner there was still no word from Karl. No one had seen him and I knew that if he was around he would surely find me. Though dinner was great, the company beautiful, the evening lovely, I couldn't shake the feelings that put me in a troubled mood. Kim didn't say much and I think she understood. Anyway, we went our separate ways at an early hour. I needed to talk to Marv.

He'd evidently had a nice dinner, maybe a few brandies and a good cigar, because he came on in a mood that I could only call flippant for Marv. "Where are you, kiddo?"

*Kiddo?* "I'm in Durango. At the Casablanca."

"Good. You find Gruner?"

"Yeah."

"He's supposed to be good. Has he been of any help?"

"Not yet but he's out working for us. I haven't heard from him in a while."

"What does that mean?"

"It means he went out to ask around about the ranch and Santana and I haven't seen or heard from him since lunch."

"So you don't know for sure if Christine is there?"

"No. Circumstantial, as they say, Marv. It seems a good assumption based on what we got in Haiti. I'm not sure we're going to get any more here. We can't get near the place to find out anything."

Silence. Then, "Let me see if I can get a bird over the place in the morning. I'll try to set it up for a regular pass. Maybe we'll get lucky. And I'll have someone go over whatever old stuff we have."

Didn't sound too promising to me. How the hell is a satellite photo going to tell me if Christine is being held at the ranch? Not wanting to dampen his enthusiasm I said, "It's a thought, Marv."

"You might be surprised to see what we get from those pictures, Jack. Anyway, we'll check it out. Anything you need?"

"Nothing at the moment." Then I remembered. "Yes. There is one thing, Marv. I know you told me that Kim came up clean. That's fine. But I still have this feeling about her. Do another check--a deep one. I think you're going to find something if you go deep enough."

"Okay. You got it. Anything else?"

There was a feeling I'd had, stronger the last few days, of an undertow, a riptide we called it in Florida, that was pulling me away from the beach, away from the safe and secure harbor that was me getting out of this and going home. Nothing tangible. Nothing that was said by Marv. But I

142

couldn't escape the feeling of being hooked on one of Marv's ingenious lures, snagged, no longer really on my own, for the moment running free, yet knowing that I could be reeled in whenever the fisherman wanted me in his bag.

And maybe my imagination was out of control.

"No. That's it." As soon as we shut down our conversation my thoughts turned to Kim. She was moments away. As much as I wanted her in a physical way, to feel the softness of her body and hold her tight against me, I was too up tight mentally. This was something new and I didn't know how to handle it. I let the thing bounce around in my head for a few moments then tried to shut it down and find sleep. It was a long time in coming.

***

The only thing that brought me out of the deep sleep I'd fallen into, after lying awake for a long time in the pre-dawn hours, was Kim banging on the door. It had been 3.20, then 4.30 by the digital clock as I glanced at the time, certain that I had never been asleep at all. But we do sleep. We do shut down. I had slept but it had not been restful. It had been the sleep of the troubled--the most common of all.

To her banging on the connecting door I said, "Do you have the password?"

After a brief pause, "Santana. Now get out of bed and let's get going!"

"Good girl. I didn't know the password. You made that up?" For a few moments the body remained sluggish, as was the habit of late, but I did get the brain moving along in first gear. After two cups of coffee it usually hummed right along at near top speed. "How about coffee! Would you order some?"

"Jack," she said through the door, as if addressing a wayward child, or as in my case, a wayward adult, "This is not Miami. This is Durango. Get up and I'll meet you downstairs for coffee."

"Durango doesn't have room service?"

"Maybe they do. But I want you up and out of there."

"Okay."

The brain was in gear—a lower one. What it told me was that I had a good thing going here in Kim, and that I had a not-so-good thing with Christine. The answer seemed obvious. First of all verify that the girl was here. With that accomplished my agreement was fulfilled and my obligation was ended—on a profitable note. That is always the best way. Then, with a pocketfull of money, go somewhere with Kim—providing

143

she would go of course, always a huge proviso—that was expensive, exotic (erotic?), and totally decadent.

Dream on.

Reality told me there might well be a totally different scenario.

I was still wondering about the reality of it all over breakfast with Kim— I had a huge bowl of fruit (to ease the guilt of what followed) and a delicious cheese omelet. I asked her to drive me out to the ranch and leave me there. "For the day?"she said. "You're going to sit out there alone all day?"

"Unless you want to keep me company."

She was finishing some fruit after a bowl of dry cereal. No wonder she had that great figure. "All day? I think I'll pass. Not much by way of shopping here but I can get some sun."

We drove out later, skirting the perimeter of the ranch property, moving around to some foot hills toward the back where I found a spot under a rock ledge, a little ways up from the base to give me the advantage of some height. It was out of the hot sun and I planned to hole up with a can of water, a pack of smokes, and watch that place all day if necessary. I had a powerful set of binoculars. The thought of Marv coming up with anything on the bird passes was nice, but not something I really put much faith in.

I told Kim to come back for me whenever she felt it. Nothing else mattered now except Christine, not food, not anything, the job was to find out if she was here no matter what. I was worried about Karl. No one had seen or heard from him since yesterday afternoon. Not a good sign here in a place like Durango. I mean, where the hell could he go?

Kim stood there looking at me as if I were some alien being.

"What?" I asked.

"You're going to sit here all by yourself all day long and look at that ranch?"

"Why not? Don't we need info for the troops?"

"Yes. Like this? Don't you find that a bit odd? A bit lonely? Most people I know couldn't sit in one place alone for hours!"

"It's an acquired talent, Kim. Doesn't bother me a bit. I'm used to watching for a long time."

"Okay," she said. "If that's what you want to do. You hope to see Christine and Santana?"

"I'd settle for Christine. Santana isn't my problem."

She finally left, still shaking her head, and I settled in to watch.

The day got hotter.

144

Time was meaningless, endless, a boring space where memories and thoughts rushed in to fill the void. I let the other times, some of them better times, come in to my mind and then pass by slowly, only so that I could see them once again, but not to stay. The past is history. Even the good is gone. I was there and I went away.

Hannah lingered for a time. Now I was searching for her daughter. And when I let myself go down that path I found a lot of mystery, questions, not about Hannah as much as about her husband. Something nagged at me about him.

I came back to my scan of the vast ranch property, moving the glasses in a slow pan from left to right. Nothing out of the ordinary day down there.

The memories.

*In those days I simply followed orders. The rationale, political ramifications, or even the morality of what I was doing didn't enter into the picture. The fact of the matter was that General Benitez was to be taken out. I didn't know then, and even if I did it wouldn't matter, that the General was democratic, for the people, and the best thing to come along since George Washington paddled across the river. He was a good guy in a white hat. So what! The powers that be felt that our interests were best served by keeping the president in office. No matter that he was communist, or whatever. Sonofabitch that he might be, he was our SOB.*

*The one thing I didn't have in those days was a political position.*

*I was flown into Costa Rica and then traveled overland into Guatemala. It was one hell of a trek across the border, between the heat and bugs and the group tracking us. But I found his camp without too much trouble and settled in to watch. For a sniper patience is not only a virtue, it's a necessity, a pre-requisite to success.*

*I watched the site, and especially the general's tent, for two days. A lot of men went in and out, but I never had him in a clear shot for enough time. Towards the end of the first day, when I was running out of patience, what with the damn heat, bugs, and my water supply already exhausted, I considered a shot through the tent when he went out to relieve himself on the backside, out of my vision.*

*But I didn't like that kind of a shot, a cheap shot we called it. That was like shooting with a blindfold on. A true shooter wants to see the end, wants to connect with a target, whatever it is.*

*This operation, my operation, was designed to be a quick in and a quick out. It was becoming long and tiresome.*

*Then in the late afternoon on the second day the general came out of his tent and gave me a good shot. It was almost perfect. The setting sun was behind me and even if I showed a muzzle flash they wouldn't see it, what* with the glare in their eyes. I drew in a long breath, then exhaled ever so slowly, letting my body relax to the point that squeezing the trigger was a natural part of the flow. I saw his head explode.

He was done and it was time to shag ass out of there.

My pickup area, in what was called a friendly zone, and which looked innocent enough in the photos, was across a rope bridge that spanned a deep ravine. There should be no problem, they said, the bridge was safe and indestructible.

Where do these people come from? These desk people with so much wisdom.

When I got to the bridge I found the supporting lines had either disintegrated, which was highly unlikely, or were deliberately cut. In either case the damn thing was hanging down into the rocky chasm and there was no way for me to get across to the rendezvous.

Morgan had a problem.

While I was working on that, without a whole lot of options, and wondering if I had been intentionally screwed--set up is the common term--the chasing guerrillas caught up with me...

Inside of 24 hours Marv sent a team in to get me out. Nothing was said one way or the other, but I have wondered to this day, based on nothing more than gut feeling, and the fact that some of the brass seemed surprised to see me come back, if Marv didn't go against the operational plan in getting me out.

One day I must ask him.

Memories.

Viewing the property with a little elevation, I was surprised at the size of the ranch, most of which I couldn't see from the road or from anywhere around the perimeter. Behind the house, which was a huge Dallas-type structure (in the TV show) with columns in front, gaudy, the whole bit, was a huge swimming pool. Further behind that area was a line of flat buildings stretching out from the main house like wings. In the middle of this was a race track. Behind those stables, or whatever they were, on one side was a heliport. And further still was a landing strip. This man had it all.

Two roving patrols in what looked like top of the line Mercedes Wagons were in a continuous circle around the entire property.

Bored, I watched and smoked.

I smiled at the thought of Claire and Harry. She loved that dog perhaps as much as I did. As big and intimidating as he might be to encounter, Harry like most Labs, was like an open, loving child, wanting only to be where you were, fed and walked a couple of times a day, and unable to

146

hurt a fly. He was the world's worst watch dog, probably prone to licking the intruder. Early on when I took him out walking I expected to see some basic traits of the hunter, a seeking instinct of the retriever, but he moved right past ducks without a pause and showed no sign of hostility--to anything.

***

For Washington, D.C. in the early days of December when it was of course cold, but sometimes at least bright and sunny, the weather was miserable: unseasonably cold, freezing rain, and on top of that dark and dreary. This was a day the elements had combined to bring out the worst in the public servants who toiled in the nation's capitol--of those who had a worst to bring out. And a good percentage did have a dark side, though they didn't have it when they came to this place of power. Perhaps the power, even the nearness of it, brought a certain darkness into the personality and the very life of otherwise bright, cheerful, honest and dedicated people.

The only ones who might be cheerful on such a day were those in the fuel oil business.

Shit he thought, then said the world aloud. "Shit." Senator Kowalski, the acknowledged king of pork, and with no apparent guilt or concern over it, a man he didn't want to be associated with for those very reasons, had him inked in to vote for yet another project in Pennsylvania. Had the man never heard of the greatest good for the greatest number!

Senator Blackwood once again shook his head and wondered how he had gotten to this low point in his life. A wealthy man when elected, he could be his own man, independent and free of the constrictions of the indebted--which was most of the politicians, and most of Washington for that matter. He had his pride and was a man of honor who was respected among his peers. Then a market downturn and a modest recession. He was suddenly not so wealthy, and not so free and independent, seeing for the first time in his office the many lobbyists and front men, listening and now being susceptible to their offers. For the first time he had to enter into the horse trading and the wheeling and dealing that was a part of the system, a necessary fact of life if one wasn't wealthy and wanted to accomplish anything for the constituents.

His pride was reduced to a veneer, like a set for a movie, only the imposing front of grand structures. He had been forced to come to terms, had learned to live with what he could only call "the grand prostitution on the hill." At some point in our lives, all of us he mused--it wasn't a matter

147

of rich or poor--we sell ourselves, perhaps unknowingly, for money, power, security, love, whatever, we sell our soul for the vague hope of something we think will make our lives better.

He could accept all of that, swallowing without tasting like a dose of salts. But he didn't like the man and hated having to deal with him.

With ill feeling he signed Senator Kowalski's petition.

And as bad as this might be it was nothing compared to Santana.

He went on to sign a batch of nothing paper work and picked up the phone to call Marvin.

It was one thing to find Christine. All well and good. What he didn't want was for anything else to be found, like anything linking him to Santana. He was walking a dangerous line here, but then the demon of gambling had been on his back for years. The gambling was something else he could have lived with and accepted, but this time he'd gone too far, extended himself to the point of financing a drug sale to recoup his losses.

Christine was being held ransom for the three million he owed Santana.

How could one sink this far?

The thought of what he'd done in a weak moment , how in a terrible instant of panic at the very thought of being broke, made him tremble, gasping for breath and feeling faint.

He was backed into a corner but he saw a way out.

Get Christine out of there and at the same time demolish the place. Reduce that house in Durango to rubble!

Marv came on the private line in a forced note of cheerfulness, hoping it would make for a short conversation. "Senator. How are things on the hill this morning?"

The Senator didn't answer in kind. "Same as always."

"Kowalski again?"

"How many fucking roads can they build in that state? But never mind that. What's going on in Durango? Has your man located Christine?"

"He has."

"And?"

"And what?"

"What is he going to do about Santana?"

"What do you want him to do?" Marv asked. "His job was to find Christine."

"Why are we dancing around here, Marv? You sent down a shooter and I want him to do his job."

"Shooting Santana was never a definite in this thing, Senator. I'm using a man who is capable, who can make that decision and carry it out, but I didn't order an execution here." *Not yet anyway. For whatever reason the senator was walking right into this thing--setting himself up for a part of the fall, if there was one.*

"Call it whatever you like. This is my operation bought and paid for and what I want is the corpse of Santana. Do I make myself clear?"

"I hear you, Senator. But there are other ways of handling him," Marv threw out, testing the waters to see how deep the senator would go. "We could do a Noriega."

"No! Talking to the press and giving out a bunch of lies? No way. He is to be silenced on the spot. Permanently."

*Could there be a connection? What could Santana tell the press? What did he know that could hurt the senator?* Marv said, "I'll see what I can do."

A silent pause. "If it's a question of money I'll pay your man."

"I don't think that's relevant, senator."

"And one other thing."

"Oh. What's that?"

"I want nothing left of that ranch in Durango. I want it totally destroyed."

Marv's turn to pause in thought. This was getting better by the moment. "And how do you expect me to do that? We're not at war with Mexico. Will you put yourself on the line for our troops going in?" *The president had given his okay. But in a blame contest, what with the man's ability to say anything to keep himself clean, and be believed, coupled with his high popularity ratings, the president would be untouchable.*

"It seems to me that we can be discreet about this, Marv."

"You want a man killed and a place destroyed--in a foreign country. Now you tell me how discreet we can be."

"Now Marv. Let's be calm about this. If you're looking for my backing, you have it. I hope it will never come to the point of blame. You did say this will be a clean operation: no American uniforms or markings, and Spanish speaking?"

"I did say that, senator."

"And we will be removing the man behind a  major source of drugs coming into this country from Mexico?"

"That's true."

"Never mind blame, Marv. We should be getting medals  for this."

"Medals? Cute thought, senator."

"Should worse come to worse the whole thing could be blamed on a rival gang war. Isn't that what you told me?"

"Right again."

"So why are we talking gloom and doom here?"

149

"Because these things can go wrong--they can and they usually do. And if that happens, this might very well come down to an investigation, a hunt with full television coverage, the whole damn world watching and looking for someone to hang. Have you forgotten Ollie North?" Marv didn't want an answer and didn't wait for one. "Don't you think the new Mexican president is going to have something to say?"

The senator sighed. "It might come to that. God help us. But it has to be done. You've handled this sort of thing before. Do the best you can and keep it as covert as possible. You know about these things, Marv."

*I sure do. Not only will I have someone to blame if it goes bad--though if things get to that stage, like facing a senate hearing committee, blame won't matter--I will have a bit of leverage, the upper hand with the senator, and he ends up owing me.* "I'll handle it, senator," Marv said.

***

A Bell chopper came in and two men in suits got out and were driven to the house. The helicopter shut down and waited.

Horses ran the track, some very fast it seemed to me. Exercise people walked the hot horses. A typical day at the Santana ranch and racing compound.

I found myself waiting for the men to return to the chopper. Except for the fact that I could be discovered at any minute, the security boys turned loose, and that I could be hunted down and shot like a dog, this watching could be a boring pastime. That scenario, among other thoughts in the back of my mind, kept me from boredom.

My position, in the shade of a rock overhang, kept me out of the direct sun and while it was far from cool, my body had learned long ago to deal with the uncomfortable heat of the tropics. It was a truth with me--my body insisted on it--that I would much rather have to deal with the heat than with the cold.

A white limo pulled up in front of the house. One man in a white suit got out and went into the house. Either this was just a day for social calls or an important business meeting was taking place. If Christine was in the house would she be moved out while business was conducted? Not likely. The place was big enough for everyone to have a room of their own. But the thought did give me hope.

I looked away then to a hawk doing lazy circles above me. What a life. Drifting, swooping, rising and rolling in the wind currents. Of course there was the matter of food to be found. He was dark, white on the underside of the wings, a big fellow, huge wing span. Rolling the wheel

150

on the binoculars to focus in on him, I could make out every feature. Could he see me? Dumb thought. If he could spot a field mouse at 100 feet up he could certainly see me!

I smoked and watched, scanning, searching every inch of the property until my eyes blurred.

I lowered the glasses, rubbed my eyes, looked down at the ranch, then at the sky and horizon, back down at the ranch. Movement caught my eye. Someone was moving at the back of the house. I quickly brought up the glasses. A woman had come out to sit by the pool. Focus. Zero in. I kept staring, trying to fine tune the image and bring in her face. These were powerful binoculars--I could see every detail of her features. I was looking at a younger version of Hannah! It was Christine.

My heart was suddenly racing like a kid at his first prom--racing at the exciting thought that I'd actually found her. I'd had my doubts along the way. But she is here!

A man walked beside her with a muscular-looking dog on a leash. That dog was no Harry. That dog was a killer.

She is here!

Even though I was sure there was nothing of any importance I could learn about her circumstances by watching her through binoculars I was so entranced, so thrilled as if at the successful end of the hunt, I kept watching, as if all would be revealed to me. And I watched because I saw Hannah in that face. I watched like a voyeur might study his fantasy romance from a distance. Yet I knew Hannah was in a past that was only a cold memory. Or was it? Do we ever completely douse the fire that blazed with an old love? Can we truly forget those moments from the past, those times when we couldn't eat, couldn't sleep, and were sure we would die without her? Do we shut it out forever?

The man with her was obviously a guard (and that dog wasn't there to fetch and play games), so she was not here on her own volitition. Beyond that? Was this a daily routine? Was there a pattern? I couldn't help but think of time and distance, of wind and sun, the weapon snug in my shoulder, the feel and smell of polished wood and oiled metal, a target centered in the blackened sights--thinking of the shot. This is what I do. Correction. This is what I used to do.

Christine is confirmed to be here in that house, which means that Jack Morgan is finished here. That should be the end of the Christine story--for me anyway. Now why didn't that ring true? Even at that point I wasn't sure that walking away, right then, would bring a kind of closure that would satisfy me, and wouldn't bring a satisfactory end that I really wanted.

151

Of course it didn't end there, couldn't end there. Little did I know, or even imagine, all that was to come before the end.

Kim driving up in a cloud of dust broke into my thoughts and I put down the glasses and turned to her. The moment I saw the expression of sadness on her face, mixed with a look of fear in her eyes, I knew that something terrible had happened. "What's wrong?" I said. "What happened?"

It came out soft and choking. "They found Karl's body."

"Karl's body? Where? What the hell happened?"

Steadier now, Kim spoke in a flat tone, as if she were far away in a sad and lonely place. "They found his body in a ditch just outside of town." She stopped talking then and I waited for the rest of it. "I only spoke to him for a few minutes in the lobby, Jack. I hardly knew the man. But you told me about him and what he was going to do for us. I feel as if I knew him. From what I picked up at the hotel, the body was bad, as if he'd been tortured. I don't know how true that is. Who would do a thing like that, Jack? Why?"

"I don't know, Kim." I knew that Karl was most likely dead because he tried to help me, help us, and probably because he went around asking questions about someone you didn't ask questions about. And for what? I found Christine myself today. The poor guy died a shitty death on a useless mission.

"Jack! Talk to me. What's going on here?"

"I don't know, Kim! But if he was asking around about Santana, which is what he said he was going to do, the suspects aren't a large group are they?" She was looking at my face but didn't say anything. "I think we can safely assume that Santana is in this. Did he give the order? We don't know. Did he even know about Karl? Maybe not. But he is at the bottom of all this."

"Poor Karl," she said.

"Yes. Poor Karl. There are lots of ways to die--some a lot worse than others. I guess there isn't a good way."

"What does that mean?" she asked after a moment. "As far as your job here."

I told her what was in the book, the agreement, the unwritten contract. "It means I've done my job and I'm finished here, Kim. From here on out, which ever way it goes, it's a problem for someone else."

"You sure about that, Jack?"

I stared at her while I tried to figure out just how I did feel. I didn't say anything because I couldn't give her an answer--not the definitive one. My head was telling me one thing and my heart another. The best thing I could do at the moment was let it lie.

152

I called Marv on the cell phone and told him the girl was here in Durango. He didn't say anything for a long moment so I said, "Why do I feel there is more to this, Marv? Is there something else?"

"Only if you want it to be more. You know your job and no one would be upset if you did it here. No one, Jack. This needs to be done." Then after a pause. "I can get you a bonus on this. Set you up for life."

"I'm already set up for life, Marv." A part of me agreed, a small part, and at this point that wasn't enough. "I'll be in touch."

"Okay. But don't wait too long on this. The whole situation could change quickly. You know about these things. If it's a go, there's a lot to be done on my end. I'll be waiting to hear from you."

*A lot to be done on his end? Was killing a man just a little?*

We drove back to town without saying a word. What was to be said? It was a time to think and not the time to talk about those thoughts, not yet the time to bring light into the dark corners.

After we parked and started towards the hotel a woman came running out towards us. She was very excited and yelling in Spanish. After Kim calmed her down and spoke with her for a few moments I got the story from Kim. "She says the police were here looking for you. They seemed very angry about the man who was killed and were blaming you for the crime. They are waiting for you in the hotel."

"Okay. Let's go talk with them. I don't have a problem with that, in fact, maybe we can learn something from them."

"I don't think so, Jack. At least not from what she says. According to her, and she seems pretty certain about it, they don't want to *talk* with you. They want to arrest you."

"Not again. My luck isn't running good with the police lately."

"Jack. This is serious. The locals are here to lock you up for the murder of Karl. This woman says the police are all on Santana's payroll anyway and will arrest anyone he wants arrested. That doesn't sound like a game we want to play. You agree?"

"Definitely," I told her. There was a familiar ring to all of this, a memory come to life. The circle was closing with me in the middle. I was in a land close to my own country, yet so foreign in that I was the hunted with no place to hide. This might well be--I considered but didn't say--the time to accept the situation for the loser that it was and get out fast. In the old days that meant that things were going sour, fast, and if I had any hope of completing the mission I had to take my shot right away, then run like hell to avoid being caught. I didn't think I was at that stage just yet, close yes, but I still had some room. I doubted that the police here would move all that quickly to find me--if I happened to show up at the hotel and they could grab me, fine, but I didn't think they would go out looking for me. And while I was beginning to get the feeling that I wanted Santana, and felt the old juices flow at the thought of taking him out, I wasn't full of the confidence I used to have, that youthful bravado and a feeling of immortality that made it all a piece of cake. But tempering that feeling with age and experience wasn't a bad thing--I'd seen kids pull off their shots way too early and miss, when a bit of patience would have paid off with a hit. No. I was reasonably sure that I hadn't lost it. What I had was a unique skill, an acquired art, that once learned could never be lost. It simply meant that I had to put more time, thought, and effort into whatever I wanted to accomplish.

I was aware then of Kim watching me closely, as if trying to read my thoughts, trying to get a handle on all of this, and on me. As I looked at her and thought about Christine, and about Karl and Santana--and about myself--it seemed clear to me that I would have to stay here and see this through to the end. In fact I wondered why it was ever in question. No. That part didn't come as too much of a surprise. What was still very much up in the air was what part I wanted to play in the finale.

As it turned out it was taken out of my hands anyway.

Kim said, "You're not sure about this are you, Jack?'

"Sure about what?"

"Sure about what you're going to do."

"No. I'm not sure, Kim." My answer was an honest one, but I don't think we were thinking about the same thing.

"I am," she said, then abruptly changed the subject. "There're not looking for me. I'll get our things out of the rooms and come down the back way."

*Now what the hell did she mean by the first part of that? What is she sure of?* "Good idea. I'm going to make a call." After I watched her go in, I moved the LR around to the back of the hotel. No one seemed to be watching the front or the outside of the building. Then I called Marv. "Things are moving fast here," I said, the instant he answered.

"Like how? Fill me in, Jack."

"For starters, Karl is dead and the police want me for the murder. You want more?"

"Let's hear it all."

"I told you that the girl is here?"

"Yes. That's good news, Jack. Did you see Santana? Is he confirmed?"

"No. It's not a definite. I haven't actually seen the man. But I'm certain he's here. People have been coming and going at that place like a convention."

I heard Marv's usual snort, which was a sort of non-verbal utterance, a comment of some kind I think, though I was never sure what it meant. "Maybe it is a convention--a drug convention." Then a long moment of quiet before he said anything. "So what are you going to do now?"

"Keep a low profile, Marv, for as long as I have to hang around here."

"You going somewhere?"

"I could leave now. You know that. My job is finished." He didn't comment on that, as I expected him to do, so I went on. "Out of the goodness of my heart I'll stay here until your team gets here. You will be sending a team I assume?"

"Goodness of your heart huh? Yes I will be sending in a team. And I would appreciate your being there to help them set this thing up."

"Is that all?"

"No. It's not all. I'd love it if you took out this guy Santana. That would make me very happy. But you don't want to get involved in that, and that's fine. *It isn't fine. I need Santana removed from the scene and at the moment I don't see that happening. I can only hope something happens down there to change Jack's mind on this. Well, there is always the team--they have orders to change that ranch to dust.*

"I respect your feelings," Marv said after a moment, not entirely truthfully. "What I do need you to do is run this thing on your end. You've seen enough of these ops and you know the score. All I ask you to do is check out the place and point these boys in the right direction. They're good troops, some of the best from Bragg. Are you sure you won't reconsider on Santana?"

"I'm a contractor, Marv, always was--and now I don't take those jobs anymore. I don't know a single one of those guys in my line of work who is normal, or who was able to settle down someplace and live a normal life--the nightmares kept that from happening. I've managed to get this far, to get past all that, and I'm not about to go back."

"Okay, Jack. I get it. But you will oversee the operation?"

"Yes I'll do that. Since I'm out of the hotel, I'll be setting up at a spot near the ranch-- a good spot with cover and a view of the whole place. The team can use the GPS (Global Positioning System) to get the exact location. Once they get here we'll set up and plan and I'll be in touch with you. They..."

Marv interrupted. "Kim still with you?"

"Yes. Why?"

"No reason. Go on."

I pushed for an answer. "Why the question about Kim?"

"Nothing really, a gut feeling--we haven't turned up anything on her. But if she is with somebody else--remember this guys spreads his poison all over the world, and he's probably on every bodys hit list--she could get in your way."

"I have the same feeling about her, but it isn't something I worry about. Whatever she is, I'll handle it, Marv. Leave Kim to me."

"Okay. Can you give me some idea of what we're facing here? I'm only curious."

"Marv, you're like an old race horse eyeing the starting gate from your stall, itching to be in the damn thing and knowing you can't be. Am I right?"

"All too true, Jack."

"They're maybe looking at a dozen or more unfriendlies. I haven't seen much in the way of weapons. It's huge compound, fenced, way out, and I would guess the guy has more inside the fence--sensors, whatever. It's not a cake walk, but I don't see a big deal here. We know who he is and what he does so we can figure on some resistance. Though it seems to me, what with his set up here--he's got the world by the balls--he may be sloppy and over confident as far as security. That's just my guess."

"Best we don't under estimate him, Jack. What's the general lay-out of the place? I still haven't been able to set up any passes with our bird in the sky." After I gave him a description of the ranch and the property he wanted to know about my weapon. "Just for self-protection," he said.

"My weapon? I'm rear echelon on this one, Marv. I'm back in regimental headquarters safe and sound, an operations planner. Why would I need a weapon?"

After a long moment of silence, "I got it, Jack. It's your call."

From something in his voice I had the feeling he was hoping that like an old war horse myself, I would respond to the bell and do what I was trained to do. I said, "How soon can I expect that team?"

"At the very best, twenty four hours. As soon as I hang up with you I'll get word down to Fort Bragg. Hopefully, if I push this thing, we can get the general's Gulfstream Jet to get the team down to El Paso, Texas. From there it's a what...? Six hour drive?"

Kim came out of the hotel with our stuff and was loading it in the back.

Marv said, "Any special gear? Anything you want to request?"

"Hard to say at this point. We'll have to watch for the right moment and move. I don't have much in the way of routine yet for the ranch, but I hope to have enough by the time they get here. Let the team bring their usual gear--they know how these things go. They might be in place for a while, so I would suggest Ghillie suits."

"I don't know how they do it: lay in hole in the ground in a camouflage suit, eat cold food, piss in a bottle, hardly able to move for hours. But they're young."

"You're right, Marv. They're young. I think that's it for now. We're out of here. Anything new I'll be in touch."

"Okay, Jack...good hunting. Keep in touch. From your observation, is the girl in shape for travel?"

"Christine?"

"Yes. Can we get her out of there in the usual way? No medical equipment?"

"No physical problems that I can see. As for mental...?"

"I get the picture. Keep your head down, Jack."

"Will do, Marv. Watch your ass."

"Those days are gone for me. My only worry now is the big C."

On that cheerful note I disconnected and went to help Kim pack up the Land Rover. Maybe we were lucky or maybe the locals were dumb because we saw no sign of the police.

\*\*\*

In Fort Bragg, North Carolina, one of the largest Army posts, including Special Forces, Colonel Franklin Cramer, Group Commander of a Special Forces unit, and Battalion Commander of five of those Special Forces units, looked away thoughtfully, nodded his own understanding, then said "Yes Sir," into the mouth piece and slowly hung up the phone. Not all that unusual to hear directly from CSA (Chief of Staff Army), he was thinking, since this CSA often bypassed the normal chain of command, but it hadn't happened much of late. What was unusual was the order for a special team, an "experienced, older team," was the way it was worded. Along with that order was the qualification to follow orders to the letter on this one. He had such a team that he could rely on and it wasn't a problem. What the order indicated was that someone, most likely a highly placed civilian, was using their political clout for what was very probably personal gain--though he couldn't see what that might be. That was usually what these things meant and it always annoyed him. He would have to go back up the chain before the day was out, filling them in on the CSA's bypass, and his two intermediate superiors would chew him out for the Chief's transgressions.

He had never served in Washington, and while such duty among the movers and shakers might bring some career enhancing advantages, he had no desire to go there. He preferred to be strictly a soldier, a good soldier, not merely an adequate soldier who played politics.

He yelled to the other room and told the clerk to get Captain Sanchez in here on the double. The captain was a good man, solid, and respected by his men, though but not the core of the team he needed for this one. Sanchez had only been here two years. What this team had was one of the best Warrant Officers in the Army, the one who took care of all the technical stuff and organization, a top Master Sergeant, and two Sergeants First Class who had a combined 50 years fifty years of experience. This is not to mention the experience of the other four members of the team. The medic was a 15 year veteran. The weapons expert 18 years. The other two had some 30 odd years between them.

The team leader reported in and stood in front of the desk. Captain Michael Sanchez, of Irish and Puerto Rican parents in Chicago, the colonel knew from a quick review of his service jacket earlier, was of average height, stocky and powerful of build, a man with a deep tan and blue eyes. Coming up through the ranks, he had been an enlisted member of a team that went into Iraq at the onset of the Gulf War, had advanced to almost within sight of Baghdad, then watched and waited until pulled back. In spite of that accomplishment, he felt cheated and deprived of his war in that he had not fired a single round at the enemy. He had a wife and four children.

"At ease, captain," the colonel said. "You have your team ready to go?"

"Yes sir. We've been ready for almost a week now."

"Good. I know the worst part is the waiting. Any questions?"

"Did I get this right, sir? Clean clothes and no weapons or ammo?"

"You got it right. You'll find out more on the other end. One important thing here, captain. Follow orders closely on this one. Keep it strictly by the book." Then on a lighter note, he added, "this is a plush job, captain: You get to fly in the general's plane down to Texas. That's pretty good duty. You'll be met there and get further instructions. You have GPS equipment?"

"Yes sir. Are we going in with anyone besides the team?"

"Not that I know of, captain. In Mexico you will meet the controller in this operation. From what little I've heard on the grapevine, your contact down there is an experienced operative, former military, and someone who knows what he's doing. That's all I know. You might think this is all a little vague at this point, and it is, simply because it isn't our operation. But I'm sure you'll find out all you need to know on the other end. Any other questions?"

"No sir."

"Good. Take care of business and get back here in one piece."

"Yes sir!"

The colonel, thoughtfully, watched him go and wondered about the captain and the lives he would have in his charge: they seemed so young--every day younger--and filled with that arrogant confidence of youth that so readily knew the rights and the wrongs--there was no gray--and so certain of their immortality as to race into the face of death. And in a way it was a glorious time, however brief. Where did it go? What happened to that innocent, simple world of our youth? To what place is the world turning now, in its maturity and wisdom of years, and taking us with it?

By any standard that Mike Sanchez knew of--and that meant cramped into a cheap seat on a commercial airliner, or jammed into an even harder and cheaper seat on a military aircraft--the flight to Fort Bliss, adjacent to El Paso, was the fastest and sweetest trip he'd ever made in the air. And that attendant! She looked Latino with that black hair and dark eyes. Even in fatigues--which aren't the most flattering of female attire--Corporal, Specialist stripes, she had a nice body. He watched, slightly amused, as some of the younger members of the team came on to her. Young or not, she handled it all deftly and slipped away from any entanglement..

In what seemed like no time at all, the plush Gulfstream touched down with a slight bump, rolled smoothly to the end of the main runway, then braked and turned off to follow a side ramp and into a little used section of the airport that was reserved for special flights such as this one.

The only light in the surrounding area were those of the plane as it came to a stop in front of a row of hangars.

Movement outside as figures moved around and under the body of the plane. Then the exterior lights went out and the cabin lights came on. Mike was glued to the window, straining to see anything outside. A huge hangar door slid open and a tall man walked out to the plane. The aircraft door opened and a voice called them out into the darkness.

When the team had disembarked and was assembled in a rough line beside the aircraft, the tall man, now visible to be in civilian clothing, spoke to the group. "Welcome to Fort Bliss," he said with a smile. He paused for a reaction that he expected--there were a few murmurs, some shifting of bodies, but no spoken words. He went on. "I am here only to facilitate your movement from here to the border. I am not giving a briefing on your objective. In fact I don't even know your assignment." A few laughs. "And I don't want to know. What I do know is that you are going into Mexico." Looking around at the men, he added with a smile, "I must say I suspect you all can handle the language. You are going south as a fishing group in two vans that are parked at the side of this hangar." He waved an arm and everyone turned to look into the dim light. "Anyone looking at the vans, or inspecting them, will see that they are ordinary vans loaded with fishing and camping equipment. What they won't see--at least we hope they won't--is a specially designed, hidden compartment under the floor boards. There you will find weapons and ammo."

He stopped to look over the group in a slow scan, settling finally on Captain Sanchez.

"Airborne! Hooah!"

In spite of the clothing, Sanchez recognized a jumping comrade. "All the way,"he replied. And with that the team relaxed a bit.

The man said, "Because of the special nature of this mission it was decided that you would fly here without weapons. Don't ask me why. I've selected what I think will be the best small arms for this team. In the compartment below the floor are some compact HK's, that machine pistol you guys like, with plenty of ammo; flash-bang, smoke and thermite grenades; a pump shotgun with a short stock; a couple of Baretta automatics; and last but not least something special--and I have no idea what it is--for the guy in charge down there. Orders for that came from way up on high. And, oh yes, maps and there are suppressors for the weapons. There is also some camo clothing without any labels. Questions?"

Sanchez said, "We don't even know where we are. How the hell do we get to the border?"

"Good question. I should have explained that my men will drive you out of the base and to a safe crossing spot on the border. From there you are on your own. I know you guys can read maps."

"Communication?" Sanchez said.

"In the van you will find your orders which contain a GPS location to set up down there, and a cell phone number. Do not use the cell phone number unless you are in trouble, in really deep shit. We don't want to pinpoint the location of your contact. Anything else?"

"Do you know the name of our contact?"

The man smiled. "I don't know his name or your name. And I don't want to know. I never even heard of you guys passing through here. I never saw you. You get the picture?"

Sanchez nodded without comment.

The man said, "Okay. That's it. Let's roll." Without another word he walked away into the hangar.

160

After a moment, Sanchez, realizing that they'd had all they were going to get here, which wasn't a helluva lot, moved the team off the tarmac to the side of the hangar and got them loaded into the back of the two vans. Drivers were already in place and Sanchez got in front with one of them. The hangar was already dark. "How's it going, ?" he said.

The driver, an older man who had the tanned, lean look of a field operative, glanced at Sanchez without comment, then started up the van and moved out to one of the service roads heading off the field. Sanchez considered that this might well be a DEA thing. He had worked many over the past few years and somehow nothing seemed to change in the drug scene. After a moment the driver said, "we'll be at the border in about 40 minutes. Not at a border crossing--a place where you can go over quietly."

"Thanks for all your help."

That was all the conversation, which didn't bother Sanchez because he had orders to read and maps to study.

In about 35 minutes--having passed through the city and now out in the country, which was black as ink--the driver suddenly turned off the paved road onto a track in the sand. They bounced around, went up and over a few sand hills then down into a gulley and came to a stop. Only because the interior light was on, Sanchez was able to make out an off-road vehicle off to one side--the driver's ride home.

"End of the line," the driver said. "Straight ahead is Mexico. The river is no more than a puddle here. You can drive right across and enjoy the wonders of 'South of the Border.' Good luck."

"Good luck to you too," Sanchez said, climbing out of the van. He went off to brief the team and set up their driving directions.

'South of the Border,' like the man said, lay straight ahead.

161

# THIRTEEN

Sometime during the night the winds had shifted, or perhaps dropped, and the air went from comfortably cool to warm and sticky. I had thrown open the summer sleeping bag. Now in the first light of morning I lay on top of the bag watching the changing colors of the sky. Kim was still asleep a few feet away.

This was quiet time--until my cell phone beeped, destroying the peaceful moment. Fumbling around in the bag under me, I found it, punched in the open key, and said a hello to whomever was on the other end. The tiny screen told me that a call was in progress--as if I didn't know that. After a few seconds a woman said: "the team crossed the border into Mexico at 0630." I looked at my watch: 0645.

It was a nice voice and I kidded her. "Why the delay in reporting?" But she had already hung up and missed my ready wit.

So, how long would it take to drive here from wherever they had crossed? I hadn't a clue. Would they run into check points (bribes) and be delayed? That would only happen if they didn't know enough to lay out a few pesos to the soldiers, which didn't seem likely--Marv said this was an experienced team. I took that to mean this was a group of sharp, seasoned professionals who would know how and when to grease a palm. Time would tell. All I could do was wait, keep a close watch on the ranch, and hope that nothing would change--like Santana deciding to move out with Christine. When I thought about that possibility, it seemed unlikely, after all this was his home and there was no obvious threat--at least that he was aware of--and I ended up feeling that I was creating scenarios and letting my imagination run wild. This was another one of those annoying signs of the aging process creeping into the Morgan body.

Since we were the hunted, in what seemed to me to be a loose fashion ( I knew what it was like to be actually hunted, hounded day and night, and running for my life), the hotel, and the city, was off-limits for us--for me anyway. We were living in the field--camping out as it were--and I felt comfortable with the whole thing. Kim took it all in stride. Of course she had been brought up in South Africa, and that is not to say that all of that part of the world is uncivilized, or even rural. But from what little she had said about her upbringing, I got the impression she had lived in the country, rather than in a city, and that would account for her being at ease with our situatioWhen I heard her moving in her sleeping bag and the muffled sounds of a body coming awake, I got out of my bag and went off searching for some small twigs and branches for the start of a fire. We hadn't taken the time to shop on our way out of town ( for good reason)--

one thing we didn't have was a propane, or any kind of cooking stove--but we did have coffee, some bread and cheese, and a pot in which to boil water. In a short time I managed to get a nice little hidden fire going (though we were beneath an overhanging rock and well away from the ranch, habit caused me to be cautious), heated water, and had two drinkable cups of coffee ready. By that time Kim had splashed some water on her face, taken care of her toiletries, done something with her fingers through her hair and looked absolutely beautiful.

The big ball of sun was coming up in front of us, the promise of another hot day, and we sat by the fire with coffee. We agreed that I would keep watch and log the activities at the ranch and she would go into town and get us some of the "basics for living in the bush," as she called it, which in a sense it was.

We had some of the bread, which was now stale and hard, and some of the cheese which was still in good condition, and didn't talk much.

My thoughts drifted off to the team coming, what they would be like, and how we would set this thing up. The larger picture, the grand strategy of this was an unfamiliar part to me--I was well versed in my special part in a plan to kill someone, finding my spot, setting up a hide, the shot, my starring role in one scene if you will, and of course the getting out. I had to smile at the idea that here I was a part of the planning of a major operation.

Of course, in looking at our situation, there wasn't a whole lot of planning for me to worry about. In the back of all my thoughts was Christine--her safety. And this team coming down here were probably the best of the bunch, no doubt hand-picked, and thoroughly trained in hostage rescue. This was their specialty. I had my area of expertise and they had theirs. I couldn't think of a helluva lot that I could even say to them. I could well be the invisible man here.

I wasn't really happy with that part. Some of us, maybe a lot, no doubt enjoyed and thrived on the thrill of command. To me, the excitement was out in the field. As much as it had troubled me over the last couple of years, the undeniable truth was that I missed the action and the feel and smell of the earth, that thrill of being the hunter, knowing again the ultimate high of being one on one, my life or theirs. Snipers know that feeling. I loved the feel of the stock in my shoulder, touching my cheek, especially the older models with wooden stocks that gave a scent and feel of their own.

This was an art, no less so than a brush creating a scene on canvas or the forming of a figure in clay or metal. In the early years, I never considered my work as anything less than a talent and there was no guilt attached about taking out someone who had to be removed from our society. I removed those who had to be removed. Only later, having found some of the wisdom that came with aging, did I get into the thinking process, questioning, daring to venture down the moral trail I'd ignored, down the path that brought feelings of guilt. While I could choose not to take that road in my youth, the thoughts came uninvited in the later years, pushing their way into my life.

Kim finished her breakfast, such as it was, then deftly worked her hair into a neat braid that hung halfway down her back. She had thick, beautiful hair. She caught me watching her and came over to give me a kiss. "Will you miss me?"

"More than you will ever know, Kim," I told her.

She wasn't sure how serious I was and eyed me for a moment. "I'll settle for a yes."

"You have my yes. Can I expect ChateauBriand for the evening meal?"

"That's French."

"Probably. It's filet mignon."

"I know what it is," she said. "And will you be cooking this filet mignon?"

"I hate to cook."

"As do I. So, since we both dislike cooking, don't expect a choice cut of meat, or a choice anything. French or otherwise. You will have to settle for take-out."

"Take-out? In Mexico?" I said.

"What's wrong with take-out? Taco to go. Every place in the world has take-out. In London they call it take-away. Wonder what it is in India? Take your chances?"

"Never been there. But I have eaten in some very good Indian restaurants."

"In London?"

"Yes. In London and in other places. Do you know London?"

"I was educated in London."

"Good for you. They did a nice job."

"Thanks, Jack. Flattery will get you everything--except ChateauBriand." She turned to leave then faced me again. "Is there some plan here, as far as Christine, that I should know about?"

"There isn't any plan for you to know about. We will be getting company, professionals, to take care of getting Christine out of there. The cavalry is coming."

"That's nice. You are going to fill me in on all of this?"

"Just as soon as you get back."

"Good. Because," she added with a smile, "I just might want to drop in on Santana myself."

"I know you aren't serious. Don't even think about it, Kim."

"See you." With that she went off to the Rover, long braid of blond hair bouncing as she went.

Right away, watching her drive off, I missed her. I couldn't help but wonder, and be a little bit concerned, with her comment about Santana. There was a lot I didn't know about her, and while that didn't bother me as far as our relationship at the moment--I felt that under normal conditions we could smooth out all the wrinkles between us--I was concerned about her getting in the way of this operation. Not because it was my operation, not an ego thing, but because I wanted to see it come off without complications and bring this to an end.

Nothing is ever really simple.

I looked down over the ranch. No sign of life. The sky went from an array of pinks into a strong yellow. It would be a boring day of watching and writing down what I saw and the time of day, as if it really mattered. The team would have been their own timetable, their own precise way of administering a swift justice to the hostage taker or takers. If it had reached the point where a team was called into action, those who had taken the hostages would die--there was no middle ground. In some of their training, I had heard of but not seen, these men practiced with a live hostage and live ammunition. This was a serious business.

Some notes were made on the movement of people and horses, the obvious stations of guards at the front and rear of the house, this in addition to the roving patrol, a rough drawing of the compound with the heliport--the beginning of another average day in the life of a drug king, perhaps his last, and as yet no sign of Christine.

Even under my overhanging rock it was hot. I had lots of water.

Christine came out, under guard, swam and sunned for a time. Not at the same hour as yesterday. No pattern there. The only regular movement was that of the roving patrol making an hourly swing through the property.

The sight of her didn't excite me as it did at first and I wondered why.

Later, Santana walked with a man in a white suit to the helicopter, which took off in a cloud of dust that didn't seem to bother him. He went to the stable area and stayed for ten minutes. Then he went back into the house without even a glance at Christine and her guard.

The air hot and humid, and still. I never thought I'd see the day that I wished for an icy Dos Equis, since I wasn't a beer drinker.

Soon it was siesta and nothing moved out in front of me. In moments I had stretched out and was asleep.

When I woke up in the already fading light, the sun dropping in the mountains behind me, I was hungry and wondered where Kim could be all this time. I waited, and thought about the team on its way. People would die, probably Santana, and others. How would our side fare? An arsenal could be waiting for them inside. Christine would be at great risk when they went in. At least I didn't have to worry about Kim, nor did I have any fears for myself since I would be out here, safely tucked away, watching and reporting as if at a football game--Jack Morgan, commentator.

I noticed that the chopper was back.

A tiny bit of breeze stirred and brought slightly cooler air from the west--a refreshing breath from the sea that found its way over the mountains behind me and down into my valley. It was so quiet that I could hear my hungry stomach growl. I started a small fire in the hope that food would be along shortly.

I turned at the sound of the Land Rover whining up the grade in low gear. Coming up right behind Kim were two vans with some business lettering painted on the side. The nine men who got out, all dark and Hispanic, though in civilian clothes, would be spotted anywhere as military, in someone's army--young and confident, there was something in the way they moved. Words were spoken, orders given, and the men started unloading the vans, piling some things on the ground in a heap, moving selected items into separate piles, the hushed talk between them, the distinct, repeated snick of bolts going home in the empty chambers of their weapons.

Kim had an armful of bags that had to be food and I was torn between tearing the bags open, and watching the team. She set them down next to the fire.

One of the men detached himself from the group and came over to me. He said, "You must be Jack Morgan." He put out his hand. "I'm Mike Sanchez. Nice to meet you."

"Pleasure, Mike. How was your trip down here?"

"Uneventful. Oh, I forgot." He went back to one of the vans and returned with a long case in his hands. "I was told to give this to you, personally."

Feeling the soft leather case, recognizing the shape, I knew what it was. "Thanks. If you don't mind we can talk after I eat. I'm starved. Do you know Kim?"

They exchanged smiles and he said, "Yes. We met on the road coming our here."

166

"Met on the road is putting it mildly," Kim said. "They damn near shot me."

"Not true. We thought she was following us so we forced her off the road to check her out."

"Well. No harm done, " I said. "Let's eat."

"If you don't have anything, we have plenty of MRE's," Mike offered.

I wasn't so hungry as to go for Meals Ready to Eat. "I think Kim has something for us."

"Good. I have questions and I want to get the men deployed tonight. If you don't mind I'll just eat here with you and we can talk."

"Fine with me." He went off to the van and I quickly attacked a roasted chicken, and at the same time eyed a container of chunky Chile that Kim had laid out. There was also a stack of tortillas, beans, strips of beef, and a six pack of Dos Equis. What a gal.

When Mike came back he'd changed into camo fatigues, as had the rest of the team--they all seemed very busy with their gear. Sitting down next to me by the fire, he tore open an olive drab meal packet and laid out the contents. It seemed to include everything one might need for a complete meal--except perhaps taste. From personal experience I'd found them well thought out and packaged and certainly a far cry from the tinned combat rations of my time. I could get indigestion at the mere thought of that sausage patty meal.

Watching him I drifted off to that leather case he'd given me. A temptation. I pushed the thought aside.

The sky had turned to a purple speckled with bright stars.

Kim watched Mike, fascinated by all that came out of the package Finally she said, "we've got more than enough. You're welcome to join us."

"Thank you, mam. But this will do just fine. My stomach is used to it by now."

"Okay," she said, slowly, not quite believing he would choose the rations over our food. "Maybe you'd like a cold beer?"

"Now that I will accept. Thank you."

Kim was our Welcome Wagon hostess for those new to the neighborhood.

The fire crackled and popped as we ate. Off in the darkness were the sounds of hushed talk of the team around smaller fires. After a time Mike said, "You have a plan for this thing, Jack?"

"A plan? Not me. You're the Hostage Rescue Team here. This is your show, Mike. I'm here to be a spotter and a coordinator. The rest is up to you."

167

He seemed relieved at not being burdened by my interference. "My thought was to keep it simple as far as communication. We have throat mikes and ear pieces--instant communication is always there. But I want to keep the chatter to a minimum in case they can monitor our frequency. I'll be Mike1 and the others numbered up to nine. Sound okay?"

"Fine. Weapons?"

He smiled at the thought. "We have a nice assortment--everything we need. And we all speak Spanish so this could easily be blamed on a rival drug gang warfare. That is if it goes bad, and I don't expect that to happen. This is a good team. We'll go in, get the girl and get out."

"I don't doubt that the team is good, Mike. But there are a few bad guys in there, and you know what they about these things: what *can* go wrong usually *does* go wrong. What's your plan?"

Mike finished his beer, set it down, then lit up a cigarette before he answered. "How many of them?" I shrugged and gave him my rough estimate. He didn't comment. "As soon as we've eaten and get our gear together, we're going to move in to positions around the house. You said there is no perimeter stuff to worry about--sensors, that kind of stuff?"

"Not to the best of my knowledge, Mike. I've been scanning the place thoroughly for a couple of days now and I don't see any indication of perimeter stuff. I think this guy Santana is too cocky and confident to worry about any serious threat to the property. Why should he worry? He's got this part of the country in his pocket."

Mike considered that for a moment, nodding his head. "Well, we'll go in easy anyway. This goes down just before dawn. We'll be in position long before that and have plenty of time to look the place over."

"I'm sure you know your job, Mike. And the girl's safety is top priority?"

Mike looked as if I'd insulted him. "Jack. That's our job. That's what we train to do: rescue the hostage. And we do our best to bring them out unharmed."

Kim had been paying close attention, her face serious, almost grim. I watched her and wondered what could be going through her mind.

Had I even a tiny clue as to what was in her pretty head, I would have done things a lot differently. As it was, there was too much going on and too much to think about to even give Kim more than a passing thought. Of course on Monday, after the Sunday game, we can all be great quarterbacks and make every call the perfect one.

The night breeze had come in and the air was cooler, dryer, a lot more pleasant.

168

Mike declined the offer of another beer, saying he had to get his stuff together and get the team moved out.

Kim had kind of pulled into herself and I asked if she was okay. She said she was, that she was just tired, and settled down on her sleeping bag, turning away from me.

I stared up at the sky, smoked, and barely heard the movement of the team going off. Then it was quiet and I fell asleep.

The receiver beside me screeched, scaring the hell out of me for that moment when I first woke up. I felt tired and disoriented, a terrible taste in my mouth, certainly not ready for this damn thing to start. Then..."Jack. This is Mike1. Jack. Mike 1. Do you read me?"

"I read you," I answered, a sigh more than a talking voice. With the procedure coming back I added, "I read you loud and clear, Mike." Too damn loud and clear I thought, but didn't say. He was out there ready to kill, or maybe get killed, and I was lying in my bag back at the base, maybe tired and grouchy but comfortable in comparison. Who was I to bitch? The luminous hands on my watch told me it was 4.30 in the black morning.

"Situation report, Mike," I said, reverting to procedure again.

"In place and quiet here. We are in a U position around the front of the house. I'm in the center. On the northern end is Mike 2. Mike 9 is on the other end. The two on the open end, in back of the house, will drop off and secure the stable area."

"Any signs of life in the house?"

"All dark and quiet."

"How about outside?"

"Nothing but the roving patrol."

"I'll scan and get back to you." We both had night binoculars but I had the overview.

"Roger."

I scanned and didn't see a thing out of the ordinary. "All clear, Mike. Let me know when you move."

"Roger that, Jack. Moving out in ten minutes."

Kim got up and walked off into the darkness. "You okay?"

"Taking care of business," she said.

I smoked and stared out into nothing.

"Mike1. Five minutes."

"Roger that, Mike1."

Where the hell was Kim?

I idly watched an Iguana--pink at that--move across my bag. I thought: *do you know where the hell* you are! *Do you have any idea of what is*

169

*happening in the world around you?* And the answer was simple. No. And he (or she) didn't give a damn.

The Land Rover started up and Kim drove off. What the hell was she doing! Was she going back to town, unable to watch? Or maybe just driving off to be away from here? In any case her timing was lousy--this thing was set to go.

"Mike 1. What's happening?"

"Nothing."

"Are you driving that Land Rover?"

"No. I'm still at base."

"The woman?"

"Yes. Kim took off."

"Why? She could screw this up. I hope the hell no one is awake in the house. From here it sounds like a Greyhound bus!"

"No explanation, Mike. Sit tight and stick to the plan."

"Roger. Out."

Without really thinking about what I was doing or why, I picked up the gun case--it was heavy, the leather soft. I slid open the zipper and expected to see my old trusty Springfield, or something of equal value as they say. Surprise. What I had was a M82A1 .50 caliber Barrett Sniper Rifle. Marv evidently had an in with the Rangers or Special Ops. A long, slightly oiled, fine piece of equipment, this one came with a Leupold Tactical 3.5-10x variable scope that would give a sharp picture in day or night. Along with it was two boxes of armor piercing ammunition. I'd heard stories about the weapon that came with detachable bipod legs, and could be fitted with a sound suppresser, but I'd never fired one nor even seen one. The ammo he'd sent would probably penetrate four inches of steel! What the hell was he thinking of? If I sent one of these rounds into the house it would pass through anything in its path, and I do mean anything, go out the other side of the house, and still be a deadly missile for up to a mile away. I could only assume that Marv asked for the best weapon available for me and figured I'd know how to use the thing. And in a sense that was a fair assumption because shooting, with any good weapon, was pretty much the same routine. The important part in this fine art was having the weapon zeroed in at a specific distance--knowing where it was true. Again, with any good rifle, this was a matter of a slight adjustment from factory specs.

I worked the smooth action of the bolt. A beautiful weapon. Holding it up, I looked through the sight at the landscape highlighted in green-- everything was shades of black and green. Adjusting the sight I searched the area around the house, looking to see if I could spot any of the team--

170

the scope so precise I could see a blade of grass. I didn't see anything that looked human or out of place.

Why was I holding this thing? And why was I loading a round into the chamber?

"Shit! What the hell is she doing? Go! Go! Go!" Mike screamed.

"Mike 1. What the hell is going on?"

"No time, Jack. Kim crashed the gate and is at the front door. Going in!"

"She what!" I screamed.

Then I heard a boom and several popping noises as the ground seemed to come alive to release clumps of earth--the team--rising up and racing towards the house. Flashes of light and the early dawn awakened with movement and noise. A window blew out of the house. A chatter from the HP's. Lights came on in the house--a steady rattle of rapid fire from inside. An answering fire, heavier, slower, the sound of American weapons.

Thinking of Kim all the while, I watched, helpless to do anything in what could be the last moments of her life. Set up and be ready to help her!

Fighting a feeling of panic, and a hopelessness that was something new to me, I set the legs of the bipod down on a flat rock, and stretched out behind the rifle. I told myself: "This is what I do. This is what I do as well as anyone else in the world, maybe better than anyone else in the world." I worked my shoulder into a comfortable fit with the stock. What were the settings? At what range had this thing been zeroed in? Too late for that. What about the wind? Distance? There was little wind and my range was about 600 yards. The rifle was probably set for 500. I worked the tiny wheel up a notch.

Great. I'm here and I'm ready. But I don't have a target. I may not get one.

The first light of dawn crept in and the whole scene took on a new dimension. Nothing else mattered to me as I stared through the scope at my fixed position on the house.

Noise and more flashes of light. The team was in full action.

And Kim? I didn't have a clue. What the hell. Was she suicidal? A nut case?

More light now. I didn't need the night scope mode on the telescopic sight. I switched it off and smoked, one hand draped over the stock--a familiar position for me. Sure I was worried about Kim. But she didn't wipe out my life. I was a shooter. I am a shooter.

Give me a target.

As if in answer to my thoughts, I saw two figures come out of the back of the house and run towards the helicopter. I scoped in for a closer look. One of them was in casual clothes and one in a white suit. Fine tune the scope. Geez. It looked like Santana! I had him dead center and it was definitely Santana. The other one had to be the pilot. I started to breath fast and lost the image. I looked away then back. Settle down. Scope in and lock on the target. Yes. I had one now.

I had time. Don't lose him.

Breathing better now. They were almost to the chopper. The pilot climbed in and Santana opened the door and threw in his briefcase. As the blades started to move I saw him step up into the cabin. He leaned forward and said something to the pilot, then sat back and buckled the belt.

Nice thought, Santana. But it won't matter. It won't save your miserable life.

I fine tuned the crosshairs. Him or the engine? I could miss him. Take the bigger target.

Where was Christine? Whatever he had in that bag was more important than the girl.

Kim came running out of the house after Santana--she had her Glock in one hand. Nearing the chopper, Kim crouched and was bringing up both arms to line up on Santana--a good, classic shooting position. I moved up to scope on him, then back--my field of vision was sharp but tiny in the larger picture.

But she was too slow and too late. He fired through the open door, then fired again. He had rushed his shots I thought, or at least I hoped he had, and there was a chance of his missing. With a horrible sinking, empty feeling, I watched her body jerk at the impact, then crumple to the ground. I focused in on her but I couldn't see much more than her body lying in a fetal position, facing away from me. I hoped for the best.

Then I had Santana centered. I moved my finger onto the trigger.

Slow it down. I didn't want to rush because I couldn't afford to miss. Fighting the adrenaline rush that comes with the territory, I forced myself into a steady breathing pace--slow in, slow out. This was all routine. No problem. Why the hesitation?

The chopper blades were whirling now. Lift off would be soon.

Santana had picked up the briefcase and clutched it to his chest. His eyes were darting all around like a deer sensing the hunter.

I had time. It would take a few moments more to reach liftoff speed--I hoped.

I sighted in on the engine compartment, just below the blade stem. I could possibly miss Sntana but would surely hit the chopper body. I inhaled deeply, then in the middle of a slow exhale I held still and squeezed the trigger. Quickly I grabbed another round from the pouch attached to the stock and rammed it home, bolt clicking shut. I put another round into the engine.

Nothing seemed to change. The blades still turned, faster now.

The chopper started to lift off the pad. Was there a trickle of black smoke coming out? I couldn't be sure and I couldn't stay focused on that. I worked the bolt and fed in another round. Now I centered on the cockpit, on the pilot. Rising shot but I followed. Unless the rifle was way out of zero I had a solid shot. I held and squeezed. It felt good and I knew it was true.

The chopper kept climbing. I worked the bolt and got ready for another shot.

Then suddenly it dipped and rolled to the right, spinning awkwardly. Trailing black smoke, it spun and dropped like a stone.

Hit!

I swung the rifle down then looked for a target around the house. I was getting into my groove and ready. Smoke poured out but no target. I shifted to the back. Someone, maybe our guys fearing a spreading fire, had opened the stalls and the horses ran wild--the innocents in panic running for their lives. From the house then, running figures who didn't get far, cut down as they ran.

Three men, probably of the security detail, ran to the patrol vehicle at the side of the house and tumbled in. Bugging out? Not nice to leave your buddies. I tracked them along the driveway and when they were about halfway to the gate I put a round into the engine, then a second, which was probably a waste because that .50 caliber slug would blow that engine apart. Their attempted escape ended with the vehicle swerving off the road into a tree. Mike's team would round them up. I had no taste for shooting humans with an elephant gun.

Then suddenly it was quiet. It was over.

The sun was up full now and the hot air was rushing in over the valley. I had to get to Kim--and Christine. I'd nearly forgotten her. I went down to the house in one of their vans. It occurred to me that the team had to get the hell out of here, fast. As these things go, this wasn't an especially noisy operation--I'd seen worse--but it had to be heard by some of the neighbors, someone who might suspect that it was more than an early morning movie shoot. It was definitely an early shoot. No pun intended.

The gate at the guardhouse hung open, abandoned, no one there to challenge me. Had they run to the house to help out? Or had they run away, in the direction of Durango? Somehow I suspected the latter.

Along the road in I saw three bodies by the vehicle that had nosed into the tree--with a little help from me--two of the bodies close by and one halfway to the gate, face down, arms flung out. At the front of the house, our Land Rover sat with the driver's side door hanging open--she had left in a hurry. The big question was why!

Directly inside the front door was a large entrance way, and off that was a larger room--now strewn with bits of furniture and chunks of glass--and a wide circular stairway to the second floor. Two doors to other rooms were blown off and lying on the tile floor. Charred curtains hung beside gaping holes that had been windows. A fire, probably started from the stun grenades, burned on a huge sofa. Off to one side, in front of a window space, was a grand piano with one leg broken, it tilted down like a shiny, wounded beast too proud to topple.

Sitting with their backs against one wall of the large room, and smoking, were three of the team. Mike sat on the bottom step with Christine at his side.

"Everything okay? Christine?" I asked.

Mike nodded. "She's fine. A bit shaken up, but fine. One of the team got it. The medic is outside working with Kim. What the hell got into her! She could have fucked up this whole operation. I should have left her out there to bleed to death."

"You don't mean that." He looked at me but didn't say anything. "I don't know what got into her, Mike. But I plan to find out. Your guy dead?" A weary nod. "Was it Kim's fault?"

He took a deep drag and let it out. "No. Freak thing. He caught one in the throat. Can you imagine? All kinds of body armor and he catches one in the throat."

"That's it for casualties?"

"One guy out back. Hit in the leg. Not too bad. There was a woman and a child upstairs. Maybe his wife and daughter? They weren't hurt. I sent them out to the stables. It's okay out there. We have them all gathered in a holding area."

"The stable area is secure then?"

"Yep. You bring down that chopper?"

"You saw it?"

"Yeah. I was trying to get loose to go out after Kim. I caught a glimpse of her going out after Santana. Never got that far. I saw the whole thing through the doorway."

174

"It was a lucky shot," I said.

"Lucky shot? I don't think so. That was a damned good shot. The work of a pro."

"Whatever. I'm going out back to check on Kim. You guys better clear out of here."

"You're right. I'll round up the team."

Debris from the house floated on the clear, green water of the pool that shimmered in the bright sunlight..

Beyond the pool, in a different setting, Kim lay in a large smear of blood on a cement walk that led to the chopper pad. The team medic was bent over her holding a bag of intravenous liquid that flowed down into her arm. She looked pale, weak, and scared, and I hated to jump on her about why she went charging into the house. It had to be done.

The medic looked up at me. " A blood pack--latest thing. I have two of them but she'll probably need more. Her wound is in the left torso area, low, close to the heart. We need to get her to a hospital, fast."

"Thanks, Doc." I bent over Kim. "You okay?" She gave me a weak nod. "Why did you do this?" Looking at her, seeing the shape she was in, I felt lousy asking her this instead of being a comfort and maybe showing a little compassion for her. But it was done.

Motioning with her head for me to get closer, she said, "I'm sorry, Jack." I waited, seeing the tears in her eyes. "I wanted him, Jack. I wanted him so badly. He killed my mother and father. He had a car bomb set up to kill the witnesses against him. My parents just happened to be walking by...just innocent people, Jack. He killed them. Killed the witnesses and killed my mother and father. I wanted to tell him what he'd done and then put a bullet right between his eyes. Can you understand?"

I did and I didn't. She had her own objective and she went after it, went after it at any cost. She put the lives of eight men in jeoprody. A trained operative, which I always felt she might be, would know better. I had to ask about that. "You alone on this?"

"Yes." She was still running on high emotion, and added, "My parents didn't even know Santana, never heard of the man, and he blew them away."

"I understand, Kim. Take it easy. Does your control know about you being here?" I was reaching out in the dark.

"No. I'm alone on this, Jack. They didn't know and wouldn't sanction my being here."

"Who is they, Kim?"

"Interpol." The word hung in the silence for a moment. "Is the team okay?"

175

"One dead. Not your fault. One injured. Everything's okay, Kim." Interpol. Gave a few answers, I thought. Not all. From what little I knew about the organization it was generally a clearing house for information-- the gathering, filing, and the disseminating of the collected criminal data among the nations. Maybe, like so many other intelligence organizations-- those that took on a life of their own, giving birth to separate territories and sectors, each with their own ruler, areas of operations, renegades, the whole bit, all becoming uncontrollable in the larger scheme of the thing-- Interpol might well be more than it was known to be.

Her breathing was weak and labored. After another long pause she said, "I checked on the girl first--shot the guy with her. Then went looking for him. Mike and the team came in then...blowing them away. They're good. I chased Santana outside. He shot me. Did I screw up, Jack? We got the bastard didn't we?"

"We got him. No more talk." I turned to the medic. "I'm going to get a chopper in here to take out the wounded--and you go with them."

"How the hell you gonna do that? I mean, this is as covert as they come and we're one helluva long way from Ft. Bliss."

"I'll do it. Stay with her."

I went in and took a fast tour of the house--bodies in almost every room-- then got Marv on the cell. Before he could say a word I told him I needed a chopper. He wanted to tell me how difficult it was to send a chopper into Mexico to bring out wounded that shouldn't be there in the first place. "I know all that shit, Marv. I don't care about your problems. Get it done. I need that chopper in here--yesterday!"

"Okay. Okay." He was quiet for a moment, then talked as if to himself. "Bliss is too far. Gotta get someone local. Who the hell has a chopper down there?" Then aloud to me, "This will take a bit of time, Jack. Fort Bliss is almost five hundred miles away! I have to find someone closer and at the moment I don't know how long that will take."

"I don't care where you get it! Do what you have to do. I want one here inside of one hour!"

A pause, then he said, "Did it go off all right, Jack?"

"Went off like a Swiss alarm clock, Marv. And what the hell did you have in mind with that rifle you sent me?"

"For old times, Jack. Thought you might get into it."

"You mean you wanted me into it. But I won't get into that now. Nor will I get into a whole lot of explaining you have to do. Now get the hell off the phone and get busy with that chopper."

"Santana dead?"

"Yes! Santana is a pile of ashes in a chopper fire."

176

"Don't yell, Jack. Anything left of the house?"

"Now what the hell does that mean? Some damage but the house is still here--pretty much."

"Can you see about getting..."

I cut him off. "I'm hanging up now, Marv. I'll be outside looking for the chopper. And it damn well better be here fast!"

Back in the living room, or whatever room it had been before our redecorating, Mike handed me a large, leather portfolio. "Blew a safe in the big bedroom upstairs and found that. Looks important. Found a lot of cash too."

"What did you do with that?"

"Left it in the safe."

"Why do that, Mike? He won't need it. And it won't be evidence. You going to blow up the house?"

"That was in my orders."

"Up to you. Do what you want. Seems a shame to blow up good US. currency. Isn't there a law about that--destroying money?"

Mike smiled. "Maybe you got a point there, Jack. Wouldn't want to break any laws."

"Souvenirs, Mike. It's the American way. I'll check out the case. How are you doing, Christine?" It was the first time I'd paid any attention to her this morning, and the first I'd really looked at her. She didn't look like the photo I had. They never do. She was pretty, but older.

"I'm fine. Who are you?"

"No one important. Mike here, and the team, rescued you. You sure you're all right?"

"These men were sent by my father? Are they American?"

"They may not look it, Christine, but they're as American as you and I. Mike here has apple pie at least once a week. Isn't that right, Mike?"

"At least," Mike said. "After my rice and beans."

Christine didn't have a clue as to what was going on. She said, "Do you know who my father is?"

"I think he  works in Washington," I said. On the tip of my tongue and ready to come out was a question about her mother.  I kept my mouth closed. This wasn't the place and it sure as hell wasn't the time.

"Yes he does," she said,  bewildered, in a far away voice.

She'd been through a lot. Looking at her and reflecting, now that it was over, I thought it sort of anticlimactic and I felt a bit depressed. There had been mystery, adventure, and even a touch of romance in the search for a beautiful young woman who was the daughter of someone I'd loved. The reality was something different. Here was just a scared little girl and it all

177

seemed so ordinary--a simple package wrapped in plain paper. An old love that was now over and gone. Forgotten?

But Kim was real.

A short time later Marv called back to tell me he'd gotten a local cowboy who owned a helicopter, and that for some big money the hotshot would fly in and take out our wounded. All well and good. I didn't give a damn about the money.

By my watch--and I'd spent agonizing minutes looking for the hands to move--it was exactly 42 minutes later, having made several walking tours around the property, and checking on all manner of things of no importance other than killing time, when a brown helicopter with crudely done Red Cross markings swung in over the hills and set down on the pad near the ranch house. When the rotors slowed and the dust settled, I looked at the young Latino pilot in aviator glasses and sport shirt, a confident, cocky expression in his smile--from my experience in this kind of operation, my guess would be that this pilot had never been closer to the Red Cross than maybe having a donut and coffee from them near some disaster he happened to come upon. He sure as hell wasn't employed by them. No one in the world would question a supposed Red Cross mission of mercy--except maybe the Red Cross.

I noticed that the chopper was equipped with external fuel tanks, something the pilot would need for any long haul.

The medic and one other member of the team quickly and carefully loaded the wounded, strapping them into stretchers that could be bolted to the floor. Christine was buckled into the seat to the left of the pilot. I had no idea where she was going from here, but she was freed and off to join her parents.

Kim looked scared, vulnerable, and so small and pale. I leaned in and wiped a smudge of dirt from her cheek. "You're going to be okay, Kim. You'll get the best treatment available."

She nodded and spoke in a whisper. "Will you find me?"

"I'll find you, wherever they take you." She struggled to raise up and I kissed her.

In ten minutes the chopper was lifting off.

She stayed in my thoughts, but there was much to do here. Mike was busy rounding up the team and getting them into the vans. Watching them pack up I remembered that the sniper rifle was still up in the hills--a problem for me to deal with. The men were shedding their protective gear and stowing weapons in the false floor of the vans. All the while, Mike's sergeant is yelling, "Move it! Move it!"

I grabbed his arm. "Don't take the main road. There's a fork to the left that will take you further to the East. But eventually you'll find a road north. The police are bound to be responding to this thing any minute. I'm surprised there're not here already. Try to keep to the back roads."

"Got you," Mike said. "We're outta here. Good luck, Jack."

Kim was gone. The team was gone. Back in my hide, I sat with my back against a rock, smoked and stared down at the ranch. While I was half lost in my thoughts about Christine, Hannah, Kim, and all of this, I saw two jeep loads of police and military pull up in front of the still smoking ranch house. They scurried around, some of them going out to the stable area, and after a few moments of discussion quickly came back to their vehicles. It seemed obvious they were going to pursue Mike and the team.

Not if I could help it. And I could.

I dropped one of the AP rounds in the chamber, worked the bolt, and settled in behind the rifle. The sun was almost overhead and there was very little breeze to contend with in the way of trajectory. Aside from my heart thumping this was ideal shooting conditions. Looking through the scope I could make out the size and depth of scratches on the hood--I could have read the vehicle serial numbers from the engine block if the hood had been open. This was a powerful piece of equipment.

The men around the vehicles were busy in animated conversation for a few moments, then got into the jeeps.

Deep inhale, let it out slowly, take up the slack in the trigger, steady on, then in a calm moment of exhale squeeze off the shot. It was a clean hit.

Even as the bullet was tearing into the engine I was already reloading. I didn't have the time and I couldn't take my eyes off the immediate target, but I could imagine the shock to those men in the jeep. In an instant out of nowhere, from a shooter they couldn't see, they were in the line of fire.

With no more than a slight swing of the muzzle I took out the second jeep. For good measure, I put two rounds into each of the tires on my side. This was like using an elephant gun on a canary, but I wanted to be sure there would be no immediate pursuit. Of course, there were cell phones and radios they might use to call for help, if they had them, and I doubted that a force of any size was nearby. In any case, no one was going to be on our tail for a while.

Where would that chopper take Kim and Christine? They were safe and I'd find them through Marv. I couldn't let myself get off on that track--far too many questions. At the moment my top priority better be to get the hell out of there. My best route, at least the shortest and quickest according to my limited knowledge of the countryside, was up over the

179

mountains and down to the coastal town of Mazatlan. Once there I could turn in the Rover and get a plane to Mexico City. Nice idea, except for the rifle. I didn't think there would be any way for me to explain that away.

While I was naturally anxious to get out of that place as soon as possible, the fact was that I had to drive back the way we'd come. This wasn't a big deal because no one was chasing me. I knew what I'd been doing the past 24 hours. They didn't. I had to keep that in mind. No wanted poster was displaying my picture. The police might want to question me in Durango but I didn't think that warranted national attention. I hoped it didn't.

I gathered up all our stuff and threw it into the Rover, carefully dismantling the bipod and removing the telescopic sight from the rifle--it was one thing to have a rifle of questionable use, but quite another to have a very obvious sniper weapon. The scope I wrapped in my sleeping bag. One last glance down to the house--they were all gathered around shaking their heads at the smoking pile of metal--and I was off.

## FOURTEEN

An older, attractive flight attendant, brought me the two little bottles of tequila I'd requested. Of course, the bosses might claim, and rightly so in the early days, that flying was sophisticated and glamorous and the attendants had to be likewise--the airlines wanted them young and pretty. That time was long gone. Except for a few in the first class seats, it was Greyhound in the sky these days and people dressed as if they were going on a camping trip.

She asked if I wanted anything with it and I told her nothing but ice.

I'd gotten this Mexicana flight to Miami without any questions or problems.

The main problem, that one in the leather case, I'd left at the American Embassy in Mexico City--not without questions. There were big eyes and lots of questions from many people. It took my call to Marv and a whole lot of phone conversation with embassy personnel before we even got started. I told the Attaché who finally ended up with the problem, that the package was a very expensive hunting rifle I'd bought, at tremendous expense, for a member of the president's staff. He asked which one--of course I didn't have any names--and I named a department. I was in over my head here and trying to keep afloat.

The head of the department I'd named turned out to be a woman. Who knew?

"Women do hunt," I'd told the Attaché.

"With a telescopic sight?"

I shrugged. "You can't always get that close to the big ones."

At that point he gave up. The rifle, along with the leather case from the ranch, was sent by diplomatic pouch to Marv's attention in Washington. The ammo I'd dumped in the mountains. One day those AP rounds might be discovered in a serious Aztec dig and pronounced to be a priceless relic of an ancient time--a rather violent time. But then maybe they would think them to be some form of writing instrument.

How nice to get back to my own little island.

Harry, wise dog that he is, was on the far shore barking as I got out of the car and loaded up the inflatable for the trip across the lagoon. Claire at the house, in her own way was waiting as well, beaming, giving me a big hug, but not barking. I had no doubt she would hurriedly fix a special dinner--I hadn't let her know I was coming home. We had a joyous reunion with Harry jumping, yipping, racing around, and all the while trying to lick me and paw me to death. The first thing I did after unpacking was call Marv.

He sounded pleased with the results, or maybe with himself. "Everything went off fine?" he said.

"How do you know that?"

"I got a report from the team."

"Did you get a report on Kim?"

"She's in a hospital at Fort Bliss. Prognosis good. What happened with her down there, Jack?"

"What did you get from the team?"

"They didn't tell me anything."

"Then I won't either. Let's say she was wounded in the line of duty and let it go at that."

"Did you find out who she is?"

"She's a lady from South Africa who lives in France. Make sure she gets the best of treatment. She did one helluva job in Durango." I didn't see any point in bringing up the fact that she went off the deep end and could have easily screwed up the whole operation. It all worked out.

"I had to pull some strings on her, Jack. She's not even an American citizen let alone not being military."

"Keep doing what you do best, Marv. On another subject. What's the idea of sending that rifle?"

"You like that Barrett? I've heard good things about that rifle."

"That's not the point. Why did you send it? You knew damn well I'd use it. You wanted me to use it didn't you?"

"Jack. Don't get upset about this. That rifle is the best. I wanted you to have the best--just in case."

"In case of what, Marv?"

"In case it worked out just the way it did. You were there to take out Santana. I had to have someone there who could do that. I needed a shooter, Jack. I needed someone there who would do what had to be done. These kids today would still be weighing the political ramifications, the moral aspect, the social-economic reactions, and the military procedure before pulling the damn trigger. You every hear of Metamphetamines?"

"Never. I'm not up on drugs."

"Well. Those are the worst. And the stuff is pouring in from Mexico-- from Santana."

"Okay. I think you're selling these kids short, but let it go. I'll forgive you for the rifle thing. But you owe me one. Did you get anything from those papers from the ranch?"

"I owe you one! You owe me for getting you back in the action."

182

"Maybe. I'll let that one go for now. What about the papers?"

"Haven't had a chance to really go over them. At first glance it could be dynamite."

"Who gets blown up?"

"Senator Blackwood."

"Really. That means Hannah as well."

"She's married to the man."

"Speaking of Hannah. Why did you tell me that she was dead?"

"Would you have left London is she were alive?"

"No."

"There's your answer. I needed you in Guatemala. Simple."

"Not so simple to me, Marv. You juggle lives as if you were shuffling a deck of cards."

"You still love Hannah?"

"What the hell difference does it make!"

"Let's get off this, Jack. I'll see that Kim is well taken care of and I'll let you know what's in the papers just as soon as I know. How's Claire?"

"She's fine."

"How's Harry? Still having those seizures?"

"It's a Lab thing. How did you know about those?"

"Claire told me."

"You're reaching, Marv. Goodbye."

## FIFTEEN

I woke up in a strange state of bewilderment and pain. I was in a hospital, the room austere, and I knew it had to be military.

Aside from feeling groggy, stiff, hurting all over, and without the faintest idea of where I was or how I got here, plastic tubing was taped to both wrists and I was surrounded by machines. Under the tape on both wrists was a large bruise that was dark blue in color. I was getting transfusions of something and I was in a hospital. But where? The upper part of my chest, and shoulder on the right side, was bandaged and throbbing. And if all that wasn't enough I was hungry and thirsty.

After a few moments of looking around and trying to focus my thoughts and feelings, some memory started to came back. Durango. Jack. The burning sensation and the shock of being shot. There was more. There was guilt.

A nurse in a starched uniform came in and stood by the bed. Her name tag told me that she was "M. Ruiz." She had gold bars on her collar. She said, "How are you feeling, Miss Durden? Or is it Mrs?"

"It's Kimberly. Please call me Kim. And you are?"

"Call me Mary."

"Okay. Mary. I feel like I've been through a war, which I lost, my body hurts all over, and I'm totally disorientated. Oh. And I'm hungry and thirsty. Aside from that I feel great."

Mary smiled. "I can take care of the hunger and thirst without too much of a problem. The body part is going to take a little time. Your shoulder wound was a clean one, which is good, should heal quickly, but you lost a lot of blood. Are you in any pain?"

"No. My shoulder is stiff and I'm sore, but no pain."

"Lucky you got in here when you did," she said smiling. "Whoever worked on you did a good job. You have any idea who that was?"

"No," I told her. "He was one of the team but I have no idea who he is." I remembered the helicopter then, the dust and the heat, one of the team working on me, trying to be reassuring, Jack standing there watching with a strange look on his face. Must have been Jack that called for the helicopter to get me out. It was coming back in pieces, fragments, like a movie trailer with scenes flashing by, too quickly to really understand, the coming attractions that have already happened. "Do you think I could have something cold to drink and maybe a couple of aspirins?"

"Of course. Do you want something to help you sleep? Or just something for a headache?"

"I'd like to sleep."

184

"You said you were hungry. Would you like me to see if I can find something for you? The kitchen is closed but I can find something."

"Don't bother...Mary. I think I'd rather sleep."

"I'll take care of it," she said and left the room.

With her leaving the flood gates opened and the memories came rushing in. There was depression and there was the guilt. I'd let my emotions overcome good sense when I went charging into that house. How stupid. I could have gotten them all killed. But the feelings were so strong, feelings of revenge I had carried for the past 5 years. He had taken my parents away from me and I wanted to take his life from him. The hate was all consuming. I had always felt that I was in control, could be in control, no matter what, was a strong person, my own person in spite of the baggage I carried about my parents. All that had come tumbling down. I was weak like everyone else. In the moment of stress, the final time when control was everything, I'd lost it.

And what would Jack think of me? I had let myself go with him. For the first time in a long time I'd let down my guard, let my feelings go free with him. I don't know if it was love. I know I liked him and I wanted to let myself go with him. He was strong and steady and on course. And he smiled and made me smile. Now, after what happened at the ranch, the way I acted, I have the feeling it is all over with Jack.

I wondered if he knew where I was and if he would call. Why should he know? How could he know? He had his own problems with getting out of Mexico. My thoughts went round and round.

Mary came back with a huge glass of water and a couple of pills. "Take these and you'll go right off into a great sleep, Kim."

"I need a great sleep, Mary."

"You've been crying. Bad memories?"

"Some good and some bad."

"Was there a man?"

"Yes. He's part of both."

"They usually are, Kim."

"Yes. But now...?"

"If he's good and he's the right one for you he'll be there in your life."

"Do you have a good man, Mary?"

"I did. But he's gone now."

I felt badly for her. "He left you?"

"No. He was killed in an airplane crash. A training flight."

***

185

There was a void, a hole in my life that I tried to fill by keeping active. I ran with Harry, fished (without Harry), swam (with Harry), and worked on the many little jobs around the house that I could easily have paid someone to do. My bank account was fat, so flushed as to become a nonentity. Money can be that way--painful when you need it and seek it desperately, a cushion of comfort and totally ignored when plentiful. Claire, who seemed to be in very good health, wanted more flowers around the house and I planted a variety that the nursery owner told me would stay healthy going into the fall. Contrary to common belief, Florida does have seasons, however faint. During the summer heat and humidity, which usually lasted until the end of October, the air conditioning was on 24 hours a day, despite being on an island with a constant breeze. The breeze was balmy and heavy with moisture. The cooler months did bring, if you had northern trees, falling leaves and the whole autumn bit--on a smaller scale of course. Plants can bloom all year round but there is still some seasonal variety to our existence.

When I called Marv one day to find out about Kim, he explained that she was a bit of a diplomatic problem and that her presence in the US was awkward to say the least. As soon as she was fit for travel, he told me, she would be flown to France to finish her convalescence at home. Why the problem and who was having a problem? I was annoyed and I told him that she had engaged in one of our operations, had served us well, and deserved the best of treatment and no immigration or diplomatic bullshit. I went on yelling for a moment until I realized that it wasn't worth getting annoyed about, wasn't worth the effort. The petty bureaucrats would need to have their little snit, let everyone know how important they were, then everything would go on as before. In the end, I told him to handle it and to see that Kim got the best of care.

To keep busy I planted all manner of colorful things for Claire. I fixed a small leak over the kitchen window. Harry had another seizure with no apparent lasting effects. A Lab thing, the vet said, not putting him on any medication at this time. I wondered how many he'd had that I wasn't aware of, when I was away, that maybe Claire hadn't seen.

About a week later Marv called to tell me that Kim had left the country. Well enough now to travel, she had been flown back to finish mending and complete her rehabilitation in France. He assured me that she had no problems while she was in the hospital at Ft. Bliss, and no hassle from Immigration or anyone else. Perhaps to impress me he told me that he had found out a little bit more about her. There was a farmhouse on the outskirts and a small apartment in Paris. I made a note of both places. Her parents, while not well off early on, were early settlers in the country

186

and offered huge tracts of land in South Africa, at a very attractive price, if they would settle there and develop the property. This all sounded like a dream come true. They worked hard and eventually prospered. During that period between survival and prosperity, the coffee bean had been tried and failed--the world might well have been ready for the product, but at this point it was too unstable to attract buyers. A later successful venture had been cattle--some of the best beef in the country--and on this they found a ready market. The bottom line was that Kim had come from an average, hard working family, who got a break. Then she lost interest in all of it, when her parents were killed, sold the property, and moved to Paris. Educated in England and France, she was now part owner of a successful travel agency and lived the good life working in the city and living in the suburbs.

While most of this wasn't news to me, I was bothered by this invasion of her privacy, and I gloated a bit in that he hadn't found out about her Interpol connection. This was assuming that there was such a connection. Why would she lie?

His other news was cause for thought. From some of the papers in that case from the ranch in Durango, it seemed that Senator Blackwood had been involved with Santana in a drug deal. Apparently he owed his end of the front money and Santana grabbed Christine as insurance. Marv wanted to go on with all the dirty details, but I'd heard enough and really wasn't interested. On top of that I had the vague feeling that this wasn't all new stuff to Marv. It was no more than a feeling. But a strong one. Pieces began to fall into place that I didn't like. How much had he known from the beginning? And why did he really ask me to go? Blackwood wanted Santana out of the picture--permanently. Who better for the job than...an old shooter? Marv knew me, knew how I'd react out of instinct at the smell of action. He laid it all out, showed me the target, even put the rifle in my hands--did everything but shoot for me, which he knew I'd do readily enough on my own. Like an old racehorse, who at the clang of the starting gate bell was ready to run the laps once again, I would smell the cordite and remember the faint aroma of gun oil, and I'd be ready to line up my target.

While I felt a bit depressed about that whole business--more annoyed with myself than anything else--I felt worse for Hannah and Christine because whatever the man was mixed up in would bring a fallout on the two of them. Poor Christine had been nothing more than a pawn from the very beginning. I wondered what kind of a man would put his family in such a position. A desperate one?

Maybe he had no choice. Though that didn't make sense. Hadn't Marv told me the senator was loaded? But what does that mean? He's wealthy now, for the moment? Did he have a fortune in old money? The good kind that never ran out. My knowledge was limited about financial matters--I left that to a professional. And I didn't play the market. About all I knew was that from the papers the market went up and down. Maybe that's what happened to the senator.

At any rate, Senator Blackwood and whatever he was into, was of no concern to me.

I moped around for a day or so, with Claire increasingly annoyed at me, then put all my attention to the house and the property. There were old jobs to be finished and new, long delayed projects to be started. The dock was in sad shape. The boat needed work. Harry and I kept busy. Well, I kept busy. Harry supervised, with his eyes closed.

Towards the end of November, a few days before Thanksgiving, I began to see items in the *New York Times*, Florida edition, that mentioned political problems in Haiti--the country always had political problems and on occasion, if nothing interesting was happening around the area, some reporter would make it into an important, new story. It was old stuff. Only the names changed. At any rate, the gist of it was that the former president, since he wasn't eligible to run, was doing all he could to disrupt and even cancel the upcoming elections. These were troubled times. A few more days went by, difficulties continued, and a general curfew was put into effect. I followed it all with some interest and concern because I pictured Amy struggling to keep the clinic going, and Al trying to make a living with that wreck of a car he had. This business would not only bring to a halt the tiny steps the country had made towards becoming a democratic government (an impossible dream?) it would throw the process into reverse.

For a time I was able, for the most part, to occupy myself with the many jobs around the property. And this worked until about two weeks before Christmas, when it all caught up with me and I knew that I had to get my life back on track and moving again--I couldn't bury myself in this house. Between what happened in Haiti and in Mexico, I'd been brought back into the world whether I liked it or not. I had been away a long time.

As well, I think the holiday spirit was upon me.

The next morning I arranged, through my bank, to have three accounts set up in Miami--one for Al, one for Father Smith, and one for Amy--into which I deposited twenty thousand dollars for Al, and fifty thousand each for the other two. I arranged for Amy to be notified through the American Embassy with instructions to pass on the information to the others.

Conditions being what they were in Haiti, it wouldn't be a simple process to get to their money, but I could only do so much. I was not about to transfer money directly into any Haitian bank.

It was a simple matter of sharing the wealth. I had more than enough money and what better way to use it? Al could get himself a decent car. Father Smith and Amy would have no trouble finding worthwhile projects to spend the money on, and in fact, their biggest problem might well be the pleasant question of what to buy first. All told, I thought it was a good deal and I felt good about it.

What I didn't feel good about was not being in touch with Kim and not seeing her. Earlier, when I had tried calling the base hospital about her, no one could give me any information. That was bad enough. Now I had to see her. I tracked Marv down and got Kim's address and phone number.

The time difference made it early morning in Paris and it would be a rush to make this evenings flight. But I wanted to see her and I wanted to be in Paris tomorrow.

I told the woman who answered the phone only that I was a friend and wanted to speak with Kim. After a few moments she came on and said hello.

"Hello, Kim. How' s the shoulder?"

"Jack! The shoulder is fine. Where are you?"

"Still in Florida. But I'd like to come to Paris. Do you want to see me?"

"What do you think? Of course I want to see you. When can you come?"

"Tonight?'

"Don't tease me, Jack. You could never make the flight this evening."

"I will if you get off the phone. I'll call you tomorrow one way or the other."

"Okay. And hurry, Jack."

"Bye. I'm on my way."

Claire was used to these things and only wanted to know what kind of clothes to get ready and if I would be home for Christmas. I assured her that I would, knowing that it was a special time for her when she had lots of church activities.

With a little bit of luck, and fast, efficient car service, I made the evening flight out of Orlando.

***

For my taste the French are a bit too...? French? It's all well and good to love ones country and treasure the customs and traditions of that country.

It is quite another thing to be rude and show no patience for those who don't speak your language. Most countries have the same feelings, to some degree, about their own country and the foreigners who visit: the improperly clothed and loud, boorish tourists. But they do spend money and that is what makes the world go round.

Anyway, I hadn't come to see the city, nor the country, nor to put up with the trying French. I was here only to see Kim. Personally, I always thought that I dressed nicely, spoke softly, and of course, spent lots of money.

Thinking of Kim, and trying to show some patience on my part, I endured a long line at customs and tried not to be annoyed with the surly inspector who had me open my bag. He found nothing of course and mumbled an apology, or something.

Upon clearing that mess of petty officials and weary visitors, I raced to a phone to call Kim. Busy. And busy again. And busy still. I could try again from my hotel. Outside the bustling terminal and into a light rain, I found a taxi and quickly settled on a fare. While I was looking forward to getting into my suite, having a leisurely bath and a nap (even being stretched out on a seat in first class is not the same as being in a bed), I was looking forward even more to seeing Kim.

Maybe I could persuade her to spend a few days with me in the suite.

My thoughts were on that delightful subject as I looked out the taxi window. Whatever was out there in the way of sights to see was wasted on me.

My hotel was the Ritz on the Place Vendome. I had stayed there before and liked both the location and the service. It is in the heart of the city and constructed, I learned in a conversation at the bar, by Hardouin-Mansart, the architect of Versailles. I wasn't sure what that meant, not having been to Versailles, but it sounded impressive. What I liked about the hotel was that each suite has its own decor, and is distinct from any of the other suites, and even more, the service was excellent--something like two employees per room whose purpose was to tend to your every need. What's not to like about a place like the Ritz?

I checked in and called her from the desk.

"Jack! Where are you?"

"At the Ritz."

"What Ritz?"

"Paris of course. Can you join me?" I doubted that she would right off, but it was worth a try and I would certainly argue my point when I saw her. "I have a large suite."

After a pause she said, "I don't know, Jack. It's a long trip."

190

"I understand.  Your shoulder okay?"

"Yes.  It's fine.  Stop worrying."

"How about this.  I'll come out there and we'll have a picnic lunch.  We can talk about us and about you spending a few days here with me.  You can show me Paris.  How does that sound?"

"That sounds fine.  How soon will you be here?"

"Just as soon as I can set things up."

"Do you know how to get here?"

"No.  But my driver will.  See you soon."

"Okay.  Bye, Jack.  Tell your driver to drive carefully.  These are narrow roads out here."

"I'll have the best.  Bye, Kim."

After a shower and shave I felt a lot better.  I called room service for a sandwich to tide me over, and had them pick up my things for pressing.  While I waited I fixed a vodka martini.

Next I rang the desk and told them told him, in detail, just what I wanted and that I wanted it now.  He totally understood my request and didn't seem the least bit fazed by my urgency.  After all this was the city of romance.

A while later, he called to tell me that all was in order, except for the picnic lunch which would be picked up on our way--ChateauBriand, rare, was not something that could be rushed.

Dressing down a bit for a country picnic, I put on a tweed jacket that I bought in London--it had the right look of country class--and tan slacks with a blue shirt.  I had put on a tie and taken it off.  I'd tried on several ties.  I was as nervous as my first prom and this was my final choice after trying several outfits.

A prim, fussy man at the front desk looked at my face, rolled his eyes and looked at me again.  Then I remembered.  At the last minute, dressed and ready to go, I noticed a razor cut and put a tiny piece of toilet paper on it to stop the bleeding.

At the curb a driver awaited me with my Mercedes limo.  Surely a coach fit for a queen.  His name was John and he assured me that on board was a complete picnic ensemble with table, chairs, umbrella, the works, and champagne was chilling in a bucket. A large box of what had to be the two dozen roses I'd ordered, lay on the seat facing me.  Did I require anything else? No.  Everything seemed to be in order.

After a brief stop to pick up the meat, which was brought out to the limo in a fancy, quilted warming pouch by the restaurant's chef, we were on our way to the country.

191

The place where she lived was about midway between Paris and Lyon, the second largest city in France and the headquarters of the 178 member states of Interpol.

Her house, located on a narrow road about a mile outside a small village, was a two story, white-washed structure, that had the look of being old but well maintained and up-graded. The front door was new, as were the windows and the large skylight I could see on one side of the upper floor. Beneath every window was a brightly painted box that held drooping flowers. Off to the right was an old barn that housed rusted machinery.

It seemed the perfect place for Kim to be living, a peaceful, charming spot, and I wondered how I could ever convince her to leave. I fixed a vodka martini from the mini bar and thought about that prospect.

The sky had brightened somewhat, still not clear, but at least not raining, and I had high hopes for a pleasant afternoon as far as weather. If it went sour we could always eat our goodies in the limo or in her house. We had options.

The front door was a bright, glossy red with a gold knocker. I banged the thing several times and put on my best smile.

In a few moments the door was opened by a woman, not Kim (my smile was wasted) who seemed annoyed at being bothered to attend to the door. Maybe that was her usual expression? Maybe she was having a bad day? More likely she was being protective--from the dark apron she had on I saw her as an employee rather than a friend.

She said, "Oui?" I told her I was an old friend of Kim's, not a total lie as far as longevity, but not totally true either, and that she was expecting me. She looked from me to the limo, then at the box of roses, back to me, and once again out to the limo. I could see her mind turning: *How bad could a man be who comes calling in this weather in a car like that, dressed like he is, and carrying a box of flowers? My husband should be here to see this. Maybe he would learn something.*

"Your name?" she said.

"Jack. Jack Morgan. What's yours?

She looked at me as if I'd asked where she kept her jewelry. After a rather long moment she said, "My name is Gabrielle."

"Pretty name."

She ignored my comment. "Wait here. She is upstairs." With that she closed the door in my face.

Ah the warmth of the French.

It what was a long time, at least for me, before the door opened. When it did and I saw her standing there--she was wearing a stained smock and her left arm was in a sling, on her face a smudge of blue paint--I said, "Hello Kim." Not exactly eloquent, but real.

I gave her the roses and she put them aside on a wooden bench. Then she said, "Hello Jack," and folded herself against me. After I had wrapped my arms around her and was holding her close, she added, "What kept you?"

"Slow driver, Kim. Are you ready for our picnic?"

"Almost. Actually you're here sooner than I expected. I'll change quickly and get a sweater."

"No hurry. No need really.. You look lovely just as you are. Besides, this is a spontaneous thing."

She kissed me and said, "That may be, Jack. But I need a few minutes-- spontaneous or not. Go upstairs and take a look at my studio while I freshen up. I'm hardly an accomplished painter. But I try. And I enjoy my work." She pulled me inside and closed the door. "I'll only be a minute."

A narrow wooden stairway led me almost directly into a large room off the upper hallway. With the skylight, and large windows along the front and side, the room had good lighting, and on a closer look I could see that this had once been two small bedrooms converted into one large studio. Against one wall were several finished works waiting to be framed, or just waiting. Her current work was on an easel in the center of the room, a landscape that was pretty good. I thought she was better with that than the flowers and still life that she'd done much more of. I was looking through the finished stuff when she called that she was ready.

She was standing by the door, the smock and paint smudge gone, with a blue sweater around her shoulders. "I'm ready for our picnic."

"You are and you look lovely. Your carriage is waiting." I took her arm in mine and we walked out to the car.

We drank champagne from Waterford Crystal and rolled along the country road. Kim had taken off her shoes and had her legs curled up under her on the leather seat. She leaned over and kissed me. "This beats Durango."

"Anything would, Kim." I kissed her and she was smiling. I said, in my best imitation of a serving butler, "More champagne?"

"I suppose. But it does taste a bit cheesy," she answered, raising her glass with little finger extended. She laughed then and said, "This is so good, Jack. What is it?"

"Just an old Dom Perignon I found in the cellar. Twelve year old I think."

"I didn't know you had a cellar."

"It's under the opera house."

We were both laughing. I put my glass in the rack on the door and reached out for her. "Is the shoulder okay for some hugging?"

She put her glass aside. "For you it is." I put my arms around her and held her gently. She looked up at me and said, "You can do better than that, Jack. The shoulder is really all right."

We rode along that way for a time, me holding her. Her hair had the scent of fresh flowers in a country garden. I said, "If you see a place that you'd like to stop, just let me know."

After a time she said, "I needed that, Jack. I needed you to hold me, needed to know that you are real."

"I'm very real, Kim. Are you getting hungry?"

Looking up at me she said, "You know, I am getting hungry."

"That's a good sign."

"That I'm hungry?"

"Yes. It means you're getting healthy again. Are you looking for a place to stop?"

"Now and then," she said. She kissed me then looked out the window. "Here! Let's stop here."

I looked out and it looked like any other country spot of rolling green land--nothing special. "This is it?"

I lowered the glass partition and told the driver to pull off the road.

After we had the table set up, everything just so--the driver had gone off somewhere not to be seen again for at least an hour--I waved an arm over the warming packet. "Ta dah!." I opened it up and we were looking at a gorgeous piece of meat. She sat there staring. I said, "ChateauBriand."

She smiled. "It had to be. Jack, you're marvelous. Very romantic too."

In a few minutes, with the meat carved, plates fixed, and another bottle of champagne opened, we toasted and started to eat under a still gray sky. I said, "Is this better than that meal in Mexico City?"

"No comparison. This is wonderful."

"You warm enough?"

"Jack. Stop worrying about me."

"Are you?" She told me that she was and we ate in silence for a time. Finished, I said, "I want to talk about us, Kim."

"You've weakened my defenses with that wonderful champagne. So I suppose it is a good time to talk." She leaned forward and smiled. "Are you going to take advantage of me?"

"Perish the thought. But I will try and convince you to come back to Florida with me."

She looked at me than away and didn't say anything for a long moment. "That's a lot to think about. I have a life here."

"I know. You have a life and a job."

"I'm on medical leave,"she said thoughtfully, "and I really don't know if I'll go back. After my parents were killed I buried myself in my work and the job served me well. Things are different now. I'm different. I have my house and my flowers and my painting."

"Sounds to me as if you are turning off the world. What about love?"

"That will come if it's meant to be." She was quiet for a moment. "I still think of Durango."

"Durango is a memory, a bad memory, something to let go of, to put into the past and never brought to light. We can't live there, Kim. It's a dark room and we have to lock the door and never go in there. We have to move on."

"It's easy to say."

"You mean it's easy for me to say? No, it isn't easy for me. I have my own dark place." Seeing her expression and listening to her voice, I realized that this wasn't the time to go into all this. Maybe I'd gone too far already. Her life had been shattered and it would take time to get the pieces back together. I had been a part of that and now I had to find my part, if indeed I had one, in the rebuilding.

"I'm sorry I brought this up, Kim. This isn't the time. We can make as much time as we need to talk about all of this. I don't have any place to go. Do you?"

She smiled and her eyes were wet. "No. I don't have any other place I want to go."

"Good. That's settled. We'll both stay in France for a while. Let's finish up this little bit of champagne and be on our way. I'll call the driver."

I lit a cigarette and we were quiet then. She got up from the table and walked a short way off in the grass, then came back and sat down. Leaning back in the chair she sighed and patted her stomach. "It was wonderful. I'm stuffed and it was wonderful, Jack."

The air was definitely cooling and I for one wanted to get us both under the covers, somewhere--if not in the same bed at least under the same roof. We had gotten what had to be the best of this day. The night was yet to come.

By the time the driver got back we were both ready to get into a warm limo and snuggle, and we did just that.

She was against me, tight in my arms. I said, "Is your shoulder okay for this?"

"It's really fine and this is the best thing that could happen to it."

"Then we'll stay just like this."

"Are you taking me home?"

"If that's where you want to go.  But bear in mind my suite is quite luxurious, and large, and has two bedrooms.  You can be private and get all the rest you want.  The food is wonderful and on top of that, I will be there to attend to your every need.  Tomorrow, if you feel up to it we can be tourists and you can show me the best of Paris."

She looked up at me.  "I think the best of Paris might be right here, Jack, with his arms around me."

"Now that *is* a compliment."  I kissed her and said, "Are you considering my offer?"

"I am taking it under serious consideration," she said smiling.  A pause, then, "You have made me an offer I cannot refuse."

"Wonderful!"

"But I do have to stop and pick up some things."

"We can buy whatever you need."

"I know.  But some personal things I want."

We stopped at her house on the way back and she went in, then came out with a small case and a hanging dress bag which the driver put carefully away in the trunk.

"You didn't bring clothes?" I kidded.

"Of course I brought clothes."

"I planned to buy whatever you might need--and even what you don't need.  We are operating here on a fat expense account."

"Your personal expense account no doubt," she said with a grin.  "I am not without funds, Jack."

"You are no doubt a wealthy woman, Kim,  But alas, your money is no good with me.  It might as well be counterfeit.  And besides, you have terrible taste.  Look at that awful meal you brought us in Durango."

She brought her right hand up to my cheek and held it there.  "But look at the great meal in Mexico City."

"*I* bought that."

"That's true," she said with a nod.  "But *I* ordered the wine."

"Correct.  Your taste in wine is excellent.  You can order all the wine you like in Paris but you cannot pay.  Any other questions?"

"Not at the moment."

Were it not for Kim, of course, I wouldn't be in Paris this time of year, with the dark days, cold rain, and the coming of snow.  I had long ago lost my tolerance for cold, or even the nearness of cold weather.  But the

196

moment is now. There may not be a tomorrow. There is really only today and Kim is a part of today.

I was in Paris because I loved that woman.

At the remembrance of Paris and the weather I thought of another time-- not in the city but in the country. I had lain in the cold, wet grass for a full day and night waiting for my target. At the last moment, with my objective in sight, the operation was called off. It turned out that my target was also an Israeli target and they had priority. They had first crack at any terrorist group in that part of the world. It was an ugly memory and a big disappointment.

In any case, since the past is best forgotten, or for the most part should be, once we have dumped the excess baggage of guilt and the like, and absorbed whatever positive things that might help us deal with the future, there is really only today.

How horrible would it be to get snowed in with Kim?

For the next two wonderful days, since the weather was not a problem, we didn't mind waiting in a queue to visit the centuries old Louvre Museum to see the Mona Lisa and Venus de Milo.

We walked the Champs Elysees and looked at the Arc De Triomphe. At night we went to the Eiffel Tower to catch the magnificent view from what had been, when it was built in 1889, the tallest structure in the world.

And of course there was a dinner at Maxim's. Though perhaps not *the* place in Paris that it was a hundred years ago, it is still nevertheless an establishment to be visited if for no other reason than the ambiance, the glitter and glamour, painted ceilings, the music for dancing, and to experience that feeling of fame from another time.

In keeping with that other time, and our own romantic mood, Kim wore a black evening dress that accentuated her blond good looks and fine figure. Many an eye was cast in her direction. No one looked at me, well, a few out of curiosity to see who rated that gorgeous creature. But I had remembered to pack my custom made dinner jacket, and while I felt well dressed, in this crowd I was merely average.

We had been quiet for a few moments as the champagne was opened and poured. That whole afternoon, and now, she seemed to be lost in thought as if struggling with a problem. I knew that I had to be at least a part of whatever she was trying to deal with. I knew because she was a huge part of my problems. These few days were a wonderful interlude, an escape, a journey away from reality to a romantic fantasy land where all was like a dream. Not that it had to end. We could go on living this way the rest of our lives. I had the money. It was great to think about as a dream.

The reality was that I didn't think she would give up her life for that, for me. Could I really expect that of her? She had made a life for herself, not without problems of course because there is no such thing, but a life, her life here in France. Mine in Florida was a much different world, a new kind of life, a whole other world. The more I thought about it the more fear I had that she would turn me down.

But then we didn't have to live in Florida. We could live anywhere. Why didn't I think that was possible?

I took her hand across the table. "You seem far away today. Are you having a good time?"

Maybe it was the champagne, but I thought her eyes were sparkling. "Of course I am, Jack. Why would you even ask?" Then after a moment, "This place is unbelievable. Didn't they film some movie here?"

"Probably."

"I'm serious. Was it Gigi?"

"Maybe."

"It *was* Gigi!"

"You would know better than I."

She looked away then and seemed to go off in thought. I said, "You seem very pensive tonight."

She looked back at me. "The Tower was great wasn't it?" She knew I was waiting and went on. "Pensive? Thoughtful? Yes. I have a lot to think about, Jack. You've asked me to share your world with you. That's a big thing." She gave me a little smile. "Two different worlds we live in, two different worlds..." she sang softly. "Do you remember that one?"

"Vaguely. But we can make those two worlds into one anywhere we like."

She emptied her glass and quickly refilled. "We could. But not tonight, Jack. No more talk. Tonight is for...love. And...shall we dance?"

We dined and danced until near closing. Kim, I thought, had too much to drink, not sloppy, pleasantly tipsy, which I attributed to a combination of our surroundings and an escape from decisions.

She stopped the taxi a few blocks from our hotel and danced along the sidewalk humming tunes from "Gigi." She sang: "Thank heaven for little girls..." I wanted to love her so much.

In her bedroom, I helped her out of her dress and got her tucked into bed. She put her arms around my neck and kissed me and in moments was fast asleep. The suddenness of her going to sleep, as I stood there looking at this incredibly lovely girl, was disappointing in a way, but she was still recovering and we'd had a long night. With more wisdom and inner strength than I knew I had, I resisted climbing in with her.

Sleep was longer in coming for me.

Some time later, having thankfully drifted off in the midst of many thoughts and concerns about us, I was awakened by movement in the room. By the faint filtered in from the street, I watched her take off her nightgown. It was the first time that I had really seen her without clothes and she was even more beautiful than I had imagined she would be at this moment. I turned back the cover and she got in beside me. "My room was a bit chilly," she said. "Mind if I join you?"

I was far too busy with my holding her and kissing her to answer such a silly question.

"That's much better, Jack. I needed to be held."

"You came to the right place. I'm actually well known for my holding."

She pulled away from me just far enough to look into my face. "Not too well known I hope."

"Only within a very small circle, Kim. Mostly kids and dogs love me. More dogs than kids."

"Oh. Well. That's okay." She moved back and curled against me. "Now you can make it dogs, kids, and one woman."

"A most beautiful woman. The *only* woman."

"You do have a way with words, Jack."

I lay there feeling her against me, loving the scent of her, and in moments I knew from her breathing that she was asleep.

My contented sleep, restful and comfortable, no doubt from the feeling that something wonderful had happened with her earlier in the night, and was still happening to me, was abruptly broken by Kim's hand jabbing and tickling me in the side. "Wake up, Jack!" she shouted into my ear. "I'm starving."

I laughed and tickled her in return. We were both laughing and rolling around like a couple of teenagers. I said, "Leave me alone, woman. I've been seriously busy holding you and it's been a short night." She was quiet then and I brought her to me, gently, not like the frenzy of before.

"A short night. But a lovely one, Jack. You're quiet good at this holding business. Was it as good for you?"

"I aim to please, Ma'am," I told her in my best Clark Gable voice. "And if anything, I think it might have been better for me."

"I do declare," she said, coming back in a fairly good Scarlett. "You say the nicest things!"

"But I do think you're right, Kim." I was back to plain old Jack Morgan. "If we intend to keep this up, this active regimen we're on, we need nourishment. Shall we go downstairs and have coffee and Croissants, then tons of ham and eggs, sausage, cheese, fruit--all kinds of energy things?"

"Sounds wonderful, Jack. But won't that let them know what we've been up to here in bed?"

"Who is them?"

"Everybody."

"Probably. Do you care?"

"Not really."

"Then we will have to get dressed," I told her.

"You're such a prude, Jack."

Early afternoon by the time we left the hotel, off to visit the Latin Quarter, so named from the language used by students in the middle ages, and made famous, or infamous, by the student protests of the late sixties. This is the Left Bank. It looks like the student haven it is with small streets, cheap restaurants, book shops, and the like. To the western end were the cafes made famous by the intelligentsia of an earlier time: Cafe de Flore, Brasserie Lipp, and the Cafe des Deux Magots.

Neither of us was really in the mood for sightseeing. We were going though the motions, looking more at each other than at the sights, pretending that we were real and forever, that our life together was without an element of uncertainty. Only later, when we were having lunch at a pleasant sidewalk cafe, did we talk about what was really on our minds.

****

About 5800 kilometers to the west-northwest of Paris lies a strip of land called Coney Island. This island, an interesting story in itself even in its delapidated state of today, with a world famous roller coaster, and boardwalk eateries, is a part of the borough of Brooklyn, which is a part of the total makeup of the City of New York. On the eastern end of this boardwalk is the city's largest Russian community--a neighborhood known as Little Odessa. Here one can find an assortment of Russian nightclubs and shops, and as well, one can find the Mafia.

Though not a member of that organization, nor with any group at the moment, a man known as Alexei Ivanov (this was not his given name) was walking home from a meeting at Cafe Glechik, a local favorite that featured good, inexpensive food.

He was in a bright mood for the first time in many months because he had just gotten a job, or at least the possibility of a job. Equally pleasing was the fact that his target was an American and that the job would be

200

done in this country. He was tired of traveling. That was all he knew at this point. But it was enough to bring a smile to his weathered face.

Alexei had made his living as a shooter, the best in his time for the KGB.

Coming back along the decaying boardwalk, Alexei came to the small house he had been able to buy, just two blocks from the ocean, and again smiled at his good fortune in being able to have such a place to live. In Mother Russia only the rich and powerful could live close to the water, were able to escape from the dirty city and know the fresh, clean air of the country. But then, they were also the ones who had enough food to eat and the ones who could afford enough heat to keep the cold from their rooms.

Alexei knew the cold. He had lived in two rooms with a brother and sister and only a tiny heater for warmth. His father, God rest his soul, had fought and died for Russia against the German hordes that threatened the land. He lay somewhere in the frozen waste outside the then gutted city of Stalingrad--a patriot and a hero to the end. At least that is what the family was told.

His brother and sister were dead when he came home from Afshanistan, victims of a rare germ, a plague, the officials had said. There was never enough money for the medicine.

An uncle, far-removed, perhaps no more than a lover of his mother--Alexei could find no formal family connection--was an officer in the Red Army. He had gotten the young boy into a decent school and then into the special training that led to an elite army unit. Alexei proved to be a good soldier and an excellent marksman.

Then, with the decline of the great Russian Republic, the utter failure of communism and the rise of graft and corruption into the system, he, like many others with a wish to survive, turned to the inner strength of the Russian mafia. He did what he knew best--he killed. With the passage of time he earned a reputation as an efficient killing machine and his talent became known to a higher echelon. He worked for the KGB and then became a contract killer for a central government committee.

But the only constant is change.

The Russian economy faltered, then came to a state near death. The change to a capitalist system, which they saw as a must for survival, would be a slow and costly move. There was no money. They army went without pay, soldiers often selling their weapons, and even their medals and uniforms for money to live.

Since there was no money to pay for the billions agreed to on a space venture with the wealthy Americans, Alexei figured there was certainly not enough to pay for a contract killer, no matter how good he was or how much he was still needed.  There would always be a need for men like him.  But there might not always be the resolve to use such men, nor the funds to pay them.

His country, in this sorry state that had befallen Mother Russia, was a place Alexei could no longer stand.  He was not wealthy but he was not truly among the poor.  He had the money to go to America.  Many of his countrymen were already there and prospering, lesser men than himself, and he had no doubt that he would survive.

He shook his head sadly at the thought of his country as he heated the water for his tea--brave, loyal soldiers, the cream of Russian youth,  some of the best trained in the world, now begging in the streets.  How could this happen?  Could it happen to the capitalists of the west?

His own lot was not so bad.  He filled the cup and watched the water darken around the tea bag.  In the summer this place was like having a dacha on the sea, just like the rich and the politicians at home. Unfortunately, his house here on a narrow plot in Little Oddessa was his only home--winters here were just like winters at home with the freezing wind blowing in from the ocean.  He was getting too old, aching in the joints now, stiff in the mornings, no longer having the feel for the clear, bracing, Russian winters.  He remembered with mixed feelings the sight of vast stretches of white, frozen land.  It took a hardy people to live in that country.

While he was not really old, he mused, he was beyond youth and the immortality they believed in, their brash naiveté that brought them quick answers to problems that had been unsolved for centuries, past the struggling middle years of work and family raising, but not yet into the skeptical, negative period of the old who saw nothing but disaster ahead for the world.

He felt certain that he could still hunt, find, and kill his quary.

Setting the cup aside for a moment while the tea cooled, he went to an old wooden chest that stood against the wall, opened it, and took out a long leather case.  He would once again disassemble the specially made rifle that was his partner, his signature, a very part of his being, inspect each part for even the most minute flaw, then clean and oil each piece.

****

I looked at Kim as she  thoughtfully sipped her  glass of white wine and stared off into space for a moment--a very normal reaction I suppose since I had just asked her to come and live with me in Florida.

Not a simple question to be sure.

I was asking her to turn her life around. In truth, I was asking her to give up her life here in France, and to walk away from everything that was familiar to her, to give it all up and live with a man she barely knew in a country she knew even less. When I thought about it, watching her face, seeing the visible signs of questioning and doubt, I wondered how I could even ask her, and secondly, why she would consider such a thing. But while lovers may be blind to a degree, seeing only what they choose to see, and that is not a bad thing, they are also filled with a bold confidence that makes all their dreams attainable. They are the masters of their world.

She came back to me with a bit of a smile. "I hope you're not expecting an answer right away. This comes as a bit of a shock to my system."

"I know you haven't been well," I kidded. "Your resistance is down. But then, isn't that the exact time to ask?"

"It isn't my physical system. It's the mental one. I'm thinking of just what it means. What you are asking."

"Simple, Kim. I'm asking you to come live a grand life with me in sunny Florida, the Sunshine State. That's my home and I'd like it to be yours as well. But we don't even have to live there--it can be anywhere you choose."

"That would be twice as bad, Jack." Serious now. "That way we would both be leaving our homes. You love your home?"

"Yes. I'm comfortable there."

"But you would leave if I wanted you to leave?"

"Of course."

"That tells me a lot. But it doesn't solve our problem."

"And what is our problem? You know that I'm in love with you." Her smile came back when I added, "Madly in love with you. Isn't that enough?"

"It is a lot, Jack. It may even be enough. I'm just not sure. I have my home and my job here, my friends, a whole environment that is comfortable and familiar. It is a big step."

"You said you might not go back to your job. Do you have to?"

"No. Not in the financial sense. I have money. The work was something I needed at the time."

"So the job really isn't a factor?"

"No. I guess not. I don't need that anymore. I have my house to take care of and I have my painting. They're important to me."

"You don't have to give those up, Kim. Keep the house. We can come here in the summer. Florida is too damn hot anyway. We can spend four or five months a year here."

"And what about your life and your work?"

"What work?"

She held eye contact for a long moment. "I know what you do--what you did anyway. Is that finished?"

"It's been finished for a long time."

"What about Mexico?"

"Mexico happened. It wasn't a planned job for me. Those days are over."

"Can you be sure? Can we be sure that is out of our lives? I checked out the senator in our files. He was active in more than one drug deal. He is dirty, Jack."

I reached acrosss the table and held her hands. "What does that have to do with us, Kim?"

"It has to do with us because you were there--in Durango. You know about the senator. And even if you don't, he thinks you know about him. Do you think he will let that go? Do you think he will let you go?"

I squeezed her hands and leaned forward to give her a kiss. "I think you are overreacting. I think you are very melodramatic, exciting, and sexy."

Her face was close to mine. "I like the last two. Melodramatic?" she added, shrugging her shoulders.

"Two out of three is good."

"Seriously, Jack. I worry about that. I worry about you."

"I think, my dear lady, that you were also in Durango. Doesn't that mean that you are just as vulnerable as I? Doesn't that mean that you are just as much a target as I? And doesn't that mean that I should be worried about you?"

"I'm a big girl."

"Not terribly. Just right actually."

"You are near impossible."

"I *am* close, Kim. Near is good in horseshoes--and Bocci, which I know nothing about. Maybe a few other activities. It's not so good in love. In love one has to be right on." She was laughing, and very beautiful. "Now what about us? I won't press you. I promised Claire that I'd be back a few days before the Christmas holiday. It's a very busy time for her."

"Claire?"

"Of course. You wouldn't know about Claire. There's lots you don't know about me and I plan to change that. Claire is a wonderful woman, a friend, who runs my house."

Kim's face went blank and she stared at me. "You have a woman in your house now!"

This was something I had to explain and I did. "Claire is my cook."

"Then she works for you?"

"Yes. But she means more to me than a cook. She's been with me a long time."

"Oh," Kim said thoughtfully. "For a moment there you had me worried. Now I understand. Is there anything else I should know?"

"Well. Harry lives with us as well."

"Harry. A man lives there as well?"

"Harry is a dog, a big lovable Lab Retreiver. You will love him. I know he will love you."

She was nodding in thought. "Is there more?"

"Yes. I have a 200 foot yacht and I keep a dozen gorgeous young women as my guests."

Taking a playful swing at me she said, "Now I know you're kidding me. You wouldn't have the strength."

I kissed her again. "You are so right. I only want strength for you. Anyway, I told Claire I'd be back. How does this sound? I'll make reservations for the evening flight tomorrow night out of Orly."

"So soon?" Her smile told me that she had asked out of surprise at the suddeness more than anything else.

"Yes. I want you with me. From what I saw of your house it's in good order--you have an efficient women there as well. I"m sure you're well organized--one who could leave at a moments notice if need be."

"Actually you're right," she said thoughtfully. "There isn't any reason I can't leave." Then after a moment she added, "You make me sound so terribly organized."

"There is nothing wrong with being organized."

"What are you smiling at?"

"Your expression 'terribly organized.' It's so English."

"I was English educated."

"And very well I might say. So, then you will come with me tomorrow?"

"Yes. I will, Jack."

"Wonderful!" I reached right across the table, then lifting her up I took her in my arms and hugged her. There was noise from around us, loud talk, then clapping--romance was still alive here. I ordered champagne for us and drinks for everyone. In a few moments the place had settled down and us with it. We were sipping Dom Perignon. "First thing in the morning..."

She interrupted. "The first thing?"

"Well," I said, grinning, "maybe the second thing. You take the car and go do whatever you have to do. You'll have all day."

205

"More than enough time, Jack. My biggest problem will be deciding what clothes to take with me."

"You don't need any."

"Jack!"

"No. What I meant was that Florida is hot and sunny. We wear a cool shirt and shorts."

"But I need more than shorts and tops."

"You need nothing, my dear," I said faking a leering, lecherous look.

She looked at me for a long moment then said, "If we're going to see any more of Paris we'd better get going."

"Must we?"

"Only because I want to show you more of my city."

"And so we will go."

We toured and then had a lovely dinner that night in my suite--I should say *our* suite because it had become quite warm and comfortable with her added touch of flowers in all the rooms. She did that kind of thing naturally and it was somthing else about her that I loved. She seemed to come into a room and give it life.

I didn't want to let her go in the morning--I dreaded a day without her. We made love and then she had to go.

All day long I wondered if I had made a huge mistake in letting her go, if only for the day. Was I that insecure? Or was it that love is so delicate? I packed and then ate and read the papers, all of them, English edition, since I couldn't handle reading French. I could get by in a very brief exchange-- if it was about eating or sleeping. As grand as my suite was, it didn't give me tv in English. I watched for a while, surfing channels, then settled on a good soccer match for a time.

Then I went out for a walk.

When I got back I considered calling her but then thought better of it. She had things to do and I'd only be interrupting.

Somehow the day passed until it was time for leave for the airport. I had to get another car, forgetting that she had my car and driver.

There were long lines for check in, not quite so lengthy for First Class, and I moved along quickly, checking in almost two hours before departure, not because of airline regulations but because I'd simply gotten bored waiting around the hotel without Kim. Paying for both, I told the girl to hold Kim's ticket, that she would be along soon to pick it up. I told her to direct Kim straight to the First Class lounge.

I bought the New York Times--the one paper that I hadn't read during the day--and settled down in the lounge. Much of the news I'd read earlier. But the Times did have a different slant and broad coverage. The world situation at least as far as their reporters saw it, seemed to be stuck in the same rut of violence and corruption. I moved on quickly to the sports page looking for anything on the Dolphins and finding little--it was a New York paper! In the Business Section things were looking just as grim: market down, lay offs, earnings and profit way below expectations. The bottom line seemed to be that the consumer had to have confidence and spend, spend, spend, or the system just didn't work. Interesting theory there, the money has to go round and round like the juggler keeping three plates spinning on tiny sticks. While I wasn't too interested in all of this I would read anything to kill time.

Still an hour before departure and no Kim.

In near desperation I turned to the Crossword. Big mistake. In fifteen minutes of work, I'd filled in three answers for my efforts and felt decidedly dumb (mentally challenged?) and inferior. Did anyone really finish these things? Harvard professors?

Getting close now. I wasn't going to have a drink until I got settled on board--what's the harm in one?

In a few more minutes we started boarding and with that I started to get worried. Could she have changed her mind? Maybe I was expecting too much of her. Asking too much. Perhaps her feelings weren't all that strong about me--as strong as mine about her. Maybe. Maybe. I had all kinds of questions and lots of doubt. This was something new for me and I didn't seem to be handling it well. I kept scanning the crowd for any sight of her. What could have happened?

Some of the brighter stars in our galaxy, biggies in the entertainment orbit, the rich and famous, were slipped on board without the public getting even a glimpse of their glow, as if their brightness would blind and cripple us. I wasn't one of those and I was standing there holding up the whole boarding process while I searched for Kim. Finally I went in to my seat. One passenger across the aisle from me was already ordering drinks.

Boarding passengers takes time on a large aircraft, and in my mind that still left time for Kim to show up, though the clock was ticking.

A final check by the attendant for seat belts and loose gear, and in moments the doors were being closed. Then they were opened. A disheveled Kim burst into the plane and plopped down in the seat next to me.

We looked at each other for a long moment without saying a word. Finally I said, "In your mad, reckless, impetuous love for me you lost all track of time?" We both burst out laughing and I hugged her as best I could within the seat belt restraint. "I'm glad you're here, Kim."

"So am I, Jack. You won't believe what happened. I'll tell you all about it after we get settled in the air. I could use a drink."

"Champagne?"

"Why not."

Our fellow passenger across the aisle, accompanied by a leggy, painted blonde--I'd heard whispers that he was a famous rock star, but who was unknown to me--was hitting a bottle of Jack Daniels pretty hard and was getting loud. The attendant shrugged, and gave us kind of a pleading look as if to say it wasn't her fault. Maybe she'd manage to sedate him later.

Kim and I ignored him and concentrated on each other as she told me about her problems in getting to the airport. "The driver was so nice--I had him running me all over as I tied up loose ends--there is a lot to done in getting away. Anyway, we got back to the house in plenty of time." She stopped for a sip of bubbly. "We were on our way to the airport when the car died. It just stopped. They're all electronics these days. Then on top of that the car phone hadn't been charging so he had to walk to the nearest village for a phone." She paused in her narrative and looked at me with a smile. "I called you earlier in the afternoon and there was no answer."

"Must have been when I went out for a walk."

"Oh. At this point I knew I was never going to be at the airport two hours before departure."

She looked tired and the champagne was hitting her hard--I'd put her under some pressure. "It's not written in stone, Kim. They are allowing for a slow check in, passports, that kind of thing."

"You were no help," she kidded. "I called your hotel again from some little village, but you had evidently already left for the airport. Not in stone? How early did you get here?"

"Early."

"You have that supercilious look on your face."

"It's a look of empathy, Kim."

"Empathy? I must need more champagne."

I ignored that and asked her to continue.

"That's about it. That's why I was late. And here I am."

"And I'm glad you are here."

We were quiet then for a few moments. There was quiet across the aisle--the rock star was fast asleep and the blonde was reading the Wall Street Journal. Figure that. I turned back to Kim. "I think you'll love Christmas..." I started to say. Kim's head hung down on one shoulder and her eyes were closed. I had the attendant adjust her seat--they went almost flat and were wide and comfortable--and got her a pillow and a blanket. She was gone. I had wanted to tell her that I was sure, well, fairly sure, since there would be sun and mild temperatures rather than the winter she would have at home. A minor detail. The important part is how you spend the holiday and who you spend it with. I was going to go into all that with her.

Then I fell asleep.

In Little Odessa the phone rang for Alexei Ivanov--the call he'd been waiting for. He would soon be traveling to Washington and he was told to be ready to leave in a few moments notice.

The Christmas holiday was a joyous occasion. The weather was mild but I heard no complaints from Kim. Claire was very busy what with cooking special dishes--mostly for Kim--and tending to her church doings. Harry was himself. He'd taken a shine to Kim and followed her everywhere--his purpose seemed to be to lick her to death. I was his forgotten master and his Christmas present went accordingly--a rather small bone. But I must say that he had excellent taste in buying Kim an emerald bracelet. Sure.

Claire was the difficult one to buy for when it came to presents. She had no interest in clothes or jewelry--for that matter she had no interest in *any* material things. Kim and I were making no progress in talking about something for her until I remembered something: several times she'd mentioned having trouble with the stove. For whatever reason I'd never gotten around to doing anything about the problem--most likely because I didn't do the cooking. So, while I wasn't exactly thrilled with getting a new stove as a present for Claire (Kim thought it was a great idea) I had a new one installed when she went off to do some shopping with Kim. When they came back and she went into the kitchen she screamed at the sight. Along with the stove was an array of the latest gadgets for her kitchen. After she'd looked at it all for a few minutes she commented that she could never learn how to use that complicated-looking microwave, and as for the ceramic stove top with no burners showing...? She didn't know about that. Of course all the time she is grinning from ear to ear. Knowing her, she'd have it figured out and using it in no time, maybe cutting some corners with the electronics but using it never the less.

Either by accident or by design, the problems started after Christmas.

Claire was busy in the kitchen, Kim was off walking, or swimming, or whatever with Harry, and I, having nothing better to do--and having temporarily lost the affection of my dog--was working on a troublesome fuel line. I could just as easily have the whole system replaced at the boat yard, replace the whole damn boat if I wanted--it wasn't a question of money--but I enjoyed tinkering, sometimes.

The cell phone that I had lying nearby chirped and I picked it up. It was Marv.

"What's up Marv?" I said, wiping off my oily hands. "Somebody unhappy with Durango?" I asked, kidding. It was a done deal after all, finished, ended in a satisfactory conclusion I thought, for the good guys anyway. If anyone was unhappy with it, too bad, though I couldn't imagine who that might be.

Marv came back in a serious tone and I knew we were on different wave lengths. "A problem has come up. Some things we need to talk about, Jack."

"Why so serious, Marv?" He didn't answer. "So talk. You're interrupting some very important work on the boat but go ahead. By the way, you have a nice holiday?"

He ignored that. "Not on the phone, Jack."

Something was drastically wrong here. I was talking to a stranger. "That serious huh? Your phone is clean."

"Yes. But yours isn't."

"That's true. Is is that bad?"

After a period of silence, he said, "You need to come here, Jack. I'm getting a lot of pressure on this Durango thing, more than I want to deal with alone. We have to talk, in person."

Far beyond a bit odd--I'd talked with this man during and after some heavy shit that had gone down, stuff that would topple a government, or at least a presidency, and he handled it without a ripple--this was a Marv that I had not only never seen, but could not imagine. I didn't know what to say. "Are you in real trouble here?"

A pause. "This is serious, Jack. Not like the old days. I could handle this crap then. Maybe I'm getting old."

"We all are, Marv. What's different now? Besides old age."

"What's different? The pressure. I'm getting it from the Director and from some of the senate. It's not like the old days, Jack. We used to have some people around with balls, men and women who didn't spend all day looking at their televison spots, watching the polls every minute, and looking in the mirrror. But I can't get into this on the phone. We need to talk. There is stuff I want to pass on to you in case something happens to me. Stuff from Durango--you'll know what to do with the documents."

"I thought that you and the Director were tight?" He didn't say anything and I went on. "Are we getting into the melodramatic here, Marv?" I was

210

trying to lighten things up and put him at ease. "What could happen to an old Jarhead like you? You're too damn tough and ornery to die. It's not your time. You're the one who told me about that business--a time to die."

"I'm not so sure about that, Jack."

"Lighten up, Marv. I'll come up and we'll go fishing."

"Would be nice if we had time for fishing. Be a little cold for you Floridians--all that thin blood. How soon can you get up here?"

"Well, I'm working on the boat right now. Nothing serious. I suppose I could get away. Kim won't like this one bit."

"She's with you?" I told him yes and he said, "You have something good there, Jack. Don't mess it up. Did I tell you she was with Intepol?"

"I think so. I think we knew about that, Marv."

"Good record. Solid background. You going to marry her?"

"I don't know. I hope so."

"Good. Now how soon can you get up here?"

"How soon do you need me?"

"Yesterday."

"Huh," I said to myself. I owed him everything--my very life. Not that he would ever put it on that basis--that wasn't his style. But it was a truth. A fact of my life. "I'll get a flight tomorrow, Marv."

"I appreciate it, Jack. I'll make a hotel reservation for you--the usual. My treat."

"As I remember, it was usually your treat, Marv."

He sounded brighter now. "I'm a classy guy, Jack. Once you get to know me."

"Not many people do."

"Bye Jack."

I finished up with the fuel line, replacing a weak spot in the tubing and tightening connections, working mostly by rote since my mind was on Marv. There wasn't a question about my going, nor did that bother me. What did bother me was telling Kim.

But before I had time to do much thinking or worrying about that Kim came down to the boat with Harry tagging along behind. She took one look at my face and asked what was wrong. As we walked back up to the house I told her the whole story, or what I knew at this point, and when I had finished she was quiet for a few minutes. Then she said, "And you feel that you have to go?" I nodded. Another silence, then, "Well then you should go. I don't like it, any of it, and I have bad feelings about this whole thing. At the same time I know how you feel. I do think that this debt you talk about is a bit over done. I'm telling you how I feel. At the same time, I'd never tell you not to do what you feel has to be done, Jack.

211

I might hate whatever it is you want to do,"she added with a smile, "and be furious at you for wanting to do it, but we must be true to ourselves individually as well as to our coupleness. Does that make sense?"

"Makes a lot of sense to me, Kim." At the house I opened the door and Harry went charging past us into the kitchen. I took her in my arms. "And I love you even more for understanding."

"More?" she said laughing. "I thought you already loved me as much as you possibly could love me."

"There's always room for growth."

"As long as it isn't physical."

"Right." But she had started me thinking. Just how much did I owe Marv? When is the marker torn up? Yes, this all started *with* Marv and *for* him. I owed him then. We went back a long way, back to the wars, back to the time when I was a kid and the world was different. The kid could have just as easily been killed as to have done the killing, except for Marv. He put it in perspective, helped me to see that in a time of madness I could do what was expected of me, do my job and survive--that was what we did in wars if we were lucky, and careful, and professional: survived, what we hoped to do. I was a tradesman in an honorable profession. He helped me to live long enough to learn my trade. Did he use me? Yes. Did he give a damn about me? Yes. He saved my life more than once. Yes. I do owe him.

She said, "How long will you be gone?"

"I don't know. Shouldn't be more than an overnighter. I don't want you spending any more nights alone."

"I don't want me spending any more nights alone either," she said with a smile. She snuggled in against my chest.

*** 

The voice on the phone, impersonal, almost business-like, and annoying to Alexei Ivanov for that very reason, told him to go now. This was the start of his mission. He would find money and other things he would need in a locker at the airport. He was given a phone number to call when he was in Washington. Everything was arranged. He was told to go to a specified hotel, no other, and to follow whatever instructions he would be given. As he listened carefully, committing it to memory, the voice suddenly stopped and the line was empty.

Nothing changes, he thought, the melodrama, the soft voice of a nameless person giving directions that would lead to the death of another, as if this were the first, or the last, and it was neither. This had gone on since the world began, the secret killing, and it would go on forever.

***

My thought was to go to Washington, see Marv right away, find out what was on his mind and hopefully end this business, then get back home the same night, or at the latest the next morning--a hotel room was in my plan. With that in mind I got an early flight out of Orlando that got me into Ronald Reagan Airport just after noon. This left plenty of time to check into my hotel for a bit of a nap and still get to my meeting. I'd checked the weather and decided to dig into my closet and get out a down coat.

A great plan that wasn't meant to be.

In my suite I had nothing to unpack other than toiletries so I fixed a drink and sat down to check the news on CNN. I watched the screen but my thoughts were elsewhere. I went back to the beginning and set my mind on rerun. This was about Christine. Christine and Haiti. Christine and Durango. Common denominator: drugs. She certainly wasn't involved in that business. What was the connection? There was no way I could see Hannah in any part of this either. That left Marv and the senator. Guess which one I picked?

Could Christine's father be involved? Could the senator be the one putting such pressure on Marv, so much so that he was cracking? A definite yes to both. But a weak point there. As long as I had known him, and that was a lot of years, no one from the president on down could shake up Marv. Why now? From where? I was curious about that because he had never been impressed, or swayed, by the power and trappings of any office in the capitol merry go round.

And so the music went round and round and came out here. Which is to say no where.

I dozed for a time and when I woke up I called the number Marv had given me. He was there awaiting my call, and quickly directed me to an address on K Street--a place new to me, he'd always been at Langley. I was impressed because this was a section of high priced lawyers and the equally high priced lobby group--the setting for some of the real power in this city. At the very end of our conversation he said something odd: "I made some great lures didn't I?" The connection was lost and that was all he said. What the hell did it mean? I redialed the number but it was busy.

Waiting outside on the street for a cab, fairly comfortable in my down jacket against the cold, miserable rain that came in strong bursts of wind and water, and still troubled about this whole thing, I wondered--which was unlike me--if this weather was a bad omen. I was getting superstitious in my old age? The cab curled into the curb splashing water and I jumped in. The driver had an ID displayed showing a Middle Eastern face with an unpronounceable name, which was fine with me as long as he at least spoke our language--English. I had to admire the Brits in London on that score because they had very strict rules about cabbies: They had to be well versed in English and they had to know the city, really know it, and the test was a tough one. In addition to those requirements, the physical appearance of the car had to be tip top--no dented, rusting clunkers rattling around London streets. My driver here qualified on the first two counts--the condition of the car was up for grabs but would seemingly, from a quick glance, get a passing grade.

My destination turned out to be an older office building that was tucked in among the shiny new cubes of concrete and glass, like a weed that had somehow slipped in among the roses. I paid the driver and dashed in through the rain to the lobby. No security here I noticed, finding Marv listed on a lineup next to the elevators under consultant on the third floor. At least he was being honest. I rode up in the empty elevator, followed the numbers down a hallway, found his office and went into a nicely furnished reception area. It was nice but oddly empty. There was a beautiful desk that should have had someone behind it. I stood there in front of the desk for a few moments, puzzled at the silence that prevailed, then when my patience ran out I called for Marv. Nothing. I tried again only louder. Still nothing. Off to the left of the large reception area was a set of doors of dark, polished wood--that had to be his lair. Could Marv be making it with his receptionist? What a crazy idea. Crazy if you knew Marv.

I pushed open the double doors and walked into what could be a small library. Behind a desk that was centered in the room was an entire wall of books. But there was no one here. A closer look told me that someone *had* been here, had been here looking for something. A wall safe hung open. A filing cabinet to the right of the desk was also ajar. Papers were strewn on the cabinet top and on the desk. Moving in for a closer look I quickly spotted the body on the carpet behind the desk. I didn't need to take a closer look, knowing full well who it was, but emotion, and yes, curiosity, led me to kneel down and take a last, close look, an inspection of my friend and mentor. Not a pretty sight. Looking at the hole in his head where any eye should have been made me gasp and choke--it's different when it is someone you know, have known for a lot of years. No pulse in the neck and the body was still warm, blood still trickling from the wound. It didn't take a medical examiner to place Marv's death at only a short time ago, maybe less than an hour. Perhaps we passed each other in the building.

Shit.

My hands shook as I lit up a smoke, trying to settle down and get into some kind of thinking mode. The big question of course was who and why. To my knowledge, taking into consideration the people I knew who knew Marv, there weren't a whole lot of possibles. But I was familiar with only a small portion of his life--I was a tiny piece in that puzzle. What this had to be was about Marv and myself and that narrowed the field quite a bit. In any case, I didn't have a whole lot of time to get into that because right away I was aware of noise and activity in the background--sounds I wouldn't have heard if the place wasn't so quiet. The sounds of police sirens coming closer.

Instinct told me that they were coming here and that I was in the center of the target area. Wake up. I was the target!

A vague picture of the thing assumed some sort of form. Was it the plan of whomever to find me here with the dead body? Crude. A plot out of the B movies, maybe even C if there was such a thing. But it was a nice move in that it would tie me up for a time with the police, maybe long enough for a different and perhaps more effective plan to be put into play. What was the plan? Did the killer, or killers, think that I knew whatever Marv knew? The reason he was murdered? Fairly obvious. From there it was a tiny step to accepting the fact that I was next on the list of people to be eliminated.

All well and good. Well, actually, not so well and not so good if I was concerned about my life span. The problem was that I didn't know an awful lot and that I was working mostly in the dark. After a moment of thought, it didn't seem much of a stretch to realize that someone expected me to be here, in fact knew that I would be here and that my every movement was being watched. My phone was probably tapped. I hadn't noticed a tail. Filled with a pang of guilt, I had to accept the fact that I hadn't been looking, hadn't been checking for a tail or inspecting my phone, hadn't been paying attention to my job. I wasn't paying attention to what was going on around me. I had lost my edge. I was in trouble for, if nothing else, not being attentive, not watching my back, not picking up on everything around me--a lapse that could cost me my life.

A cardinal sin in my business.

After one last look around--though I didn't know why I looked, nor what I was looking for--I ran out into the hall and down a back fire stairway. I came out onto the street from a narrow alleyway on one side of the building. Two police cars and lots of activity in the front.

The consistent, annoying rain was in the growth process of becoming sleet. When fullgrown it would be a heavy snowfall. Following that pattern, being a lover of the heat and sunshine back home, both the weather and my life here were in a downhill spiral--I was running down a dirty little alley in the freezing sleet of Washington, DC.    It wasn't something to brighten my mood.

One block away from the building I stopped to catch my breath, hailed a cab, and told him to drive around for a while--I needed time to think. The cab was warm and actually comforting in some small way. The driver's ID card, a relatively new one, displayed on the partition between us, showed him to be a bearded man with a name I wouldn't even try to pronounce, and which probably meant he didn't speak a whole lot of English. Which was fine with me because I didn't plan to have a conversation--the last thing I needed was some friendly, talkative driver when I wanted quiet.

My hotel as a place of refuge was out, in fact even going back there might be dangerous. What did that leave? I was in someone's sights. A look out the back window (now I was looking) showed lots of cars, windshield wipers slapping, and headlights. A police car screamed by with lights flashing. Going to have a look at the latest homicide? At Marv? If I had a tail I didn't see one. But he had to be there. Or she? Sadly, I too was being caught up in the oxymoron of politically correct.

I wasn't about to go back home just yet since that would lead to Kim, and as well it wouldn't give me any answers nor solve anything here. I was starting to want some answers. No. This had to be settled here. What I needed was a safe place to go--a hide, like in the old days, a place to curl up and watch for the enemy, pick the time and place, wait for my shot. The cabin! Marv's place in the Virginia mountains. How many people could possibly know about the cabin? Damn few. Perhaps only me. It suddenly seemed like a great idea, perhaps the only answer, but the problem was that I wasn't all that sure I could find the place again--it was years since I'd been there. I found my way by landmarks--I didn't know from street names or highways--turn right at the large rock--look for the red farmhouse near a stand of white birch. As I thought about it I was sure that I could find it.

I had the driver drop me near a car rental. After I paid him and tipped him handsomely, I went inside to try and convince the woman behind the counter that I should be rented a car for cash. Sounds simple but it isn't--those people like a credit card just in case there are some heavy,

216

unexpected charges down the road, like the car being totaled. With the help of a large cash deposit against damage, I won out.

Most likely no  place in the city area was safe for the fugitive I had suddenly become and I knew that it wasn't a good idea to go back to the hotel. But I wanted my things and this time I'd be a little more alert and careful.   Trying to move right along and get out of there, I quickly cleared out the bathroom of my stuff and went down to check out.  I had my car and I was ready to roll. The delay at the check out counter was annoying--their system was down. While I thought it was odd for a first rate, expensive,  hotel to have a computer problem like this, I had other things on my mind and really didn't think too much about it at the time.

Looking around the lobby I didn't see anyone who might be interested in me. Eventually I got checked out of the hotel, drove over the river in what was now snow into Arlington, and there picked up Route 66--I had no idea what highway I wanted to take--it looked familiar and I knew to take it West towards the mountains. Once I got out in the boonies I knew that I wanted a main highway to the South. Again, I'd know it when I got there. Numbers didn't mean a thing to me.

***

In the hotel Jack Morgan had just left, the man in room 612 lay on the bed watching a rerun of a popular western series of several years back. Alexei loved American television: the men were strong and bold and the women were beautiful, far more beautiful but thinner than Russian women who seemed coarse in comparison. A bottle of Stoli vodka sat next to him on the night table--the damn stuff is made in Russia and we can't even buy it, he thought angrily. Right now his life was good, as good in many ways as the wealthy party officials, those back home with their place in the country, the *dachavita* as one of his control officers had called it in  a moment of disgust at the injustice of their system.

Alexei had a large cash advance on this job, and there was time before the kill, waiting time to enjoy himself.

The woman knocked at the unlocked door. He told her to come in and she stood at the open doorway for a moment looking at him then around the room. He clicked the mute button on the remote control to send the television picture into silence, watching for a moment in amusement as the stoic hero faced the beautiful heroine, mouth moving without words, then he turned to the woman at the door as she walked slowly across the room towards the bed. She was expensive, he thought as he watched her move, with the full figure he wanted and paid dearly for, blond and mature,

217

nearing forty he guessed, maybe past, and the hair was probably not her true color, but he didn't care. Money had little meaning at this point in his life, a time when there probably weren't all that many days left--one never knew. He planned to enjoy whatever was left. And even this, he thought in a moment of sad reflection was small repayment, sorry compensation for a lifetime spent, used up was more appropriate, in the service of the Motherland, of months in the heat of the Caribbean, in the foreign corners of a hostile Europe, the sweltering stench of Africa, and in the dusty, barren, lifeless hills of that Godforsaken place that was called Afghanistan where his country had met a humiliating defeat at the hands of what they considered turbaned rabble. The proud, well equipped and well trained men he'd served with there, the elite of the Russian army were now were begging in the streets, selling their uniforms and medals. It was all a great sadness that was too much to even drown with drink. But he tried.

Tomorrow might never come. There is only today.

She stood looking down at him on the bed. "You a smoker?"

"Sometimes. Feel free. Are you a drinker?"

"Sometimes," she said, lighting up a slender, filtered cigarette. She inhaled deeply, savoring the taste for a long moment then let out the smoke through her nose--a true lover of the habit and one who would never consider quitting. "Russian vodka? Is that good stuff?"

"We think it is."

"Are you Russian?"

"Yes. It is my country."

"I'll try some--with ice. You have ice?"

"Yes I have ice. But we drink it straight down...what you call neat?"

"I wouldn't know." She sat down on the edge of the bed. "You Russian huh? No funny stuff here. No kinky Russian stuff."

He looked at her curiously, not fully understanding her words. "Funny stuff?" he said, pouring vodka into a plastic glass. "I don't know funny stuff. We drink. We smoke. We make love."

"You mean we screw. Let's take it one step at a time." She swirled the ice around in the glass before taking a drink. "Not bad. We drink. We smoke. We screw. That's what we do. You get the picture here? No extras and no funny stuff. That's what you paid for."

He sat up on the bed, smiled, then drank down a half glass of vodka. "I get the picture, as you say. I think I would like one of your cigarettes. And that money"--he waved an arm at the table beside the bed--"is for you."

Sitting down on the edge of the bed, she held out the pack for him, lit the cigarette and watched him for a moment. While he certainly isn't young, she thought, he's in good shape--there is a strength and a youthful vitality about him. This man is no softy. Might be fun.

Up close she seemed much older, worn, tired and painted, thought Alexei, watching her pick up her money. The structure was crumbling but the face of it, the front, was made up to look new, or at least maintained--like a movie set--an illusion.

She smiled. "You have a name, Russian?"

"Alexei."

"Alexei," she said thoughtfully. "That sure is Russian."

"And you? What do we call you?"

After a moment. "You can call me Lara."

"Lara?"

"Yes. Didn't you see the movie?"

"What movie?"

"Dr. Zhivago of course." He gave an unknowing shrug. "No matter." She suddenly leaned over and kissed him firmly on the lips. She started to undress.

Then the phone rang.

The voice told Alexei to be ready to go at any moment. His target was in motion and being tracked. When a location was established he would be advised. Before checking out of the hotel he must stop at the desk where a package would be waiting for him giving the exact destination. He was reminded that a successful mission--the killing of the subject--would bring a sustantial bonus.

The line went dead.

The woman, now nude, was opening his robe. "Bad news, Alexei?"

"Not so bad...Lara. But we must hurry because I may have to leave at any moment."

"Aw. A quickie. I was getting to like you, Ruskie."

"Well then, my Lara, show me quickly." A thrilling time, he thought, so much excitement for his old heart: delicious sex with this creature and then the hunt. It had been many years since he had felt like he did this night. She leaned down and swished her hair back and forth over his stomach and he groaned.


*** 


There is nothing quite so dark as the mountains, I thought, straining to see the road on a starless night. On top of that the wipers were engaged in a furious battle with the sticking snow on the windshield, and losing the contest at the moment. But I had great hopes for victory as I launched my counter attack and went up to the final highest notch on the defrost fan.

What is the temperature in Florida, right now? Idle thought. Fantasy.

I had a rough idea of where I was, knew that I wanted to head South eventually, and that from there, maybe ten or twelve miles, I had to be especially alert for the stand of birch trees next to an open space next to a large red barn--the nearest town was Mortonville? Not much to go on but I had a vivid picture in my mind of the turn off from the main highway, then the dirt road leading down to the cabin. About 10 yards behind the cabin the land dropped off sharply. In the ravine a stream where we had fished. Was it still flowing? Still visible from the back porch?

The road South turned out to be Route 81.

Not surprisingly I missed my turn off, what with the weather and the dark night, and had to turn around and go back. It all came back when I found the right spot to turn off Route 81 and then found the dirt road. Nothing seemed to have changed. Marv had told me that his cabin was on the edge of a tree farm and he liked the idea of being surrounded by woods and nature. That side of him had baffled me at first--it seemed in such contrast to his work. We are all complex creatures.

Marv was one of those who had more imagination than to leave the key under the front door mat--he left his under a flower pot by the back door. The rooms smelled of damp wood and I shivered at the cold inside of the cabin. First thing was to get a fire going.

The large main room was dominated by the long fireplace that gave both warmth and a sense of  character to the place. Off that room were the kitchen on one side, with an adjoining work room, where Marv had all his gear, and on the other side were two bedrooms, each with a tiny bathroom. Both bedrooms had baseboard heating, as did the kitchen. A fireplace was great to sit and look at, Marv said one night when we were sitting in front of it with a drink (I had just returned from a job in Columbia), but as far as heating the damn cabin, forget it.

Once the paper took hold and the wood started to crackle and pop in the fireplace, and my blood started to circulate again, I settled down in front of the fire with a large single malt scotch. Vodka was my drink but Marv loved scotch and that was what he stocked. He had what must have been a priceless collection of old, rare, single malts, many of them 25 years old. Now that is old, smooth stuff. And I had to admit that it was some pleasant  drinking. I suppose his two passions in life were his scotch collection and his fishing lures. As far as I knew he had never married.

I warmed before the fire, sipped, smoked, and tried to figure things out. I missed Kim.

Marv had been killed, no, murdered, there is a difference, because...? He knew and could tell things that someone didn't want the public to know. That led nowhere! Marv knew lots of things that the world should never know! He had intimate knowledge of events that the president didn't know! And wouldn't want to know. The man was a walking file of secrets. But I didn't think he was murdered because of the past, not the distant past anyway. That made no sense at all. My thoughts went round and round and eventually came to Durango, Christine, and Hannah. Then what...?

Go back. Who could have murdered Marv? Not Christine or Hannah. Who did that leave?

Then I remembered my last conversation with Marv...about lures. Odd that he'd say that, out of context as it were, and it stuck with me. I went into the room off the kitchen and looked for his tackle box--it was a monster plastic box full of line, lead weights, wiggly things, hooks, you name it. Memory was tugging at me and making this a painful thing.

Suddenly something else came to me, a thought cutting in amidst the memories--a basic bit of tradecraft I'd forgotten.

I put on a jacket, hat and gloves and went out to inspect the car. Of course, the rental car! I had been held up at the hotel check out counter. Why? I thought it odd at the time but let it go. It didn't take too many minutes of crawling around under the car in the snow to find a bug, a tiny listening device snug up against the side of the gas tank.

So I would have company soon. There hadn't been a tail--didn't need one. Just follow the bouncing ball to find Jack Morgan. The question was who would come and when? I couldn't even venture a guess about the first part and the second was up for grabs. In this weather anyone would have trouble finding the cabin, even if they knew where they going, and I was sure no one knew about this place. Well, fairly sure.

Back inside, I sipped the warming scotch, smoked, and took stock of my situation. I was forewarned and thereby forearmed, so the saying went, and that could provide the edge in my favor. First I took out the tackle box and set it on the table--I had plans for that fishing line.

While I was digging around in the tackle box, pulling out things and putting them aside, sinkers, lures, hooks, floats, an asssortment of fishing gadgets, I noticed a tray near the bottom and pulled it out. On the very bottom of the box, beneath all that junk, was an envelope that, when I took it out and examined it , was addressed to me. In Marv's handwriting: *Jack. You will know what to do with this.*

And as I read, I knew what he wanted me to do and what I would do. If I was still alive.

I was a long time looking through the papers he'd assembled for me--a long, thoughful, time of regret and memories. It was time to move on. Next I went to examine the book case with the false front that Marv had opened so easily when I was there, looking to show off his collection of guns. I'd be in good shape if I could just get the damn thing open. After opening the glass front of the cabinet he'd reached in under the shelf to open the shelf itself--it swung open to the side. Of course I'd been across the room and didnt' see exactly where the control was located. I slid my hand all along the bottom of all the shelves. Nothing. I repeated the process twice and still nothing. On a third try my hand accidenty bumped the shelf bracket. It moved and presto!

Inside were several bolt action rifles, a shotgun, and a lever action Winchester. Hanging by itself was a beautiful Walther PPK, the fine weapon made for the German police. Boxes of ammunition were lined up carefully on the bottom shelf. So far so good.

I fixed another drink and sat down at the table with the tackle box. On a sheet of scrap paper I laid out my operation. I drew a circle with the house in the middle. The stream behind the house, maybe 30 feet across, cut my circle in half, reducing my danger area to the 190 degrees, or half the pie, in front of the house. I doubted that anyone would approach from the rear through the icy water. I wouldn't. Of that space in front, about 30 degrees was cleared directly in front of the house--another no-approach area. That left a cone of roughly 80 degrees on either side of the front.

Since the road came in from the highway on the left, looking out, that section was the most likely area of approach. They would hardly drive past the house then come in from the right.

The dense section of young trees to the left of the house was the zone of defense. Simple enough. But what did I have in the way of equipment. Unfortunately for me, Marv didn't stock trip flares, grenades, sensor devices, a few nice little mines, nor anything of that nature. No NVGS for my night vision! What was he thinking of?

I prowled around the room then went into the kitchen. My mind was at work but I didn't see much to work *with.* Then I spotted a container of tin cans and bottles that were tossed there for recycle but never made it outside for the truck to pick up. Suddenly I had a plan.

Outside, what little I could see was white, swirling with snow. The road was just about invisible. Was there a brave soul who would come looking for me here in this?

Yes. If they were paid enough. As well, this ugly weather could all end quickly and bring a clear dawn. The time for me to work was now.

After putting on as much winter clothing as my body could hold, and still be mobile, I gathered up a spool of line and a plastic bag of tin cans and went out into the tree line. It was slow going, and awkward with gloves on, but I eventually had a perimeter line of cans hanging on fishing line that, when disturbed, would jingle-jangle and make a fair racket. All well and good. But I wouldn't hear the cans if I was in the house. I'd have to keep watch on the road and when I saw headlights approaching, go out quietly and listen for the noise to locate my visitor, or visitors. Not the greatest of plans by far, but it was workable and gave me a slight edge if all went well.

By this time the snow was tapering off and the sky clearing--we would have a hunter's moon, or an assassin's moon in this case.

\*\*\*

Damn this weather and damn these poor directions, thought Alexei, taking another pull at the vodka and finishing what was left in the bottle. Must be the same stupid ones who planned the war in Afghanistan. That same voice telling him that he would find a map in the car. He had his target and he must go.

As much as he needed the money it would have been nice to spend the entie night with the woman.

So here he was in the dead of night, trying to drive in this blinding shit of a snowstorm and at the same time follow a map. He had to admit that he was a little bit drunk and he must be careful not to attract attention from their highway patrol. He had seen worse weather and he had drank much more vodka. Not to worry, as they said here in the US of A.

His map was a good one, giving him exact mileage in tenths for each stretch of road and turn off. Only a fool would get lost. He did.

After having lost an hour on this miserable shit of a road, he was back on track and was coming at last to the turnoff that would take him in to the house. They could have waited until morning, he grumbled to himself. At least the damnable snow had stopped, the sky cleared, and he could see where he was going. The house should be less than a kilometer up this road.

\*\*\*

223

I fixed a pot of coffee and ate some canned food from the kitchen cabinet--nothing fancy, sustantial stuff. Even with several cups of coffee I was having a hard time staying awake so I alternated betweeen standing watch, actually sitting, on the front porch, and sitting inside where I could warm up and watch through the window. By my watch it was 4:30 in the morning, just about the toughest possible time to try and stay awake, that period when the body knew damn well it should be asleep.

It was quiet in the cabin and of course my thoughts wandered between short periods when I know I nodded off. I thought of Kim, fast asleep at this hour, the nice moments together in Mexico and Paris, and the great times we will have summering in France. There was a lot going in my life now, substance, a meaningful relationship, something all new to anticipate. But first there was this.

I had my jacket on a nearby chair, pockets full of ammo for the lever action Winchester, along with hat and gloves, and the Walther PPK tucked in my belt. Marv had loved the small Walther PPK (Police Pistol) that was first made in 1929 he told me, and said that it was a favorite among the field men in the Agency. He laughed when I called him Double O Seven, the most famous user of the handgun.

Suddenly there were headlights on the road--just a quick flash of them and then black just beyond the tree line. I quickly put on my coat and the light material shooting gloves, grabbed the rifle and quietly slipped out the front door and down the steps. The light was left on intenionally. My idea was to get just inside the tree line to the right of the house and from that position I'd be shooting across the open area in front of the house to the opposite side. Not a great plan. Not even a good plan. But with the limited terrain I had to work in --the circle with the house in the middle was split in half by the creek in back--it was the best I could come up with. A factor more important than any plan, no matter how ingenious or detailed it might be, was the invaluable edge of surprise. This one element could make the difference between being the killer or the killed. Big difference if you're one of the participants.

I was moving bent over and at the same time looking off to my left for any signs of life. I missed an icy patch and went down hard on my back. I felt sure it could be heard all over the area. But I was so bundled up that the only thing that got hurt was my pride.

I settled in to watch and wait, staring across the clear stretch in front of the house to the trees beyond. I had worked the Winchester action in the house to get one round in the chamber ready to go. Of course this would have all been so much simpler, and easier for me, if Marv had the foresight to stock a pair of night vision glassses. But why cry over missing NVGS? Visibility was excellent in that bright moonlight, except that I was looking into a stand of trees where it was nothing but darkness.

Who was the shooter and how good was he or she? Equipped for night vision? I hoped not.

Movement in the trees. The slight sound of snow crunching under foot. I still couldn't see anything. Would the vapor from my breath give me away? It was so damn clear and cold. I pulled the jacket collar up around my face and breathed down into it.

Hopefully this little exercise in the moonlight wouldn't last too long--I didn't want the Winchester freezing up. Nor did I want myself freezing up.

A first rattle of tin cans--the outer line. I have to admit I felt good knowing that my crude perimeter alarm was working. I was watching and listening, straining the senses, my heart thumping away, the adrenaline pumping, but I worked at trying to stay calm as I brought the rifle up to eye level, resting it in the V of the tree trunk and a small limb. In a moment, if the shooter kept to the same course--and I saw no reason for him to change direction from his target, which was the light in the window--I should hear the noise from the next and last line of cans, those closest to the end of the tree line.

If.

There is always the *if*. It is impossible to plan for every eventuality. We can only hope the *ifs* go in our favor.

A rattle. I thought I saw a body move in among the trees and I fired--too quickly, poorly aimed, and just plain dumb. I should have waited. I was jumpy. Now the shooter knew that I wasn't in the house. Beating myself mentally for the error, I was still staring into the trees and hoping for a hit when there was a simultaneous crack and something tore into my arm with the force of a sledge hammer. I was hit. I was paying the price for my impatience. The arm didn't hurt, it was just numb, and the jacket had a neat hole. Either my hurried first shot was a complete miss, or it was a graze, and neither one had anything to do with the final score. In our game, played without the cheering fans, the only score that counted was the one final, fatal hit.

Dropping down in the snow, still annoyed at myself but determined to settle down and get back on track--let's face it, it was that or die here, and I wasn't ready for that--I looked again at the hole in my jacket but didn't see any blood. Maybe it was too damn cold. I rolled to the right and got into a new postion. Another crack and a puff of rock. I could smile at that because I knew now that the opponent was jumpy and rushing his shots as well--he didn't see me there, he fired at where I'd been and where he thought I was still holed up.

Just how jumpy was he? While I reached up and shook a branch, I searched the trees for any sign of movement across the patch of light between us. This time I saw the muzzle flash of reaction. I quickly got up on one knee and fired. I heard a scream.

I had to assume from my blind shot in the direction of the muzzle light, and the scream, that the shooter was at least superficially hurt. We were both hit now and it sort of evened things up. I didn't want to fall too far behind on points.

I made some noise moving fast to the right, then backed deeper into the trees and moved in the direction I'd just come from, hoping the shooter would pick up my movement in the wrong direction. I watched and waited for the shot that never came--he didn't go for my fake. Nothing for several moments. Then I heard movement. He was moving away. Back to the car? He had been hit. Was he giving up? I stood up for only an instant then dropped to the ground. Nothing.

His car was around a bend off to the left and I made my way across the road and waited in a gully, a spot from which I could just see the car--with the moon clear of the clouds I could see the shooter.

It was cold. Damn cold. My cheeks stung and the tips of my fingers were numb. Not good. I needed a steady pull on that trigger at the precise moment of my shot. Numbness in the arm but no blood showing so I didn't think that amounted to much of anything.

No noise except for the wind blowing through the trees--no human sound.

I guessed that he was heading for the car and I waited.

I heard a noise behind me, to the side, off to my 5 o'clock position. Turning, I saw a redish-brown fox dart off into the woods. Good hunting.

Movement then from out of the tree line up in front of me, a hesitant, wary move of a dark body. I let him come out and move around in front of the car. Unlike the quick fox on the hunt, the figure I watched was slow, bent over, hurting, looking for a safe haven.

I had him lined up for a head shot, making it intentionally high in case the cold, or the wind, however slight, caused a drop in the trajectory. I took in the slack in the trigger. He was at the car door now and it was my last chance to make the shot before he got into the car. Why the hesitation? What the hell! Pull the damn trigger. No. That was a human, not a wounded animal. He's leaving in peace. Leaving in peace? Cut the bullshit. There's a mad dog out there who came here to kill you. Wake up! We care so much about animals and are so full of feeling as to put them

226

out of their misery. Why not offer the same compassion to humans who are not only hurting, but are mad and totally anti-social as well? There are no redeeming social graces from an assassin. I was looking at a human who came here to kill me, far worse than a pitiful, wounded animal.

The argument with myself went on for only an instant before I made a decision.

The shooter opened the door, took a long last look in my direction, almost as if knowing I was there but also knowing, hoping, almost sure that I wouldn't take his life. He was wrong. My shot took him above the ear and blew the top of his head away. He was gone, no longer any threat to my life, and another part was ended. Would there be more? Was someone else always waiting for a shot at me? Somehow I didn't see myself as all that important. What happened here was connected to Christine and her father. There was no world plot to get rid of Jack Morgan. But there was other, unfinished business that I had to tend to before this was all over. Maybe it would never be completely ended for me.

Back in the house, feeling cold, tired, and depressed, I put the guns away, except for the PPK which I decided to keep, threw some wood on the fire and poured myself some scotch. The hit on my arm was nothing more than a scratch, more damage to the jacket than to me. Who was that shooter? I sipped, smoked and reflected. I could trudge out into the cold, look at that by now frozen body, the destroyed face, pull aside his heavy clothing and check his ID. But to what end? What could it tell me about the person? I wouldn't know his place of birth or his history, his journey through life. And besides, it would be phony anyway. This was our world. Even in the shadows we were not real. I felt that I was halfway out of that world and nearing some kind of normalcy. It only bothered me when I chose to delve into that deep darkness of the assassin, and when I looked there I knew it wasn't me.

Was the cold dead body perhaps an old professional like me? Had he found his way out? Was there a wife and children waiting for him to come home with money to buy nice things? Or was there nothing more than an empty flat that would be no brighter for his presence? What did it matter?
He was dead.

# SIXTEEN

The fire had gone out, the cabin quiet and cold, and I wanted nothing more than to get back to Kim, who aside from being the woman I loved, was my new found stability, a life ring thrown out to me in the surging seas. Of course before Kim I didn't even realize that I was adrift. My life seemed to be in order, some form of order anyway. I lived well and I was content-we can't miss what we've never had. I had become accustomed to living with what I now knew was an empty space, a void waiting to be filled. She came in and gave everything a new meaning. With the thought of her in mind it didn't take long for me to be packed up and out of the cabin.

As I drove down the snowy road, with one last backward glance, I couldn't help but think of Marv, my friend and mentor, the man I'd known for most of my life. We had spent many hours in that cabin, and in the nearby countryside, fishing, talking, thinking, planning, at times we were quiet, letting the world move on without us, at other times in serious talk of life and death-of taking a life. We were businessmen charting the course for our survival-only we talked of countries rather than companies, and take-outs rather than take overs.

Planning my moves as I drove, I was confident, but not certain, that thanks to Marv I had the facts and figures that should be enough to destroy any public figure-in normal times. But were these normal times? The public had become immune to the lies and scandal of our elected, accepted it as a part of the whole package that was often referred to as the lesser of two evils from the voting booth. I knew what had to be done. One way or the other he was finished.

The sun was strong and bright, glistening on the snow and the wet roadway where two grooves were cleaned by the procession of tires plowing through the snow. On either side of the path was about a foot of snow. It was a crisp winter morning and I saw, surprisingly, some beauty in that.

My doubts about having enough evidence against the senator were more than offset by the satisfaction I felt in bringing him down. This wasn't like the cold, impersonal kill that was my trade-the bullet finding its target and a life ended. No. This one had meaning and it was very real. I had crossed over the line.

What I wasn't happy about, in really a minor way, was that Hannah was in the middle of this, caught up in the eye of the storm. From what I remembered of her she could be strong and she would survive. But I was

228

the one bringing it all, th one causing the storm. I was bringing a bad time into her life.

Traffic was light in the early morning before full light, that time when headlights and tail lights were an essential, and I moved along nicely at a reasonable ten miles over the speed limit. I cut that back when I passed a car stopped on the side of the road with a trooper's car behind, lights flashing in that disco thing the lights did on top of the car.

A lot of things were on my mind as I drove back into the Washington area, to Georgetown to be precise, where the senator lived, as did Hannah and Christine. Of the three, I was most uncomfortable at the thought of seeing Hannah, uneasy at having to deal with the old feelings, remembering the lies I was told and the false, abrupt ending to our relationship. Christine I hardly knew and I had no feelings about her one way or the other. She happened to come into my life and was promptly out of it. The senator I knew even less, the difference being that I did have feelings about him, lots of them, and none were pleasant. He was a negative. Hopefully, he would get exactly what he deserved. Hannah, on the other hand, was an affair of the heart, and without closure a that, the hardest to deal with and the most painful. There was Kim now but memories linger forever. I wasn't in love with Hannah, loved her maybe in a distant way, but why did I still care what hurt came into her life now? Simple: I cared if I was the cause. I thought about it all and could rationalize my guilt away in an instant: it was her life and her doing-she married the man. And so it all went round and round. Fortunately, deep in thought as I was, I didn't run off, out of the ruts and into the heavy snow.

I smoked and hung to a steady 5 miles above the limit--not that there was much traffic but it was in the safe zone. No rational, sane, well adjusted trooper would bother a driver on an early, cold, week day, snowy morning doing five above the speed limit. Of course, there were other troopers...

I had a map and I was trained to read maps-a long time ago, so long ago that it was depressing. Finding the senator's house wasn't exactly a challenge to even my tired brain.

Impressive colonial house set behind a brick wall-I had expected nothing less. I drove into the circular driveway and parked in front of the house. Not a light and no sign of life. They were all nestled into their snuggy beds, warm, comfortable and content. Being tired and dirty, cold, and in an ugly mood, I was about to end all that contentment. I had to admit that I was looking forward to taking the senator down a peg or two.

Taking a deep breath and grabbing the envelope full of documents, I stepped out into the brisk morning and went up to the bright red door. The door knocker was a gold fixture with the letter B engraved in the center. I banged it a few times and waited. After a few minutes I repeated the process. Just as I was pulling my hand away Christine opened the door and looked at me for a long moment.

"I know you," she said as a smile spread across her face. "You were in Mexico."

"That's right, Christine. You've got a good memory. How are you?"

I remember faces. I'm fine. But I've forgotten your name."

"Don't know that I ever told you. It's Jack. Jack Morgan."

"It's nice to see you again, Jack Morgan."

"Most people stop at Jack."

"Of course," she said, showing an embarrassed grin. "Did you come to see me?"

"Partly," I lied. "But I need to talk with your father."

"I don't know if he's even up yet. But I'll check for you. Come in, please."

A woman's voice from upstairs. "Who is it, Chris?"

"Nothing mother. Someone to see daddy. I'll take care of it."

"At this time in the morning! Who is it?"

"I'll take care of it, mother."

"Who is it, Chris?"

Christine looked at me then upstairs and shrugged. "He was in Mexico, mother."

"Christine! A lot of people were in Mexico. Enough of this. Who is it to see your father?"

"His name is Jack Morgan."

Not a sound for a few moments, then someone coming down the stairs. The stairway was around to the right and I couldn't see her until she came into the foyer. Hannah.

"Hello, Jack."

"Hello, Hannah." For two people who had loved, and shared, this wasn't an emotional, heart-rendering opening to our meeting, I was thinking as I looked at her. But I didn't have any brilliant opening. She was older, the years showing in more lines, hair not as deep in color, but she was still the beautiful woman I'd loved in London. As she would always be with that classic face.

Christine was perplexed, looking from one to the other, feeling that something was going on here, as we stared at each other, some happening that she couldn't fathom. Overcome with the strange vibes she was getting, and dying of curiosity, she broke the silence. "What is it, mother? You two know each other?" Still the silence hung heavy in the air. "Mother. Answer me. Do you know this man? What's going on here?"

230

"We know each other," I said. "I knew your mother a long time ago."

"Is that true?" Christine demanded. "Does this have anything to do with Mexico?"

Hannah looked away, then down, still silent.

"Christine," I said carefully, "this has nothing to do with Mexico. A coincidence. Nothing more. I knew your mother in London. A friend of mine-not not your mother, she had nothing to do with my being involved-a asked me to go look for you. I was doing a favor for a friend. End of story."

"End of story," Christine repeated slowly. "I don't think so. I think someone owes me an explanation."

"Maybe you're right," I said. "But this isn't the time. I need to see your father. Your mother can fill you in. Will you see if he's up?"

All through this Hannah had said nothing. But then, what was to be said? "I'll go get him, Jack." she said finally. "Do you want me there?"

"No. This is something strictly between me and the senator."

"Not between us?" she asked.

Better that it isn't, Hannah, I thought. I shook my head and didn't say anything. With that she turned and went upstairs. After a few silent moments of Christine and I just looking at each other, she called down to tell me that the senator would see me in the study. Christine would show me. That quickly, Hannah had become the cold, impersonal, dutiful senator's wife showing a caller into the study. And that was fine with me. We were the past, history, old and soon to be forgotten. I had lots of thoughts about this meeting during the drive in from the cabin: wondering if there were any feelings between us and how I would feel seeing her. Aside from the awkward beginning, and the shock of actually seeing her after all these years, I found that there was no live emotion left, not even warm embers to fan. It was just as well. But there was a feeling for Christine. My instinct told me that she was someone I could like-for that matter she could be my daughter. I let that thought die quietly and quickly.

She walked ahead of me down a hallway of white tile, then off to the right past tall, wooden doors into a dimly lit room, flicked on a wall switch, then turned to me. "I hate dark rooms," she said with a smile.

"Sometime I hope we can talk. I think there is a lot we should share and I hope you'll keep in touch after this. Do you think we can find the time to talk?"

"Sure, Christine. We'll find the time. Not here, but if you come to Florida..."

"I will! I'd love it. The sun and beaches. Promise?"

"It's a promise."

231

The room was a bit darker for her absence-she seemed the type of person to brighten any environment. Or maybe it was my dark mood moved by her youth and vitality. I'd come here in a tired, dirty, aggravated, even bloodied condition and I was surprised they even opened the door. I must have looked like a homeless person invading their sanctuary. To Hannah's credit, and to Christine's, they took no notice of my sorry state, or at least didn't show any reaction. I wanted this to be over and finished.

An impressive room, I thought, looking around as I waited, taking in the massive desk that looked like mahogany, tall-backed leather chair, bookkeepers lamp with the green shade, wall of books behind the desk-the entire room bespoke money and quietly elegant taste. Was this his influence or hers? I was looking over the books when the senator came into the room. I turned to look and study the man whom I had pictured as some kind of monster, the villain in this, the man who married Hannah and the man I was preconditioned to hate. He was a disappointment as my villain, too ordinary, for this setting anyway, in a dark blue robe and slippers over pajamas. But he did look tired and drawn, worn out, with deep circles under his eyes. I could almost feel sorry for him. Almost.

I let him come to me and I said, "I'm Jack Morgan."

A pause while he put out his hand-which I didn't take-and he said, "I know who you are. Hannah has told me about you." That surprised me. "How can I help you,?" he added.

"It's not me I came to help."

"You lost me there. You came to help me?"

*No. I came to bury you.* "Think about it for a minute, senator. I was in Durango. I'm the one who found your daughter and sent her back."

He was cool, or trying to be-a crude actor struggling with his part as a polished gentleman. "And I appreciate that, Jack. May I call you Jack?" I didn't answer and he went on. "You did a great job and I appreciate having her back. She is the treasure of my life."

Now why do I have trouble believing that? "I'm sure she is, senator," I lied. "You do know why she was in Durango?"

A curious look, then " Why she was in Durango? She was kidnapped of course. The man wanted money for her return."

"But you never gave him any money. You never paid any ransom. In fact, you never paid him for the drugs he shipped to you." I looked for a reaction but didn't see much-he was growing into his part. "Your daughter was kidnapped because you owed the man a couple of million dollars! Isn't that true, senator?"

"I don't know what you're talking about. In fact, I think you should leave."

"No coffee?"

"I can call the police."

"I don't think so. You'll be talking to the police soon enough."

He walked to the French doors that looked out onto a large patio, stood for a moment, then turned back to me. I lit a cigarette and watched his moves. He said, "Where did you get this ridiculous business about drugs? Are you claiming that a United States senator dealt in drugs? Do you realize the seriousness of such charges? Do you realize that even the hint of such a thing would ruin my career?"

"Yes to all of the above, senator."

He stared then glared, his eyes wide. "How dare you make such an accusation!"

"It's easy when you're dealing with the truth, senator. My guess is that your fortune, at least the fortune you were reported to have, went down the tube, for whatever reason, and you had to come up with some money fast. What could be faster than cocaine? I don't know how you got hooked up with Santana and I don't care-it doesn't matter. What matters is that you did get hooked up with that sewer in Mexico and you dealt in the dirt and slime that was their product. Do you want to hear more?"

He fumbled in his robe for a cigarette and lit one. After a few deep drags he seemed to gain confidence. "Do you know, Mr. Jack Morgan, that I could crush you in an instant? Do you realize that I'm a member of a powerful group? A body that is more powerful than anyone can imagine, one that can destroy you. I can do that, Mr. Morgan. I can turn your life into a living hell."

"What happened to Jack?" I was tired and fighting to keep my eyes open. I lit up and watched his face. "Now you listen for a moment, senator. While I fully realize the power of your exclusive group, one that not only makes its own laws and governs itself, and gives regular raises to an already obscene salary, but also enjoys a handsome pension for life. Oh yes, I know the power of your group. You've created your own kingdom while we slept—the innocents trusting in your honesty. We've made some mistakes. But fortunately, there is a large group in our population that is awake now and wants the kind of clean government they took for granted. I think they'll be kind of pissed at you and what you've done in this drug business. And I don't think they'll like the idea that you put your own daughter in danger because of your...shall we say transgressions."

He seemed caught up in his own rage and ignored me. "You even *mention* such unsubstantiated charges and you will be finished, Mr. Morgan. Your life will be over."

"Unsubstantiated? Does that big word mean that I can't back it up?"

"You're a fool, Mr. Morgan. You can't prove any of this!"

"On the contrary. I can prove every bit of it. I have bank records, statements, surveillance pictures, phone conversations, the whole ballgame. I can wrap you up like a Christmas present."

A long silence was broken by Hannah knocking, then coming in with coffee on a silver tray. She said to me, "Yours is black with one sugar." We made eye contact as I realized that she'd remembered. He watched the exchange silently.

Don't complicate things, Hannah, I was thinking as I stirred the coffee and drew in the aroma. Don't try to rekindle what is better off left as cold ashes. I said, "Thanks. This is just what I needed." She left without a word.

After a time he sighed and put the cup down, his body deflated. "What is it you want, Mr. Morgan? Is it money? Do you have your hand out with all the rest of them?"

"Money! I'm insulted. I think you know what I'm doing in your house. I think you know very well why I'm here and what you have to do about your mistakes senator. Do you want to see these documents I brought? Is it necessary?"

"I don't know what you think you have that might affect my life." The coffee cup shook in his hand. "Others have tried to ruin me and they failed. So I really don't know why you went to all this trouble, Mr. Morgan. You're on a fools errand and I'd like you to leave my house. Now."

"Fools errand? I don't think so. What's in those papers ties you in with Santana and the drugs, a nice neat trail from Mexico to you. There are bank records, phone taps, you name it. We have it, senator. So I suggest you cut crap and this phony innocent pose of yours and get real. We're not on one of the staged, network news interview programs where you know the questions and you know the answers, those shows where you come across as oh so clean and bright and knowing. This is the reality. What I have here in documented proof in this envelope is where you went bad, senator. What I have is the end of your public career, the end of you. And you know what? It couldn't happen to a more deserving person. This is justice, senator. Is that word still in the memory bank? I'll just leave this with you," I said, putting the thick envelope on the desk. "Don't worry about losing or destroying those papers because that would be a waste of time. The originals are in a safe place and I can make lots of copies."

This was pure guess work on my part in assuming that the originals were in Marv's safe deposit box—the logical place to keep them. But he didn't know that. Let him sweat. I had taken the chance, laid it all out there for him to hopefully stew about, and I had either dropped the bomb that would bring him down or he'd fight it and possibly survive to go on doing his rotten thing.  In thinking about it, his surviving was a definite possibility, given the prevailing liberal attitude of the moment.  Look at what the previous president got away with.  That wasn't a happy thought but it was out of my hands.  As far as I was concerned this was the end of it for me.  Having nothing more to say I got up and went out to the entrance door.  Christine was waiting there.  "Can I really come visit in Florida?" she asked.

"You bet.  Anytime you want to come.  The invitation is always open."

"That's super," she said and gave me a big kiss.

I hugged her and said, "You're super.  Come anytime you like."

Hannah, watching,  stood further back in the shadows of the hallway.  But she didn't say anything.

*** 

My trip home was reflective and all of a sudden I wasn't filled with any certainty in my life.  It would pass.  In any case, my feelings aside, the story would have ended there except for Haiti.

## SEVENTEEN

Harry was a traitor, a fair weather friend.

He now followed Kim, dogged her every move, and was always to be found by her side. If I called he'd come, but reluctantly and after a moment of indecision, as if granting me the honor of his presence. At times when he lay at her feet we'd make eye contact and he'd break off, in guilt I thought. You can't trust animals.

It was on the morning after I got back, over coffee, with Harry sprawled out nearby, that I told Kim about my trip to Washington, the cabin, the senator, all of it. I could feel that it was an unresolved problem between us and it was a relief to get it out. I hoped this would clear the air and we could move on. After a few moments of thought, she said, "Hardly seems a proper ending."

"What do you mean?"

"I mean that he's getting away with it, isn't he? Even if you gave that information to the press what good would it do? He could lie and buy his way out of any scandal. He could look right into the camera and deny it all. It's been done. The public doesn't want to believe that a public figure has gone bad. It reflects on their judgement at the voting booth."

"I didn't know you cared about politics."

"I don't care about it at all. I care about people."

"What you say is true. He could ride it out, counter it with a bunch of lies, and come out clean. It's a possibility. But I don't think he'll get away with anything."

She looked at me curiously. "I don't follow."

"Just a feeling. I can't tell you why."

"I'm not following you here but we'll let it go at that."

I hoped she was sincere in that comment.

Three days after I got home the senator was found dead in his study from a self inflicted gunshot to the head. Kim gave me a knowing look when we saw it in the papers. I didn't gloat. I'd won. But it wasn't much of a victory when I thought about Hannah without a husband and Christine without a father. Telling myself that they were better off without him didn't help. It came to me then that I had turned the corner and reached the end of my killing.

The story was, naturally, front page stuff that went into the family background, baby pictures, the whole bit. The media was in a feeding frenzy over this story and I couldn't but help feel a touch of guilt as I read one article after another.

236

A few days later, partly based on a nice extended forecast for the whole area, and partly because Kim was sick and tired of me moping around, we took the boat on a days run to the Bahamas. I have a 35 foot Bentley that had been custom made with teak wood and fully equipped with the latest of everything. She was a beauty—someone's floating dream with low hours on her and well maintained. I considered myself very lucky to find her still available in an estate sale in Ft. Lauderdale. The sale was closing the next day. The widow, I was told, anxious to sell everything off and be on her way to Europe, would take almost any price. It wasn't a question of money. There were literally hundreds of boats for sale in that town, and when you add in the whole southern coast of Florida, you'd be talking thousands of boats on the market. For me it was a matter of finding the *right* one. It was like buying a house: when you see that special one you know it.

Kim was carefully stowing the lunch Claire had made, and I was checking the ice and bait, when she said, "This is a first for me, you know. I'm excited at the thought of deep sea fishing." She laughed. "Suppose I get one too big for me to handle?"

I closed the ice chest and put my arms around her waist. "You mean like me?

"You're not to big for me to handle. I'm talking fish, Jack."

"We'll worry about that when and if you get one. You have great expectations, lady."

"And why not? Besides fishing I have other things in mind."

"Oh. Like what?"

"Like is there a cabin on this boat?" I nodded. She knew that there was. "And in the cabin is there a bed?" Another nod. "Well then, we can do more than fish."

I held onto her for a moment without a word. She had on tan shorts and a pink top and looked gorgeous, as usual. I kissed her and hugged a bit tighter.

Laughing, she pulled back. "Skipper, you better tend to your boat chores or we'll never get out to sea."

Reluctantly, I let her go.

Getting out into the ocean by way of the Sebastian Inlet, a narrow passage with rocks on both sides and surging waters within—the only access in this area—was sometimes a hairy bit of seamanship. Many a boat had smashed into the rocks, some from being underpowered, and there was little hope for them, and some from not knowing when to use what power they had.

Kim watched me maneuver through the rough water with a look of concern. "A piece of cake," I yelled down from the bridge. She looked from me to the water, then back again without comment.

Once we got a good ways out, past the deep blue run of water that marked the Gulf Stream, I put the boat on auto pilot, belted her in the chair at the stern, got us a couple of cold beers, lighted up a nice illegal Cuban cigar and sat in the other chair watching her. "Don't you have anything to do?" she said, with a glance at me. "Some boat thing?"

"There is nothing for me to do now but watch you."

"Isn't that dull? Why aren't you fishing?"

"I would much rather do just what I'm doing."

"I know what you have in mind and it will have to wait until I catch my fish."

"If you do."

"I *will* catch my fish."

There was nothing to say to that comment.

She was patient and didn't seem annoyed as the time passed without a strike. Earlier, I'd heard the fishing boat captains bemoaning the calm seas and poor fishing as they chatted on the radio, so I wasn't surprised that we ran into the same conditions. The sea was deadly calm, not a wisp of a breeze, and the day was hot. I already had the cabin closed up and the air conditioning humming.

"Why is nothing taking my bait, Jack? Maybe I lost it?"

"Reel it in and I'll check. Nothing's biting."

"Is that from some inner sense that you have?" she said with a smile.

"Not at all. I've been on the radio. All the boat captains are bitching about the lousy fishing conditions."

"That's cheating, Jack."

"That's being informed, my dear."

"Semantics. Where's your sense of adventure? I thought you were like Hemingway, with this deep natural feel for the ocean and all that, this terribly macho thing between man and fish."

"It's fiction, Kim, fiction and a lot of booze. I sometimes wondered if the old man actually caught anything."

"You're destroying illusions, Jack. I've read Hemingway and I liked his stuff."

"So did I, except for Africa. Robert Rourk did a better job with "Something of Value.""

"You're well read."

"I try. I'm not *well* read in the sense of the so-called classics. I read what I enjoy. Does it surprise you that I'm a reader?"

238

"Yes, sort of a surprise in a way. You're complex, Jack."

"Aren't we all?"

"Look at that!" she yelled, pointing off to the starboard at a large brown, flat shape in the water.

"A sea turtle."

"They're big aren't they?"

"Huge. And maybe very old. They have a long lifespan."

"You think we'll live to be very old, Jack?'

I shrugged without an answer. I wasn't sure that living a long life was good if one was living as nothing more than a vegetable. But I didn't want to go there—it was too nice a day.

Kim was hugging the rod with both hands and staring hopefully at the sea when she got a hit—we'd been on a dull, four hour run, almost halfway to Nassau at that moment.

"Ooh.!" she screamed as her rod bent in half. "I think I have something, Jack!"

"Hang on. Take up the slack in the line slowly—lean forward and wind the reel as you come back in the chair. Take your time. Let him run but keep him under control. Bring him in slowly."

"Keep him under control! Are you crazy? It's pulling me out of the chair! I've got a whale here!"

Not a whale, but indeed she did have something: a good-sized Wahoo that still glistened in brilliant colors when we finally got it aboard after a 15 minute battle. All too quickly though, when out of the sea and the life ebbing away in captivity, the colors faded. It was a good catch—turned out to weigh near 18 pounds. If we were on the way home I'd try to keep it—Claire did wonders with fish—but there was no way to keep the thing for the day, let alone overnight. Maybe we'd catch something on the way home. In any case, she got her fish. With that wish satisfied, we were then able to enjoy the cool cabin, specifically the bed.

Entering the harbor of Nassau wasn't a problem for me; I could slip in and tie up without a problem. For the big cruise ships it was a different story. We were tied up at the dock in town and I watched one enter the narrow channel. She did a very slow, careful 180 degree turn, which was a feat of seamanship and modern technology in itself, then backed into one of the new concrete piers that had just been built for the tourist trade. After getting tied up fore and aft, she would spew out some two thousand passengers on the tiny island. There was room for two large ships at the dock

239

In days gone by, the British Colonial , located within a spit of where we were docked, was *the* place in Nassau. Royalty had stayed here. James Bond had been here—Sean Connery had filmed a water skiing shot off the hotel pier. Lying on the hotel beach, one could watch the ships enter the harbor a mere 50 yards away. While Kim did raise her eyebrows and smile at the mention of the movie star, she wasn't too impressed with the place. Hilton owned the hotel now and a massive renovation was in progress. They would probably try to bring back the glorious past in rebuilding, but I feared that could never be. The past was gone. Connery was now old and gray, or maybe bald.

Just up the hill from the BCC (British Colonial Club) as it used to be known, was a restaurant on West Hill Street by the name of Graycliff that was an interesting story in itself. Located in a 250 year old mansion, with the restaurant on the main level and a few select rooms on the second floor, Graycliff was the best in Nassau, one of the top restaurants in the Caribbean, and in fact was rated as one of the best in the world. Impressive reputation. But in reality it was very low key, rather plain, and unassuming in appearance in the best of the old, wealthy English tradition. Aside from being the only 5 Star restaurant in the Bahamas, and having excellent food, and a spectacular wine cellar that ran into the thousands of bottles, it had a world renowned collection of hand made Cuban cigars.

Oddly enough no jacket was required.

After our fabulous dinner, a light, lively white wine for her and a red for me, and a cigar, Kim and I went down the stairs out of the main house, through a fairly dense garden, and out to the pool that was ringed with simple bungalows. No one was around the pool and we peeked into the bungalows for any sign of life. It seemed that we had the place to ourselves.

"Did you know that Winston Churchill often stayed here during the war?"

Kim laughed. "I never knew that. How do you know these things?"

"I try to keep informed," I told her, putting an arm around her waist. "Can you picture Winnie floating in the pool with his big cigar, puffing away?"

"I can't. But it sounds like fun. Why don't we try it?"

"What? Smoking a cigar?"

"No, silly, going for a swim. There's no one here."

"Kim, we're here for dinner. We're not guests."

"Jack. Lighten up," she said grinning.

"No bathing suits, Kim."

She reached up and kissed me. "Do we need them?"

I held her tight, feeling every bit of her body pressed against me, from her mouth right down to her thighs. "No. We definitely don't need bathing suits."

After getting undressed we carefully stacked our clothes on a chair in what we thought was some semblance of order, but in reality was probably a jumbled mess, and then, laughing as if we were the only ones in the world, jumped into the water.

We swam and laughed and played, splashing each other like a couple of kids, then in a quiet moment she was against me. Reaching between my legs and grabbing me, she said, "I think Winnie is here. At least there is something big in the water."

"A cigar?"

"I don't think so."

"I thought he was dead."

"No way. He's very much alive." With that she arched her back and slid down onto me.

We had a late, leisurely breakfast and then forced ourselves to go on a tour of Nassau. We could have easily spent the day in our room. The driver I'd hired was friendly and informative but I found the whole island to be a bit depressing what with the fast food places and the poor in the streets. This wasn't the Nassau I remembered. But then, memory often works in conjunction with our feelings, giving us what we'd like rather than what was the reality.

After the tour which took us from one end of the island to the other, and a delicious seafood lunch on the dock, our driver took us over the bridge to Paradise Island, where we both almost happily lost money in the gambling room. This pleasure palace that was Paradise Island, with the expensive trappings that defied description, was something new to Kim and she seemed in awe of it all, not because it was expensive, but because of the sheer glitz, the obvious commercialism of it, the decadence as she called it.

But we had a good time and it was a great trip.

The next day we were on our way home.

## EIGHTEEN

A week later we were having breakfast on the patio on another beautiful morning. Harry was where else? Sitting at Kim's feet. She called my attention to an article in the New York Times. "Did you see this about Haiti?"

"What about Haiti?"

"More problems. The president has postponed the elections, again, and there is talk of a general strike. A curfew is in effect and the army is in the streets. This reporter thinks the country is about to explode."

"So what else is new? Haiti is another place, one of many, where history repeats itself over and over again and improvement just doesn't seem to happen. I'd probably be called a racist if I even mentioned the thought that they are just not ready to govern themselves. It's not a question of race. It's a question of a large percent of the population not having the education to function as a democratic society."

Kim looked up at me over her reading glasses, which she at first hated to wear in front of me. "The same could be said of Africa, Jack. The worst is blacks prejudiced against blacks."

The next day Kim jolted me with another news item. She had petted Harry then went back to the paper. "Still bad news from Haiti." I looked at her and waited. "Says here that an American priest was picked up by the police for being out after curfew and later died in jail."

*A priest? There aren't that many in the country. I didn't want to go there and my voice betrayed me.* "Is there more?"

"What's wrong, Jack?"

"Nothing. What else does it say?"

"Not much. That seems to be all they know at this point."

I tried not to think about Haiti, but it was in my thoughts no matter what I tried to to to keep busy.

Two days later the worst came true.

In shock as I see the headline, and devasted by the thougth of what could be happening, or already happened, I read: "The priest," the article stated, "Father Smith, who claimed he was on an emergency call to visit a dying villager, and picked up by the police after curfew, died in prison from a heart attack according to Colonel Sauvain, head of the palace guard and someone who not only is close to the president but is in charge of all police actions." The article went on to say that Colonel Sauvain was under a US federal indictment for drug smuggling but that the Haitian government was not cooperating and would not honor the indictment.

*How's that for biting the hand that feeds!* They wouldn't have a government if it weren't for us!

Could this be true? Father Smith? It was like a sledgehammer blow to the chest.

Kim looked up from her breakfast and said, "What is it, Jack?"

"A good friend is dead in Haiti." I went on to explain about my time there, about Father Smith and Amy.

"Are you sure it's the same man?"

"Has to be."

I grabbed the phone and called Amy. After about ten minutes I got connected. "Amy?"

'Hello. Who is this?"

"Amy. This is Jack. Jack Morgan. Can you hear me?"

"Jack! Yes, I can hear you. Nice to hear from you. How are you?"

"Never mind that. What's the story with Father Smith?"

After a pause she said, "He's dead, Jack." Another pause. "He didn't die from a heart attack."

"What *did* he die from?"

"He was beaten, Jack," she answered, her voice wavering and soft. "He was beaten by the police until he died."

"How do you know that?"

"Because I went to see his body. I got that man Price from the embassy to take us to the prison. The police weren't too happy about it, and Colonel Sauvain tried to keep us out, did his best to keep us from seeing him. Price was adamant. And we got in."

I was starting to boil. "You saw the body?"

"Yes. There were bruises all over his chest and back."

"And what did the colonel say about that?"

"He shrugged and said that prison was a rough place."

"That's all he said?"

"Yes. It's a terrible thing, Jack. I don't know what to do, if there *is* anything to do."

"There's nothing you can do, Amy. I'm terribly sorry. Is there any family or anyone for you to contact?"

"No. He was all alone as far as I know."

*He wasn't alone and there is something I can do.*

"I'm coming down, Amy. I'll be in touch."

"What is it, Jack?" Kim asked as soon as I hung up.

"Father Smith didn't just die. He was beaten to death!"

"Oh God. Are you sure?"

"I'm sure."

243

"What are you going to do?"

"I don't know yet. But I have to go there."

She looked at me for a long moment. "Is this more of the same? Is this more of what you told me was finished? Is this more killing?"

"I don't know, Kim. I just don't know at this point."

"I don't want more of this, Jack. I don't know if I can take more of this. You're asking a lot of me and I don't know if I can be here for you."

"I hope you don't mean that, Kim. You're my rock and this is something I have to do. Can you understand?"

"What I understand is that the man I love is into killing. No. Make that *still* into killing."

"That's not fair, Kim. All I said was that I have to go there. I never said I was going to Haiti to kill anyone."

"What else do you know? This is your profession, Jack. I don't condemn you for that. But I thought it was over. I thought we could make a new life together, without that business being in the way."

"We can, Kim. Trust me on this. You don't know this Colonel Sauvain, but I told you about him. Either directly or indirectly he's responsible for Father Smith's death—his murder. Do you want to see him get away with that? The Haitian government won't do anything. Do you want to see him walk away as if it never happened? Is that what you want? You wanted Santana to pay."

"That was different, Jack—that was my family." She didn't say anything for a few minutes. "No, that's not what I want. I want to see him punished for what he's done. But does it have to be you? Are you his judge and jury?"

The tension hung thickly in the air between us.

"Is there any other? There *is* no judge and no jury in this, Kim. He is a government to himself and no one is going to touch him."

"You're right," she said slowly. "I see that, Jack. I really do. I guess it's that I worry about you. I don't want anything to come between us. I want us to go on being together."

"We will be together, Kim. I promise. Trust me to handle this one last thing that has to be done."

She hugged me, then walked out the door heading down to the river. Harry was right behind her. As I watched her walk away, my mind was elsewhere, thoughts spinning in lots of directions. In among it all I began to see the hint of a plan concerning one Colonel Lucien Sauvain. What I saw was something new for me, something different, but it was bold and daring and the more I thought about it the more I liked the idea.

244

Back when I was a bit younger and struggling to set up an air freight business in Miami, I came to know a man in a similar situation. We shared the learning experience that making a living with airplanes is not an easy way to go, maybe the hardest work with the least profit. But we both loved the idea of airplanes and flying, though he was a pilot and I wasn't—it's a form of mental illness that is yet to be fully understood. In any case, I don't remember just who introduced us or how that part of it came about, but we became good friends and eventually partners. In retrospect, I wonder if the introduction wasn't a planned event.

His name was Guy Morrison. To look at him you would never know that he was part Cuban, the part on his mother's side of the family, because he was blond and fair from his Norwegian father. He was a good looking guy and we came to call him Guy Madison after the movie actor who made a career in B movies. Guy had a gorgeous wife, Julia, and four children, but he was always ready to go off on any kind of adventure, now matter how wild or crazy. He had made countless trips to Cuba, none legal, and fit into the scene in Havana like a native. I, on the other hand, went off on my own occasional outings to places unknown to him. It was an odd arrangement but somehow it worked. In time I was making a lot of money, tons of it, and I walked away leaving the business to Guy.

At any rate, Guy was a pal and someone I could depend on. He was also a Marine. I called him in Miami.

"Morrison here," he said. "We cover the Caribbean and the world. What do you have and where do you want to fly it to?"

"What a pretentious statement. You cover the world? Is this the movie actor?"

"Movie actor?" A brief pause. "Is this Jack?" I told him it was indeed his old friend Jack. "How the hell are you? Semper Fi! What's up?"

"I have a job for you."

"You have a job for me? That's a switch. What do you need?"

"Do you still have that Cessna?"

"The Caravan?"

"Yes. The one you got at the drug sale. The one we fought about for days." At a time when money was tight and business scarce, Guy went to a DEA auction and bought this airplane. Granted, he got a bargain: the plane originally sold for a million and a half, reasonably equipped. Guy, that is we, got it for a quarter of that price, which was still a lot of money for us. We went round and round on that purchase. He was out to convince me that the aircraft was a one of a kind that could do anything: take out the seats and it had a lot of cargo room. We could go either way with this airplane, cargo or passenger and it was economical to boot, so he argued. This is a plane, he said, that was designed for "unimproved" airfields and was a real workhorse. It seemed to me that he had personal goals in mind with this plane—like another Bay of Pigs—but in the end, after seeing how reliable and economical it was to operate, I came to agree with Guy on the purchase. I wouldn't have if it hadn't been a bargain price, and even at that I choked when I saw the invoice.

At any rate, the Caravan proved to be worth every penny. We worked that airplane almost into the ground and she kept on flying.

He laughed, probably also remembering our fights over the plane. "The one we used to fly down to Cuba?"

"Yes that one. But you better not talk about going to Cuba. It is illegal you know." He'd made personal flights and "company flights," and was almost a commuter into the troubled island.

"Ha. Stupid thing. Only because the country isn't big enough or rich enough. Do you see us not dealing with China? Or even Vietnam? They tell me that the beach above Da Nang is the latest big time tourist development over there. Can you imagine that? The dollar talks, old buddy. Anyway, not illegal for me. I'm Cuban."

"About half Cuban, Guy."

"Whatever," he said. I could see him shrug in that way he had. "So. What about my airplane?"

"We need it to fly down to Haiti."

"Haiti! Why the hell would you want to go there? There's nothing happening there, Jack. Now I know a place out near Veradero Beach in Cuba..."

I interrupted. "Guy, this is business."

"Business! I didn't know there was any business down there—not since we put that crook back into office."

"They're all crooks, Guy. I need you to fly me down there right away. Are you free?"

"For you I'm free. And there's no charge, Marine."

"I'll pay, Guy, for the plane and the gas."

"No way, Jack. We go in as a team."

"You don't even know why I'm going."

"Doesn't matter."

"Like I said, it's business, and there is a man I want to see."

"You want to see him for the last time?"

"That's one way to put it."

"Do you need weapons?"

"Just handguns, Guy. No heavy artillery. This is a hush job."

"A snatch?"

246

"Maybe. Depends. I've got a Walther PPK, but not much ammo. I could use a suppressor."

"If you do it right you don't need much ammo. But I can get anything we need."

"Not *we*. You are strictly the pilot. You are not in this, Guy. You fly me there. You wait for me. Then you fly me home."

"We'll see about that. Every one man operation I ever knew was nothing but bad news. It takes two, Jack."

"To Tango yes. But not here, Guy. We aren't dancing. The only one I might dance with is Colonel Sauvain."

"That big wheel in Haiti? I read about him in the paper. Is that your target?"

"He's my target."

"Then you definitely need a partner! That colonel is no one to be fooling with, Jack. He's a heavyweight down in that backwater. You better count me in."

"Guy, this is not for you."

"Whatever you say. I'll only be a backup."

I knew it was near impossible to keep a man like Guy out of an operation, once he knew it was happening, so I factored him in as just that—a backup. He was correct. I did need someone to watch my back. "How soon can you get up here, Guy?"

"Where are you again? Vero Beach? Sebastian?"

"You can come into Sebastion. That's about ten minutes away from my house."

"You live on an island don't you?"

"I'll meet you at the airport. Give me an ETA."

"I can get out of here early tomorrow morning. Figure I'll be up there by 11am at the latest. Give me your number and I'll call you when I get into Sebastian."

"Sounds good to me."

"Oh. By the way. How's your love life these days?"

"None of your business. But it's great. How's Julia?"

"Julia is wonderful, Jack. She's a great lady. Did I mention that she might be pregnant?"

"No. What do you mean by she might be pregnant? You either did it or you didn't, Guy. Isn't it about time for you to slow down with the children?"

"You may be right old buddy. I am getting old to be a pappa, let alone the thought of how old I'll be as a grandfather. Can you picture me behind a baby carriage? Where did those young, good days go, Jack?

Those days when we were hot and ready to go every night?" With barely a pause he changed the subject. "How far is it to Haiti?"

"I'm not sure. Best guess is around 600 nautical miles, give or take, from Miami that is."

"Okay. No problem. The Caravan, cruising at 10,000 feet, has a range of close to 900 nautical miles, depending on the cargo weight, of which we'll have almost none going. We'll get down there no sweat but we'll have to fuel up in Haiti. I'll work it out. And I'll bring some toys we might need. See you tomorrow."

"Okay but no heavy stuff, maybe a few flash bangs, cuffs, you know the drill. See you, Guy."

*"Adios amigo."*

He was standing by the plane—which now looked a bit older and shabbier than I remembered—with a syrofoam cup of coffee in one hand and an unlit cigar in the other. Unlike the airplane, he looked about the same. Switching the cigar to the other hand, he gave me a one-armed hug. "Good to see you, Jack. You look exactly the same."

"What did you expect?"

"An old fart," he said with a big grin. "This woman of yours is keeping you young."

"How do you know there's a woman?"

"Because without one, old buddy, you'd be just that: an old, dried up fart. Take it from me, I know."

"How would you know with so many women?"

He put a hand up defensively. "No more, Jack. There's only one. Julia is the woman. You look good, Jack. Let's get aboard. I want a smoke. And you can tell me about your woman...and about this operation of yours. We're gassed up and ready to go."

Once aloft I appreciated both his flying skill and his friendship because I saw the one and felt the other. Helit up his cigar and puffed away, adjusting throttle and trim as if without a thought. "So," he said, "first the woman and then the mission. You found this woman of your dreams?"

I smoked and watched his face. "You make it sound like I was pretty damn particular."

With a glance at me, "You were particular, Jack. You wanted a special woman."

"Don't we all?"

"Sure. We all want that certain woman. But it seemed like you wanted something from another planet."

"You're probably right, Guy"

248

"So now you have her?" That special one?"

"Maybe."

"So, tell me. What about her?"

"Her name is Kim and she is originally from South Africa, but she hasn't lived there in a while. Has a home outside of Paris. She is not only beautiful, savy and smart, but she's a good shot and can hold her own. I think she is someone rare and special. And before you ask, the answer is yes. I would love her to be my wife. Now, let's get off my romantic life. What goodies did you bring?"

"Wow. This one you'd actually marry? I'm impressed. Okay. I've got two Mac 10s and lots of ammo in case you want to spray the area if we have a lot of traffic. But in this case it would be bad news if we ran into a crowd. I have a couple of grenades, smoke and flash, and ammo for your PPK. Oh. I also came up with two vests. You never know. And I have some plastic cuffs. How long do you figure for this? I told Julia I'd be back in a week at the most."

"A week should more than do it. We're landing in Port-au-Prince and the target has a home there. I don't see more than a couple of days. I know the location of his house. We go there and get the bastard. No big deal."

We flew in a cloudless sky over a vast stretch of blue water as if no one else existed.

Guy said, "Sounds too simple. Also, what do you mean by 'get the bastard'? We gonna kill him or take him?"

"I'm not sure about that."

He turned to give me a long look without comment. After a few moments he said, "It makes a difference—I mean about killing or taking. If we're going to waste him it's in and out. If we're going to do a Noriega and take him along with us to USA wonderland, where he gets a free orange coverall, it takes longer. You get my drift?"

"I know what you're saying and I don't have that nailed down yet."

"I think you'd better do that pronto."

My mind drifted to last night and the way Kim had at first been wild and passionate, then soft and clinging, as if there wouldn't be a tomorrow. She fell asleep in my arms. I was lost in that thought when Guy brought me back to now. "We're about 20 minutes out of PAP. We going in legit or do you want me to set down in the boonies somewhere?"

I said my thoughts aloud. "Going into the airport might be a problem with our cargo. The odds are good that they wouldn't even look at the plane—but they might. There's ID and that whole bit. And then there's the problem of coming back out. We might have even more interesting cargo. No. Swing around the city and head out on a highway to the north. There's plenty of space out there and I'm sure we can find a place to put down."

"Okay. You got it. But take a very close look at any landing site you think we can use—we don't want a busted landing gear. The struts are reinforced on this Piper but I still have to be careful. Remember, we have to get out of this place."

Guy ignored the radio calls from PAP and went down low over the water, then picked up the highway that would take us out to Amy's place. I said, "Not too much farther out." I was searching the ground—it all looked so different from the air—looking for both the clinic and a decent open space. "There's the clinic. Throttle back and come around again. There! That flat area behind the school. See it? What do you think?"

"That's a school? You gotta be kidding. What I think is that it looks too damn short," he yelled back.

"How about using the road?"

He didn't answer right away but came in low, above the road. "Hang on."

We hit the road with a thud, then rolled along the highway. He brought the plane right into the front yard of the clinic. The people waiting in line scattered and ran for their lives. Guy was grinning from ear to ear as he shut down. "Not bad huh, Jack? I haven't lost my touch."

"You sure haven't, Guy. That was a beautiful job. But I don't know that I can take too many more of these landings of yours."

Guy gave that shrug. "Looked good to me. Oh you faint of heart."

Amy came out of the clinic and walked towards us. She had a concerned, curious expression which changed when she recognized me. She was dressed in what I remembered as her usual: stained white coat over a shirt and tan shorts. "Jack! Great to see you! What *are* you doing here?"

"I came to see you," I told her as she threw her arms around my waist. I held her until her trembling stopped. After a few moments she stepped back and looked at me, then at Guy. "This is a good friend, Amy," I said by way of introduction. "Guy, this is Amy."

Before kissing her hand and giving her a big smile, he said, "My pleasure, Amy." He could do that kind of thing and make it seem perfectly normal. Turning to me he said, "Where did you find this beautiful woman?"

"Guy. Gimme a break. I think it might be a good idea to hide the plane behind the school."

250

"Why the secrecy?" Amy asked. Since I didn't see any point in telling what we were really doing here—she would probably tell me how dumb it was, and she'd be right—I told her that since we didn't go into Port-au-Prince and check in with customs, we were in the country illegally. She shrugged as if that was no big deal. "Do you think they know, or even care who is in this country?"

"Maybe not," I said. "But I'll play it safe just in case."

Without asking for volunteers, several people joined myself, Guy, and Amy, in pushing the plane behind the school. There wasn't much natural cover around by way of branches or whatever, but the simple fact of getting the plane out of sight from the road was enough. As far as tomorrow, or any kind of plan about Sauvain, I didn't have a clue; it was something I would figure out in the morning. While I was filled with the warm, comfortable feeling of being back with Amy, and being in the company of these good people, I was at the same time saddend that Father Smith was missing, that he was gone forever. I tried not to let that overshadow everything, but it was hard to do. He was a good man and I missed him and I swore that I would make someone pay for happened to Father Smith. You don't do that to good people and get away scot free.

There was a nice dinner that evening and then we all turned in early. Guy and I shared a room in the back of the clinic.

After early to bed we were early to rise—not as early as Amy, however, who must rise with the first cock crowing, even before the sun comes up, or maybe she never sleeps—and I was on a second cup of coffee after breakfast in the kitchen when we had a visitor. I heard the loud voice out in the hallway and Al came marching into the kitchen. He exchanged creole greetings with the help then came to me and gave me a bear hug.

"How are you boss? You need me to drive? My new car is great." Then he spoke out loud to everyone in the room. "This good man bought me a new car."

I didn't say anything for a moment because I was actually speechless. How the hell did Al even know I was here? On top of that I was embarassed at him mentioning the car. Everyone was looking at each other and at me and wondering what was going on.

"Al," I told him, "don't call me boss. It's embarassing. How did you know I was here?"

Al smiled and said, "No problem, boss. You came back and I'm here to drive. Where do you want to go?" He turned serious then. "We going to get Sauvain?" I didn't say anything. "He is the one who killed the good man, Father Smith. He is the one who killed a lot of Haitians. He is a bad man. I know that you came back for him. I will help you."

The topic of Colonel Sauvain, in any aspect, even the mention of the name, wasn't something I wanted mentioned in the presence of Amy. I knew where she would take it and I didn't want to go there. In the hopes of maybe slipping it by, I quickly introduced Al all around and he sat down at the table with us and had coffee. I could feel Amy glaring at me before she spoke. "What is this about Sauvain?" When I didn't say anything she went on. "Is that why you're here, Jack? Because if it is then it's wrong. It makes you no better then him. Violence is never the answer."

We all looked at each other as if wondering what to say without starting an argument. I let the silence hang for a moment. "You're right, Amy, when you say that violence isn't the answer. But I won't say never. Sometimes we need strength to overcome evil. Sometimes violence has to be used to bring about justice. I'm not talking violence here, if it can be avoided, and I'm not talking vengence. I'm talking justice."

Another long, awkward silence.

Then I said to Amy, "Do you have a problem with justice?"

"Justice is something different to everyone, Jack. Your justice could be injustice to someone else. Your right is very wrong to someone else."

We were going precisely where I didn't want to go. I said, "Amy. I'm not going to debate this with you nor get into the spiritual, moral, legal, emotional, political, whatever aspect it might have to some people. You're not involved and you have nothing to do with whatever I do here in Haiti. You'll have to trust me to do the right thing."

She let it end there and breakfast sort of drifted into an uneasy conclusion—Amy and the staff went off to their appointed stations, and Al, Guy, and I were left. Al asked, "Where're we going, boss?"

"We're going into the city. Do you know Colonel Sauvain's house?"

"I know it. I know it well."

For just a moment, a brief instant, it occurred to me to wonder why he would know the house of one Colonel Sauvain. This couldn't be common knowledge. Did the average, everyday citizen know where the Head of the Palace Guard lived? Did they care? It made me wonder if Al was more than a simple taxi driver, but then, I doubted that from the start. "What I want to do is go there, Al, and take a long look at the place."

"I can tell you that it is a house with guards. It will not be easy to go there."

I assumed that he meant it wouldn't be easy to penetrate the house. "You ready?" I asked Guy.

"Never readier. Lead on, boss."

"Not you too with this boss business?"

Guy laughed, "It's the price you have to pay when you are in power. Al knows what he's doing. Let him do it."

"That's not what I asked."

"Don't ask. Let's go look at this Colonel Sauvain's house. Unless it's Fort Knox, and I don't believe there are many of those here, we'll find a way into that sucker and we'll come out with him. What we need, Jack, is a good, thorough recon. We have to know what we're doing here or we could be dead meat."

"A delicate turn of phrase. But I agree with that."

The drive into Port-au-Prince and up into the hills that overlooked the city, was both familiar and depressing—this was, unfortunately, a land without change, a country stuck in poverty and despair. It seemed to me that I could return in ten, twenty years and find everything the same, and if this was a land of milk and honey, a place of peace and some measure of prosperity, not even prosperity, just decent living conditions, then that would be fine. But it wasn't good and it wasn't fine.

The house, if it could be called that, a fortress was more appropriate, was set on a dead end, paved branch off the main dirt road so that there wasn't much to be seen from sitting in a car on the road. I told Al to back off down the road to a curving point where the house was a bit more visible. We opened all the windows, since Guy was smoking a Cuban cigar, and looked at the house. It was hot.

Guy said, "It would take Seals or an A Team to get into that place from the road."

Looking down the mountain behind the house, I said, "It doesn't look any easier trying to get at it from the back side, up that ravine. Must be a hundred yards damn near straight up."

"We could do that if we have to. I don't see a lot of options here, Jack."

The more I looked at that climb the more I realized that we had to find some other way. Even if we made that climb, up through the rocks and the trees, and got into the house, and got our man, then what? Take him out the same way? Either that or get into a major battle with the guards. I don't think so. And that's assuming that we have a live body to take out. Did I really want a live body to take out? In my present mood, and when I brought in Father Smith, I'd take out the colonel without a blink. My thoughts were buzzing around. I smoked and gave Al the pack.

Finally after about ten minutes of nothing but sweat and smoke, I said, "Let's get out of here. We need to put some thought into this. Anybody hungry?"

"I thought you'd never ask," said Guy.

"Let's stop at the Sans Souci for lunch, Al."

"Good, boss. There is that pretty woman there. What was her name?"

"I don't remember her name but she was very nice—brought me ice for the bruises after I got out of jail."

"And was that all?" Guy said with a grin. "Just ice?"

"You haven't changed, Guy."

"I hope not."

"I think her name was Claudette."

"Oh. Suddenly you remember her name. What else do you remember?"

"Guy. I remember and I wonder at the day we met. Where did I go wrong?"

"Your life began when you met me, Jack. I introduced you to the finer things in life. Without me you would have lived and died a virgin."

"Hardly. You introduced me to promiscuity. You brought me into other evil things."

Guy threw up his hands in mock indignation. "Jack. You bite the hand that fed you, the hand that gave you banquets if you'll pardon the expression."

"I don't. And I won't go there. Ah, here we are and just in time, Al. You're lucky to be in Haiti and far away from Miami and persons of questionable character like this."

Al had laughed through the whole conversation between Guy and I. He said, "I think you two are very good friends. That is good. We need friends."

At the hotel, Al didn't want to come in with us because he wanted to keep an eye on his car, which was a sensible attitude to take, what with a new car in Haiti. But we totally ignored him and dragged him in with us for lunch. Inside, Claudette was behind the lobby desk and all smiles, greeting me as an old friend. She wanted to know if we would be staying at the hotel. I told her no because at that time I hadn't thought about it. Later I was to change my mind. But that was after a great lunch and a couple of Rum Punches and more discussion.

Al wasn't drinking but he did have one of Guy's cigars, as did I. We were sitting around the table out by the pool, kind of full and satisfied, smoking, and not saying much. Luke came by and wanted to know if we wanted a refill on the drinks. I told him that it was far too early to get into seconds.

As for Sauvain, who was never too far from my thoughts, I wasn't happy with the situation here, at least not what I saw so far. We were either faced with a frontal assault on his house, which was out of the question—I

254

didn't have a battalion here, there were two of us—or coming at it from a long, difficult climb up the ravine. The advantage in that was, of course, that wonderful element of surprise. The downside was coming out that way, making our way down that rough terrain, perhaps with the colonel, and I wasn't sure about that at this point. It would be easier to kill the bastard. Why was I even hesitating? But that was a different problem.

Guy turned to me and said, "What are your thoughts, Jack? Got a plan yet?"

"No. I see two options at this point and I don't like either one of them."

"That's not good."

Rather than saying another no, I didn't reply.

"Coming up from the back side is no good? It's steep but not something we can't do."

"Then what? Suppose we get in and get him. Do we take him down the ravine with us? That would be a bitch."

Guy frowned. "Who said anything about bringing him out? I thought you wanted to *take* him out."

Al was listening and watching our faces.

"I'm not sure about that."

"Not sure? What the hell does that mean, Jack? Do you know what you want to do here? I'm not going in on some half-assed operation without a plan, without a damned good plan."

"You don't have to, Guy. I only asked you to fly me in and out. You don't have to be a part of this."

Guy was quiet for a moment, realizing perhaps that he'd over reacted. In a softer tone he said, "I didn't mean that, Jack. I'm sure you'll come up with a good plan. If you want to take out the bastard we'll take him out. If you want to bring him back we'll do that. I'm with you all the way. You go. I go."

"Thanks, Guy."

Purely by accident, back in our Miami days, our airfreight days, Guy and I found out that we were both contract employees of CIA. We never knew how each other functioned, or why really, never worked together, but we shared that common bond. Guy liked to say, usually after a few drinks, and only between us, that we were both contract players for that big production company in Washington. It always brought a laugh.

So, we shared a lot and I wasn't surprised at his attitude now, nor his loyalty.

"Like I said, Guy, I'm not impressed with anything I see at this point. I don't like the set up. What do you think about an around the clock watch on this guy? We can get a better picture of his life and habits, what he does and where he goes, and when. We need something here."

"Makes sense to me. We can stay here. Is Al in on this? If he is we can go three, eight hour shifts and cover this guy like a blanket."

I turned to Al who'd been silent. "What do you say, Al? You want to be in this with us?"

"I was never out of it, boss."

"Good. I'll get us three rooms here and we can get started right away. What about your wife and family, Al?"

"I'll get word to her and she'll understand."

"But you'll be losing money without your car on the road."

"No problem, boss."

"Yes, there is a problem with that, Al. You'll be paid $100.00 a day. No arguments." This was more in a week than most Haitians made in a year. But he was worth every penny of it.

"You can't buy friends," he said. "I am your friend and I will go where you go. Money has nothing to do with this."

There wasn't an answer to that so I let it go. I'd brought plenty of cash and I forced Al to take three, one hundred dollar bills as a start. I told Guy he'd be paid as well.

He threw up his hands in mock indignation. "Your money is worthless to me, Jack. I'll let you pay for the fuel but that's it. Don't try to buy me, old buddy. I'm with Al: you can't buy friends."

And so we started our round the clock supervision of Colonel Sauvain in his daily activities.

After three days we had nothing: he went from the police barracks to his home, and only changed that routine once when he went to the police firing range. The barracks were out. Taking him on the road in an armored car with two guards was a daunting prospect, and something I thought was an unnecessary risk. Of course we could carry this on indefinitely and sooner or later find a weak spot that we could exploit—but there was a time element only in the sense that I wanted justice, now. What I needed, and had trouble finding, was patience. There would be an opening and I would be ready.

On day five Amy came to the hotel. She had come into the city to visit some friends and to do some shopping and figured she would find me at the Sans Souci. She was right. Guy and I were at lunch by the pool. I hadn't been sleeping well since the start of these regular watches, wasn't in the best of moods, and I wasn't particularly happy at seeing her. Guy was...well, himself. He stood up and held her chair for her and asked if she wanted a drink before lunch. Luke, our waiter, hovered nearby as always.

"Nothing to drink for me," she said.

"Have you had lunch?" I asked.

"I ate earlier."

"You mean breakfast?" She didn't answer. I had Luke bring us a menu and between the two of us, mostly me, ordered up a substantial lunch for her. I thought she always looked hungry and tired. Maybe that was because she was a giver rather than a taker. And maybe I envied that sort of person. I know I respected her.

Guy quickly picked up on the atmosphere, accurately sensing that something between Amy and I was hanging in the air, and said that he had personal things to take care of and excused himself from the table.

We were alone.

A long moment passed. She said, "Maybe I'll have that drink, Jack. Just one."

"Rum Punch? Luke is the best."

"That sounds great."

We didn't talk until her drink came. I said, "So, how are things going at the clinic?"

She smiled. "A whole lot better with the money you sent. That was a nice thing you did. The need never ends, of course, but you gave us a lot to work with. I can't thank you enough."

"You don't have to thank me."

"But I want to thank you. We were able to buy new equipment and fix up the kitchen." She looked at me and smiled. "It was fun buying new things." I didn't say anything; it was enough to see her so happy. She must have been like a kid in a candy store. "More importantly though," she said, "I could finally buy a lot of medicine that we needed badly, real drugs instead of the cheap imitations that we had to buy before, drugs that killed as many as they cured. We can save some lives now, Jack. You made it possible for us to do that. Isn't that great?"

"It is great, Amy. I'm happy for you."

"You should be happy for yourself." I let that go. "Did you know that Colonel Sauvain controls the import of medicines?"

"How the hell can he do that?"

"He can do a lot. He controls almost everything in this country."

*Maybe not for long.*

After a long moment she said, "But I really came her to apologize."

"Apologize? For what?"

"I was judging you and I have no right to do that. I sometimes slip into a rightous period, when I think I'm the only one doing what is right—everyone else is out of touch and wrong. Do you know what I mean?"

"Not really. You said what you felt. We all see things differently."

"True. But people are not just good or evil. We're a bit of both. You may want to do something violent about Colonel Sauvain but that doesn't make you bad person. You gave all that money to help these people so there is a lot of good in you."

"I'm glad to hear that."

"You know what I mean. And like you say, sometimes the good have to be strong and use force. The meek might inherit the earth but it will be a long time coming," she added with a grin. "After they fight for it."

We both laughed.

I said, "So, if you came to apologize, I accept. But I still say that it wasn't necessary. How's your lobster salad?"

"Delicious. The best I ever had."

"And the Rum Punch?"

"Even better. But I won't have another one."

"Are you going back to the clinic tonight?"

"Yes. I really have to get back. I have some more shopping to do and then I'll be on my way. I don't want to be driving in the dark." After a quiet moment she said, "As far as the colonel, I'm sure you'll do what has to be done. I wish you well. By the way, have you considered that someone might recognize you? You *were* thrown out of the country."

"That was all a misunderstanding," I told her lightly. "They only wanted to give me an escort to the airport. And thanks for you well wishes. The only two who might know me are Sauvain and the embassy guy. Sauvain doesn't matter and the embassy guy…"

"What's wrong?" she asked.

"The embassy guy is here. Don't turn around. Roger Wilson of the American Embassy just came in for a late lunch."

"You're kidding."

"I wish I were kidding. So far he hasn't looked this way."

It was only a matter of moments before the observant civil servant started to scan the tables. He caught my eye and could have moved on—but he didn't. He kept staring at me and then finally got up and came to our table. With a cursory nod to Amy he quickly sat down and said, "Are you crazy!"

"Possibly. What's your problem?"

"Mr. Morgan, you are *persona non grata* here. Do you know what that means?"

258

"Latin is not my thing but I can guess. Is it a pasta dish? Doesn't sound good." I took out my passport and put it on the table in front of him. "And who is this Mr. Morgan? I think this is a case of mistaken identity."

He picked up my green passport, opened it and studied the photo, all the while shaking his head. He said, "Tom Swift? Do you really expect to get away with this?"

"Get away with what? I'm a tourist visiting Haiti. I don't know who this Morgan character is that you mention, but it has nothing to do with me."

He spoke to Amy. "Sister, are you a part of this? Do you know what he's doing?"

Amy smiled. "I haven't known Mr. Swift for very long but he seems nice. Has he done something wrong?"

Exasperated, Roger said, "He has done everything wrong!"

"Can I buy you a drink, Mr? What is your name?"

"You know damn well what my name is, Mr. Morgan." Then he sighed as if accepting defeat. "Oh, what the hell. Yes, I'll have that drink."

"Wise decision. What was the name?"

"Wilson. Roger Wilson. Make it a rum punch."

"You got it," I said. "And you know my name. This is Amy."

The drinks came promptly—I'd ordered another round. Amy frowned at me for just an instant, then gave me a smile. I think she was having too much fun to leave. A few silent moments passed as we dealt with our own thoughts, and questions.

Roger spoke first. "I don't know what you're doing here, Mr. Morgan. And I don't want to know. I suppose it isn't a great problem of identity because who knows you here besides myself and Colonel Sauvain? No. I don't see that as a problem. I do see a huge problem if in your activities—whatever they may be—you are picked up by the police for any reason. Then you will have put me in a very difficult position, one in which I can offer very little help, officially that is. Do you I make myself clear?"

"Perfectly, Roger."

"But that doesn't mean I won't try to be helpful to a tourist. I'll do whatever I can to make your stay enjoyable."

We both knew what he was saying. I'm not sure about Amy. "I know I can count on you, Roger."

After he finished his drink and left, I said to Amy, "Seems like a nice man. You know, you could do your shopping and then come back here for dinner."

"That is a very tempting offer, Jack. Very tempting. But I really have to get "Okay. Drive carefully. I might see you in a couple of days." She

259

didn't comment on that but thanked me for lunch and left. It was a typically muggy afternoon and after a big lunch I was ready for a nap before I relieved Al. Using a rental in adddition to Al's car, we were on 18 hour coverage from 6am to midnight and Al was on the middle shift. I'd go on and relieve him at six in the evening at whatever spot he indicated by radio. We had the colonel very well covered. But so far I didn't see any cracks for us to use. I felt certain that it was a matter of time, and being watchful and patient, until we found a way to get him. Without good recon, as in any situation, we could be in big trouble if this blew up in our faces from not knowing all there was to know. It had happened countless times the world over. Not only was it dangerous not to be fully informed, but in this case, it could be an international incident. I didn't really give a shit about that but it would be annoying to anyone connected with me. While they might be few in number, they were a precious few.

My shift passed in its usual boring manner with nothing happening out of the ordinary.

Not until the following afternoon, or early evening, did things suddenly go from the dull to interesting when Al checked in with some news. It seemed that the colonel had made an unusual stop at the Sacred Heart Cathedral just down the hill, halfway into the central part of the city.

Despite the grand name of cathedral, *Sacre Coer*, while being the largest church in Port-au-Prince, was in fact a crumbling structure of cement block and cracked wooden pews. Even with the floor length doors of painted wood, on both sides open, the interior of the church was hot as hell, even with the ancient ceiling fans laboring away at the heat. It was a simple church both in design and function. Staffed by French priests, who were here long before anyone else, it served about half of the catholic population in the city. A school was nearby and it was an everyday sight to see the children in uniform moving up and down the cobblestone road. This was a poor country so I always marveled at the sight of these neatly dressed boys and girls. Perhaps there was little food or money, but the parents found a way to see that the children looked presentable.

After the colonel left the church, Al being very curious at this development, this change in what was a very orderly and ordinary routine, went in to talk with the priest, one Father Bouchard. It took some creative dialogue (lying) by Al to get the information out of the suspicious priest, but the windup was that the colonel had set up a private time for confession. While he didn't get the exact time, Al did get the day of the week. We had an opening.

Father Bouchard, as he had done several times in the past, was in Sacred Heart only for a short time to fill in for the pastor who was off for a vacation and a seminar in Miami. His parish was normally across the border in the Dominican Republic where all things were different. Each time he had come here and filled in for the Monsignor he was shocked and dismayed at the conditions, not only of the people, but of the buildings and roads—everything signified the deep poverty that filled the land. It was all something he chose not to dwell on whenever he was asked to come here. He always accepted, but it was with an inner feeling of dispair that made him uncomfortable the entire time.

An old friend, and a sort of unofficial spiritual advisor, though he would never admit that to anyone, was Sister Anne Marie—he would always think of her that way even though he knew she had left the order. They had met, and become friends, some years ago when he went to her clinic looking for medical advice on a rash he was unable to cure. The rash remained a problem, but they spent hours talking about the church and things spiritual and religious. She impressed him with her sound basis in their religion and a keen mind on social problems.

Troubled now, what with both the odd questions from the huge Haitian, and the feared Colonel Sauvain—known even across the border—coming to him for confession, he called Sister to talk about his feelings. They spoke French since he was much more comfortable in his native language.

"Handle it like any other confession, Father," she said in response to his question. "As far as you're concerned he's like anyone else."

"I understand that, Sister. What concerned me was the man asking about the colonel, asking many questions. This struck me as odd."

"Describe this man, Father." He did and she was silent, thoughtful for a moment. Could this be what she thought? Was Jack involved. Her instincts told her yes to both. The question for her was what to do, if anything. She asked for the day and the time of his confessions. "Not to worry, Father. It's nothing out of the ordinary. How long will you be staying?"

"Only until the end of the week. Long enough, Sister."

"Next time you come maybe you can get out to see us at the clinic."

"I can only hope that there isn't a next time. Perhaps I will be called home. Goodbye Sister. And thank you."

*"Au revoir*, Father."

The next morning we suspended our watches and had a breakfast meeting about the colonel and his meeting with the priest. He would go to confession at 5:30 that afternoon. Not much time. But it seemed like the appropiate time to strike. Guy and Al agreed. Al was eating a huge bowl of fruit and a croissant. Guy and I had an American breakfast of bacon and eggs.

I said, mostly thinking aloud, "So, there is a driver and two guards."

"That's correct," Guy said. "No problem there. They don't seem too sharp to me."

"Okay. You and Al could take care of them and I can be inside as the priest in the confessional. He comes in, we knock him out and take him. What do you think?"

"Some confession," Guy said smiling. "How are you going to do that? Knock him out, I mean," Guy asked.

"What do you have in that medical kit? Any chloroform?"

He shrugged. "No got. We have morphine!"

"That will take time and I have to give him a needle. No good. Too slow. He's not going to be sitting there letting me do whatever I want."

Guy said, "So shoot the bastard. What's the problem?"

"I can get it," Al offered. He got a skeptical look from us. "I know some people at the hospital here. If they have it I can get it."

"But do they have it?" I asked.

"I'll find out this morning."

"Good. We'll assume that part goes off without a hitch. The guards are disabled and we take off with the colonel in his car. No one's going to question his car."

"You gonna take him? Not kill him?" Al said.

"I've thought about that, Al, given it a lot of thought, and I've decided to take him back with us." What I didn't go into with Al, nor discussed with anyone, was the trouble I had making that decision. My instinct, my training, all that was bred into me, told me to take him out and thereby exterminate one more pest. Someone had to do this and I'd always done a good job. Now there were doubts, not about my ability, but about doing what I did. I was older, true, but the eye was still good and the hand steady. There was no doubt in my mind that I could still hit my target, any target at damn near any range—if that was what I wanted to do. No, the doubt was within. The problem was in the morality of it and perhaps the mortality. I had begun to realize that my time too was limited. I'd taken lives and now mine was a lot closer to the end. I couldn't put my finger on it, nor pinpoint the exact problem, but for whatever reason    I no longer felt that it was my place to take a life, any life. Call it old age. Call it another meaning to life. Call it anything. All I knew was that I wasn't the one to kill anymore.

Maybe it was time to hand the dirty job over to someone younger—there were plenty of them waiting in the wings of that grand theater of life.

Al nodded. "Whatever you say, boss. At least he'll be out of Haiti. That's good enough for me."

"Don't worry, Al. Colonel Sauvain will get all that's coming to him." What I didn't add was that I *hoped* he would. I wasn't sure of that fact. Justice doesn't always prevail. But I was getting ahead of myself. I'd made up my mind and the plan was set. As in any operation, I mused, there is a lot that can go wrong in this one, and probably will. The unexpected will happen and threre isn't a damn thing I can do about that but have a good plan and be prepared. We used to say that the key to a successful operation, as far as lives and the objective, was in having good men who could adjust and adapt. Nothing that I was ever involved in went strictly according to plan.

Except Kim.

Breakfast finished, we broke up our meeting then and went our separate ways. Guy said he would feel better keeping an eye on the colonel even though we knew his routine for the day. "He could always change his mind," Guy said. "This confession isn't written in stone."

"Good thought, Guy. I'll stay here at the hotel in case either of you need to contact me for any reason. Al and I will meet here at 4.30 and catch up with you at the church at 5.00. Sound good?"

They both nodded and took off.


To my way of thinking, Al and Guy had the better end of this: they had something to do and keep them occuppied—I could only think, wonder and worry, which when I thought about it was just one more symptom of the aging process.

But I fought that and took a long walk down to the central square of Port-au-Prince. The warmth of the sun was one thing—very often a pleasant happening. But here the oppressive and uncomfortable heat came from the street and the buildings, from anything that lived or merely stood in this environment. This was the baked in heat of centuries that tried to escape out into the air.

In moments I was soaking wet from a brief but heavy shower that stopped almost as soon as it had started. I didn't even bother taking cover. Nor did the merchants hide from the rain. A street vendor all too quickly sold me a sweet drink in ice that did nothing but make me thirsty.

Continuing along the broad avenue, I was offered all manner of goods to buy and the only thing that even interested me was a mahogany figure of a drummer boy, tempting because while the price was high, the piece had a stark, haunting quality in the carving. This sort of thing never interested me before but for some reason I looked at it and knew that I wanted the figure. I could have probably negotiated the price, downward, and my price, any figure I chose, would have been accepted. I didn't want to bargain. Mahogany at one time had been an abundant natural resource—taken for granted as was everything else (and why not?)—that these people thought would last forever without any effort on their part. Wrong. Without reforesting and soil conservation the fertile land turned to nothing more than sand. So I had thought of this as I talked with the vendor and he benefited.

I walked on and on.

By the time I had circled back and was on the road to the hotel, the sun was out and  my clothes were almost dry. My watch read 2pm which meant time to kill before our final meeting. I went straight up to my room without a glance at who might be in the lobby rooms.

If anything, the sudden rain had brought even more humidity and the air in the room was close. I stripped and showed then lay down on the bed. As I watched a gecko move ever so carefully up the cracked plaster wall, as if life depended on stealth, and well it might, my thoughts drifted and the memories flooded the space.

*I was in some cold country in Europe which right away pissed me off, waiting in the same position for the entire night, freezing, kidneys protesting, and hungry. Why can't these people die in the sun? But then wasn't I the one to decide the locale of their demise? Didn't I pull the trigger? Enough of the head trip.*

*My position was high up, overlooking the city center, and secure enough that I could smoke—a small blessing. The target would come out of the building directly in front of me and present himself in full, plain view of my sights. The distance was 1500 yards, 15 football fields, an extreme range, difficult, one that required perfect planning as far as wind and distance, but not an impossible assignment. There were closer positions I might have taken. The problem was that all the sites closer to the shot, the buildings along either side of the street,  had been carefully inspected by the army and police and were under constant guard. So my choice was at the end of the street, a rather long distance the guards would surely feel was too far away to be a threat. My thinking proved to be correct because there was no security anywhere near me. A piece of cake.*

*No one told me the target would be surrounded by women and children.*

*I smoked and watched the scene through the telescopic sight. Armored cars and police vehicles moved into place along the street. Even at this early hour a crowd had started to gather behind the barricades. I had no mind for politics—in fact I made it a point immediately before an assignment not to read any newspapers nor watch TV—but in the back of my mind somewhere I seemed to recall reading, well before I got the job, that the target would be attending some sort of peace conference with global significance. Weren't they all? Ironic, I thought, that the target was one who constantly made headlines talking about peace, but somehow never brought his rhetoric into reality. But that was of no interest to me.*

*Time passed and I eventually saw the crowd building, and even at this distance could almost feel the excitement at the scene.*

*The doors opened and there he was coming out into the pushing, bustling mass of security, news people, staff, and those close to the source of power.*

*I brought him into the scope and fine-tuned his image. Directly in front of him was a woman holding a baby who kept crowding into my sight. He seemed to be trying to wave her off, in a smiling, gentle, and no doubt political manner. But she persisted in staying in his face. My shot had to be now.*

*Get out of the way woman!*

*The baby's head kept coming into the small space. It had to be now.*

*There was only a crease, the thinnest area my shot had to take without hitting the woman or the baby.*

*I took the shot then kept my eye glued to the scope only long enough to verify the hit.*

*I could suddenly see the faces.*

***

Al woke me up banging on the door. I let him in and he was smiling with good news. "I got it, boss. I got the stuff you wanted."

"The chloroform?"

"Yes. I have a cousin works at the hospital."

"Another cousin? You had one working at the factory."

"Have many cousins, boss."

"That's great, Al Should make things easier. I'm gonna take a shower and I'll meet you downstairs in a little while. Anything from Guy? Any problems?"

"Not that I know of."

In the church sanctuary I put on the priest's white robe, tucked the sealed plastic pouch with the chloroform into my inner pocket, then after a final check on my appearance went out into the church. Earlier, Guy had a conversation with the priest and convinced him that he would be much better off if he was out of the way for a while. He was locked up in a storage closet in the back of the church.

The church itself was quiet, the only noise being the creaking sound of the huge fans whose long wooden blades did nothing but push the hot air around. I went down off the altar and made my way up the aisle, past the rows of wooden pews, to the confessional booth at the rear. As I was opening the door of the confessional someone came into the church.

Just what we didn't need. I turned to watch a Sister in full white habit, hood covering the head, carefully make her way in and sit in the first row. She knelt in prayer. What do we do now?

We go ahead as planned.

I was too concerned with my own situation, and the Sister, to hear whatever happened outside. Must have gone well though, because in a moment the colonel came walking in, alone. I watched him long enough through the partly open door to be sure he was coming to the confessional, then closed the door and sat down inside. I was soaked in perspiration in the small confined space. My hands were wet and I wiped them on the robe. I had to be able to move quickly with the pad.

Our plan called for Al and Guy, one or both, depending on how it went outside, to come in and help me with the colonel. In the confessional, I slid open the partition between us and mumbled some words, to which he gave the required response. Though it was dark in the booth I did have enough light to see that his head was down in concentration and that meant it was time for me to make my move. The idea was to get the chloroform-soaked pad out my pocket and into my hand. I would get out of my side of the booth, open the door to the other side, taking advantage of his being occupied with prayer, then quickly grab him and smother his face with the pad.

Nothing seemed to go right. I got the other door open but the damn pad was caught in the robe. I stumble into the booth, opening the door with one hand, the other trying to free the pad, he looks up, amazed, and we tangle and go down onto the floor together. The colonel is strong and quick and before I know it he is up and out the door.

Where the hell is Al? Or Guy?

I got up and looked out to see the Colonel running down the aisle. Neither Al or Guy is in sight. We have problems.

Suddenly the Sister gets up from her prayer and steps out into the aisle at the exact moment the colonel is passing by, they collide and go down. I'm clear by this time and run down the aisle with the pad in my hand. I'm down on the floor wrestling with the man and holding my own, barely,

266

when the colonel is lifted away. Al to the rescue. We get him knocked out and ready to leave. Guy comes in.

It all worked out.


Outside, Amy stops by her car parked under a tree, takes off the white robe, smiling all the while, throws the robe in the back seat, gets in and drives off.

The three of us, four with the prisoner, are not far behind Amy on the same road out of town. Al, with a big smile, says, "We got him, boss. He's sleeping like a baby back there."

Guy stops puffing on a cigarette. "Good plan, Jack. Went like a breeze. What are we going to do with him?"

Ignoring his question for the moment I said, "What happened to that Sister? Anybody see her?"

They both shook their heads. Guy said, "I never saw anyone."

Al said, "One minute she was there, the next she's gone. Wasn't paying much attention to her."

It was a minor puzzle that I let go. "What are we going to do with him?" I said, turning to Guy. "We'll dump him in Florida." I got a glance from both of them at the vague answer, but no comment.

Darkness was total as we pulled into the clinic. In this latitude the night came completely in moments. I saw lights in the clinic as we drove by and wondered who was about. Was it Amy? I would have loved to see her again, but I thought it best that we were up and out here as quickly as possible—we had important cargo to be delivered, and Guy was as good at night flying as he was in the daylight. At about the time Al and Guy got finished loading the cargo and checking the aircraft, seemingly out of nowhere, people appeared to help us turn the aircraft—several of them were carrying torches to light up our departure lane. This would always be a place of mystery, I thought, watching them in wonder. In moments we were warming up and ready to go.

I hugged Al and told him to take care of that new car.

As I was getting aboard Amy suddenly showed up behind me. She got a hug, then backed off from me and said, "That was me in the church."

I looked at her and we both burst out laughing. "I knew it was you!" I said.

"No you didn't."

"Maybe I hoped it was you."

"Well, it was me and we got him. The people will be much better off with him out of the country. Whatever you do with him, just make sure he doesn't come back."

"Don't worry about that, Amy. You won't see him again. And thanks...for everything."

"Thank *you,* Jack. Have a good flight. If you ever come back to Haiti..." She turned and walked away without finishing. But I knew what she would have said.

The author is a graduate of Girard College in Philadelphia. During the Korean conflict, as it was called, he served 8 years between the U. S. Coast Guard and the U. S. Marine Corps; 3 years in the U.S. Coast Guard, most of that time on weather patrol in the North Atlantic. During his 5 years with the Marines he served a year in Korea, and over two years in Haiti where he met and married his wife, Barbara.

He lives in Florida and can be contacted by e-mail: jimtfl1@aol.com

Printed in the United States
91068LV00003B/73/A